*To Madge Duncan-Sutherland with thanks
for all her help and support*

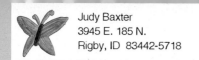

Paul Doherty was born in Middlesbrough. He studied History at Liverpool and Oxford Universities and obtained a doctorate at Oxford for his thesis on Edward II and Queen Isabella. He is now headmaster of a school in north-east London and lives with his wife and family near Epping Forest.

Paul Doherty is the author of the Hugh Corbett medieval mysteries, the Sorrowful Mysteries of Brother Athelstan, the Canterbury Tales of murder and mystery, the Ancient Egyptian mysteries, the Journals of Roger Shallot, THE ROSE DEMON, THE SOUL SLAYER, THE HAUNTING, DOMINA, THE PLAGUE LORD and MURDER IMPERIAL, all of which have been highly praised.

'Extensive and penetrating research coupled with a strong plot and bold characterisation. Loads of adventure and a dazzling evocation of the past' *Herald Sun, Melbourne*

'An opulent banquet to satisfy the most murderous appetite' *Northern Echo*

'Paul Doherty has a lively sense of history . . . evocative and lyrical descriptions' *New Statesman*

'Teems with colour, energy and spills' *Time Out*

'Vitality in the cityscape . . . angst in the mystery; it's Peters minus the herbs but plus a few crates of sack' *Oxford Times*

'As always the author invokes the medieval period in all its muck as well as glory, filling the pages with pungent smells and description. The author brings years of research to his writing; his mastery of the period as well as a disciplined writing schedule have led to a rapidly increasing body of work and a growing reputation' *Mystery News*

An Evil Spirit
Out of the West

Paul Doherty

headline

Copyright © 2003 Paul Doherty

The right of Paul Doherty to be identified as the Author
of the Work has been asserted by him in accordance with
the Copyright, Designs and Patents Act 1988.

First published in Great Britain in 2003 by
HEADLINE BOOK PUBLISHING

2

Cataloguing in Publication Data is
available from the British Library

ISBN 978-0-7553-0338-0

Typeset in Trump Medieval by Palimpsest Book Production Limited,
Polmont, Stirlingshire

Printed and bound in Great Britain by
Clays Ltd St Ives plc

Papers and cover board used by Headline are
natural, recyclable products made from wood grown
from sustainable forests. The manufacturing
processes conform to the environmental
regulations of the country of origin.

HEADLINE BOOK PUBLISHING
A division of Hodder Headline
338 Euston Road
London NW1 3BH

www.headline.co.uk
www.hodderheadline.com

PRINCIPAL CHARACTERS

PHARAOHS

Sequenre:
Ahmose: } war-like Pharaohs of the
Tuthmosis III: Eighteenth Dynasty (1550–1323
Hatchesphut: BC) who founded the great
                             empire of Ancient Egypt

THE ROYAL HOUSE (OF AMENHOTEP III)

Amenhotep III,
'The Magnificent':   Pharaoh of Egypt for about
                           thirty-nine years during which
                           time the Kingdom of the Two
                           Lands reached its high pinnacle
                           of power

Tiye: Amenhotep III's Great Queen
                           and Great Wife: a native of
                           Egypt, daughter of Thuya and
                           Yuya, from the town of Akhmin

Crown Prince Tuthmosis: heir apparent of Amenhotep III

Prince Amenhotep: the Veiled One (also the Great
                           Heretic; the Grotesque) –
                           known to history as Akhenaten,
                           younger son of Amenhotep
                           and Tiye

Sitamun: daughter of Amenhotep III and
                           Queen Tiye

CHILDREN OF THE KAP (ROYAL NURSERY)

Horemheb: General
Rameses: Horemheb's great friend
Huy: leading courtier/envoy of
                           the period
Maya: Treasurer during this period

Meryre:	Principal Priest of the Era
Pentju:	Royal Physician

THE ROYAL HOUSE
(OF AKHENATEN)

Akhenaten/Amenhotep IV:	Pharaoh
Nefertiti:	Akhenaten's Great Queen and Wife, daughter of Ay
Meketaten Meritaten Ankhesenaten/ Ankhesenamun Tutankhaten/ Tutankhamun	} children of Akhenaten
Khiya:	Mitanni Princess, one of Akhenaten's 'junior' wives

THE AKHMIN GANG

Ay:	First Minister of Akhenaten, father of Nefertiti, brother of Queen Tiye
Mutnodjmet:	younger daughter of Ay
Nakhtimin (Nakhtmin/Minnakht):	half-brother of Ay

OTHER OFFICIALS

Hotep (Amen-Hotep):	First Minister, close friend and principal architect to Amenhotep III
Rahimere:	Mayor of Thebes
Bek } Uti:	Royal artists/ sculptors
Tutu:	Chamberlain

Introduction

The Eighteenth Dynasty (1550–1323 BC) marked the high point, if not the highest point, of the Ancient Egyptian Empire, both at home and abroad; it was a period of grandeur, of gorgeous pageantry and triumphant imperialism. It was also a time of great change and violent events, particularly in the final years of the reign of Amenhotep III and the swift accession of the 'Great Heretic' Akhenaten, when a bitter clash took place between religious ideologies at a time when the brooding menace of the Hittite Empire was making itself felt.

I was very fortunate in being given access to this ancient document which alleges to be, in the words of a more recent age, 'the frank and full confession' of a man who lived at the eye of the storm: Mahu, Chief of Police of Akhenaten and his successors. Mahu emerges as a rather sinister figure responsible for security – a job description which can, and did, cover a multitude of sins. This confession seems to be in full accord with the evidence on Mahu that has been recovered from other archaeological sources – be it the discoveries at El-Amarna, the City of the Aten, or the evidence of his own tomb, which he never occupied. A keen observer of his times, Mahu was a man whose hand, literally, was never far from his sword (see the *Historical Note* on page 587).

Mahu appears to have written his confession some considerable time after the turbulent years which marked the end of the Eighteenth Dynasty. He kept journals, which he later transcribed, probably during the very short reign of Rameses I (*c*. 1307 BC). Mahu's original document was then translated in the demotic mode some six hundred years later during the seventh century BC, then copied again during the Roman period in a mixture of Latin and the Greek Koine. His confession, which I have decided to publish in a trilogy, reflects these different periods of translation and amendment; for instance, Thebes is the Greek version of 'Waset', and certain other proper names, not to mention hieroglyphs, are given varying interpretations by the different translators and copiers.

Mahu's confession does not, unfortunately, clarify certain vexed problems of the period. For example, just how long did Amenhotep III reign? Did he allow his son to become full Co-regent during his lifetime? How long did Akhenaten actually reign? Nevertheless, Mahu's account does bring to life the bloody struggle which tore Egypt apart almost 3,500 years ago. It vividly describes the intrigue and conflict, the vaulting ambition of men and women who fought to the death over the dream of Empire.

Paul Doherty

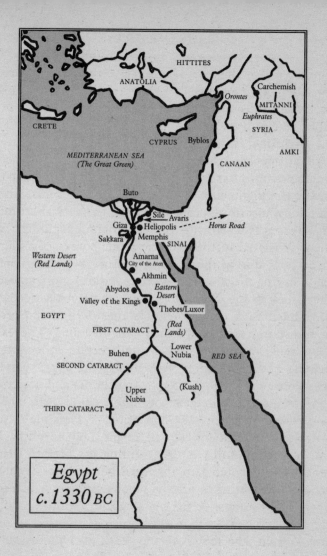

HITTITES

ANATOLIA

Carchemish

MITANNI

Orontes

Euphrates

SYRIA

CRETE

CYPRUS

Byblos

AMKI

MEDITERRANEAN SEA
(The Great Green)

CANAAN

Buto

Sile ← Avaris

Horus Road

Giza ● Heliopolis

Sakkara ● Memphis

SINAI

*Western Desert
(Red Lands)*

Amarna
City of the Aten

Akhmin

Abydos ●

*Eastern
Desert*

Valley of the Kings ●

Thebes/Luxor

EGYPT

FIRST CATARACT

*(Red
Lands)*

Buhen ●

Lower
Nubia

RED SEA

SECOND CATARACT

(Kush)

Upper
Nubia

THIRD CATARACT

Egypt
c.1330 BC

'O you who takes away hearts
and accuses hearts.'

(Spell 27: *The Book of the Dead*)

Chapter 1

I have swallowed their magic.
I call on their spirits.
My thoughts race like chariot teams ready for war,
Hot for the heat of battle.
I taste their blood in my mouth.
I see their Kas come before me,
Released from the Underworld,
Ready to haunt me.
I speak of those who have gone before,
Gulped by Eternal Night,
Swallowed by the destroyer,
Their souls hacked up like joints in the cauldron.
The star-riven darkness parts
A name slips back, memories, images,
And yet it's like crossing shifting sands,
Or peering through the heat haze of a desert.
I stand and watch them come
But I cannot make out their form or face.

So many names, so many souls, so many thoughts,
so many memories,
So, so long ago.
Only you, Rameses, Lord of the Two Lands,
Strong in arm and form,
Horus Incarnate, Master of the Twin Crowns,
Keeper of the Diadem,
Mighty Pharaoh.
You should know, for you were with us,
in spirit from the beginning.
This is my hymn to you:
'The Heavens are Overcast
Their Lights are Darkened.
The pillars of Heaven tremble,
The bones of the Earth Gods shatter.
The earth is quiet under your feet.
The creatures of the world
Have seen our Pharaoh
Appear in power.
The King is Master of Wisdom,
He is Possessor of Men's Necks.'

Ah well, so the fire is laid. A fire burns away the dross of the years. So, who am I? Why, I am Mahu, former General of the great Pharaohs, friend of the great Pharaohs, now I dwell alone in a little mansion beside the Nile where palm trees throng. Over their green-skinned tops I can make out, through the mist, the dim ghosts of mountains. Those mountains know the secrets. They hold the truth about the One whose name cannot be uttered, and the rest. Oh yes, the rest.

I have begun my confession on the nineteenth day of Akhit, the Season of the Inundation; the waters of the Nile are fat and swollen, sweeping life into the Black Lands. The Dog Star has risen high into the eastern sky; now it has gone, as have the white flashes of the ibis bird. All memories! The Pharaoh's scribes have also come and gone, so has the Eyes and Ears of Pharaoh: with his cobra eyes and beak-like nose he reminds me of General Rameses, thin lips always twisted in a smirk – or was it a grimace? Even now Rameses' ghost stands in the shadows with the rest, watching with those close-set, ever-shifting eyes.

They have brought me food, writing pens and ink pallets, rolls of papyrus, a horn knife and a smoothing stone. They have also found the journals I kept over the years: these will serve as pricks to memory. I am to write down all that has happened. They want my confession, so Pharaoh shall have it – once the dross of the past has been burned away, bringing back those glory days of the Magnificent One, Amenhotep III, his fat paunch and coarse thighs gleaming with perfumed sweat. Amenhotep the Magnificent, Lord of the Two Lands, Wearer of the Divine Plumes, sitting on a pleasure stool, his own daughter squatting libidinously on his lap, long legs dangling down, in one fair hand a blue lotus which had flowered at noon and in the other a silver-edged whip. Next is Queen Tiye, small of face and fierce of heart, a Queen whose dreams were haunted by her mysterious god. Ah, and here comes Maya! Old Smooth-Skin with his perfume-drenched robes and face painted more heavily than any heset girl from a temple. Ever-smiling Maya who liked to dress in women's clothes, his face as bland as the full moon and a heart just as changeable. Maya's lips were wet, red and full as if he had sucked on blood, that sneering mouth ever ready to sing his own praises: *When I began I was very good*, so ran the inscription on his tomb, *but when I finished I was brilliant*.

The shadows shift, to reveal Pentju the physician, cunning and just as dangerous. Behind him is Huy, the glory of Pharaoh, followed by Horemheb the great warrior, with his thickset body, square stolid face and the eyes of a ferocious panther. Rameses? Ah well, Rameses always stands in Horemheb's shadow. And the others? Oh yes, they'll appear. Nefertiti, 'the beautiful woman has arrived'. She walks, as she always did, her magnificent head tilted back, those strange blue eyes peering out from under heavy lids. She is followed by her daughter Ankhesenamun, just as eerily beautiful and just as treacherous. Ankhesenamun wears her perfumed wig bound by a golden fillet; her sloe eyes are ringed with black kohl; a silver gorget circles her beautiful throat, and her braided, beaded skirt slaps provocatively against those exquisitely curved thighs. She wears one gold-topped sandal whilst the other is held effortlessly in her hand. Behind her is gentle loving Tutankhamun, innocent dark eyes in a smiling boy's face. Dominating them all, like a brooding cloud which covers the sky, is the Heretic! The Veiled One, whose name cannot be uttered. They all come to Mahu, and where does Mahu begin but at the very beginning?

I was born popping like some rotten seed out of my mother's womb, so rough, so hard she died within the month, or so common report had it. My father Seostris, a Standard Bearer in the Medjay, was not present at my birth. Surely you know who the Medjay are? Auxiliary troops from the South. Many years ago, during the Season of the Locust, the Medjay decided to throw their lot in with the Egyptians when they waged war with fire and sword, by land and sea, against the Hyksos: barbarians who turned the Delta town of Avaris into their stronghold and threatened to bring all Egypt under their heavy war-club. So impudent did they become, that the Hyksos Prince sent a message to the Pharaoh of the time to keep the hippopotami in his pool quiet because they disturbed his sweet slumbers in Avaris.

The brave Sequenre took up the challenge, launching a savage war only to be struck down in battle. The struggle was taken up by his son Ahmose who, like fire running through stubble, marched against the Hyksos and reduced them to ash. The gilded Egyptian war-barges smashed the Hyksos defences along the Nile, and Ahmose's troops burst into Avaris and burned it to the ground. My ancestors, the Medjay, were with Egypt's troops and, for such help, an eternal pact of friendship was sworn between the two peoples.

My father was a Medjay from the moment he left the egg. A born soldier, he did not bother with me. My memories of him are vague: a stout man with a shaven head, dressed in a leather kilt and jerkin, marching boots on his feet, a war-belt fastened about his waist, a quiver of arrows slung across his back. A man proud of serving Pharaoh, he had received the Golden Collar of Honour together with the Silver Bees of Courage for slaying enemies in hand-to-hand combat in battle. (I still own these medals of bravery; the heavy gold necklace and the small silver bees carved in a cluster from a lump of pure silver with a jewelled hook to fasten on your tunic.) I remember him showing me the *khopesh*, the curved sword which he used against the People of the Nine Bows, those myriad enemies of Pharaoh who envied Egypt's riches and lusted after her rich soil and fair cities.

Father visited me occasionally, sometimes accompanied by an aide who carried his ceremonial shield. He would crouch down and stare coldly at me, eyes wrinkled up after years of peering through the heat and dust of the Red Lands. From the beginning I was lonely. I lived with my father's sister, Isithia, a hard-faced, sinewy woman, sharp-eyed and bitter-tongued. A childless woman whose husband had gone North on business and never returned. I could understand why! He certainly left Isithia wealthy enough, the owner of a country mansion surrounded by lofty thick walls. One of my constant memories is playing on the steps leading up to its porticoed entrance with its palmetta decoration in blue, green and ochre-red. Around the house were slender columns carved to represent green papyrus with red roots and golden capitals, a shadow-filled peristyle which provided welcome shade against the heat. The rooms inside had polished beam ceilings and tiled floors: a vestibule, an audience chamber, other rooms and polished wooden stairs leading to upper chambers. Isithia and I would sit on the broad roof, away from the heat, to catch the cooling breath of Amun. All around the house stretched verdant gardens, fed by a canal from the Nile, shaded by climbing vines and edged with flowers. A beautiful place, its paths were lined with trees of every variety: kaku palms, sycamore, persea, pomegranate, acacia, yew, tamarisk and terebrinth. Elegant coloured pavilions stood around the garden where you could sit to enjoy the different flowers and scents. In the centre gleamed a square pool of pure water with blooms of white water lilies floating on the top. Even as a boy I could sit for hours and observe them, how the blue lotus would flower at dawn, curl at midday and sink beneath the water whilst the white lotus only flowered after darkness fell.

I very rarely left that house and garden. I used to stand on the roof next to the corn bins, resting against the latticework built around the parapet to keep me from falling off. Not that Isithia cared all that much for me. She was a cold woman. The only creature she ever showed affection for was Seth, the ugly Saluki hound – a fierce war-dog from less gentle days, and in my youth a rare breed. Where Isithia went, Seth always followed, and where Isithia went, so did her fly whisk. She hated flies and mice. Every hole, every crack through which vermin could creep, were liberally coated in cat fat.

I recall her sitting, fly whisk in hand, in her high-backed armchair, its legs ending in four panther paws. The chair suited her. Isithia was a panther with narrow eyes and receding chin. A tall woman, she dressed in flowing gowns and embroidered sashes. She very rarely wore a wig or, indeed, her silver-edged sandals which a servant always carried behind her. If the nights turned chilly, she'd drape a fringed shawl about her shoulders. She distilled perfumes and medicine and sold them to select customers, often making trips out to the Valley of the Pines to collect those herbs and concoctions she could not grow in her own gardens. In the main these produced enough fruit and vegetables to make us self-sufficient, with crops of onions, leeks, lettuces and water melons. Isithia rarely went to the market but hired the best cooks to buy and serve fattened duck and geese. I always drank the freshest milk, sweetened with honey from the hives of pottery jars kept at the end of the garden and, when the bees were found wanting, the milk was sweetened with carob seeds. If I was naughty I'd be given nothing except the pith of a papyrus stalk to suck. Isithia never hit me though sometimes she'd seize me by the shoulders and shake me. She led her own private life: her customers came at night – women for potions and sometimes men. I used to hear the sound of beating and cries but whether they were of pleasure or pain I could not tell.

Isithia's servants were *shemsous*, or personal slaves, who wore a collar with a hieroglyph denoting their status – rolled-up matting on a stick. They were as terrified of her as I was – wary of her tongue and fly whisk. There were also a few slaves or *bekous*, men and women captured in war who were made to work in the gardens and live in sheds not fit for cattle. On one occasion two of them escaped. My father pursued them, caught them but never brought them back. Wielding authority over these was Api, Isithia's *wedpou* or steward, dumb as an ox but just as faithful.

Isithia was undoubtedly rich. Her strongrooms held vases of oils and unguents: henna, iris, fir, mandrake and lotus, all kept in sealable chests with ebony and gold veneer in silver mountings. I don't know whether Father even recognised the truth about his sister, or the silent terror she instilled in me. Sometimes at night, on the eve of an inauspicious day, Isithia would stand on the portico quoting blood-curdling verses from *The Book of the Dead*. Flanked by fire cauldrons she would sprinkle the darkness with oils and herbs, Api standing in the shadows behind her. Isithia's voice would carry low and terrible through the night.

'Go back! Retreat!
Get back, you dangerous one.
Do not come against us.
Do not thrive on my magic.
Go back, you crocodiles of the South.
Go back, you who feed on faeces, smoke and want!
Detestation of you gnaws at my belly!'

One night I even glimpsed her in the garden squatting over a dish of glowing charcoal strewn with herbs. Her kilt pulled up, she crouched like a woman would over a latrine, mouthing curses into the night. Isithia practised *hek*, the magic of the dark. She was always terrified of the *aataruu*, those evil spirits out of the West. Only the gods know what her past contained; her soul must have been heavy with the nastiness. She hardly spoke to me except to quote proverbs about the need for peace and security. I remember one of the verses well. She made me learn it by rote.

It is so good when beds are smoothed

And the pillows well laid out for the officers,
When the need of every man is filled
with a sheet and a shade
And a securely closed door for someone who slept in
a bush.

In my later years, going through the records, I discovered that Isithia's former husband had been an army officer. Perhaps she was terrified of the chaos war might bring. Occasionally I tried to ask her about Mother but she forced a quick smile and told me to keep quiet. I asked about my birth and she pounced like a cat would on a mouse.

'You were born between the twenty-third and twenty-seventh day,' she waved her fly whisk at me, 'so you must always be wary of snakes and crocodiles.'

On reflection, oh how right she was! I asked what god should be my patron? What divine being protected my birth? She pushed her face close to mine in mock sadness. 'Strange you ask that, Mahu. Strange to answer. No god.' Again, how right she was!

My memories should be sweet: a clean house with its bathrooms, hard-tiled stoolroom and well-decorated chambers. The air was sweet with the fragrance of kiphye, juniper, cassia and frankincense, and plentiful incense, the divine perfume of the gods, burned in spoons, their handles carved in the form of human forearms. Food was plentiful, delicious meals piled high on reed dishes. Yet I cannot recall anything sweet. No children ever visited us. I was given an education of sorts. The first hieroglyph I drew was the *sebkhet*, an enclosure with battlements that represented my life as a boy, locked in an enclosure.

On rare occasions Father arrived and took both my aunt and me across the Nile to the *Todjeser* – the Necropolis. I loved such occasions: the fast-flowing Nile, the cooling breezes, the pungent smell from the thick papyrus groves, the flashes of colour as ducks and wild birds rose up and wheeled against the blue sky. Sometimes the roar of the hippopotami would echo along the banks. I'd feel a shiver of fear as my father pointed out the crocodile pools. Occasionally, I'd glimpse the gold-topped obelisks and carved mountings of the temples of Thebes.

'That is Waset,' Father would whisper in my ear. 'Pharaoh's city. And from here you can see . . .' And he'd list the temples but I couldn't really care. I was just so pleased he was close to me. Eventually the crew would make ready to land at the Great Mooring Place. Above us soared the peak of Meretseger, the brooding goddess, and those craggy cliffs which could change colour so dramatically. These loomed over the City of the Dead and its warren of tombs, the Valley of the Nobles, the Valley of the Kings, the places where the dead came. We'd disembark on the quayside, pass the huge statue of the green-skinned god Osiris and go up through the winding streets of the City of the Dead, a place of horror and delight where the stench of natron, the heavy salt from the embalmers' shops, mingled with the more pervasive stink of corruption. Yet we'd turn a corner and glimpse beautifully carved caskets and coffins or elegantly sculptured canopic jars. The embalming shops, cabinet-makers and coffin suppliers did a roaring trade. As in life so in death. The rich could buy the best but the corpses of the poor were everywhere, nothing more than dried-out skeletons, draped in skins lying on floors or ledges. Not for them the Osirian rites of the embalmer but the cheap juice of the juniper pumped up through the rectum, the entire corpse pickled in natron. The very poor were given some cheaper, even more corrosive, substance, before being dried out in a natron bath wrapped in a dirty sheet and housed with scores of others in some coffin room. I noticed my aunt's whisk was even more vigorously at work as the flies buzzed everywhere. Great black clouds of them seemed to haunt her.

At last we were free of the city and going along the rocky, crumbling path to the Valley of the Nobles. At its entrance we were greeted by the Master of the Necropolis carrying his staff, its top carved in the shape of an *ankh*, the symbol of life. He was flanked by two priests wearing Anubis masks, which the Master introduced as *Wabs* or 'Pure Ones'. They took us along to my father's tomb, the House of Eternity which sheltered his wife's corpse and would, in time, shelter his, Isithia's and mine. Even then I uttered a silent prayer that, in death, I would be free, as far away from her as possible. We entered a courtyard. Inside, a small stela proclaimed the message:

The Great Enchantress has purged and purified her.
She has confessed her sins which shall be destroyed.
Homage to thee, oh Osiris.
He who hears all our words,
who washed away our sins,
has justified her voice.

This was the first clear reference I had ever seen to my

mother. My father squatted down and pointed out the words *Ma a Kherou*. 'Do you know what that means, Mahu?' 'No, sir,' I replied. My father smiled slightly, a rare occurrence. 'It means "Be true of voice". Will you be true of voice, Mahu?'

'Why, yes, sir.'

That was the first promise I ever really made and the first one I never really kept. 'Was Mother . . . ?'

'Your mother was a good woman,' Father replied.

He took my hand, another rare occurrence, and led me round to the other side of the squat stela to read out the confession from *The Book of the Dead*.

'"I have not ill-treated people. I have not taken milk from the mouths of little children".' (I glanced sharply at my aunt.)

Under this there was a picture of my mother's soul being weighed on the Scales of Truth. My aunt took great delight in naming the demons, also carved there, ready to seize my mother's soul if the Scales went against her: Great Strider, Swallower of Shades, the Breaker of Bones, the Eater of Blood, the Shatterer of Shades. I tried to grasp my father's hand but he gently pushed me away. Standing up he ruffled my black hair.

'Don't worry, Mahu. Your mother is in Yalou, the Fields of the Blessed, under the protection of the great Osiris.'

He led me across the courtyard to the small temple faced with columns. The Master of the Necropolis unsealed the door. For a while we waited for the torches to be lit and my father led me proudly into the vestibule.

'This, Mahu, is our House of Eternity! We have prepared it well.'

The walls of the entrance chamber were decorated with scenes from Father's life: being received in audience by Pharaoh to be presented with the Silver Bees. Father hunting out in the desert, driving his chariot towards a herd of antelope. Father in a papyrus thicket, boomerang at the ready, waiting to bring down the gloriously painted water birds which burst out at his approach. Other more touching scenes were recorded: my mother, lithe and graceful, anointing him with perfume or pouring water into his hands.

We left the vestibule and went down a narrow passage-way; its walls on either side were decorated with scenes of souls being taken to Abydos, of worshipping the gods, of offering them dishes of fruit above lighted braziers. At the entrance to the burial chamber Father paused to talk to the priests, making sure that the *Ka* priest, the Priest of the Double, offered prayers and libations to the gods on the anniversary of my mother's death. At last we entered the burial chamber containing four sarcophagi. To the left stood my mother's, dark-red and covered with quotations from *The Book of the Dead*. I was fascinated by the *wadjet* eyes painted just under the sarcophagus lid. I ignored everything else and went across and pressed my cheek against the cold stone. When I looked up, my father was staring down at me, tears in his eyes. My aunt, however, still stood in the doorway, the only time I had ever glimpsed her really fearful. I wished to crouch down. Burial chamber or not, I could have slept by that tomb. However, my father picked me gently up and led me out.

On our way back across the Nile, Father asked me to speak with true voice. Was I well? Was I happy?

'I am, sir,' I replied.

'And are you not happy to live in the Land of Tomery?'
He used the old term for the Kingdom of the Two Lands,
the realm of Egypt.

'Of course, Father.'

'Then what is wrong, son?'

My aunt's obsidian-like eyes caught my gaze, but
sheltering by my mother's tomb had strengthened me.

'I am lonely, sir.'

My father laughed and ruffled my hair. I thought he'd
ignore me but, in the riverside marketplace, he stopped
and bought me a pet monkey, an agile little creature with
bright mischievous eyes who clung to me and screeched
noisily. My aunt whispered a joke, how it would be
difficult to tell us apart. I was delighted. I called my pet
Bes after the ugly household god, and when my father left
I hardly noticed. I loved little Bes. He truly was a brother.
Indeed, I took pride in the jokes, made by my aunt and
taken up by the servants, about the resemblance between
us. I bought Bes a little shawl and a silver medallion
with the *debens* of copper I had saved. I didn't actually
do this in person. An old servant called Dedi went to
the marketplace for me. She was a *bekou*, a slave who
did the laundry and who somehow knew a great deal
about monkeys. Bes was the delight of my life. A greedy
creature, the very aroma of duck or meat cooked in onion
and garlic would send him chattering wildly whilst a piece
of sliced melon made him dance with joy. Where I went,
Bes followed.

My aunt came to hate him.

'He attracts the flies,' she snapped.

Bes grew very wary of her copper-tipped whisk.

Isn't it strange where dreams come from? Memories drift in and out of our hearts like incense across a sanctuary. Our memories are traces of ghosts, things that were, or even might have been. My aunt's house was always dark yet tinted with yellow as if one of those great sandstorms had blown in from the Red Lands. My childhood was like a wall frieze with a yellow background against which all those around me, including Bes, acted out their roles. I can still recall that little monkey, his jerky movements, the silver chain glittering around his neck, the naughty face and darting eyes. I also remember that fateful day so well. Dedi was filling the vase of the water clock: it was decorated with carvings of the baboons of Thoth, ringed with twelve lines to signify the hours of the day. I was explaining all this to Bes, chattering like a monkey to a monkey, one of the few occasions I ever did so in my aunt's house.

'You see,' I pointed with my finger, 'it takes one hour for the water to sink from one line to the next as it trickles out of that small hole at the bottom.' Bes jumped up and down on my lap. Dedi started laughing at me, not in a mocking way; her fat face crinkled up, her eyes, like two slivers of black glass, bright with merriment. I rose and embraced her; she was one of the few people I touched. She smelt of dust and soap. Dedi stopped what she was doing, put the jug down and gave me her endearing gumless smile. I heard a patter behind me and looked round. Bes was streaking like a pellet from a sling through the doorway towards a piece of juicy melon lying there. That monkey could never resist melon. I shouted and ran after him, but Bes grabbed the melon and scampered across the courtyard.

I had almost reached the doorway when an agonising scream, followed by a low growl, made my stomach lurch. I could hardly step through that doorway. Even then I knew what had happened. Someone had let Seth the great Saluki hound out. Bes was already dangling between his jaws. The cur was shaking him as a cat would a mouse; blood spattered the pavements. Bes's arms hung limp, his head strangely sideways, the small medallion glinting in an ever-widening pool of blood. A nightmare image as that hellhound shook the little corpse like some bloodsoaked rag.

My screams seemed to come from far off. Servants came running, led by Api. He grasped Seth's collar and pulled him away but made no attempt to retrieve Bes from his jaws. Dedi put her arms around me. I pushed her away and looked up. My aunt was staring coldly down through a latticed window. Dedi tried to comfort me but I was inconsolable. She ran away in a patter of sandals and, a short while later, brought back Bes's corpse wrapped in a green, gold-edged cloth. We buried him beneath the shade of a sycamore tree. Then I wept for the first and last time. Dedi, grey-faced with anxiety, sat cradling me. I was all but eight summers old. My eyes couldn't leave the freshly dug earth. Dedi had even found a small *ankh*, a life sign, and pressed it into the black soil.

'Cruel she is,' Dedi whispered.

I knew what she meant. The melon near the doorway, the waiting Saluki hound, Isithia's vicious gaze fixed on me.

'She was always cruel,' Dedi continued.

Something pricked my memory. I felt a shiver as if I'd been doused in cold water. Dusk was gathering. The sky was scorched with slivers of red. Dedi led me deeper into the garden under the shade of a beautiful willow, its branches curving down as if to drink the water from the narrow canal. Here she knelt and dug at the earth. She brought out a lightly coloured pot-shard and, with stubby fingers, traced its strange markings.

'I can read,' Dedi murmured. 'I am, I was, of To-nouter.'

I recognised the phrase for the Land of Punt, the Incense Country.

'I was captured in war and brought back here during the Time of Starvation by your father's father. I can read.'

'What does it say?' I asked.

'"Go away from me, Meret. Let your spirit not haunt me".'

'Meret was my mother. Did she,' I gestured back at the house, 'leave that there as she left the melon?'

Dedi cackled with laughter and reburied the pot shard.

'Your mother often came here, that's why Isithia has placed the curse beneath the tree. Cruel she was to her, cruel as she is to you.'

I heard a sound and turned. Dedi, mumbling in terror, clambered to her feet but there was nothing except the whispering branches in the gathering darkness. Nothing? So I thought, but the next morning Dedi was gone, and I never saw her again.

My aunt left me alone to brood on Bes and Dedi. My anger soon cooled. I decided to hide my feelings and mix with the servants. Akhit, the Season of the Inundation, came and went followed by Peret, the Season of Sowing, and Shemou when the sun burns hot and the servants fight against the vermin which swarm into the house. My aunt hated this time of year as the flies hovered like black clouds and the rats thrived fat and supple. I loved such confusion and did my best to help it. I found a rat's corpse, bloated with poison, and hid it in the whitewashed toilet, its limestone seat fitted around a hole over brick containers filled with sand. I tunnelled deep and placed the rat beneath the sand. Two days passed before my aunt realised what had attracted the horde of flies and gave off the terrible stench. A short while later I managed to find some poison. I hid some duck, soft and tender and coated with venom, near Seth's kennel.

'An accident!' the servants later cried. 'The hound must have eaten bait meant for the rats.'

My aunt grieved, but that night I went out in my linen shirt, stood beneath the willow tree and whispered softly to the breeze about Dedi and Meret.

The death of the Saluki hound was only the beginning of my aunt's troubles and my own liberation from her. Two days later a dusty, sweat-streaked messenger bearing the cartouche of Pharaoh arrived at the house. He was taken into a hallway to be cleaned but, even as a slave bathed his feet, he gabbled out his message: my father was dead! He had recently been promoted to a full Colonel of the Chariot Squadron known as the Vengeance of Anubis with the direct responsibility for the protection of the tombs in the Valley of the Nobles. A gang of skilled robbers had broken into one of these through the adjoining mortuary temple. Once inside, the robbers had stripped the gold sheets from the faces, fingers and toes of the mummies, seized the amulets and ointment jars. They had compounded their blasphemy by setting fire to the mummies of children so as to provide light for their plundering. The fire had burned fiercely, and smoke had curled out through a venthole so the alarm was raised. The robbers fled out into the Red Lands, my father following in hot pursuit.

'Like a hawk,' the messenger proclaimed loudly, 'plunging on its quarry.'

The robbers, a sizable gang, eventually took refuge in a rocky outcrop served by a spring. My father laid siege. Aided by Sand Dwellers, he had eventually stormed the outcrop. Those robbers who were not killed in the skirmish were impaled on stakes thrust up into their bowels or bound in thornbushes drenched in oil and set alight. A few were sent into Thebes to await punishment whilst my father returned triumphant. He had only been slightly wounded; an arrow had clipped the side of his neck. However, its barb had been drenched in snake venom and, despite the help of the regimental leech, by the time they reached Thebes, Father was dead. My aunt didn't cry but, gnawing at her lip, demanded my presence and, escorted by a retinue of servants, led me across the Nile to the *Wabet*, the House of Purification, up above the Libyan plateau just beyond the Necropolis. Our journey was fruitless. We arrived only to find that a great honour had been bestowed on my father by the express order of Pharaoh the Magnificent One. My father's corpse was already across the Nile being cared for in the House of Death at the Temple of Anubis, a soaring temple which lay just east of Ipetsut, the most perfect of places, the great temple complex of Karnak where Amun-Ra the Almighty, the All-Seeing Silent One, or so they said, dwelt in dark mystery.

I did not know why my aunt dragged me to these places of death. Oh, I know what the priests say, they are also the Springs of Life, the first part of the journey to the Fields of the Blessed. Isithia didn't care about that. Perhaps it was revenge? Yet, on reflection, it was an enjoyable day. I was taken through the *Waset*, the City of the Sceptre, the splendid Thebes – what an experience! Most boys of my age knew the city like the back of their hands but, for me, it was like entering another realm. An experience I'd never imagined: the throngs of people, the dust haze, and the marauding flies against which Isithia's notorious whisk was used like a weapon.

I'd always regarded Isithia as a Demon God lording it over her household, but in the city she was just one being amongst many. I saw men and women I could never have imagined: Negroes in their plumed head-dresses, shoulders draped in jaguar skins. Mercenaries from Canaan, Libya and Kush. Some wore horned helmets, stout boots on their feet and wicked-looking weapons thrust through belts and sashes. These brushed shoulders with merchants from the islands, Desert Wanderers and Sand Dwellers whose faces and bodies were hidden beneath folds of cloth. Hesets, temple girls, danced and flirted, their beautiful faces framed by thick braided wigs, all decorated with white stones and gorgeous head-bands. They wore gauze-like gowns above leather braided skirts. Every movement was part of some dance as they clashed *sistra* and shook tambourines in a slow, sinuously moving line of beauty.

The many markets enthralled me. Smells from the ointment- and perfume-sellers mingled with the tang of freshly cut antelope steaks which hung dripping from hooks or were being vigorously grilled over charcoal fires. Bakers offered strange-shaped loaves smelling fragrantly of spices and fresh from the ovens. Water-sellers, yokes fixed across their shoulders, cheap cups dangling from cords round their necks, forced their way through, bawling for custom. Shaven-headed priests, eyes ringed with black kohl against the heat, moved through the crowds like a shoal of fish amidst gusts of incense. Ladies in palanquins chattered in different tongues, their brilliantly-plumaged tame birds chained to a pole. A thief, caught red-handed, was being beaten on the feet next to a barber's stall set up under a palm tree. Elsewhere, the market policemen with their trained baboons had caught another sneakthief, who screamed abuse as a baboon bit deeply into his thigh. A million colours dazzled the eyes. Shifting images came and went as we twisted and turned through narrow streets or trod across blazing white squares and courtyards. Oh, how I remember that day! I could have stopped and stared till the sky fell in, but Aunt pulled me on.

At last we were through, going up the basalt-paved avenue to the Temple of Anubis. You must have seen it? Lined by huge statues of the crouching Anubis dog, their bodies, heads and paws black as night, their pointed snouts and ears picked out in brilliant gold, rich red ruby eyes glowing in the sunlight as if these creatures were about to rise in snarling anger. I recalled Seth the Saluki hound and glanced away. We pushed through the throng towards the great *pylon* or entrance to the temple. This was flanked by two huge statues of Anubis the Lord God of the Necropolis, the Master of the Death Chamber. For a young boy who had never seen the like before, it was an awesome spectacle. Above the gateways soared flagpoles, their red and green streamers dancing in the breeze. Crowds of worshippers, many of them carrying small reed baskets of food, were also pouring through to pay their devotions. The heady aroma of food made me realise I had not eaten. In outright defiance, I stopped and cried out that I was hungry. I could tell by my aunt's face that she was prepared to argue but her servants were similarly famished so she agreed to stop by a small booth. A few *debens* of copper bought trays of *mahloka*, its green leaves crushed and mixed with onion, garlic and strips of roast duck, followed by pots of bean soup and eggs cooked long and slowly so as to be melting soft and creamy in the middle. We squatted under an awning and ate, my aunt chattering to Api. As we were eating, another servant took me across to read the inscription of the mighty war Pharaoh Tuthmosis III:

> *I made those who rebel hurl themselves under my sandals.*
> *They heard my roaring and withdrew into caves.*
> *I trampled on the Libyans and the vile Kushites.*

Oh yes, I remember that day so well! A shabby fortune-teller, a wizened man, eyes yellowing in a weather-beaten face, sidled up to curse my aunt in a language I could not understand. My aunt jumped to her feet and replied just as fiercely. I didn't understand, but a servant later whispered that the fortune-teller had cursed my aunt with the Seven Arrows of Sekhmet the Destroyer Goddess.

'Why?' I asked.

The servant pulled a face, cupping a hand over his mouth to whisper, 'He claimed she has no soul.'

I don't know what really happened but, if I had a piece of silver, I would have rewarded that fortune-teller.

We finished our meal. Sounds from beyond the *pylon* drifted down – not the singing of choirs or the humming prayer of priests, or the sweet music of the harpist and lyre-players, but hideous screams. Curious, we hurried up to the gateway and into the great temple forecourt. I stood astonished at the sight. Executions were rarely carried out near holy places but on this day, the Magnificent One had made an exception. Kushite mercenaries, members of my father's regiment, were dealing out punishment against the last of his killers. The temple forecourt had been cleared, its visitors marshalled into one long column stretching up to the great copper-plated, cedarwood doors. At the far side of the forecourt a stake had been driven into the ground and the thief, impaled through the rectum, writhed in his death agonies. A herald, armed with a conch horn, oblivious to the blood-drenched ground and the hideous screams, loudly proclaimed the penalty for plundering tombs and murdering Pharaoh's servants. Two other robbers, stripped naked, were being basted with animal fat. More members of my father's regiment, sea-soned warriors in their leather kilts, baldrics and striped bright head-dresses, were preparing great leather sacks held with cord. These last remaining assassins from the tomb-robbing gang were to be bound in the sacks, taken to the great river and thrown into a crocodile pool.

My aunt seemed impervious to the hideous death agonies and the dreadful scenes. Beating the air with her fly whisk she approached an officer, a standard-bearer of the Chariot Squadron. In a hoarse voice she explained who we were. Immediately we were surrounded by soldiers and priests – a strange contrast of soft skin and sloe eyes with the tough and grimy war veterans, eyes red-rimmed from tiredness and desert dust. I recall a mixture of sweat, exotic perfume, hardened leather and perfumed linen robes. My aunt was treated as an object of veneration whilst I was caressed as the Son of the Hero. A priest gabbled his apologies, how we were not supposed to wait but I knew Aunt, she always liked to make a grand entrance. We were ceremoniously ushered across the second court which boasted a giant statue of a jackal-headed Anubis. A priest explained that it had a movable jaw so it could speak to devotees and utter an oracle. Around the courtyard were fountains, each with a sacred stela, a statue over which the water could flow and so become holy, a sure remedy against poison. I, remembering the Saluki hound, didn't think there were such remedies and stopped to examine one. My aunt pulled me away. I could tell by the curl of her lips that she was not impressed.

I wondered why my aunt was so apprehensive about approaching the temple until I entered it and realised that this was my first time in a true House of Worship: Aunt Isithia's house had few statues or tokens of the Divine Ones. Isn't life strange? I have never thought much of the gods but the Houses of Eternity in which they are supposed to live always impressed me. The hypostyle or hall of columns: rows of papyriform pillars with their bell-shaped bases and bud-forming capitals painted in glorious red, blue and green and decorated with triangular patterns. Bronze-plated doors, emblazoned with inscriptions, opened smoothly and silently on hinges set into the wall. I truly felt we were entering a place of magic.

Every so often we were sprinkled by a priest with drops of holy water from a stoup and cleansed by brushing the images of Pharaoh inscribed on the wall. Paintings and decorations were everywhere. The air was thick with incense and pierced by a low chanting which echoed eerily through the columned passageway. We passed Chapels of the Ear where pilgrims presented their petitions and eventually reached the *Wabet*, the Place of Purification. At the express order of the Magnificent One my father would begin his journey from here to the eternally fresh fields of the Green-skinned Osiris. A great honour! Even the most expensive embalming houses in the Necropolis could not be trusted with the corpses of the great ones. A priest once confided to me in a scandalised whisper how even the bodies of beautiful women were kept for a few days to allow decomposition to begin so they would not be violated.

The steps we went down seemed to stretch for ever. The cavern below glowed with light. Priests, some with shoulders draped with jaguar skins, others with their faces hidden behind jackal masks, moved through the billowing smoke. The air was rich with spices. The object of their veneration was the body of my father, stretched naked in the centre of the chamber on a sloping wooden slab. He looked fast asleep except for his grey skin and the dark wound in his neck. His corpse had already been drenched in natron. Surrounded by incense-burners, a lector priest, eyes half-closed, swayed backwards and forwards as he chanted the death prayers. I had to stand and watch my father's body be embalmed. The ethnoid bone in his nose was broken, the brains pulled out, the eyes pushed back and the cavities filled with resin-soaked bandages. Armed with an Ethiopian obsidian knife a priest made the cut in my father's left side and drew out the liver, lungs and intestines. The inside was washed with natron and stuffed with perfumes. All the time the prayers were chanted and the incense billowed. I was not frightened, whatever my aunt intended. I was fascinated by the priests in their white kilts and robes, shaven of all hair, even their eyebrows, their soft skins glinting with oil. Afterwards, when we left, I did not feel sad. My father was gone and these secretive priests in that sinister chamber with the brooding statues of Anubis meant nothing to me.

We honoured the seventy-day mourning period whilst the preparations were brought to an end. Father's corpse was pickled in perfume, his heart covered with a sacred scarab, tongue lined with gold and two precious stones placed in his eye-sockets. He was then bound in bandages. On the day of his burial I joined my aunt and a legion of mourners and singers to accompany Father across the Nile to the House of Eternity. He was placed in his sarcophagus. We had the funeral feast and afterwards on our journey back across the Nile my aunt leaned over. I had studied her well and so had remained totally impassive throughout the entire ceremony. At the end she asked if I was upset.

'Madam,' I replied, 'I am not sad.'

'Because your father has gone,' she gabbled, 'to the Field of the Blessed?'

'No, dearest Aunt, I am happy because my father's ghost will now join my mother's beneath the willow tree in your garden.'

Isithia's face went slack. I savoured for the first time how revenge, well prepared and served cold, was sweeter than the richest honeycomb.

'You have seen her there?' my aunt breathed.

'Often,' I replied, round-eyed in innocence.

She moved away. I glanced at the swirling water of the Nile.

'Oh swampland,' I whispered, reciting a famous curse, 'I now come to you.' I glanced quickly at Isithia. 'I have brought the grey-haired one down to the dust. I have swallowed up her darkness.' I realised, even then, that my days in Aunt Isithia's house were closely numbered.

> How fair is that which happened to them.
> They have so filled the heart of Khonsou
> In Thebes,
> That he has permitted them to reach the West.
> In peace, in peace, all fair ones proceed westwards
> in peace.

Despite my tender years, these were the verses I sang under the willow tree. I even managed to find gifts to place there: small coffers made out of papyrus, miniature wooden statues which would act as *shabtis*, servants to help my parents in the Fields of the Blessed. I turned the area around the willow tree into a small shrine. To be perfectly honest, it was not so much out of filial affection, more to taunt Aunt Isithia. Oh yes, I knew I would be going but I just wanted to help her make that decision. I spent more time under that willow tree than anywhere else. Accordingly, I was not surprised when, within a month of my father's burial, I had joined the Kap, the Royal House of Instruction at the place known as the Nose of the Gazelle in the sprawling, unfinished Palace of the Malkata. The Malkata was a jewel, the House of Rejoicing, the Palace of the dazzling Aten built by the Magnificent One, Amenhotep III, for his own pleasure. It lay just beneath the western hills, so at evening the palace was suffused with the dying rays of the sun. It was an impressive imperial residence, but as a boy of no more than nine summers, I didn't care about its splendour. Children are strange! I was not aware of the coloured pillars, the flower-filled courtyards or the ornamental lakes. All I cared about was the fact that I was leaving Aunt Isithia! I was to be in a new place, the school attended by Pharaoh's son, the Crown Prince Tuthmosis, and the chosen offspring of certain high-ranking officials. My place there was the Magnificent One's final tribute to my father. Only later did I learn that Aunt Isithia wielded considerable influence, not to mention her rod, over certain of Pharaoh's ministers.

The House of Instruction stood at the far side of the palace and, looking back, I smile wryly. I was in the most

splendid palace under the sun, being given a foretaste
of life in Osiris's Great House and Territory. However,
I was more concerned with my new surroundings and
new companions. The House was a one-storey building
built four square round a large courtyard which boasted
a splendidly built fountain, a small herb garden and a
multi-coloured pavilion. The building was mud-bricked,
stamped with the name of the Crown Prince; plastered
within, whitewashed without, its flat roof was served
by outside stairs, its doors and lintels made of wood
and limestone. One part served as a dormitory: its beds
were crude cots, wooden frames with stretched leather
thongs to support a straw-filled mattress. Each bed was
protected by a canopy of coarse linen veils against the
flies, with sheets of the same texture and a rug for when
the nights turned cold. The floor was of polished acacia
wood so bright you could see your face in it. Beside
each bed was a simple fold-up camp chair and a plain
stool fashioned out of sycamore. A chest of terebrinth
wood stood at the end of each bed to contain clothing
and other personal belongings. Down the centre of the
room ranged small dining tables bearing oil lamps. The
windows were mere wooden-edged squares in the wall,
boarded up with shutters in the winter or latticed screens
in the summer. One part of the building was a schoolroom
during inclement weather. In the spring and summer,
unless it grew too hot, we were taught outside. The rest
of the building served as offices, kitchens, wash places
and schoolrooms.

The overseer of the House of Instruction was Weni, an
old soldier-cum-scribe with a plump round face, thick

fleshy lips and heavy-lidded eyes. From one earlobe hung a gold ring; cheap jewellery decorated his fingers and wrists. He looked the typical fat fool but he was sly, ruthless and, despite his porky appearance, light on his feet. Weni was a former member of the *Nakhtu-aa* or 'Strong-Arm Boys', a crack infantry unit known as 'the Leopards of the East'. A highly decorated veteran, successful in hand-to-hand fights, he always wore a Gold Collar and the Silver Bees for killing five Mitanni in hand-to-hand combat and cutting off their penises as proof.

Aunt Isithia made sure I was aware of Weni's reputation as she dragged me through the palace grounds, whispering and nipping me, determined to exploit this last occasion together to heap petty cruelties and insults on me. She kept mentioning the Mitanni penises. When I met Weni, he glared down at me as if he would take mine. He was sitting on a bench in the courtyard, his *shemsou* or personal slave holding up a parasol against the midday sun. Grasping me by the shoulder, he spun me round. His hard eyes studied me carefully.

'I knew your father.' His gaze shifted to Aunt Isithia. 'You can go now.'

Isithia scuttled away. She didn't even say goodbye, I didn't even look. I decided to stare around and received a blow on the ear.

'*I* will tell you,' Weni whispered, leaning forward, 'when to look away.' His grim face relaxed and he gently caressed my earlobe. 'I never did like your Aunt Isithia – she's a cruel bitch! Some people say she drove your mother to an early grave. Well, go and unpack your things.'

There were about twenty-four boys in the Kap, sons

of the Magnificent One's friends or the offspring of his concubines – known as the Royal Ornaments. The principal boy was Crown Prince Tuthmosis, a tall, twelve year old with the eyes and face of a hunting bird. We were organised into four units of six. Tuthmosis was not with us on the night I met the Horus Ones, the members of my unit. We all bore the seal 'HA' with the hieroglyphs of a hawk and a rod etched on a small copper tablet slung on a cord round our necks. There were five in all, boys who were later to be my friends, rivals and enemies. Horemheb, Huy, Pentju, Maya and Rameses – I vaguely remember a sixth but he died of fever. I always think of us as the 'Six'.

My companions were roughly one or two years either side of my age. Horemheb was the undoubted leader; pugnacious and hot-eyed, his lower lip jutted out, his chin too: even as a boy he had muscular thighs and a barrel chest, and his skin was slightly lighter in colour than ours. Rameses struck me from the start as a bird of prey, with those cold, ever-shifting eyes and beaked nose over thin bloodless lips. Huy was Huy, graceful but arrogant. He always stood, feet apart, hands on his hips. He looked me up and down from head to toe, eyes crinkling with amusement. Pentju. Ah yes, even then he was ever-watchful. With his narrow, pointed features under a shock of rather light hair, Pentju reminded me of a mongoose. Maya was plump and always smiling; even then he could walk more provocatively than a girl. We all dressed in linen tunics and loincloths: Maya wore his like a girl with his tunic nipped in at the waist, legs oiled, feet shod in delicate sandals. Meryre joined the unit a few weeks after I did – a sanctimonious bastard from the start with his holier-than-thou face and permanently raised eyes as if he was in constant prayer to the heavens.

Sometimes I become confused. Did Meryre join us from the beginning, or am I getting mixed up with someone else? We were supposed to be a unit of six but the numbers fluctuated. What I do remember clearly is that first night I felt as if I was surrounded by a host of enemies. They pushed me around, went through my possessions and pulled the sheets off my bed. I then had to be initiated. My hands were bound, I was blindfolded and they poked and prodded me to recall their names. My little body turned black and blue and the game was only terminated by our evening meal of bran and artichoke followed by semolina cake. I remember it because it was so enjoyable. I was eating, free of Aunt Isithia's glare.

'Eat quickly,' Horemheb growled, scooping some of my semolina cake from the bowl. 'If you don't eat quickly, we'll eat it for you.'

How cruel children can be. They had the rapacity and ferocity of a starving hyena pack. Once the meal was finished the rest sat in judgement over me.

'We all have nicknames,' Huy murmured, one finger to his lips. 'So what shall be yours?'

He then introduced us. Horemheb was the 'Scorpion General'. Rameses the 'Snake Shadow'. Pentju the 'False Physician'. Maya was the 'Heset' or dancing girl, Meryre the 'Pouting Priest', Huy the 'Ignoble Noble'.

'I know,' Rameses whispered, head slightly to one side. 'Just look at him! His brow juts and so does his mouth.'

He tapped me on the end of my nose. 'He looks like a baboon.'

My initiation was complete. From then on I was known as the 'Baboon of the South'. After that I was accepted. I had learned my first lesson in the House of Instruction, the golden rule of all politicians: be as cunning and ferocious as the rest, show no pity and ask for none. Weakness only provokes attack. My formal schooling began every day at dawn. Weni roused us and force-marched us down to the icy waters of the canal. Then, whatever the weather, we'd run back naked, dress and eat a quick meal of oatmeal and sweetened bread. All the time Weni and his instructors, pinch-faced priests from the local temple, quoted proverbs at us.

'Don't eat too much. Don't drink too much. Yesterday's drunkenness will not quench today's thirst.'

The day's schooling would then formally begin. We learned the mysteries of the pen, the palette, of red and blue ink. We practised on *ostraca* or pot shards and limestone tablets before graduating to finely rubbed papyrus. We studied the *Kemenit* or Compendium and wrote out how marvellous it was to be a scribe. We learned the language of Thoth and paid lipservice to Sheshet, the Lady of the Pen. Our tutor's favourite instruction was: 'Be a scribe, and your body will be sleek. You will be well fed. Set your heart on books. They are better than wine.'

Our teachers certainly believed in the old proverb 'A boy's ear is upon his back; he hears when he has been beaten'. We'd sit cross-legged in the schoolroom or out in the courtyard, our writing palettes on our laps whilst the instructor would walk up and down ever ready to rap fingers or backs with his sharp ferrule. During the heat of the day we'd rest and continue our schooling as the weather grew cooler, followed by games, skittles, tug-of-war or jumping the goose. Whatever we did was fierce and cruel. I soon hardened myself. The seasons passed. Sometimes, Aunt Isithia came to visit me. She seemed to have aged; she was smaller, more wizened, and tried to flatter me with ointments and unguents from the storerooms. My present to her on the great festivals was always the same, a wooden carving of a monkey with a fly on its shoulder. I always informed her that I was very happy, that I was most fortunate to be in the Kap. I told her nothing about what happened there. None of my unit were friends, the only close relationship was that between Horemheb and Rameses. For the rest it was petty cruelty. I remember my first beating when Maya dared me to write this poem.

I embraced her,
her legs were wide.
I felt like a man in Punt.
The land of incense,
immersed in scent.

I was beaten because the hieroglyph for 'embrace' was the same as for a woman's vagina. The sharp-eyed priest thought I was mocking him. I always retaliated. Maya loved his sandals and I received another beating for creeping out of bed at night and smearing them with oil.

Naturally, as the time passed, our interest in girls grew, though no one could boast of any experience, except

Panhesy. He claimed he had read certain treatises and, ever clever, fashioned wooden puppets with movable arms and heads. Male and female, he made them act in close embrace which provoked smirks from Maya and sniggers of laughter from the rest. Weni discovered this and punished us, not for the toy, but for 'stealing out of barracks' as he termed it in the dead of night, lighting a fire in the grounds (a dangerous act), and taking strong beer to drink. He put us all on 'battle rations', a hideous punishment for young boys who woke like starving jackals and only lived to eat. Filling our stomachs was the only time we were silent as we bent over our reed baskets of chicken cooked in olive oil and onion sauce, garnished with chick peas and cumin. Now we had to starve. Horemheb decided to retaliate and tried to steal the bread of another unit. When Weni discovered that, we all received six strokes of the cane. He informed us that even 'battle rations' were suspended; we would now be given only dry bread and water for a week.

We were getting older, more cunning and sly, less reluctant to accept Weni's authority. Pentju was skilled at stoking our anger. We forgot that he had fashioned the puppets or that Rameses had actually stolen the bread. Weni the overseer at the House of Instruction became our mortal enemy. Now Horemheb had been given a Danga dwarf, a gift from some relative in the Delta. In theory Weni should have objected but, being an old soldier, he was superstitious and slightly wary of the dwarf: a thickset little man who reached no higher than my shoulder, his head and face almost hidden by straggling black hair, moustache and beard. The Danga couldn't sleep in the dormitory but had to fend for himself outside, whilst during lessons and games he crouched like a dog in the shadow of the wall. Horemheb always doted on the dwarf: the only person to whom he showed compassion, saving food and drink whilst also imposing an arbitrary levy on our rations. Horemheb held a 'council' as he called it, the dwarf squatting next to him. The oil lamps had been extinguished, the moon had fully risen and the rest of the dormitory were asleep as we sat in the far corner listening to the faint sounds from the rest of the palace.

'I am hungry,' Horemheb moaned, 'and so is the dwarf.'

'We are all hungry,' Huy whispered.

'It's Weni's fault,' Pentju accused hoarsely.

'But where can we get some food?' Meryre demanded.

The Danga dwarf muttered, a guttural whisper. Horemheb cocked his head. The dwarf repeated what he had said. Horemheb smiled and patted his stomach.

'I'm starving,' he repeated. 'And what I'd do for a piece of *roast goose!*'

At the time I didn't know what he meant but two days later I found out. Weni had a goose called 'Semou', sacred to Amun: a noisy aggressive bird always dropping dung and pecking the nearest piece of soft flesh. I never discovered the full story but the goose disappeared and, from the smug smile on Horemheb's and Rameses' faces, I gathered they were the culprits. The dwarf also, a miniature grotesque with his flowing beard and sunken features, looked remarkably happy. Weni was furious and naturally suspected the Horus unit.

By now we had been joined by Sobeck, the son of

a powerful merchant prince of Thebes who imported incense from Punt and cedar from Lebanon. 'Sobeck the Sexual' I called him; even as a youth he was always hungry for girls. He'd managed to weave his way into Horemheb's affection and I suspected he was part of the coup against the goose. Nevertheless, we were all to blame. At midday, in the baking heat of the sun, Weni decided to hold court. Crown Prince Tuthmosis, as leader of the Kap, was present, dressed in a short tunic and holding an embroidered fan which bore the insignia of the Kap. He would act as Weni's official witness. We were all stripped naked, the dwarf included. Weni rigorously inspected us, sniffing at our mouths and hands for any sign of grease or cooking but the 'criminals' as Weni called them were cunning; they had washed themselves thoroughly, though they had forgotten about the dwarf's tousled hair and beard. Weni fell on him like a hungry vulture. He sniffed the little man's hair and beard and slapped him harshly across the face.

'Criminal! Thief! Murderer!' Weni bellowed.

He dragged the dwarf from the line, pushing him forward for Tuthmosis to inspect. The Crown Prince confirmed his judgement: the dwarf smelled of goose.

'Give us the names of your accomplices,' Weni demanded.

The dwarf, trembling with fear, shook his head and made matters worse by urinating over Weni's feet. The overseer grabbed him by the hair and dragged him across to a bench. He was forced to lie face down. Weni grasped a rod. Horemheb made to protest but Tuthmosis pushed him back in line. Weni turned threateningly. The dwarf's wrists and ankles were seized by Weni's assistants. The rod came back.

'Master?' I stepped forward.

Weni paused and turned. 'Yes, Mahu? Are you the culprit?'

This was the one time I could tell the truth.

'No, Master.'

'Then why are you speaking?'

I went down on my knees and knelt in the dust.

'Master, the dwarf is innocent.'

'What!'

'I gave him the goose grease.'

Weni forgot the dwarf and, striding over, dragged me to my feet.

'I did not eat the goose,' I stammered. 'Nor did the dwarf. As you know, my Aunt Isithia distils potions and unguents. She gave me a pot of goose grease.' I caressed my sidelock, the mark of my youth as well as membership of the Kap. 'It is good for the hair.' I gestured at the dwarf. 'I gave some to him.'

Weni stared narrow-eyed. 'And where is this goose grease?'

'In a pot in my chest.'

Weni gestured with his head and one of his assistants hurried away to discover the truth. Aware of the others standing next to me, I closed my eyes. The dwarf was moaning. Tuthmosis was sucking on his lips as if to control his smirk. I just prayed that the pot of goose fat would be found, and whispered a prayer against ill luck: 'Perish you who come in from the dark. You who creep in with your nose reversed and your face turned back.'

'Master, he has told the truth.'

I opened my eyes. Weni was holding the small pottery jar, sniffing at it suspiciously.

'Did you use this?' He pulled the dwarf up and made him stand on the bench. The dwarf looked quickly at me, nodded and muttered something Weni couldn't understand.

'He uses it on his hair and beard,' Horemheb shouted. 'It keeps away the flies.'

Weni strode across and slapped Horemheb on the face. 'Speak when you are spoken to.' Then he turned to me. The fury had drained from his face; his eyes had a cold, calculating look.

'Well, well,' he murmured. 'You are well named Mahu, Baboon of the South.' He gnawed at his lips. 'Let the dwarf go.' Weni's gaze never left me. 'We'll all take a good run down to the water and have a swim. Afterwards you can eat.'

He strode off, followed by Tuthmosis and his instructors. We just sat down in the dust. I had to, my legs were trembling. A short while later we were taken down to the canal to bathe. No one said anything until we returned. I was standing by my bed drying myself off, more interested in the fragrant smells coming from the portable stove out in the courtyard. Horemheb and Rameses came sidling over. Horemheb held out his hand.

'Baboon of the South, I shall not forget.'

I clasped his hand and that of Rameses, and that was all Horemheb ever said. I learned two powerful lessons that day: how to win friends and how to survive. From that day on, the petty cruelties stopped and I fashioned my own philosophy. I would not be too bright to attract the teasing of my peers nor too dumb to provoke the anger of my teachers. I would be Mahu, he who lives by himself and walks alone. Horemheb never forgot and, I think, neither did Weni. From that day I felt strangely marked but I took comfort in the proverb I had learned in the schoolroom: Trust neither a brother nor a friend and have no intimate companions for they are worthless. The quotation from the *Instructions of King Amenemhat* was most appropriate. I had acted on impulse by myself, I had confided in no one either before or after; I had made friends or at least allies without making enemies.

I became a student skilled in the hieratic and hiero-glyphic writing, the preparation of papyrus, and the use of calculations, especially the nilometer. With the rest I studied the glories of Tomery and, of course, theology – the worship of the gods and the cults of the temple. All things centred around Amun-Ra, the silent God of Thebes who, over the years, had become associated with the Sun God and was now the dominant deity of Egypt. We were instructed in the mysteries of the Osirian rites, of the journey through the Underworld, the *Am-Duat*, as well as the difference between the *Ka* and the *Ba*, the soul and the spirit. It all meant nothing to me. The gods were as dry and dusty as the calculations for assessing a *kite* of gold or a *deben* of copper. Women, though, were a different matter.

The years had passed, our bodies had changed. We no longer played skittles, or jump the goose or tug of war, but became more interested in stick fighting, wrestling, boxing – anything to dissipate the energy which seethed within us. Weni, of course, noted the changes and turned a blind eye to our sweaty forays beneath trees and in bushes with kitchen girls and maids, those who crossed our courtyard carrying pots or jars, swaying their hips and glancing sly-eyed at us. Of course Weni tried to give advice, but his attitude on women could be summed up in that proverb he lugubriously repeated: 'Instructing a woman is like holding a sack of sand whose sides have split open'. Weni's experiences with women had not been happy ones! He certainly never had the honour, or blood-freezing experience, of meeting women such as Tiye, Nefertiti and Ankhesenamun. I once repeated Weni's advice to Nefertiti, at which she bubbled with laughter, and pithily replied, 'You don't have to instruct a woman, Mahu. She is already knowledgable.'

One word of advice Weni gave us which Sobeck later ignored to his peril. 'Have nothing,' Weni roared at us, one stubby finger punching the air, 'have *nothing* to do with the *Per Khe Nret*, the Royal Harem, whoever they are, wherever they come from! They are the Sacred Ornaments of the Magnificent One!'

I listened bemused. The Magnificent One was encroaching more and more into our daily lessons, not only his name and titles but his power, whilst Prince Tuthmosis was finding his feet and wielding authority amongst the young men of the Kap. I, in turn, was becoming more curious about my surroundings. Years away from Aunt Isithia, I now began to crawl out of my shell or nest, the House of Instruction, and my first foray formed one of those threads which would later bind my entire life. I had been out with a kitchen servant, a sweet girl with beaded head-band and pretty gorget. We had gone deep into the orchards, then she left whispering how she would be missed and flitted away like a shadow through the trees.

I lay for a while staring up at the branches and listening to the early morning call of the birds. It was one of those inauspicious days, decreed by the Priests of the Calendar to be touched by Seth the Red-Haired God. Accordingly, there would be no instruction, no school, nothing but boredom from dawn to dusk. I had stolen out, met the girl and now wondered if I should go back. Instead I decided to explore the orchard and, for the first time, approached the Silent Pavilion. I had heard of this place from chatter in the dormitory and the drill ground but had paid it no attention. It lay some distance from the Residence. It wasn't really a pavilion but a two-storeyed house peeping above a high, whitewashed wall. From my vantage point I could glimpse date palms, sycamore trees and terebrinths. A canal from the Nile had been dug in to water the grass, gardens and herbs. I crept closer, moving silently amongst the trees, and discovered that the Pavilion had only one entrance – a spiked double gate of heavy wood painted a gleaming black.

I approached the gate but froze. It was guarded by Kushite mercenaries, in fringed leather kilts, copper-studded baldrics across their chests; there were at least a dozen of them, some armed with the *khopesh* thrust through their sash, others with spears and shields bearing the insignia of the Isis and Ptah Regiments. A few archers also patrolled the area, heavy composite bows in their hands, quivers of cruel barbed arrows slung across their backs. They all wore the imperial blue and gold head-dress which stretched from their forehead down to the nape of their neck, each warrior displaying the Gold Collar of Bravery and the Silver Bees of Valour. Yet, even from where I crouched, I noticed they were all disfigured: one had an eye missing, another had suffered a deep scar which ran across his face and down into his neck: a third had his left cheek shrivelled, the eye pulled down as if he had escaped from some hideous fire.

The sun had risen though a faint mist still clung to the trees. I had just decided to withdraw when I heard a shout, that of a boy playing in the courtyard beyond. I also noticed the heavy rutted tracks of a cart marking the entrance to the gate. Mystified, I crouched back and listened more intently. Again the shout. Memories flooded back of Aunt Isithia's house. Was this a similar situation? A boy playing by himself, guarded by adults?

I returned to the Residence. When I questioned my companions they were equally mystified, though Rameses smirked slyly, rubbing that beaked nose as if he knew a secret but was unwilling to share it. Huy whispered something about being careful, how the Silent Pavilion was forbidden territory. I went to see Weni, who was sunning himself against a wall, a jug of dark beer in his lap – an increasingly common sight. We had begun to lose our fears of him. He was slower; sometimes his speech was slurred, whilst he depended more and more on his subordinates. Since the incident of the goose he had shown me a little more respect. When I asked him about the Silent Pavilion, he sat up, slurped from the beer jug, opened his mouth to bellow at me but then shrugged.

'Sooner or later,' he mumbled.

'Sooner or later what?'

Weni stared slack-jawed.

'Who's there?' I asked.

Weni blinked and swallowed hard. He gazed round the courtyard then tapped his nose. 'The Veiled One,' he slurred.

'Why is he veiled?'

'Because he's ugly like you!'

'Who is he?' I asked.

Weni smiled drunkenly and waved me away.

I was intrigued. A boy living all by himself, kept away because he was ugly? And why those cart tracks? And the disfigured guards? Early the next morning, long before dawn, it must have been the eighteenth or nineteenth day of the Inundation, I stole out of the dormitory and took up my position near the Silent Pavilion. The guards were easily distinguishable in the glaring light of fiery pitch torches dug into the ground. The dancing flames illuminated the spiked gates as well as the grotesque wounds of those who guarded it. I waited.

The north wind, the cooling breath of Amun, began to subside. At the first gash of sunlight a conch horn wailed from beyond the gate, a harsh braying sound which sent the birds all a-flutter. The torches had now burned out. I was moving to ease my cramp when the conch horn wailed again. I recalled hearing it on a number of occasions in the House of Instruction but had always dismissed it as just another eerie sound of the palace. The double gates opened and a covered cart, pulled by four red-and-white oxen, garlands between their horns, lumbered out. Two Kushite archers led these, another sat on the seat guiding the beasts through the gate. On the cart stood what looked like a *naos*, a tabernacle. I could make out a wooden frame and a shape beneath hidden by drapes of the finest gauze linen. Pots of incense in the cart glowed and sent up perfumed clouds. The cart, followed by its escort, turned east towards the river. I followed. It entered a small glade and drew to one side.

The day was already bright with the glowing rays of the rising sun. Steps were brought to the tail of the cart and the veil lifted. A figure emerged, head and face hidden by a linen mask. A roll of similar material hung over a long, unnaturally thin body, the legs and arms strangely elongated. Whoever it was wore no ornamentation except for a red arm guard embossed with silver studs. I glimpsed sagging breasts and a protruding stomach. As the figure clambered down, his legs and arms, as well as the fingers of the thin hands appeared almost spidery. He wore no sandals, exposing long slim feet, with toes like that of a monkey. So this was the Veiled One?

The figure turned its back on me and went to squat cross-legged on blood-red cushions the guard had already laid out, two pots of burning incense placed either side of him. He sat, head down, towards the rising sun. A low, melodious voice began to chant a hymn which would one day ring through Egypt and shatter its gods.

'Oh you, who come beautiful above the Horizon.
Oh you, whose rays kiss the earth and bring it to life!
All glory to you!
A million jubilees, Greatest and Only!'

I crouched transfixed. The rest of the retinue were now

squatting in a semi-circle behind this figure; his appearance might be strange but the voice was strong, rich. I had heard hymns and poetry chanted before, but not with the passion which suffused these lines. Was he a worshipper of the Aten, the Sun Disc, a cult gaining popularity amongst the wealthy nobles of Thebes?

The face veil was now pushed back. Leaving my position, I stole quietly through the trees to outflank the guards and obtain a better view. I settled beneath a holm oak. The figure seated on the cushions lifted his head; revealing a face with elongated chin, narrow eyes, and a sharp nose above thick full red lips, his high cheekbones emphasising the narrowness of the eyes. And yet, although the face was strange, it possessed a singular beauty. Again the head went down and the hymn was resumed.

'Oh you who come from a
Million, Million Years.
Who sustains all life on the earth
Who hears the petals break and smells the lotus,
All praise to you.'

The hymn was taken up by the escort, a low, melodious chant followed by silence. The young man had something in his lap, a blue water lotus. I moved closer. The Veiled One turned to his left, beckoning to the Captain of his escort who hurried forward. A few whispers and the Veiled One returned to his meditations. The sun was now rising fast, bathing the glade with shifting light. I was about to withdraw when I felt a sharp point digging into my neck. I whirled round. A Kushite, one eye missing, stood holding his spear, its point only inches from my face. On either side of him were two archers, arrows to their bows, the cords pulled back tight and taut. They gazed impassively down at me. I couldn't speak. I was frightened both of them and of breaking the silence.

The Kushite leaned down, grabbed me by the shoulder and pulled me to my feet. I was dressed only in a loincloth, a linen shawl across my shoulders. He pulled this away, whispering to his companions in a tongue I couldn't understand. My loincloth was felt.

'I have no weapons,' I stammered.

'Bring him with you.'

The Veiled One was already moving back to the carts. He took his seat, the steps were removed, the cushions and incense pots placed back and that strange procession returned to the Silent Pavilion. I had no choice but to follow. One of the Kushites had tied a rope around my neck. He didn't treat me cruelly, but held it lightly as one would walking a pet dog or monkey. The black gates opened and I entered a square, brick courtyard cut by the canal; a small fountain splashed in the middle. There was no garden plot but an abundance of flower baskets, full of fresh cuttings, their fragrance already filling the air and attracting the hunting bees. The front of the house was like any wealthy nobleman's, porticoed and columned with Lebanese cedar, brilliantly emblazoned with different insignia and approached by well-cut steps. The cart stopped in front of these. The Veiled One got down and, escorted by his strange retinue, swept into the house. He moved more freely now, not so ungainly but with a natural grace and dignity as if, aware of his disabilities, he was determined to emphasise these rather than hide them. My guard stared down at me.

'Shall we crucify you now?' His voice was guttural.

Despite his grotesque wounds and the fierce glare of his one eye, the harsh mouth was smiling.

'What shall we do with you, Monkey-Boy?'

I hid my fear and glared back.

'Monkeys,' he leaned down, 'can stay in trees.'

'A monkey can look at a king!' I retorted.

The Kushite laughed and cuffed me gently on the ear. He undid the rope and pushed me towards the steps. The inside of the house was cool, its walls limewashed a faint green, no paintings except for the richly ornamented borders at top and bottom. Servants clustered there: men and women, about four or five in all. They, too, were disfigured. In Thebes they would have been dismissed as Rhinoceri, men and women who had lost their noses and ears as a penalty for some crime. Usually they would be banished to a dusty village or commune or even exiled to an oasis, some rocky culvert in the Red Lands. These, however, looked well fed and clothed and were welcoming enough. My shawl and loincloth were removed. A servant brought a jug of water. My body was carefully washed and anointed, lips and hands lightly coated with stoups of salted water. I was being purified as a priest would be before entering the Inner Sanctuary of a temple. A fresh loincloth was bound around me, a linen robe, cool and crisp, draped over my shoulders, and strange long sandals fastened to my feet. I was then taken into the inner hall – a beautiful elegant room, its roof supported by four pillars painted green and red. Here the walls were finely decorated but, as I waited in the shadows just beyond the doorway, I realised the paintings were like nothing I had seen in the Temple of Anubis. There was no formal stylisation; here the raging lion was lifelike as if ready to leap from the wall. The birds in their brilliant plumage were about to fly. Everywhere were symbols of the Sun Disc, either in full glory or just rising above a dark-blue horizon. Sometimes they were winged, sometimes not. A fireplace stood in the centre of the room; at the far end was a daïs protected by a grey curtain. Someone propelled me forward, the curtain was dragged back. The Veiled One sat on cushions with his back to the wall, a small table in front of him. I was pushed to my knees and nosed the ground before the daïs.

'There is no need for that. There is no need for that.'

The words came slowly, the voice low. 'Let my guest join me.'

I went up the steps. The Veiled One lifted his head, revealing his strange elongated eyes, yet their stare was entrancing, and it distracted my fears. I was no longer aware of the spidery fingers, the long hands on the breast or stomach bulging against the embroidered linen robe. Just those eyes, full of passion as if the Veiled One was going to chant one of those hymns as he had in the glade. His sensuous lips were parted: his tongue sticking out slightly as he studied me closely, like a judge weighing what I was worth, trying to discover in one glance who I really was. He smiled, slightly lopsidedly, a graceful movement of those long fingers gesturing at the cushions on the other side of the table.

'You'd best sit down, hadn't you?'

The cushions were thick and soft. The table was of beautiful acacia inlaid with ebony and silver whilst the pots and jars were of the finest quality, containing small chunks of crisp duck, sauces, herbs, and bread cut into thin strips. The cups held wine not beer. When I tasted it I coughed and drew back. The Veiled One laughed softly.

'The best,' he murmured. 'From the rich land of Canaan. They say the earth is black there, so rich you gather two crops in one year. Come, come, eat!'

He gestured at the fresh reed basket before him. I was not frightened but wary. He served me himself, delicately wiping his fingers on a napkin.

'You are purified and cleansed.' He leaned across the table and I became aware of the Veiled One's true features. He wore a blue and gold head-dress, a silver pearl dangled from one earlobe and a flowered pectoral hung about his neck. On his left hand glittered a ring bearing the symbol of the Sun Disc.

'You are too shy,' he murmured, eyes squinting as if he was short-sighted. 'But not shy enough not to pry.'

'I wasn't prying.' I swallowed quickly.

'Then what were you doing?'

'I was curious.'

'Do you know who I am?'

'The Veiled One.'

'And why am I veiled?'

'Because they say you are ugly.'

'Do you think I am ugly?'

'No, sir.'

'Do you know who I am?'

I shook my head.

'My name is Amenhotep. I am the second son of the Magnificent One and his beloved wife, the Lady of the House, Queen Tiye.'

I hid my nervousness by lifting the wine cup and gulping noisily.

'You've never heard of me? I was born like this,' he continued evenly, 'kept in the Royal Nursery away from the Kap. Do you think I am strange? I have no real name. I am simply the Veiled One – he who lurks in the shadows.' He broke from his reverie. 'And who are you?'

'I am Mahu, son of Seostris, the Baboon of the South. I, too, am called the Ugly One.'

I spoke louder than I intended. I heard a sound from behind the veil; the Kushite archers were still there armed and ready. The Veiled One, however, just lifted those long fingers, palm upwards in the sign of peace. He stared at me for a while, that long, solemn face, the unblinking eyes and then he began to laugh. At first it was a sound deep in his throat, then throwing his head back, he laughed loudly, clapping his hands softly together.

'Mahu the Ugly One, the Baboon from the South!'

He picked up a piece of duck, dipped it into the herb sauce and, leaning across, gently fed me. 'I like you, Mahu, Baboon of the South. You are a child of the Kap. Now tell me about yourself.'

I had no choice. I chattered like a bird on a branch about Aunt Isithia, my father, my years in the Kap, Horemheb, Rameses and the rest. The Veiled One turned his head slightly as if he had difficulty hearing. He stopped eating and listened intently, now and again interrupting with a sharp question. When I had finished he leaned back against the cushions, head against the wall, cradling his wine cup.

'I hate beer.' He looked at me from under heavy lidded eyes. 'How old do you say I am?'

'About my age.'

'Which is?'

'About fourteen summers.'

'Have you had a woman, Mahu?'

'Yes,' I confessed.

He leaned forward, his face rather vexed. 'But not last night?' His voice became rather petulant. 'Not today, not last night. You have been purified.' He stared intently through the linen curtain behind as if seeking assurances from someone beyond it. Then he relaxed and laughed noisily.

'I cannot take a woman.' He glanced down at the table. 'They say I am unable to.' He gestured towards his groin. 'A curse from the gods. What is your favourite god, Mahu?'

I was tempted to reply the Aten, the Sun Disc.

'Well?' The Veiled One's head came up, a curious look on his face.

'I have no god.' The words came out. Tell the truth, I thought.

'No god?' He reached over and caressed my cheek. 'Are you sure, Mahu? Not Seth or Montu, Isis or Ptah? Why not? If you repeated those words in the House of Instruction . . .'

'I'd be beaten,' I replied, the wine now making its presence felt. My face felt flushed, my tongue thicker and heavier than I would want.

'No god.' The Veiled One blinked. He turned to his side and brought out a small beautiful coffer of sycamore wood with bands of copper, its corners inlaid with silver and gold. He moved the platters and cups, placed this gently on the table and pulled back the lid. 'Here are the gods, Mahu.' He lifted out small statues of all the great deities of Egypt, except their heads had been removed: Osiris, Isis, Anubis, Seth the Destroyer, Montu of War. 'Baubles!' The Veiled One weighed two in his hand. 'Plaster and stone and nothing else. They laugh at me, you know?'

His face had changed, no longer beautiful with his jutting mouth and those half-closed, glinting eyes. 'The shaven pates, the soft heads, the priests – they told my father to keep me away, to place me here so here I have sat, Mahu.' He threw the statues back in the box.

I was tempted to ask him about what I had seen in the glade earlier that morning but decided to hold my peace. Abruptly his mood changed.

'Come on, finish your meal.'

I did so even as he filled my wine cup. I was becoming alarmed at this strange person with his changeable moods. Sometimes he would talk to me directly, at other times he would break off and turn to his side as if there was someone I couldn't see sitting next to him. He would eat quickly but tidily, wiping his lips with his fingers, cleaning them on a napkin. The questions came thick and fast.

Had I entered the House of War? What was it like to lie with a girl? Which of the boys were my friends? Did I ever visit my aunt? His mood turned ugly whenever he mentioned the priests. I fought against the drowsiness, a sense of oppression. At the end of the meal the Veiled One rested back against the wall.

'Shall I share a secret with you, Mahu? My brother Tuthmosis, he is kind.' He wagged a finger at me. 'I am glad you respect him. You must go soon.' He played with the ring on his finger. 'Mother will be here shortly. I shall speak to her about you but ask her not to tell Father. The Magnificent One,' his voice turned rich with sarcasm, 'does not like my name to be mentioned. If he'd had his way, I would have been drowned in the Nile. Mother argued differently. She says I am touched by the gods. We have our secrets.'

'But you do not believe in gods?'

'True,' the Veiled One murmured. 'For the time being true.' He cocked his head slightly. 'Do you believe in magic, Mahu?'

'I know some tricks,' I replied.

The Veiled One giggled, fingers covering his mouth. 'Well, you'd best go.' His hand fell away. He stretched across and ran a finger around my lips. 'I have met you and wish you peace Mahu, Baboon of the South. One day we shall meet again.'

'Your son has acted for you.
The Great Ones tremble
when they see your sword.'

(Spell 174: *The Book of the Dead*)

Chapter 2

My encounter with the Veiled One was brief but startling.
I wondered if something might happen but no reference
was made to my secret visit nor did I receive any message
from the Silent Pavilion. My encounter also coincided
with 'the children of the *Kap*' (though we were young
men now) being more included in the life of the Malkata
Palace, as Crown Prince Tuthmosis matured. What the
Veiled One had told me quickened my interest in his
parents whom I'd glimpsed from afar; now I listened
avidly to the gossip. Old Weni, who was growing more
and more dependent on the beer jar, was an excellent
source of stories, if he kept sober. Not content with the
henket or barley beer, he had moved on to the *sernet*, rich
dark beer which would soon bring you into the presence
of Hathor, Lady of Drunkenness.

I would often join him in the shade of an olive grove
near a rather dank pool where the leaves were thick and
lush. He'd lounge back against a tree, a basket of garlic

sausage or grilled chicken covered with celery sauce on his lap.

'Oh yes,' he'd slurp, tapping his fleshy nose and winking at me. 'The Magnificent One is truly blessed by Amun. He had a harem.' Weni stumbled over the words *Per Khe Nret* 'The House of Women'. 'Princesses from every nation under the sun.' He smacked his lips. 'Mitanni, Hittites, Babylonians, Nubians, Libyans, the fairest of the field to satisfy his every whim.' He'd slump closer, eyes glazed, breath thick with the smell of beer. 'But the real power, I'll tell you the real power. It's his wife, the Great Queen, Mistress of the House, the Divine One Tiye.'

'Where's she from?' I asked.

'She's not a foreign princess.' Weni squinted up at the sky. 'Pharaohs have always married foreign princesses but the Magnificent One was captivated by her since the days of his youth. Tiye the Beautiful.' He shook his head. 'And she was exquisite, Mahu. Oh,' he caught himself, 'she still is, small but perfectly formed, with strange red hair and those almond-shaped eyes. If she was a cat they'd glow in the dark.'

I lifted my hand for silence. Strange, isn't it, how the relationship between teacher and pupil can change? Weni was becoming more and more dependent on me. The rest would tease or taunt him but I would talk to him and use the gifts I had received from Aunt Isithia to buy him a jug of beer. I'd do errands for him, fetching this or fetching that. I was growing as cunning as a mongoose and intended to use him to learn more about the Malkata. Horemheb had once said a strange thing to me. I'd made some funny remark about an official at the court. Horemheb was tying up his sandal and chose to do it close to me.

'Watch what you say, Baboon of the South,' he whispered hoarsely. 'Around here, even the trees hear.'

I had taken the warning to heart but that olive grove, as always, seemed deserted. If anyone approached, the undergrowth and leaves would betray him.

'Lady Tiye?' I prompted.

'Lady Tiye.' Weni shook his head drunkenly. 'Generous with favours, Great King's wife, Beloved of Nekhbet. She's from Akhmin, hundreds of miles to the North, in the Ninth Nome of Egypt where they worship Min the God of Male Fertility. Lady Tiye was a priestess there. They say,' his face came closer, 'she knows more about the art of love than a legion of courtesans.'

'And the harem?' I insisted.

Weni waved his hand as if wafting away a fly. 'More for show than anything else, though rumour has it that, as he gets older, the Magnificent One's tastes have developed. He likes to watch some of his women dance whilst the others fondle him.'

'And the Divine One's children?'

Weni was too sly to reveal a hidden scandal.

'Oh, there's Prince Tuthmosis,' he glanced out of the corner of his eye, 'and some daughters.' He glared blearily at me and turned the conversation to how soon I would enter the House of War.

'My days will end and yours will begin,' he'd add mournfully. 'I'll be sorry to see you go, you clever goose.' A reference, of course, to the disappearance of his beloved pet. However, I could play Weni at his own game and I wouldn't be drawn.

The real leader of the Kap was Crown Prince Tuthmosis, a hard-bodied, lean young man with an imperious face and manner and a grating voice. About two months after my meeting with the Veiled One, the Prince gathered us together and announced that we would stay in residence here but enter the House of War under the direct supervision of Hotep the Wise, his father's close friend and councillor who rejoiced in the title of God's Father, Scribe of Recruits, 'Overseer of all Works'. Hotep was a legend: a commoner from Athribitis in the Delta, he'd been promoted high in the Royal Circle. He was the overseer of the building works of the Magnificent One, from the Great Green to beyond the Third Cataract: temples, statues, shrines, palaces and obelisks all to the glory of Amun-Ra and his son, Amenhotep the Magnificent.

A week later Hotep arrived, tall and thin-faced, with patrician features. He must have passed his sixtieth summer. He dressed like a priest, head all shaven and devoid of any ornaments. He was joined by Colonel Perra of the Maryannou (the Braves of the King), seconded from the Regiment of Seth, a burly young man with a thickset body and the harsh face of a professional wrestler. He would be our tutor in the arts of war. Weni was ignored, pushed aside to sit on his bench and drink beer. Hotep gathered us in the courtyard and, with little ceremony, stood on a bench. He carried a small fan in his right hand which he kept tapping against his thigh. For a while he just stood studying each of our faces.

'I am,' he began in a carrying voice, 'a truly excellent

scribe. The first to calculate everything in To-mery. I have been inducted into the gods' books. I have studied the words of Thoth. I have penetrated the gods' secrets and learned all their mysteries. I have been consulted on their every aspect. I have directed the King's likeness in every hard stone, supervising the work of his statues. I never imitated what had gone before. There has never been anyone like me since the founding of the Two Lands.'

Hotep the Wise paused, a smile on his lips. 'I have taken a vow to Ma'at. My words are true. And why do I tell you this? You are children of the Kap. Soon you will enter the service of the Divine One. You will work in the House of Rejoicing and the will of the Divine One will be your pleasure. In doing his will, if you imitate me, you will find great favour. Do you understand?'

We were kneeling before him on the hard ground and made obeisance, noses pressed into the dust.

'Good!' Hotep climbed down from the bench. Colonel Perra told us to stand, and we hurriedly obeyed. Hotep moved down the line, pausing to speak now and again. He stopped before me and tapped me lightly on the cheek with his fan.

'You are Mahu, son of Seostris.'

'Yes, Your Excellency.'

The day was hot, the sun had risen high and we had been exercising before God's Father had arrived. I was coated in dust and aware of the trickle of sweat down my face.

'A good soldier, your father.'

'Yes, Your Excellency.'

'And you are nephew of Isithia, the lady of the fly whisk which she can wield so expertly.'

I caught his look of cynical amusement and wondered if he had been one of my aunt's clients as well as the reason for me being included in the Kap. He moved closer to me, away from Colonel Perra. 'Mahu the Baboon,' he whispered. 'A young man who knows his way around the palace, who can creep through the trees like a shadow.'

I stiffened and recalled Horemheb's words. Hotep tapped me again on the face. 'Do you have anything to say, Mahu?'

'He who spits in the sky,' I quoted the proverb, 'will find spittle on his head.'

Hotep grinned. 'So you have nothing to say?'

'Except that I am honoured by your presence, Your Excellency, and that you have deigned to take notice of me.'

The smile disappeared. 'Oh Mahu, Mahu, don't worry, I have taken close notice of *you*.'

He moved on to Sobeck standing beside me. This time his voice was louder. Sobeck had grown into a handsome young man with a boyish smile and a lazy charm; a superb athlete, his hard, golden-skinned body often attracted the attention of the girls, as well as Maya's who pined for him like some lovelorn maid.

'Sobeck.' Hotep, I am sure, intended me to hear. 'Do you know the story about Babylon, Sobeck?'

'Which story?' my comrade replied.

'About the Royal Harem. When the King dies he is buried in a deep pit. Those who have served him follow him there taking poison, being wafted to the Far Horizon by the music of blind harpists who will also accompany him into the West.'

Hotep glanced quickly at me. I stared ahead. Colonel Perra had gone back further up the line to talk to Horemheb.

'You've heard the proverb, Sobeck,' Hotep continued. 'If you wish to keep the friendship of any household you enter, as either a visitor, a brother or a friend, whatever you do, never approach the women.' He tapped Sobeck on the chest. 'Remember what I said.'

'Yes, Your Excellency.'

Once we were dismissed I took Sobeck aside.

'He was warning you,' I accused.

'No, he was threatening,' Sobeck laughed, 'and I think he was doing the same to you.'

'You should be careful,' I advised, grabbing him by the shoulder. Sobeck glanced at my hand but I didn't take it away. 'There's a spy amongst us.'

'How do you know that, Mahu?' Sobeck fluttered his eyelids. 'What have they found out about you?' He tapped me playfully on the cheek and walked away.

I now regarded my companions with unease. Sobeck made no attempt to hide his love affairs but Hotep had been hinting at something more than mere dalliance with a kitchen girl. I was different. I thought no one knew about my meeting with the Veiled One. Then I recalled squatting in that glade. How did the Veiled One know I was there? Were he and his escort so keen-eyed? Or had he been warned that he was under observation? The morning I was taken to the Silent Pavilion everything had been prepared, as if he'd been waiting for me.

Hotep's arrival brought other changes, a quickening of

pace like that of a drumbeat. The children of Kap had always taken part in the festivals. The Departure of Osiris, the Festival of Intoxication, Opet, the Feast of the Valley and the Festival of Beautiful Meeting. We had always associated these great days with food: loaves of bread, round, triangular or conical, enriched with eggs, butter and milk, and sweetened with coriander and cinnamon. After the bread came succulent water melons, sliced pomegranates and luscious bunches of grapes, with fresh gazelle or sweet hare meat, accompanied by the finest wines, either the Irep Neffer, the very good wine, or the Irep Maa, the genuine wine. We'd eat and drink till our bellies bloated, sampling these wines laced with honey, spices, myrrh and pistachio resin. Gorging ourselves on this plunder from the royal kitchens, we'd sit out in the courtyard, the night lit by aromatic jars or pottery bowls full of oil, their floating linen wicks glowing brightly against the dark. The only time we'd pause was to repeat the lines taught us by Weni:

'Ankh, Was and Neb;
All life, power and protection for the Divine
One.
Ka Nakht Kha Em Ma at,
Amenhotep the Fierce-Eyed Lion,
The Strong Bull appearing in truth,
Lord of the Two Lands,
Scourge and Smiter of vile Asiatics.'

Afterwards we would chant to the Goddess of Intoxication:

'Oh sing to Hathor the Golden,
The Lady of the Turquoise.
Send sweet pleasures for the Lord of the Two Lands,
Protect he who lives in truth.
Make him healthy in the East of the sky,
Prosperous on the far horizon,
Let him live for a million jubilees.'

We would all sing this, swaying on our feet but, of course, the Divine One was a distant figure, glimpsed on his royal barge, *The Dazzling Power of Aten*. He'd be adorned in his Coat of Jubilees and Robes of Rejoicing, brilliantly coloured as if a thousand butterflies and gorgeous flowers had clustered together. A distant figure, he and the Great Lady Tiye would sit on their thrones under ornate canopies, adorned with heavy jewelled pectorals, gold armlets and bracelets. They were always surrounded by fan-bearers, protected from the sun and the wind by gloriously thick pink-dyed ostrich plumes drenched in perfume. We'd glimpse his crown, blue, white and red as well as that of the Great Wife Lady Tiye's, a solar disc between the Horns of Hathor, with tall feathers, a spitting uraeus – a dazzling image of swiftly passing colour and glory.

We regarded this magnificence as we would the beauty of the stars, always there but very distant. Hotep changed all that. He wanted to impress upon us that not only were we part of such glory, we had been born to serve it. He took us on well-conducted tours of the great Malkata Palace, be it the Magnificent One's funeral temple or the splendid harbour he had built for Lady Tiye's barge at Biket-Abu.

We were taken through the well cultivated wall gardens and into the palace proper, a residence of vivid colour with painted tiled floors which depicted the People of the Nine Bows, the enemies of Egypt, captives under the imperial sandal. The walls and pillars of the palace were festooned with green spirals, golden bull heads, leaping red-and-white calves, and luscious paintings of the rich papyrus groves of the Nile with its flowing water and brilliantly plumed birds.

We were allowed to gawp at private chambers where beds, their frames inlaid with ebony, silver and gold, glinted in the polished light of the gleaming black or dark brown wood. Hotep encouraged us to sit on cross-legged stools with leather-cushioned seats, their feet carved in the form of panther, leopard or lion's claws. We'd stroke brilliant blue and silver cushions full of feathers, silken and soft to the skin, and study wall hangings with fringes of thick colours, or handle vessels of silver and gold, faience and alabaster, moulded in the shape of exotic animals or beautiful women. The words *Ankh* and *Sa*, Life and Happiness, were everywhere. Above doorways or windows the guardian vulture Nekhbet spread gloriously coloured wings. We visited tiled bathrooms and toilets, sunrooms and a well-stocked library, the *Per Medjet*, the House of Books. Of course, everywhere were scenes depicting the Magnificent One crushing his foes, riding like the God of War against his enemies. He was a rampant Sphinx under whose cruel claws tattooed Libyans, earringed Nubians, Syrians in their flowing robes or the sheshnu, the Desert Wanderers and Sand Dwellers, trembled in fear. Hotep was a clever man. Every week he'd take us around the palaces to view the glory and drink in the power of Egypt. For this we had to live – and for this we might even have to die.

We also prepared to enter the House of War. Colonel Perra was a brute of a taskmaster. Our studies were over and a harsher training began. The service of Montu the God of War was, in the words of Colonel Perra, to be our constant food, our constant wish, the very breath of life. He paraded us dressed only in our loincloths during the noonday heat and always began with a quotation from a famous work called *The Satire of Trades*.

'A soldier,' Colonel Perra roared, 'has to be beaten like a carpet, cleaned of all dirt and impediment. He campaigns in Syria and marches over the mountains. He carries bread and water on his shoulders like an ass. He slurps from brackish pools and sleeps with one eye open. When he encounters the enemy he must fight like an animal caught in a snare. He becomes a whirling piece of wood. He becomes ill and sick. His clothes are stolen and he eats dust every day of his life. That, gentlemen, is part of being a soldier. But, remember, there is the other side. The name of a brave man will never vanish from the face of the earth. You are here to serve Pharaoh, a magnificent soldier, the descendant of a magnificent soldier.'

'I think,' Sobeck whispered, 'we are going to know this speech by heart.'

'The Divine One's grandfather,' Colonel Perra continued in a roar, 'was strong of arm, a master of bowmen, rich in glory. So was the Divine One's father while he whom we now serve, Lord of the Two Lands, makes the people of the earth tremble at his move. Why?' Colonel

Perra walked up and down the line, striking each of us with his swagger cane. 'Because of the might of Egypt, because of the glory of its regiments and the power of its army! When we go to war we are like raging panthers, lions on the hunt, eagles in the sky. You will be part of that glory.'

I assure you there was little glory! Day after day of route marches, running in a heat which seemed to have gusted up from the Underworld. We would go without bread and water, to camp in the Red Lands. Yet this was only the beginning. Roused at dead of night, we were ordered to drill. On one occasion we were marched down to the Great River; a war barge took us across, but instead of beaching we had to jump into the cold, fast-flowing water, curb our panic, the heartstopping terror, and make our way to shore. It was an experience I came to dread. Sobeck always helped me. Yet the current was very strong and, on one occasion, Horemheb's Danga dwarf, hair and beard now greyed, having insisted on accompanying his master, was swirled away in the darkness. Hideous screams shattered the silence. He had been swept into a crocodile pool and the next morning the only remains we found were part of his head. Huy cracked a joke about the curse of Weni's sacred goose. Horemheb just glared at him and, from that moment, Huy was his enemy. Horemheb hid his grief well and accepted it as part of the harsh training we all had to undergo. Rameses told me he had made an offering to a mortuary priest and dedicated a statue to Danga but, apart from that, Horemheb made no further reference to the dwarf or his hideous fate.

Colonel Perra was equally unperturbed. In fact, our

training became even more rigorous. We learned to fight with the mace, the axe and the *khopesh*. Hours were spent standing at the butts practising with the composite Kushite bow, loosing arrow after arrow, with their cruel barbs and goose-feathered flights into a target of soft wood. Sometimes we'd fight in sandals, other times barefoot. If it was cold, we'd sometimes go naked, or just wearing a loincloth with a leather groin guard. In the hot season Colonel Perra made us walk in tight-sleeved Syrian coats of mail. Some of us were not cut out to be soldiers. Maya, Pentju and Meryre were hopeless – unable, as Colonel Perra remarked, to tell one end of a war-club from another. Nevertheless they provided constant amusement to Weni, who had now become a mere spectator. He'd sit on a bench drinking his beer and chortling with laughter. As for me – well, I was indifferent with the sword, spear, dagger or bow. Indifferent because I didn't like using them. Indifferent because I didn't want to be hurt.

The others excelled, particularly Horemheb. He proved himself to be a born fighter, a skilled archer, excellent with hand weapons. By now, he had filled out, and sported strong muscular shoulders and arms, a slim waist, powerful thighs and legs. Nothing seemed to trouble him, neither the heat of the midday sun nor the biting cold of desert nights. He was a man born with the breath of Montu in him. Rameses was just as good, though more cunning, a little faster on his feet. Of course not all of us had our hearts set on being warriors. Meryre wished to be a priest, Maya and Huy hoped to enter the House of Scribes, while Pentju wanted to be a physician. Sobeck, always laughing, asserted his wish to be the Overseer of the Royal Harem. Nevertheless, as a unit we were skilled enough. The Crown Prince joined us as the Kap had shrunk, due to death and departures, to no more than eighteen, whilst the Horus unit under Horemheb and Rameses outshone the rest. Tuthmosis was a constant reminder of the Veiled One, not so much his face or form, but that calm calculating look in his eye. I secretly wondered if the Veiled One would send me a message, a gift, engineer some form of contact – or should I go back to him? In the end, I did not have to do anything; the Veiled One came to us.

Tuthmosis always joined us in the morning just after our run when, under Colonel Perra's lashing tongue, we'd prepare for the daily drill. One morning, however, quietly and without much pomp, a conch horn brayed out beyond the walls of the Residence. The gate opened. Tuthmosis led in the cart, pulled by red-and-white oxen, bearing that frame, draped in a gauze veil, behind which a figure sat. The retinue of Kushites followed led by the one-eyed man. He grinned evilly at me and raised his hand, as if we were longlost friends – a salute not lost on my comrades. They stood fascinated as Tuthmosis climbed onto the cart and pulled away the veil. He then did a strange thing: despite being elder brother and Crown Prince, he bowed before the Veiled One sitting on his thronelike chair. Then Tuthmosis turned to us, hands held up like a herald.

'Behold,' he proclaimed, 'my beloved brother.'

He did not give him his proper name, the same as his father, Amenhotep, but the translation of that name, 'Amun is Satisfied'. We, of course, clapped, bowed in greeting, and pretended not to be surprised. The Veiled

One sat, his face open to the world. His body and face were a little plumper; a sidelock of reddish hair hung down over his left ear. The face was the same, possessing its own uncanny beauty: high cheekbones, sensuous pouting mouth and those well-spaced almond-shaped eyes that glowed like Syrian wine. He didn't move though his glance took us all in: his eyes caught mine, face creasing into a faint smile. He raised his hand as a sign to continue, long fingers splayed out. Perra roared at us to prepare for our drill and, as we did so, the Veiled One sat on his throne watching us intently.

We finished just before noon and rested in the shade of the trees drinking watered beer and chewing hard bread. Tuthmosis joined his brother on the cart, squatting on a makeshift footstool, feeding him with his own hand as they chatted and joked together. The Veiled One's shoulders shook with laughter. A deep, heavy sadness filled my heart. I had glimpsed something I had always wanted yet knew I would never have. I would have given the length of days to be in that cart joking with them, to be part of something, to be loved and accepted. I half-rose. Sobeck, who must have been watching me, grabbed my arm.

'Sit down, Baboon. Don't enter the panther's cage.'

'Physician, swallow your own remedy,' I retorted.

The moment passed and we fell to quarrelling, interrupted by Pentju who wanted to tell us a filthy story about men-starved temple girls pleasuring each other.

The Veiled One stayed for the rest of the day and returned each morning. Many years later he confided how his father had reluctantly agreed for him to join the Kap and enter the House of War. Sometimes Hotep arrived and sat on a chair beside the cart. Although he always treated the Veiled One with great respect and honour, he actually seemed more interested in watching us lash and cut each other. In truth Hotep came to assess our worth, to choose and confirm which path we followed. Huy was marked down for the House of Envoys, Maya for the House of Scribes, Pentju for the House of Life, Horemheb, Rameses and Sobeck for the House of War. Hotep shared this information with us as we sat gasping on the ground, letting our sweat cool. He'd walk among us, sometimes crouching down to whisper his advice, punctuating his statements with elegant movements of his hands. He never approached me. I didn't know what was intended and, in truth, I didn't care. I was more hurt that the Veiled One made no attempt to welcome, greet or salute me whilst I did not dare tell my companions about my earlier meeting with him.

In the privacy of our dormitory, or barracks as we now called them, we'd discuss and share the gossip of court. In the main the consensus was the same, though I never made any contribution: the Veiled One was a monstrosity.

'Perhaps he likes young men?' Meryre smiled, glancing girlishly at Maya. 'That's why he comes to watch our soft flesh sweat.'

'Do you really think that?' Horemheb demanded. 'I looked at him and thanked the gods for Tuthmosis.' Rameses nodded in agreement.

'No, I don't,' Meryre replied. 'But,' his voice fell to a whisper, 'I think the Veiled One is a symbol of the anger of the gods.'

Pentju put the Veiled One's strange appearance down to his mother being frightened by spiders or scorpions when she carried him in the egg. Huy openly wondered what effect his appearance would have on Egypt's allies when their envoys visited the court. Sobeck was more pragmatic and wondered whether the Veiled One was the result of some love potion his mother, the Great Queen Tiye, had indulged in. Of course these opinions were exchanged in whispers. No one would dare speak like that in the presence of Colonel Perra or, even worse, Tuthmosis. Only two people remained quiet, myself and Maya. I remembered that.

Our military training stretched into five seasons. The Veiled One was always in attendance, even when we moved down to the royal stables to acquaint ourselves with the horses – beautiful, sleek animals trained for the chariot squadrons of Egypt. We made the usual offerings to Reshef and Astarte, deities of Syria, the homeland of these swift, elegant carriers of war, as well as to Sutekh, the Egyptian Lord of the Horses. I loved that part of my training. I had no fear of horses, even those bloodied in war, arrogant and proud with their arched necks, flared nostrils and laid-back ears. We were trained and drilled in the use of harness, the head collar, noseband, blinkers and, especially, the straps, one across the top, the other under the horse's belly; it was important for these to be fastened clear and smooth with no knots or obstacles. We were shown how to hang the blue and gold streamers or war tassels, how to fix the pole cap between the horse's ears to carry plumes, feathers or artificial flowers which would display the colours of the regiment. After that we moved on to the chariot itself, with its semi-circular platform and curved wooden sides with a thin rail above it. We studied these instruments of Egypt's anger and glory, both horse and chariot. Colonel Perra told us we had to learn how to put both parts together, then use them so we would merge as one: driver, chariot and horses, the most deadly weapon of war.

Now I was a poor archer, ever ready to fumble with the flaxen bowstring or hard shaft of reed. Sobeck my companion proved to be an indifferent charioteer so we decided on our respective roles and I found my gift for war. At first I was clumsy but I grew to love the rattle of the chariot, the speed and power of the two horses and the exhilaration of a charge with streamers flying and horse plumes nodding. Like all young men I believed I had been born to ride in a chariot. My real education began after a number of nasty accidents when both Sobeck and I had either to jump clear and, on one occasion, even onto the back of the horses when a wheel buckled and cracked against a rock.

I became a charioteer, a master of the chariots, an expert in their construction. I studied their fabric, the imported elm and birch, as well as the tamarisk, which provided the wood for the carriage, the axles and the yoke. The six-bolt wide-spaced wheels placed at the back of the chariot were of special interest; their construction gave the vehicle more speed and mobility, their hubs and rims protected by thick red leather. The craftsmen described the body of the chariot, how it could be covered with copper and electrum and emblazoned with any insignia, whilst a floor of closely knit thongs heightened the experience in a full charge of standing on air. We learned how to position the quiver of arrows, the embroidered container for javelins as well as the leather pouches placed at the side of the chariot containing food and water for two men.

I chose my own horses, two bays, the Glory of Anubis and the Might of Montu. Believe me, nothing was more glorious than the 'Squadron of the Kap' in full battle honours, blue and gold plumes dancing between the horses' ears, their necks, backs and flanks protected by leather coats of the same hue, to which war streamers and tassels displaying the same imperial colours danced in the breeze. Our chariots, polished and emblazoned, would move in a straight line across the pebble-strewn hard plain to the east of the Malkata Palace, on the very border of the Red Lands. There were ten chariots in all, Prince Tuthmosis' and Colonel Perra's included. We advanced in a line, wheels creaking, horses neighing, streamers and plumage dancing, all a-glitter in the blaze of the sun. Sobeck standing beside me was dressed the same as me in a leather kilt, marching sandals and a coat of Syrian mail across his shoulders. I looked to the left and right, revelling in the power and glory of this moving line of war. The whole scene would be watched by the Veiled One sitting in his cart under an awning surrounded by his Kushites. Near one of the wheels of the cart, Weni, looking pathetic under his parasol, squatted on a camp stool and nursed his beer jar.

The drill was always the same. Colonel Perra would move forward and his tedjet, or fighter, would intone the war hymn.

'All glory to Amun who dwells beyond the Far Horizon!

All glory to his Son, the Strong Bull in the South,
who has received his favour.'

We would repeat the refrain. The paean would be intoned.

'All glory to Montu,
All glory to Horus, the Golden Hawk who is blind
yet sees.'

Each time we repeated the refrain, the chariots would move faster. The half-moon standard on Colonel Perra's chariot would rise and fall as it broke into a charge whilst we followed in fast pursuit. The earth rumbled under our wheels, the sky echoed to the crack of our whips, the sun bathed us in its glory as we broke into a breathtaking gallop across the grey-red ground, loosed like shafts from a bow, like hawks swooping through the air. All life, all thought, word and action narrowed down to that glorious cascade of charging horses and chariots. We would reach the arrow butts and the air would hum with our flight of arrows. Then we would be past, charging onto the narrow straw-filled baskets. I'd stand feet apart, slightly stooped, reins wrapped round my wrists, guiding and coaxing, singing out to my two beauties. I praised their speed, their fire. I'd watch their heads plunge and rise whilst, at the same time, keep a keen eye out for any obstacle or be ready to take any advantage of the ground. I was full of the heart-throbbing music of the God of War.

Beside me Sobeck leaned against the rail, his body taut, prepared to pull back the bowstring and, when the quiver was empty, stand, javelin in hand, ready for the next target. Once we dealt with that we'd turn, determined to outrace each other, though, of course, never pass Colonel Perra. It was a heart-stopping, blood-thrilling, death-challenging charge back across the desert to that waiting cart almost obscured by the shifting heat haze. Once we had reached the line there would be jubilation, laughter, teasing and taunting. Tuthmosis would climb onto the cart and embrace his brother, a gesture which always provoked a stab of envy in me.

One day, during the boiling heat of Shemshu, in the thirty-second year of the Magnificent One's reign, the Veiled One rose and, resting on his cane, its head carved in the shape of a Nubian, he clambered down from his cart. Veil pulled back, he walked along the line of chariots, impervious to the dust still clinging like a cloud around us. He stopped at every team and talked softly to the horses, letting them nuzzle his hand which, I suspect, was smeared with the juice of crushed apple. He looked at each of my companions, then passed on. He had certainly grown; the protuberant belly and breasts and broad hips were more pronounced; although his hands and feet remained delicately long and thin. His face was still striking, the cheeks slightly sunken, the lips fuller and those almond-shaped, well-spaced eyes luminous and liquid. He walked slowly but gracefully. A Kushite carrying parasols and sandals came hurrying up behind, only to be summarily dismissed. Silence reigned, broken by the creak of a wheel, the snort of a horse and the low buzz of flies hovering over the dung. Above us circled vultures, their broad wings dark against the sky. The Veiled One stopped before me and lifted his head, revealing a beautiful smile, warm and generous, and eyes bright with excitement.

'I will take Mahu, the Baboon from the South.' His eyes held mine. 'He shall be my tedjet.'

Sobeck immediately clambered down. I glanced at Colonel Perra who just shrugged. Weni was giggling behind his hand. Tuthmosis stood a little distance away, hands on his hips, a knowing look on his face.

'I will be the driver.' The Veiled One did not shout but his voice carried, an imperious command which no one dared question. He asked the names of my horses and, when I told him, he whispered to each, caressing their necks, letting them hear his voice and smell his sweat. He glanced up. 'We forget how horses can smell so keenly. But come, before they cool!'

The Veiled One let his shawl slip away exposing copper-skinned shoulders, their blades protruding, his back slightly bent. Resting on his cane, he walked along to the chariot and clambered in, ignoring my gesture of support. He slipped his cane into the empty javelin container and grasped the reins, spreading his bare feet, clicking his tongue. I sensed that his skill was as great as mine though the chariot was strange and the horses new. He stood next to me, misshapen yet graceful, careful not to brush or knock me. Beads of sweat ran down his neck, and his body exuded a sweet cloying perfume. Clear of the veil I now noticed how strange his head was: the sloping forehead, the egg-shaped skull, the strangely elongated neck. His movements were carefully measured. He backed the chariot out, turning it for the long run, urging the horses forward. Once we were some distance away he reined in and turned his face to the sun, staring up narrow-eyed. I wondered if his sight was as strong as our own.

'Praise me, Father,' he raised a hand, 'as I have praised you who existed before all time began. Bless me, Father, as you have been blessed by all creatures under the sun. Support me, Father, Lord of Jubilees, Ruler of the Years, beautiful in aspect. Let the rays of your power guide my heart with an iron hand. Oh, Joyous One, listen to your son the beloved.'

The others could not have heard him. He turned and winked at me.

'So we meet again, Mahu.' He clicked his tongue and urged the horses on. 'Even though I have watched you from afar.' He then glanced over his right shoulder and spoke in a tongue I couldn't understand, as if someone else was standing on the far side of the chariot. Sharp guttural words. I wondered if it was Akkadian, the language used by Pharaoh's scribes when writing to his vassal kings. He spoke again and turned back. 'You are not frightened, Baboon of the South?'

'Should I be?' I grasped the chariot rail.

The Veiled One chuckled. 'Do you know a funny story, Mahu? Can you tell me one?'

I racked my memory. 'An old woman had a very garrulous husband. He would never stop talking even when asleep.'

Again the chuckle. 'Every day,' I went on, 'she used to lead the cart on which he perched down to the market.'

'And?' The Veiled One grasped the reins more firmly.

'One day a passer-by ran up. "Oh ancient one," he yelped, "your husband has fallen out of the cart." "The gods be thanked," the Old Woman replied, rubbing her ear. "Why is that?" the passer-by asked. "Because for a moment I thought I had gone deaf."'

The Veiled One threw his head back and bellowed with laughter, loud and clear. He then urged the horses forward, snapping the reins, calling out their names, sometimes lapsing into that strange tongue. I was about seventeen summers old, the Veiled One a little older, but he drove like a Lord of the Chariots. Undoubtedly he had been trained yet he possessed a gift and I realised the chariot freed him of any disability; he could now fly like the Horus falcon. He stood slightly stooping, his arms, wrists and hands displaying surprising strength and skill. There is a time as any soldier knows when a war chariot, both horses and driver, become united, long like a spear speeding through the air; you are not aware of the barb, shaft or feathered flight, just its swift death-bearing beauty. The Veiled One urged the horses on. They galloped as one, their direction straight. He guided them round the potholes and ruts. I clung to the rail aware of the ground racing away beneath us, the buffeting breeze and the Veiled One immersed in the thrill of the charge. Now and again he would whisper under his breath. We reached the targets, turned and streaked back like a javelin to the mark. We slowed down, but then picked up speed again and the Veiled One, leaning slightly to the left then the right, made the horses perform the most complex twists, as any war chariot would in battle, slicing deep into the enemy foot. At last we stopped just in front of our admiring audience who cheered and clapped. The Veiled One grasped his cane and clambered down. A servant hurried up carrying his shawl, veil and dark leather wallet. The Veiled One grasped this, opened it and handed me an amulet of jasper, cornelian and red sandstone: it was carved to depict the two celestial hills of the Far Horizon with the sun rising between them. He pressed this *aknty*, this Sun-in-the-Horizon amulet into my hand, stroked my finger, winked and walked away.

Later that day we celebrated, though Tuthmosis and the Veiled One were not present. Colonel Perra had also gone to the palace to convey the Squadron's congratulations to the Princes. Naturally we discussed the Veiled One's skill, his strange, ungainly movements yet his mastery of the horses. Horemheb looked a little jealous, not so much of me, but rather that he had been outclassed: however, he had the good grace, once the beer loosened his tongue, to praise the Veiled One's prowess. Naturally I was teased and taunted. The beer jug was passed round. We stretched out our hands to the brazier, welcoming its heat against the cold night air. Weni, of course, was already drunk – clasped, as we say, in the arms of Lady Hathor. He abruptly put the jug down and, picking up a soiled napkin, covered his face and pretended to be the Veiled One driving the chariot, flailing his arms and hands around and provoking bursts of laughter from everyone except myself and Maya. Encouraged in his parody, Weni persisted, demanding what would happen if the Veiled One engaged in battle with a sheet across his face? Or, what if his chariot crashed? Again the imitation.

'Would he go hobbling round the battlefield?'

I emptied my beer jug onto the ground and walked away.

The following day was a festival. There was no drill but we went down to the stables to tend to our horses, and check the harness, frames and wheels of our chariots. I was immersed in memories of the previous day; the amulet I kept in a wallet, and now and again I would walk away, take it out and study it carefully. I stayed late that day, long after the others had left. Sobeck came hurrying down.

'Mahu, you'd best come!'

'What's the matter?'

Sobeck wiped sweat from his face. 'Weni has been found dead, drowned in a pool.'

I recalled that olive grove, the dark reed-filled pond, Weni leaning against the tree, beer jug in hand. I hurried back to the barracks where Weni's green-slimed, water-drenched corpse had already been laid out on the bench on which he had so often stood to lecture and berate us. Death is always pathetic but Weni's was even more so. He lay, eyes, nostrils and mouth clogged with brackish mud, his loincloth sopping wet, trickles of dark water running down his legs. With his swollen belly he looked like a landed fish and his face had the same look of surprised horror. I took a napkin and covered his features and recalled what Weni had done the previous day. Orderlies brought a stretcher to convey the corpse to the House of Death. The others drifted around, muttering amongst themselves. Meryre had tried to intone a mortuary prayer but the others were not interested.

'Get him prepared quickly,' Horemheb bawled at the orderlies, 'before he begins to smell.'

I crouched down and took the ring from Weni's stubby fingers. He'd always been proud of that, a gift from the

Magnificent One's father. I placed this on the corpse and looked carefully at the nail of that finger, plucking at the little strips of leather. The corpse was removed. I walked around the barracks through the side gate and into the olive grove. I found Weni's tree; the beer jug lay cracked on the ground beside it. The muddy edges of the pool were marked with the feet of those who had pulled him out. I noticed something gleaming in the grass and picked it up. It was a small copper stud, certainly not from the war-kilts of anyone in the Kap. I had seen such studs on the war-kilts of the Veiled One's Kushite retinue. I weighed this in my hand and got to my feet. Weni was an old soldier, a drunkard, but sure on his feet, careful what he did. Going back to the olive tree, I sat down and imagined Weni sitting there, half-drunk, those dark shapes creeping through the trees. A sharp, short struggle, the jug being thrown to the ground, Weni being dragged to the pool and forced in, his head and face held underwater until all life left his heart. I recalled Weni laughing mockingly the night before.

'Is there anything wrong?'

I whirled around. Sobeck stood staring at me curiously.

'No, no, nothing.' I got to my feet and threw the copper stud into the pool. 'No, there's nothing wrong, Sobeck, at least for the moment.'

'Such is he who has decayed,
All his bones are corrupt . . .
His flesh is turned into foul water.'

(Spell 154: *The Book of the Dead*)

Chapter 3

In the second month of the summer season shortly after the Festival of the Valley in the thirty-third year of the Magnificent One's reign, the Land of Egypt went to war. Fires were lit in the Temple of Montu and the priestly chorus of Amun-Ra began their verbal assault on the assembled deities of Egypt. The Word of War had come from the King's own mouth to be carried the length and breadth of the Kingdom of the Two Lands. The vile Kushites in the Eastern Desert had risen in revolt. They had put small garrisons to the sword and slaughtered the workers in the mines and settlements which produced the copper, gold and amethyst which had been placed there for the Divine One's use. The reports brought by the Sand Dwellers were truly horrific. Royal roads had been attacked, imperial messengers butchered and the honour of Egypt gravely insulted. The King's messengers, fleet of foot, took the decisions of the imperial will to every corner of the kingdom. The Kushite rebels were to be crushed.

Hotep himself, God's Father, came down with Colonel Perra to announce that the entire division, the 'Glory of Amun', of 5,000 men, not counting mercenaries, foragers, scouts and commissariat, would be despatched to deal with the rebels. The Horus unit, the Children of the Kap, would be included. Hotep raised a hand to quell our excitement as we crouched around him in the courtyard.

'Both Royal Princes will join the expedition. We depart in three days.' He raised his fan, spreading it out with one flick of his wrist. 'You, too, will go with them and bring glory to the Divine One's name.' His clever eyes searched each of our faces. 'We live for Pharaoh! We die for Pharaoh!' he added.

We thanked the Divine One for this opportunity to demonstrate our loyalty. Once he had left, accompanied by the palace guard, Colonel Perra provided further details: the Veiled One would be a member of the Horus unit. Weni's untimely death was now forgotten. My suspicions were suppressed in the stirring preparations. We all readied to leave, though Maya fell ill of a fever. We found him sweating in the early hours, his fat body shaking so much he was despatched to the House of Life.

'We won't miss him,' Horemheb muttered.

I doubt if any of us would have missed each other. Weni's corpse had been embalmed and despatched to the Far West without a second thought. Maya sent us messages of good will and begged Sobeck to visit him but he was caught up in the frenetic preparation of war. Armour was distributed, weapons brought out of store, chariots readied, the horses carefully checked by leeches from the Royal Stud. The regimental units began to mass in the fertile Black Lands north of Thebes. Hotep was given the temporary title of 'King's Son of Eastern Kush', with all the powers of a viceroy. We took our oaths of loyalty in the incense-filled outer courtyard of the Temple of Montu where the unit received its standard, the falcon head of Horus perched on the back of a crocodile. The Divine One himself deigned to show his face and the citizens of Thebes lined the Avenues of Sphinxes and Rams to throw flowers and greenery as we left the city in full battle regalia surrounded by the priests, choirs and imperial orchestras providing string music.

The army moved South by barge and boat, then force-marched to the great Fortress of Buhen just above the Second Cataract. By the time we reached it we were all sore, bruised, tired and dusty whilst the army could only be described as chaotic and confused. The High Command, the Viceroy, Scribes of the Army and the Lieutenants of Chariotry stayed in the fort whilst order was brutally restored. Both foot and chariots had organised into corps of companies of fifty under a pedjet. Our commanding officer was nominally Crown Prince Tuthmosis with Colonel Perra as second-in-command, being Standard Bearer of our platoon of fifty chariots. Our unit, now called the 'Glory of Horus', was composed of ten chariots, a small squadron with Horemheb as Captain.

The entire army paraded on the hard flat ground in front of the fortress, magnificent in its battle array. The Menfyt came first, the grizzled, battle-hardened veteran infantry in their stiffened body armour, wearing groin guards, *khopesh* swords thrust through their sashes, and carrying spears and shields, the latter adorned with the insignia of their unit. Behind them came the frightened raw recruits, similarly dressed – the Nakhtu-aa, the 'Strong-Arm Boys', who, in conflict, would stiffen the battleline. On our flanks marched irregular troops, hordes of Nubian archers, white plumes in their curled, bobbed hair, leopard or lion kilts around their waists, coloured baldrics stretching across their left shoulders then wrapped round their waists to form a sash. They wore thick, white tight collars round their necks and bracelets of a similar colour on their wrists. There were others: mercenaries from the Islands in the Great Green dressed in leather and carrying rounded shields and long swords, Libyan archers, virtually naked except for a phallus guard, their shoulders draped in ox or giraffe skin. All around these paraded the true power of Egypt led by the Maryannou, the Braves of the King, squadron after squadron of war-chariots, moving to the sound of rumbling wheels and neighing horses, a vivid array of different colours.

Trumpets blew and the royal standards, depicting different gods all paying obeisance to Amun-Ra, were lifted. Priests made sacrifice on the makeshift altars and the order of march was issued. Three corps, ours in the centre, were to advance east to secure the mines, re-fortify the settlements and mete out Pharaoh's justice to the rebels: any enemy taken captive was to be executed immediately.

We began our slow advance into hostile territory, Colonel Perra in charge. The Veiled One, travelling in his cart, was attached to our unit which was sent far ahead of the rest. We moved forward across a landscape so heinous I thought I was in the Underworld: boiling sun above grey, arid land, broken by the occasional oasis, or small village.

Dust devils stung our eyes and filled our mouths. We progressed slowly, dependent on water, foraging both for ourselves as well as the horses, oxen and donkey trains. We left the protection of other great forts, 'The Repelling of Seth', 'The Defence of the Bows' and 'The Power of Pharaoh', a slow-moving column of chariots, carts, horses, donkeys, oxen and men. At first the trumpets blared and different units sang ribald songs about each other, but soon the fiery heat sucked the life and breath out of us. Our feet, despite the leather marching boots, became scarred and stubbed by the hard ground. Above us the sun, our constant torturer, like a hole of fiery gold in the light-blue sky, moved along with us. Clouds of shifting dust and storms of sand, whipped up by the wind, made us look like a troop of ghosts moving across the arid Red Lands. The heat haze played tricks with our eyes, and taunted our hearts as well as our tongues with the prospect of cool running water. We piled our armour onto the carts and fashioned makeshift masks and hoods for our heads and faces, rubbing thick black kohl around our eyes. Sobeck quietly joked that we were now all 'Veiled Ones', though Horemheb pointed out that the secretive Prince, travelling in his chariot, asked for no special favours.

We kept to the fortified royal roads built years previously across the Province of Waat. Our scouts went out before us armed with maps to locate the wells and any source of running water. Of the other two divisions moving parallel to us we saw no sign. Their mission was to secure the amethyst mines in the North, ours was to reassert control of the gold and copper mines.

The rigour of the march shattered any illusion about the

beauty of war. No longer were we glorious chariot squadrons moving majestically across the plain to confront an enemy; now it was nothing but a searing trudge through a boiling cauldron, dependent on brackish water, hard bread and stringy, salted meat. We'd camp at night near some well or oasis. The stars hung low in the dark velvet sky whilst the biting cold made us pray for the heat of the day. All the beasts of the blackness closed in around us, attracted to the smells from our cooking pots as well as the fresh flesh of our oxen and horses. Yellow-skinned, dark-eyed lions coughed and roared. Jackals bayed like some demented choir at the moon but the greatest danger were the hyena packs, striped or spotted, great ruffs of hair round their necks. They would come in very close, so we'd catch their stench, hear their grunting and watch their amber eyes glow in the dark. They were ready to brave the fire, or the danger of an arrow through the darkness, to steal in and attack the horselines or oxen pens. Hideous neighs and dreadful animal screams would pierce the night. Trumpets sounded as the alarm was raised and archers brandishing flaring torches hurried to drive the night prowlers away.

We soon grew used to the horrors of the night, only too pleased to sleep on the ground and forget our present troubles. We would be kicked awake long before dawn to continue our march, and be given coarse biscuit to chew on with a couple of mouthfuls of watered beer. We'd kneel to pray to the rising sun and honour the Divine One with a hymn thundered out to the heavens:

'Greetings, Perfect of Face!

Possessor of Radiance
Whom Montu has exalted!
To whom Thoth has given the beautiful visage of
the gods.
Your right eye is the evening sun.
Your left eye is the rising sun.
Your eyebrows the Nine Gods.
Your forehead is Amun.
Fair of form are you,
Fierce-eyed lion,
Smiter of Kushites,
Crusher of the Vile Asiatics!'

After that our gruelling march would resume until the heat of the day grew so oppressive we would stop to camp. The Veiled One's cart, no longer protected by his Kushites but by a unit of the Strong-Arm Boys, trundled in front of the donkey-train. He made no contact with me or anyone else until six days after leaving Buhen, in the first coolness of an afternoon whilst we camped at an oasis. Exhausted after finishing a march of about thirty miles, I was with the rest, crouching in the shade of a tree ready to share out bread and water. Any teasing or taunting, superficial conversation or arguments had long since ceased. We had neither the energy nor the inclination for them. Only three things mattered: food, water and sleep.

I was chewing on a crust when I received an invitation to join the Veiled One in his rectangular scarlet pavilion standing to the left of the makeshift altar to Amun-Ra where our standards were piled. The pavilion was quite small, erected so the vents caught the breeze. The Veiled

One sat on a pile of cushions fanning himself vigorously. The small acacia table before him bore two reed platters of gazelle meat, bread and dried fruits, and a jar of white Charu wine. The pavilion was deserted. Some chests and boxes lay about. A clumsily erected camp bed screened by sheets stood in the corner, weapons were slung from a hook on a pole: a bow, a quiver of arrows, a leather corselet and a helmet of the same material. The Veiled One, however, was not dressed for war but in a gauffered linen robe with an embroidered sash. Beside him lay a curved sword and dagger, their blades glinting in the light of the oil lamps. He followed my gaze and smiled.

'It looks impressive, Mahu, but we have to be ready.' His smile widened. 'Even though we know the rebels won't attack.'

'Where are your guards?' I asked, obeying his gesture to sit at the other side of the table.

'Left in Thebes,' he replied lightly. 'Can't be trusted, or so my father says.' He leaned across the table and pushed a small piece of gazelle meat into my mouth, his dark eyes glowing with humour. 'We all know that's nonsense. One of the reasons Egypt has been able to conquer Kush and Nubia is that their inhabitants hate each other more than they do us Egyptians.' He bit into a piece of meat and I noticed how even and white his teeth were. He chewed his food slowly. The flap of the pavilion had been pulled back so he could watch the sun set behind the heat haze. He bowed his head and murmured a prayer then looked up, as if he was recalling something.

'You are wondering why I am here, aren't you?' He lifted his cup and toasted me. 'The answer is, I asked to come. Mother thought it was a good idea. Permission was granted surprisingly easily. I wonder,' he laughed dryly. 'I do wonder if the Magnificent One wants me back?'

I continued eating. The food was better than my own meal. Servants came and went, faint noises echoed from the camp: shouting, the neigh of horses, the lowing of oxen, whilst the wail of a conch horn marked the hours. The Veiled One asked about the Horus unit and the horrors of the march.

'I feel so secure in my cart.' His eyes held mine. 'I have to sit there, whatever the heat, whatever the dust. Now, how about this campaign, Mahu?'

We discussed its finer points. The Veiled One showed a surprising knowledge, voicing the same concerns raised by Horemheb.

'Our squadron is too small and too far ahead.' He grasped his wine cup close to his shoulder and leaned across the table. 'The nearest support is over thirty miles away, either to the North or West. We could easily be trapped and ambushed.' He drank from the wine cup. 'We could all be killed.'

'You, too?' I asked. The wine had emboldened me.

'Not me,' he replied lazily. 'I shall not die here. My Father will protect me. You carry the scarab I gave you?'

I nodded.

'Nor will you die.' He drained the wine cup and grasped his walking cane. 'Now it is cooler, we should go out.'

He crossed to the bed and picked up a pair of leather marching boots. Without asking I knelt and helped him put them on. He then demanded two military cloaks and, when they were brought, flung one at me. I'd heard the clatter and the neigh of horses as I finished the meal and found that a chariot had been prepared for us, a simple unadorned carriage with two horses. These were splendid creatures, with firm haunches and long legs, strong and black as the night. The Veiled One climbed in and handed me his cane. I took it and placed it in the javelin container. I wondered what was going to happen but was reluctant to ask. It was not yet sunset so the camp was still busy. No one stopped us as we rattled along the trackway past the horselines and quartermaster wagons into the brooding grey-brown desert. The sun was beginning to sink though it would be some time before it disappeared behind the horizon and the darkness came rushing in. The air was still hot and dry. The Veiled One clicked his tongue and shook the reins. We passed the picket lines; he then reined in and took the leather water jar from the pouch of gazelle skin attached to the side of the chariot. He pulled the stopper, handed it over and watched me drink.

'Good?' he asked, lifting the reins.

'Fresh,' I replied.

The Veiled One nodded. He waited a while then with one hand took the water jar from me and drank himself. He had used me as his taster. No wonder he was so confident that he would not die. He pointed with the waterskin to the distant mountain range which rose above the heavy haze.

'They change colour in the sun,' he remarked. 'And become so hot even the precious stones are transformed.'

He let the horses walk; the chariot swayed and creaked as the desert ground dipped and rose, treacherous land with its gullies, shallow valleys and rocky outcrops. The

Veiled One made the chariot twist and turn. The horses were nervous and so was I. Dark threatening shapes appeared, then vanished. The silence was oppressive, abruptly shattered by a howl, roar or the scream of some bird. I checked the bow and quiver of arrows. I eased the javelin in and out of the container. We passed scouts and foragers returning to the camp. Some were empty-handed, others carried the meagre game they had slaughtered. Soon we were by ourselves. No camp behind us, nothing but the sun, reddening the sky and that grey, dangerous land. The Veiled One nudged me playfully.

'They say we will soon be in the heart of enemy territory; until then we are safe.' He stared up, whispering to himself. 'My mother takes me out to the desert. She always has since – well, since I can remember. I like the desert. No mean streets, no pomp or ceremony.'

The horses whinnied and the Veiled One reined in. In a small rocky gully we glimpsed bones white and shattered, cracked and chipped; a skull lay next to a boulder like some broken toy. The Veiled One handed me the reins, grasped his cane and climbed down. He walked over and sifted amongst the bones.

'No copper or bronze,' he remarked as he squatted down. 'They must have been Neferu – raw recruits, deserters. They left the camp and fled in the wrong direction.'

The roar of a hyena did not disturb him.

'What do you think, Mahu?' He picked up a thighbone already turning yellow. 'This once belonged to a man. We know where his flesh went, into the belly of a hyena. But where is his *ka*? According to the shaven heads,' he pointed the bone at me, 'the *ka* of this man will never reach the Fields of the Blessed: his body hasn't been mummified, the blessing of Osiris is lacking. He has no heart, so how can he be judged on the Scales of Truth? Do you think he deserved that? Or doesn't it matter?'

He rose, resting on his cane, threw the bone away and came back to the chariot, lost in his thoughts. 'What do you think, Mahu?' he asked softly. 'What happened to the *Ka* of that man?' He rubbed his fingers together. 'Is it like smoke after the fire has gone out? Is that all he meant? Or will his *Ka* go somewhere else, to a place we cannot see?' He drew his eyebrows together, refused my offer of help and climbed back into the chariot. 'And what happened when he reaches the Fields of the Blessed? They must be crowded. Don't you have any answers, Mahu?'

'I am a soldier, not a priest.'

'"I am a soldier not a priest",' the Veiled One mimicked, face only a few inches from mine. He kissed me abruptly on the cheek. 'Do you know what I think?'

I stared back.

'I think the priests lie. They make up stories to keep their power strong and their bellies full. I don't think there is a *Ka*.'

'Nothingness?' I replied. 'That's possible.'

'No, I did not say that.' The Veiled One gathered the reins. 'I think there is a Blessed West and the souls, of the chosen ones, like flames of fire, go there.'

'And who chooses them?' I asked.

'Why, the *One* who has chosen them from all eternity.'

'And how do you know you are chosen?'

Intrigued, I waited for an answer, watching the sun

sinking fast, splintering the sky with red and gold rays. The roar and growl of night prowlers echoed on the strengthening breeze, and I caught that hideous stench of rotting meat. We had entered another small gully; the rocks around us, transformed by the setting sun, were no longer part of a landscape but something else which had sprung to life with a brooding menace.

'How do you know you are chosen?' I repeated.

The Veiled One turned the chariot round, flicking the reins. 'You know you are chosen, Mahu – just as today, I have chosen to eat and drink with you and share my thoughts with you.'

I stared up at the rocky escarpment and caught the moving outline of a large head and ruffled mane. The Veiled One followed my gaze.

'Don't be anxious.' He urged the horses up the escarpment and back onto the level plain. In the far distance the fires of our camp sparked and faded. The darkness was coming down, as it does in the desert, swift as a hawk from the sky. I looked to the left and right; shapes were slinking alongside us, watching the horses, searching for any weakness. I was concerned but the Veiled One began to sing:

'Oh you who are beautiful on the horizon
Whose loving power never sleeps.'

He urged the horses into a gallop, guiding them skilfully back into the camp. Grooms and servants came hurrying up. Grasping his cane, the Veiled One climbed down and looked up at me.

'You wonder why, Mahu, Baboon of the South, but in time you'll learn.'

He walked away. I returned to my campfire. My companions had eaten well on a quail Horemheb had brought down. Now they were settling in for the night. I took my blanket, rolled myself in it and lay down, my head against a leather pannier. Horemheb asked me where I had been but I pretended not to hear.

Two days later, the enemy struck – but not to the bray of trumpets or standards flying. No, they came pouring out of a gully like locusts streaking towards our carts: warriors, black as night, armed with shields and spear, running silently, taking advantage of our column half-drowsy under the relentless sun. We barely had time to grasp our weapons then it was shield against shield, sobbing and cursing, hacking at oiled bodies, dodging and feinting. No glorious chariot war but a grim hand-to-hand struggle. Our unit was between the carts and the horses. The enemy had struck before we'd even realised it. They tried to break our line of march, dancing to the left and right, thrusting with spears, grim figures of death.

The swirl of battle pushed me back towards the carts, away from my companions. I grasped my shield and slippery-handled *khopesh*. I was knocked, spun around and came face to face with a Kushite standing on a cart, ostrich plumes in his hair. He'd speared the driver and, weapon up and shield to one side, was preparing to jump down. We clashed in a bloody sweaty embrace, his breath hot on me. A war-painted face, glaring eyes, body soaked in oil. There was a fierce tussle, but then he stumbled on a corpse. I drove my sword into the soft part of his neck, ripping through flesh and muscle. He fell, body slackening, blood gushing out of his nose and mouth. I thrust him away; my stomach felt heavy and sick, my legs were trembling. I had killed. Bending over, I hacked off his right hand, lifting the bloody flesh up to the sky. I forgot my pains, the heaviness in my chest and belly, but now attacked with fury, eyes half-closed, lashing out to the left and right.

The attack faded, our assailants retreating like shadows under the sun. Some of our men were wounded grievously and had to be despatched with a dagger-thrust across the throat. The Nakhtu-aa, the Strong-Arm Boys, did this, moving quickly along our column, speaking gently to those who were beyond our care and slicing with a knife. There'd be a gargle, a last sigh, as they turned the body over. Our unit was safe. Horemheb had killed four times, the bloody hands piled at his feet, Rameses twice and Sobeck once. Rameses had the bloodlust on him. I am not too sure whether it was from anger or fear. He was insistent that the enemy dead be mutilated and, when I objected, he just shrugged and, moving off, began to hack at bellies. The enemy wounded were bound hand and foot, pushed out into the hot sand and buried alive. Two were saved for questioning, spread across fires and tortured but they were brave and told us nothing. Sobeck cut their throats and left their flesh to burn. The vultures were now flocking in above us, black shapes against the blue sky. Perra ordered all the enemy dead to be decapitated, their heads placed on stakes thrust into the sand.

A lector priest led us in a hymn of victorious thanks to

Amun-Ra: 'Oh you who are All-Mighty, All-Seeing and All-Powerful . . . !'

Our dried throats croaked the words then we moved on. The column was now battle-ready, scouts and flankers out. I was congratulated on my kill. Horemheb noted the severed hand and placed it with the rest, a grisly pile for the hyenas to eat once the scribe had estimated the number slain. I made enquiries about the Veiled One: he had taken cover in his cart, untouched and untroubled – the Nakhtu-aa had seen to that.

As the days passed, such attacks became common, the enemy taking full advantage of the terrain with its hidden gullies, outcrops, ravines and shallow valleys. The attacks were always the same bloody, terrifying hand-to-hand clashes. The Kushite chiefs were intent on damaging our carts and causing as much destruction as possible amongst our horses and oxen. A second column began to follow us, the lions, hyenas and jackals and, above us, Pharaoh's birds, the vultures, all keen on the bloody trail we left behind us.

Even at night we were not safe. Figures, like wraiths from the Underworld, leaped across our defences, scrambled under our carts, bringing death with a swift spear-thrust. Horemheb came into his own now; albeit not as experienced, he proved to be a better combat officer than Perra. Every night when we camped he insisted on digging a shallow ditch and throwing up an escarpment on which the Menfyt placed their war-shields to form an interlocking wall. The night attacks stopped but, during the day, they still came, these stealthy warriors, fighting for their homes and families. We killed and killed again.

My number of hands increased. My fears disappeared, the trembling stopped. I was a butcher doing what I was supposed to do. In truth I was more concerned at betraying my fear in front of my comrades than to the enemy.

Horemheb declared himself proud of our unit. No one mentioned how Pentju and Meryre always disappeared during these attacks though, I suppose, Meryre prayed and Pentju did tend to our cuts and bruises. Horemheb said he would recommend me for the Gold Collar of Valour. I shrugged, more desperate for pure water, soft bread and succulent meat. The Veiled One sent me another amulet, of purest gold, depicting a rampant sphinx trampling an Asian. The gift was delivered secretly. I did not show it to the rest but kept it close, as I did the other, during that long frenetic march. The number of our dead rose. Corpses were given quick burial but the Horus unit remained untouched. Pentju took a cut across his cheek which Horemheb claimed would mark him for life as a brave man. Pentju didn't understand the sarcasm. Meryre, ever gabbling his prayers, lost a tooth from a slingshot. Huy took a spearthrust in the fleshy part of his leg which made him dance, as Rameses remarked, 'like a temple heset'. Sobeck remained untouched: a cold, resolute fighter, quick and deadly as a striking snake. Horemheb and Rameses positively thrived, as Huy murmured, 'like the true drinkers of blood they were'. As the attacks continued, Horemheb and Rameses often came to confer with me; 'The Mighty General', as I now called Horemheb, studying me with those small black eyes in that strong face, Rameses, his perpetual shadow, smirking behind him as he clicked his tongue, nodding at my replies. The mood in our corps had changed and Horemheb was deeply worried.

'I am concerned,' he confided one night, as we sheltered in a small oasis eager for its water which the Kushites hadn't polluted. 'I am most concerned, Baboon of the South,' he repeated. 'The Kushites are great in number, more than we thought. It's as if . . .' He played with the bracelets on his wrist.

'It's as if what?' I snapped. I was tired and they had stopped me on my way to fill a waterskin. I wasn't in the mood for military strategy.

'It's as if the Kushites are concentrating on us.' Rameses finished the sentence for his companion. 'Their attacks are persistent. Two other corps are also moving East, the Glory of Ptah to the North and the Vengeance of Isis to the South.'

'We also know,' Horemheb took up the complaint, 'that behind us are the supply wagons and reserves, not to mention our main force. The Magnificent One's ships are sailing down the coast yet the enemy seem to be massing solely against us.'

'Perhaps they know you are here?' I teased.

Horemheb tapped me on the cheek and walked away shaking his head, his evil genius trotting behind him.

Eventually we entered the mining area and discovered the true devastation caused by the Kushite attacks. Whole villages had been wiped out, houses burned, the small temples polluted, the inhabitants slaughtered in every way the human heart can devise. Men, women and children had been bound hand and foot, placed in thornbushes which were then saturated with oil and set alight. Corpses, stripped by the vultures and animals, were impaled on stakes; the wells were swollen with carcasses. Miners, priests, officials and soldiers had been bound, staked out under the blazing sun or buried alive. In one village we found a cauldron, taken from the mine workings, filled to the brim with severed limbs.

We secured the mines, left a protective force and moved on. Horemheb's agitation deepened. Our force was being slowly reduced and we were now in the heart of enemy country. We entered their villages, abandoned and deserted, except for the old and weak who had been left behind. Rameses delighted in lining these people up, then moving quickly down the line, slitting one throat after the other. We came across refugees, or so they claimed, destitute, naked and unarmed. Horemheb ordered the war-chariots out to disperse or crush them. The Horus unit became the cutting edge of our corps, the point of the spear, the razor edge of the sword. As our tally of dead rose, the Veiled One's words came back to haunt me. What did it really matter? We were nothing but marauders moving across the landscape of Hell: the life-force of those men killed was a mere puff of breath, smoke from a dying fire, glimpsed briefly then quickly forgotten.

By the middle of the hot season we had secured all the mines, pushing the Kushites back until they were forced to make a stand. Our chariot squadrons were deployed, we made the offering to Horus; incense was burned on a scalding rock, we intoned the litany of supplication and hitched up our horses, now not so plump, ribs showing through their dusty coats but still eager and ready for war.

We deployed in a line of battle. The Veiled One sent a messenger to Colonel Perra: he wanted to be with us. Perra shrugged and, shamefaced, Horemheb ordered Sobeck to stand down whilst we waited for him to arrive. He came leaning on his cane, walking in ungainly fashion in his leather kilt and jerkin. He wore no sandals and his head was now completely shaven: the reddish-haired sidelock had gone. The Veiled One had decided he was now an adult, a warrior. He climbed into the chariot beside me, grasped the reins, nodded to his left and right, then passed his hand gently up and down my arm.

'You wonder why?' he murmured. 'Because I have to, Mahu. My Father wishes it.'

I was sweat-streaked, thirsty and tired.

'Your father?' I asked. 'The Magnificent One?'

'The One I love, Mahu, who is in the very air I breathe.' He wrapped the reins round his wrists and glanced away. Colonel Perra and Horemheb were now moving their chariots forward, standards displayed.

'Horus the Victor!' a lector priest intoned. 'Spread your wings above us. Devour the enemy! Let your heart be with us!'

The refrain was taken up by the rest. I remained silent. The Veiled One whispered a different prayer to his Father, face turned towards the sun. Ahead of us lay the Kushite host, formed into three distinct battalions across the desert, blocking our advance. They carried their own grisly standards, long poles bearing the heads of slaughtered Egyptians, and their raucous war-chant echoed across the plain. I was aware of the sweat, the clinging dust, the shifting heat haze, the hordes of flies.

I briefly thought of Aunt Isithia and wished she was with me, to suffer from the flies. The Veiled One was singing softly under his breath. Horemheb was eager to move, the Horus squadron taking pride of place in the centre of the battleline. Perra, shading his eyes, seemed anxious.

'The Kushite line is moving,' the Veiled One whispered.

I strained my eyes. The heat haze hung like a shifting veil between us and the enemy. At first I thought my eyes were playing tricks.

'They *are* moving,' I replied. 'They are retreating!'

They were gone. Horemheb was furious. He insisted on a pursuit, and a shouting match broke out between him and Colonel Perra, who was determined that we would stay in line and not follow.

'It's a trap,' he warned Horemheb. 'Only the gods know where they have gone or what they can see.'

In the end he had his way. Our battleline broke up and we drifted back to the camp. The Veiled One threw the reins at me, grasped his cane and left the chariot without a second glance. We fortified the camp and made ready lest the Kushites attack. Colonel Perra was now in constant communication with the army high command. Now the province behind us was clear of a hostile force, messengers could move quickly backwards and forwards. Late that evening, just before darkness, a chariot pulled by the finest horses in the imperial stables clattered into the camp. The messenger reported to Colonel Perra, who came to discuss the matter with Horemheb and the rest of the Horus unit. Colonel Perra was anxious and dust-streaked. Despite his personal bravery and military bluster, Perra depended heavily on Horemheb for advice and guidance.

'I have news,' Perra peered down at us squatting in a circle round the fire, 'from the Viceroy himself.' He held up the sheet of papyrus, kissed the seal mark and showed it to us. We bowed our heads. 'The Kushite chiefs have sued for peace and are eager to surrender. Early tomorrow morning I am to go out to accept their surrender.'

'I'll come.' Horemheb got to his feet.

Rameses of course joined him.

'That's why they vanished, wasn't it?' Huy remarked. 'A last act of defiance.'

'I don't care about that.' Perra made a cutting movement with his hand. 'Horemheb, you will stay. I will go with five chariots and some Nakhtu-aa. You will be left in command. Oh,' Perra smiled grimly at me, 'and you are to come with me.'

'He will not accompany you.'

I whirled round. The Veiled One, dressed in a beautiful gauffered linen robe, sandals on his feet and a blue and gold striped head-dress covering his scalp, stood resting on his cane beneath a palm tree. He walked slowly forwards.

'Colonel Perra, you received a message? I was not informed!'

'My lord.' Perra coughed and cleared his throat.

'I accept your apologies.' The Veiled One's voice was terse and clipped. 'But you will not take Mahu. He will stay and guard me. The Strong-Arm Boys are to accompany you.'

Colonel Perra glanced at Horemheb who shrugged.

'Your wish is my command.'

The Veiled One turned and marched off into the darkness.

The next morning Colonel Perra left. He and the accompanying four chariots clattered off, the Nakhtu-aa running beside them. Horemheb was anxious. He insisted that the camp remain on a war footing: shields up around the defensive perimeter, carts pulled across the entrance, every unit ready for battle. At first I thought he was showing off to the rest of us. I had been taken aback by the Veiled One's intervention and wondered why, but he never sent for me or asked me to stay near him.

As the day grew on I began to share Horemheb's unease. In the late afternoon a look-out cried that Perra was returning. I joined Horemheb on the perimeter. The entrance carts were pulled back as the chariots emerged from the cloud of dust, men running alongside them.

'Well, it's over,' Pentju sighed behind us, 'and the gods be thanked. We have done our service to Pharaoh and now we can go home, the ever-conquering heroes.'

I and others drifted away as Horemheb went down to the gates to await the Colonel. I was by the pool wetting my lips when the alarm was raised. I raced back on the path. Horemheb was screaming; the carts had been pulled across and the chariots swung through. A nightmare. The driver was not from our corps but a Kushite wearing Colonel Perra's head-dress and uniform. Each chariot had a thornbush attached to it to raise the dust and conceal the surprise attack. Perra and his group must have been slaughtered and their chariots and uniforms taken to penetrate the camp. Horemheb's warning had given us some respite. Conch horns and trumpets wailed. Every man was still ready for battle but the Kushite foot burst into the camp and a bloody hand-to-hand struggle took place amongst the trees. The first chariot contained only two, those behind more warriors, whilst enemy foot raced up the escarpment knocking aside our shields, eager to cause devastation. Chaos ensued, not so much a battle but separate fighting as our units clashed with this group or turned to face another. Corpses bobbed in the still water of the pool. Cooking pots and carts were overturned, a small well-armed group of Kushites reached the horselines to hamstring our mounts.

Horemheb saved the day, organising a phalanx of Menfyt and leading them forward to clear the camp. I struggled through the press, lashing out with sword or club or whatever weapon was at hand. A Kushite who had speared one of our lector priests slipped around a tree, lance back, shield slightly down, exposing his soft belly. I ducked and rushed in, thrusting my dagger deep, pushing the body away and moving on. I glimpsed Pentju beneath a cart, eyes all tearful. The swirl of fighting became less intense. Stumbling, searching for a sword, I glimpsed the Veiled One's pavilion, no guards before it as everyone had left their posts. I lifted the flap and entered. The Veiled One was on his knees trying to strap on his leather kilt, fingers fumbling with the thongs. I heard a sound and turned. Two Kushites had slipped through the entrance: they separated, shields up, moving their spears backwards and forwards. I glimpsed the Veiled One's *khopesh* and grasped it with two hands. One Kushite closed but he was nervous, leading with his shield. I crashed into him and knocked him aside; the other, slightly crouched, jabbed at me with his spear-point, but missed. I lashed out, slicing off his arm just beneath the elbow. The man staggered away, blood spurting, face contorted with pain. I turned, the other one was scrambling to his feet. I swung the *khopesh* and its razor edge sliced deep into his head, cutting through the top part of his skull, shearing it away as if it was the top of an egg. The pavilion was rent by screams, hot blood spurting, splashing my leg. I closed, hacking down with my sword on the Kushite's chest. I was screaming, sweat pouring down me.

'He's dead, Mahu! He's dead.'

I paused, gasping like a swimmer who had fought a fast-flowing river. The Veiled One was kneeling beside me. The Kushite whose arm I'd severed was trembling, eyes glazed, jabbering in a tongue I couldn't understand. The Veiled One knelt beside him, nodding gently as if he understood every word. I raised my sword but the Veiled One lifted his hand. He talked quietly to the man as if unaware of the trembling, the fear-filled eyes, the blood spurting like water from a cracked jug. My battle frenzy passed. The Kushite whose skull I had sliced lay slightly to one side, his chest a mass of wounds. I squatted down, clutching my dagger. The Veiled One was still talking quietly to the other. The man's eyes rolled back in his head, his tongue seemed thicker. He kept repeating the same words. *'Deret nebeb Ra.'*

'Egyptian,' the Veiled One smiled across at me. 'He keeps saying those three words. Listen.'

The man, fighting for breath, repeated them as if lost in some nightmare, unaware of his surroundings.

'*Deret nebeb Ra.*'

'Fetch Ra's Basket,' I translated. 'It doesn't make sense.'

'He has the words wrong,' the Veiled One smiled up at me. 'He means *nuber* not *nebeb* – gold not basket. They were bribed to attack, told to look for gold, easy pickings in this tent. I wonder who told them that?'

'Well, it doesn't matter now.'

'No, it doesn't,' the Veiled One replied and, lifting his dagger, cut the Kushite's throat.

'The sky thunders,
The earth quakes,
Because of you.'

(Utterance 337: *Pyramid Text*)

Chapter 4

The eating-house of the Residence had been transformed for the occasion. Painters had skilfully drawn battle-scenes on the walls in eye-catching dark blues, deep reds and golden yellows – all depicting the glories and bravery of the Horus unit. Our battle standards, displaying the Ever Blind Yet All-Seeing Horus triumphant over a fallen Kushite, rested against the wall on either side of the door. We sat on the softest cushions before small tables on which alabaster oil jars and scented candles glowed against the darkness. On the other side of our tables sat a line of beautiful temple girls in braided, perfume-drenched wigs, sloe eyes ringed with green kohl, bracelets dangling on their wrists, jewelled rings glittering on their long sensuous fingers, gorgets of amethyst round their soft throats. They came from the Temple of Isis and were called 'the Hands of God': they were well named! All were draped in linen veils which only enticed rather than concealed their beauty. These soft-eyed, red-lipped girls

119

with their tender glances and soft sighs were a constant paean of praise to the heroic Horus unit. Baskets of flowers and pots of myrrh, frankincense and cassia perfumed the air. In the far corner musicians with lyre, harp, flute and oboe provided soothing music to pluck at the heart and stir bittersweet memories.

At the top of the room in their robes of glory and scented wigs, jewellery glittering at throat, ear and finger sat God's Father Hotep flanked by the Veiled One and Crown Prince Tuthmosis. They were our hosts, the newly proclaimed Maryannou of Pharaoh, Braves of the King. Hotep sat impassively. The Veiled One had drunk deeply. He looked bored, playing with his food, strips of tender pork, beef, chicken and duck, tapping his nails against the silver goblet. Around his neck dangled a Collar of Valour as he had killed two of the enemy in hand-to-hand combat during the expedition.

I made no mention of my role. Once the two Kushites were dead, I had rejoined the bloody struggle taking place in the rest of the camp. I blinked and glanced away. We had been well entertained as a reward for our bravery. Sinuous dancing girls with flashing eyes, clicking castanets, naked except for a loincloth had performed feats of agility, their long black hair sweeping the ground and stirring our lusts. We were all there: Maya, plump and soft-skinned, staring calf-eyed at Sobeck. I ignored the heset opposite me, her flirtatious glances and coy, soft touches across the table. I closed my eyes. A month had passed since I had returned from 'The Cauldron' as we now called the desert. We had arrived home, lean, dark-skinned warriors who had bloodied themselves in the heat of battle. We had been given a hero's welcome, the Silver Bees of Bravery and the Gold Collars of Valour being bestowed on everyone in our unit. Maya had been so incensed with jealousy he had gone out and bought himself a cornelian necklace, a shimmering myriad of colours to hang round his own throat. Our deeds had been extolled by heralds and poets all over Thebes. Colonel Perra's death was viewed as an act of gross treachery for which the Kushite princes paid a terrible price. We had only survived their brutal ambush due to Horemheb; his vigilance and ruthlessness had kept us prepared. Our assailants were driven off, scouting patrols were despatched, then we retreated, faces towards the enemy, falling back until we reached the support corps, the 'Splendour of Isis' near the oasis of Koroy.

Tonight's celebration was the last of many. It not only marked the official end of the campaign but our education at the royal court. Tomorrow Horemheb, Rameses and Sobeck took up their commissions in the Sacred Band, an imperial regiment under Hotep's direct command, which guarded the temple complexes of Thebes. Huy was to enter the House of Envoys, Pentju and Meryre the House of Life, Maya, the treasury, the House of Silver. And me? I opened my eyes and smiled at the girl opposite. Tomorrow, I reflected, would take care of itself. The room was stifling, so I rose, bowed towards the High Table and went out into cool, fragrant night air. I stared up at the stars, brilliant gems on a dark cushion and wondered what I really would do. A sound made me jump. I turned round, my fingers going for the knife which wasn't there. Imri the one-eyed Kushite, leader of the Veiled One's personal guard, emerged into the pool of light. He bowed sardonically, one hand on his chest. 'I did not know,' he said, and glanced at me from under his eyebrows. 'I did not know you were one of the heroes.'

'A change,' I taunted, 'from when you put a rope round my neck.'

'Now you have put the rope round many a Kushite.'

'You were not there?'

'I would have been.' Imri stepped forward. 'Egypt is my home; my master has my loyalty.'

'Then why didn't you come with us?'

'Orders from above.' Imri winked his good eye and gestured towards the palace.

He walked back into the darkness. I wanted to be alone, away from Imri's careful gaze, the raucous chanting of the eating-house. I decided to walk on. Since my return from The Cauldron, I had grown to love the cool greenery of the evening, the whispering olive trees, the sound of running water, the comfortable silence, unbroken by the prowlers of the night. I also wanted to think and plan – but about what? Where was I to go? What was I to do? I had fought as a soldier, the stench of blood was never really far from my nose and mouth. My sleep was plagued by nightmares. I could not do that again, at least not for a while.

I found myself walking down towards the Silent Pavilion, keeping to the line of trees. Surprisingly its gates were open, the courtyard bathed in pools of light from glowing braziers and oil lamps. People were about to leave. I hid behind a sycamore and watched a group of courtiers protected by Nakhtu-aa, swords drawn, shields up. Yet, despite the ring of protectors, the group looked relaxed. A man of middle height walked between two women, the rest appeared to be retainers. The elder woman was Great Queen Tiye – I recognised those high cheekbones and full lips, the hard sensuous mouth. The other woman was much younger. Just outside the gate, she stepped into a pool of light; pausing to listen to something her male companion said, she threw her head back and laughed. My heart skipped! My soul, that hidden force within me, surged to meet hers. It was the first time I had experienced such passion and, indeed, the last. The sheer exhilarating beauty of that face!

In my wine-drenched frenzy I thought she was staring directly at me, hands clasped, head slightly tipped back, hair cascading down, a jewelled-braid band about her brow, beautiful sloe eyes under heavy lids, that laughing, merry mouth. Despite the darkness I saw it all. A soul on fire with her own beauty! Nefertiti! *Nefer* means beautiful and the name was created for her. Till that night I'd never loved and, since that night, I have never really loved again. Don't mock, don't ridicule. Each soul has its song, each heart its purpose. Nefertiti was my song, my purpose. You'll say it is ridiculous. I thought it was miraculous. A vision by moonlight, a face which took in all my longing: all my hurts, all the stupidities and the waste – I could forget them all, looking at her! On that evening I stared on the face of my eternity and became lost in it. I still am. Don't mention courtship, getting to know someone, nurturing feelings. What nonsense is that? If death can come in a heartbeat, why not the profoundest love? I just watched openmouthed. The vision laughed again, a merry sound which touched my soul and taunted it with what could have been, what might have been. Then she was gone, my beautiful queen of the night!

I stood for a while leaning against that sycamore trying to control my breathing, the pounding of my heart. I had glimpsed beauty before, the eye-catching elegance of the temple girls, but this was different. At the time I wondered who she was. Tuthmosis had sisters but she couldn't be one of these. I reckoned she must have been in her seventeenth or eighteenth summer, perhaps a little younger. Her skin looked golden, not as dark as Queen Tiye's, so was she from beyond Egypt's borders? Yet the way she walked and acted showed her to be very much at home with the most imperious of Egypt's queens. The gates of the Pavilion closed. I heard the bar falling into place. Were they visiting the Veiled One? Yet he was absent, drinking and carousing with us or pretending to. Was she the reason he looked so glum, so downcast? I turned and walked slowly back. The noise from the eating-house had grown, drowning the musicians and the singers. The door was flung open and Sobeck, followed by Maya, came staggering out. They brushed by me lost in their own tangle of words and crossed to a grassy verge where they both urinated cackling with laughter, sharing some obscene joke before lurching back.

'Sobeck.' I caught his arm. He turned blearily.

'What is it, Baboon?' He swayed on his feet.

Maya, just as drunk, tried to hold him straight.

'Sobeck, you've been careful since your return?'

My glimpse of that beautiful woman had provoked anxieties about my companion, the nearest I had to a friend. 'Sobeck, you've been nowhere near the imperial harem?'

Sobeck tried to speak, tapped the corner of his nose and, bawling with laughter, allowed Maya to take him back to the door.

I walked a little further. Huy came out with two hesets, disappearing into the darkness and soon the silence was broken with cries and pretty screams. The door opened again. I turned, half-expecting the Veiled One, but Hotep came out, fan in one hand, a strangely carved amethyst goblet cupped in the other. He held this up and toasted me, acknowledging my bow.

'It has a sacred emerald in it.' He drained the cup and pushed it towards me, twisting it so I caught the light of the emerald within. 'A sure protection,' he murmured, drawing closer, 'against poison. It changes colour if any foul potion or substance is mixed with the wine.'

'You fear assassination?'

I was still immersed in the vision of beauty I had seen, impatient at having to talk to anyone. Hotep's patrician face creased into a smile. 'Power and murder walk hand-to-hand.'

'A fine celebration.' I gestured towards the light-filled windows through which the candles and oil lamps glowed. 'Colonel Perra would have been very impressed.'

'His corpse was never found.' Hotep slipped the fan into a small pocket in his robe and caressed the cup. 'The men responsible were impaled, their sons sold into slavery. Those who survived were brought back to Thebes.'

'How many?'

'Only a few survived the march,' Hotep grinned. 'And

their skulls were shattered by the Mighty One at the Temple of Montu. You must remember, you were there?'

Of course I, along with the other Maryannou, had lined up at the foot of the temple steps. At their top the Divine One, the Magnificent Person, slouched on his throne, his protuberant belly and breasts easy to see beneath his *nenes*, the Coat of Glory, Pharaoh in all his magnificence! He wore the blue war-crown of Egypt and sat under a gold, silver-tasselled awning. Next to him on a stool sat Queen Tiye in a cloak of shimmering feathers – the Coat of a Million Colours as it was called. On her head the vulture head-dress was stiff, white plumes either side of the sun disc. Around the imperial couple, in all their glory of gauffered robes, glossy animals' skins, shawls and kilts, clustered the leading priests, courtiers and army officers. The Magnificent One, throned in judgement and grasping the flail and the rod, was ready to dispense judgement to those who had dared lift their heads against his sandal. From where I stood I had a clear view of the Magnificent One's sagging cheeks, deepset eyes and pouting lips, which moved incessantly as he tried to soothe the abscesses in his gums.

The courtyard behind us was packed with notables, skins oiled and perfumed, their fragrance mingling with the scents of flower-baskets and jars of burning perfume. They had all come to see judgement dispensed and the blood flow. Trumpets blew, standards were raised and lowered as the Kushite prisoners, arms and hands bound behind them, mouths gagged, were forced up the steps. The Magnificent One rose, grasped his great war-club with its oval-shaped head. The prisoners knelt along the top step. The Magnificent One, assisted by Hotep, moved down the line. He grasped a tuft of hair specially prepared on each prisoner's head; as he did so, more trumpets blared. The club was swung, skulls were shattered amidst muffled screams and the steps ran with blood as the crowd hailed the might of their Pharaoh. Colonel Perra's death was being avenged.

'It's a pity his corpse,' Hotep broke into my reverie, 'and that of the others were never found.'

I recalled that Kushite in the Veiled One's tent, arm sliced off, blood gushing, body jerking, the guttural whisper crying out those strange Egyptian words: *'Deret nebeb Ra.'*

'What are you thinking, Mahu?'

'Nothing,' I lied. Before I left that tent the Veiled One had sworn me to silence. I studied the cunning face of this hollow-eyed patrician. 'Did you come out especially to show me your goblet?'

'No, I didn't.'

'So what do you want with me?'

'My thoughts exactly,' Hotep replied. 'What are we to do with Mahu, Baboon of the South? The army, the writing office? What about the House of Secrets?' He passed the cup from hand to hand. He was about to continue when the silence was broken by more cries of pleasure.

'Huy has slaked his thirst for soft flesh.' Hotep glanced at me. 'And how will we slake your ambitions, Mahu?' He wagged a finger in my face. 'But come, let's return, the formal addresses have to be given. Huy!' he called into the darkness. 'Your host awaits you.'

We returned to the stuffy perfumed eating-house. Huy,

all dishevelled, staggered in to be greeted by jeers except from Maya who glared at him like a jealous girl. Horemheb, festooned with his honours, rose to his feet, banging the rim of his goblet on the table. He held his cup towards Hotep and the two Princes.

'May the grace of Amun be in your hearts,' he intoned. 'May he grant you all a happy old age and that you pass your life in joy and honour, your lips healthy, your limbs strong.'

I saw the Veiled One pull a face.

'Let your eyes be keen,' Horemheb continued, 'your raiment of the finest linen. May you ride in a chariot, a gold-handled whip in your hands, drawn by colts from Syria whilst slaves run before you to clear your way . . .'

On and on Horemheb prattled.

'May your scent-maker spread over you the odour of sweet resin and your chief gardener offer you garlands. May you remain secure whilst your enemies are brought low. The evil men impute to you does not exist. You speak with true voice and are honoured among the gods.'

Horemheb then raised his goblet in toast and all followed suit. Hotep delivered a pretty reply. Toasts were drunk, after which God's Father rose and, followed by a rather drunk Tuthmosis, one arm over his enigmatic brother's shoulder, made his farewell to the men. For a while the girls entertained us and a blind harpist sang a sad song:

'Men's bodies have returned to the earth since the beginning of time and their place taken by fresh generations.

As long as Ra rises each morning so long will men beget and women conceive and through their nostrils they will breathe.

But, one day, each one that is born must go to his appointed place so let's make it a happy day.

May we be granted the finest of perfumes, lilies and garlands to bedeck our shoulders. Let us be true of voice . . .'

We cheered the singer to the roof then he, the hesets and the musicians were all dismissed with gifts and assurances of friendship. The children of the Kap, the Unit of Horus the Glorious, were alone for the last time. We sat in silence for a while, each recalling the passing time, invoking memories of our first days there. Meryre led the recitation of past events and we were on the brink of becoming maudlin when Rameses banged his dagger against the wall.

'The wager was offered,' he shouted, his snake-eyes glittering with malice. 'The wager was offered. Has it been taken?'

Horemheb was smiling. I could have cursed both of them. In their eyes Sobeck was a rival, a man as warlike and brave as both of them, which is why Rameses had baited the trap.

'Well, have you?' Huy glared blearily down the room at Sobeck. I glanced at my companion. He thrust Maya away and fumbled in a leather bag concealed beneath the table. He scrambled to his feet and held up a statue of pure alabaster on a gold and silver base.

'The statue of Ishtar,' he bawled.

Horemheb and Rameses clapped.

'I have won the wager,' Sobeck boasted.

I closed my eyes. Sobeck had returned from The Cauldron eager for perfumed flesh and to renew his acquaintance with Neithas, one of the lesser concubines in the imperial harem but still one of the Royal Ornaments, forbidden even to be touched by another man. One night, shortly after our return from the war, Sobeck had boasted about the favours Neithas had granted, and regaled us with stories about the Magnificent One's sexual appetite. How sometimes he liked to be beaten and whipped or taken in the mouth. We had listened greedily to the lurid stories of the harem and the Magnificent One's private pleasures. Rameses had then sprung his trap. He accused Sobeck of lying and taunted him to produce proof. Now I knew Sobeck met Neithas in the olive grove where Weni used to slurp his beer, nevertheless I kept silent as Sobeck protested about his prowess and said that he spoke with true voice. Rameses, however, refused to be mollified: he accused Sobeck of lying, provoking him to prove his conquest. Sobeck had agreed. He promised that one of the precious statues of Ishtar, kept in wall niches either side of the doorway to the Royal Harem would be his. Only a Royal Ornament, a concubine of the Magnificent One, was allowed to hold these.

'Well, Rameses?' Sobeck shouted. 'I have the statue and each of you must provide me with a horse, that was the wager. I promised I would show you tonight and so I have!'

We all nodded in agreement, yet Huy, Meryre and Pentju, drunk as they were, realised how dangerous this conversation had become.

'We didn't think you'd do it,' Rameses purred like a cat. 'We thought you were only joking.'

Maya, one hand on Sobeck's knee, was staring up at him.

'Aren't you jealous, Maya?' Horemheb called.

Maya leaped to his feet and ran crying into the darkness followed by cat-calls and jeers. Sobeck, carrying the statue, followed whilst the rest of us returned to our drinking.

I slept late into the following day, well past noon and woke to find the dormitory empty. My companions had either risen early or returned to their own homes in the city. I shaved and bathed, going out to sit on Weni's bench in the courtyard. The rest of the Residence was deserted. My throat was dry so I drew a pot of spring water from the well. I sat in the shade wetting my throat and hoping the pain in my head would go. The events of last night's banquet came and went but I was really trying to recall that beautiful face. I was in the Valley of Ghosts, memories clustered all around me. Weni cradling his beer jug, the priests armed with their sticks, watching us write. Horemheb and Rameses as close as twins, heads together. In the past I had chosen to be alone, an hour here or a day there, but now I was alone because I was by myself, lonely, bereft of friends and family. I thought of going down to the city, to visit the Mistresses of the Temples, but the previous evening's celebrations had provided enough excitement.

I kept recalling the Beautiful Woman. I wanted to see her again, gaze on her smile, rejoice in her presence, listen to her voice. I felt no embarrassment. I was more pleased not only because of what I had seen but because of what I felt. The others in the Kap used to ask me if I had a heart, and that always recalled the chilling words of the fortune-teller about Aunt Isithia. I remembered my father striding in and out without a second glance for me. Was I cut from the same wedge? A man with no feeling? The Woman of Beauty had changed all that. I spent that entire day in the Residence sleeping or wandering around. One or two servants came to clear up and move things in or out. They provided me with a little food. I was very concerned that none of the others had returned, though when I checked, the coffers and chests were empty. They had taken everything with them, leaving no trace of their long stay.

The day dragged on. I was sunning myself against the wall when the conch horn wailed, followed by the creak of wheels and the lowing of oxen beyond the walls. I slipped on a robe and quietly left, not through the main gate but a side entrance. I kept to the trees which lined the path down to the olive grove – what I always called Weni's place. Perhaps it was my military training, those long searing weeks out in The Cauldron, but I sensed danger so I kept in the shadows.

As I waited and watched, a sombre procession came into view. I turned cold with fear at the sight of the executioner of Thebes, a jackal mask over his face, the *nafdet*, the symbol of office over his shoulder, a long black pole with a gleaming axe-head. He was dressed in a red leather jerkin with kilt and boots of the same colour. I had glimpsed him before on my rare visits to the city when the Jackal Man, as they called him, carried out Pharaoh's justice along the quayside near the Great Mooring Place. Behind him trooped a line of acolytes, similarly dressed. A frightened, wizened lector priest gabbled out prayers. Two carts, guarded by Libyan mercenaries in black animal skins, grotesque masks over their faces, came next. Each cart bore a stout wooden cage. In the first a young, dark-skinned woman, naked but for a leather skirt, crouched in terror, hands bound before her, a gag in her mouth, eyes bright with fright. In the second cage prowled a large feral cat, thin-ribbed but vicious and snarling with hunger. On the first cage was pinned a scrawled notice: *Neithas, Adulteress, Traitor*.

I slipped back to the Residence. I knew what was about to happen. Sobeck's lover had been caught. She would be slung in the cage in the olive grove where she had betrayed the Magnificent One. The cat would be put in with her. I crouched like a frightened boy in the dormitory even as the hideous screams began. They continued till late in the evening when the poor woman eventually died, or the executioner took pity and dealt her a killing blow. I was more frightened than I ever had been in The Cauldron. Where was Sobeck? How had Neithas been discovered? Was it Rameses who had informed on them? Horemheb? Or the spy in our midst? I recalled Sobeck regaling us with those juicy morsels of gossip about the sexual prowess, or lack of it, of the Magnificent One. If the court learned that, every one of us risked a hideous death. Is that why the Residence was deserted? Had my companions been arrested? I drank more wine than I should have done and fell asleep, only to be aroused roughly by Huy holding an óil lamp, his face riven with anxiety.

'You've heard the news?'

'And the screams,' I replied. 'Where is Sobeck?'

'They were both caught returning to the palace,' Huy replied. 'Judged and sentenced immediately by the High Priest of the Temple of Amun-Ra.'

'And Sobeck?'

'In the Chains,' – a reference to the palace prison. 'He has been sentenced to be put to the Wood.'

'Exposed!' I gasped, struggling to sit up. 'Sobeck out in the desert?'

'The Magnificent One was furious.'

'Do they know about us?'

Huy shook his head. 'The others have sent me. They want you to visit Sobeck. You are his companion.'

I argued but at last agreed. Huy made to leave.

'One other thing,' I called. He came back. 'If they were caught red-handed,' I swung my legs off the bed, 'then there must be a spy amongst us!'

Huy just stared at me and left.

I dressed in a gauffered robe, my colours and decorations clear to see. They gave me safe passage across the palace grounds. The Chain's cellars and dungeons lay below the royal barracks. Again the guards let me through down into a stiflingly hot, sombre corridor. A man and woman, cloaked and hooded, their lined faces wet with tears, pushed by me. I guessed they were Sobeck's parents.

The masked gaolers under the command of one of the executioner's assistants, a tattoo of the *nafdet* high on his right arm, did not question me but opened the door to Sobeck's cell, a small stone room with a narrow vent high in the wall. On the far side, a slab of raised, rough stone served as bed, table and stool. The ground underfoot was mud-strewn and smelt like a midden-heap. Two lamps of cheap oil glowed beneath the garish curses drawn on the wall for the benefit of prisoners, about how the anger of Amun-Ra would consume them:

'He will give you over to the King's fire and the day of his wrath. His uraeus will shoot out flames at your face. Your flesh will be destroyed, your body consumed. You will become like a serpent of the Underworld on the morning of New Year's Day, dead and rotting. No more will you be able to pursue the offerings of the dead. No one will pour out water for you. Your sons will not succeed to their inheritance. Your wives will be violated before your very eyes. On the day of slaughter you will be put to the sword. Your body will shrivel with waste for you shall be hungry and yet have no bread.'

Sobeck, dressed only in a loincloth, sat beneath this hideous scrawling. He was dirty, his face and body covered with cuts and bruises. He grinned and spread his hands.

'Why Mahu, Baboon of the South. I would like to welcome you.' He stared round. 'I never thought I'd regret leaving The Cauldron.'

I could only stand and stare.

'Silent as ever,' he breathed. 'What have you come for,

Mahu? To see if I have talked?' He pulled a face and shook his head. 'Tell them not to worry, especially those two vipers Horemheb and Rameses. I was drunk.' He rubbed his face. 'I was stupid.' He screwed up his eyes. 'Neithas?'

'She's dead. I heard her die.'

Sobeck bent his head, shoulders shaking.

'To be put to the Wood. Ah well.' He lifted his head, tears in his eyes. 'You've heard the poem, Mahu?

> 'Let's live and love.
> Sun sets and sun rises,
> But when our brief day has set
> There's nothing left but
> Sleep and perpetual night.'

He smiled grimly. 'But that wouldn't affect you, would it, Mahu? You have no heart, to live and love.'

I recalled that beautiful face. 'I might have.'

'They wanted the statue back,' Sobeck continued as if he wasn't listening, 'but I was so drunk and Neithas was so terrified she didn't tell me so I don't know where it is.' He got up, walked towards me and put his hands on my shoulders. 'I was a good companion, Mahu?'

'You were.'

'Look at you,' he breathed, 'black tight hair, a handsome face and those deepset eyes like a monkey on a branch.' He let his hands fall away. 'Will you help me?'

'How can I? What influence do I have?'

'The statue!' Sobeck went back and lay down on his bed. 'Find the statue, then do what you can!'

*   *   *

When I left the Chains and returned to the Residence, it was late afternoon. I sat in the porticoed entrance trying to recall what Sobeck and his lover would have done. Undoubtedly they were betrayed. Justice would have been fast as well as terrible. The Magnificent One would not wish to make a great show of being betrayed by a Royal Ornament.

A sycamore tree at the far side of the Residence caught my eye and I recalled Aunt Isithia's garden, Dedi singing beneath the tree, bringing out the piece of pot-shard on which my aunt had scrawled her curse. I got to my feet and went into the olive grove. Both the cages had been removed but the reek of death remained; splashes of blood still stained the grass, rutted and marked by the carts. Where, I wondered, would I take a young woman for courting and have my pleasure?

I went deeper into the olive grove, vigilant for any soft shady grass which could be used as a couch, away from the path but not too far, not in the dead of night when the two secret lovers would not dare use an oil lamp or carry a flaring torch. A little brook ran through the grove to feed a small pool nearby. Eventually I found the place I was looking for. The grass was well-shaded from the sun by the thick branches of the olive tree. The lovers had drunk from the rivulet whilst they had left pathetic traces of their stay, small beads and a soiled linen cloth smelling of perfume. I went round the olive tree, dug at the soft, recently-turned earth and plucked out the statue.

The following morning, dressed in all my glory as I termed it, I presented myself at the gates of the Silent

Pavilion. Imri allowed me through into the courtyard where servants and retainers were lounging. A chariot had been unhitched and a palanquin rested on the ground. My heart leaped. Had the Beautiful One returned?

'My Lord is with his mother and His Excellency God's Father, Hotep,' Imri explained. He led me across the courtyard, around the side of the house and into a well-watered fertile paradise of a garden. The flowerbeds had been enriched with black Canaan soil in which flowers of every description blossomed to give off their fragrance. Small pools with lush reeds and water plants glittered next to shady alcoves and herb plots as well as a small lawn where a baby gazelle grazed. Behind a screen of sycamore trees stood a brilliantly coloured pavilion approached by steps, its door panels pulled aside to catch the sun. The Veiled One was sitting at a table within, his mother on his right, Hotep on his left, laughing and talking, picking at the silver dishes laid before him. Imri told me to wait and, going ahead, knelt at the foot of the steps, nose to the ground. I couldn't catch his words. The Veiled One ignored him, staring at me, a faint smile on his face. Imri waved me forward. The Veiled One threw me a cushion on which to kneel. I caught this and made obeisance. Hotep lifted his cup so as to shield the lower part of his face. I caught the Queen staring curiously at me so again my head went down.

'Very good, very good, Baboon of the South,' the Veiled One laughed. 'You may now raise your head and look on our faces.'

The first one I stared at was Queen Tiye, a woman I had glimpsed from afar. She was of middle stature, her body rather thin but very elegant. She was dressed in robes of purest white, an embroidered shawl across her shoulders, a shimmering necklace of cornelian around her throat. On each of her fingers sparkled a precious gem. Silver bangles clattered on her wrists. It was her face which held me: very feminine, with strong, laughing eyes but a firm mouth, lips slightly drooping as if in disapproval. She'd kept her own hair; this was neatly dressed and caught up under a shimmering net of mother-of-pearl. She delicately popped a piece of meat into her mouth.

'Is this the one, my son?'

'The Baboon of the South,' the Veiled One agreed, 'son of Seostris, a Colonel of the Medjay who performed great service . . .' the Veiled One glanced at me sardonically, 'in the Eastern Deserts. Why, Baboon, have you come bounding up my garden path?' The words were harsh but the voice was soft. Again I bowed.

'None of that,' the Veiled One reproached me. 'You'll give me indigestion. One thing I can't stand are bobbing priests.' He paused. 'Or baboons.'

'Your friend has been taken up.' Hotep lowered his cup. 'Sobeck is to go to the Wood for daring to raise his eyes, let alone anything else,' God's Father sniggered, 'against a Royal Ornament.'

The Veiled One clicked his tongue in mock disapproval though I could see both he and his mother were amused by what had happened.

'The girl is dead,' I declared.

'And so she should be.' The Great Queen's voice was sharp and clipped. I caught the trace of a faint accent. 'If you drink the wine and eat the salt of the Royal House you do not share it with commoners.'

'She died brutally,' the Veiled One remarked. 'I went down to see what was left of her in the cage, and her body was badly mauled. They killed the cat with arrows.'

Tiye waved her fingers, a sign she had heard enough.

'So, if you haven't come for the girl,' the Veiled One teased, 'you must be here to plead for Sobeck?'

'I had a dream last night, my lord.'

The smiled faded from the royal faces.

'I was down by the Nile, it was dark and swollen. The sky had turned red; I realised I was going to be visited by a god.'

'Did you really?' The Veiled One moved his head slightly to the side, a look of mock astonishment on that strange face. 'And what was your dream, Baboon?'

'I saw the waters part. A huge crocodile emerged with the Jackal-Headed One riding on its back.'

The Veiled One's head went down. He was laughing, though both the Queen and Hotep remained grim-faced.

'He told me where to find the stolen statue of Ishtar,' I continued in a rush. 'I was to dig it up, return it to the Magnificent One and seek his pardon for the sins of Sobeck.'

'And you dug it up, of course.' Hotep held his cup in one hand and waved the other airily.

'I did. In the olive grove where they met.' I produced the statue from a sash in my robe, lifting it so it gleamed in the light.

'You could be arrested,' Hotep remarked lazily. 'They might say you are an accomplice.'

'Then I shall call witnesses, Your Excellency. They will report that I have no friends or accomplices.'

The Veiled One pointed a long spidery finger. 'And you discovered the statue? Leave it there on the steps.'

'Why have you come here?' Queen Tiye demanded. 'Why not take it immediately to the court?'

'I am not favoured to look on the Divine One's face, Your Majesty.'

'So you are going to ask my son to do it for you?'

I didn't reply but stared at the Veiled One. He looked angry.

'My lord?' I begged.

'Sobeck violated my father's honour. The power of Pharaoh is not to be mocked.' He flicked his fingers. 'Withdraw and await.'

I bowed my head in surprise, fighting hard to control my temper. I recalled that pavilion in The Cauldron, the two Kushites bursting into the tent, spears eager for his blood. I rose, backed away and joined the noisy throng in the courtyard. They were watching a monkey perform tricks; the little fellow reminded me of Bes. I must have been there an hour when Imri returned and grasped me by the shoulder. As I got to my feet, his grip tightened.

'You really should have a rope round your neck,' he whispered. Then his face broke into a smile. A patch now covered the hole where his right eye had been; the white of the good one was slightly yellow and flecked with blood.

'You never asked,' he rapped out, 'where I lost my eye?'

'I was never really interested.'

141

'Out in the Red Lands.' Imri ignored the insult. 'A stone from a sling found its mark in me – and that's why I am here, Mahu. Only those with disfigured faces guard my master.'

'And?' I asked, trying to break free from his grasp.

'Why are you here, Mahu?' he asked softly. 'What is it between you and my master?'

'Are you asking because of him or because of yourself?'

Imri relaxed his grip and patted my cheek gently as a father would a child. 'I am just curious. But come, His Excellency wishes to talk to you.'

Hotep was sitting on a turfed seat just within the garden gate and, surprisingly, Crown Prince Tuthmosis sat beside him. I sank to my knees. Hotep did not tell me to rise. I glanced up. Tuthmosis' face was red with anger. He glared at me as if I was an enemy and I knew my request had made him mine. He swung his foot and kicked me viciously in the side.

'You plead for a criminal?'

'I plead for a friend.'

'Who happens to be a criminal. Look at me, Baboon.'

I stared up. Tuthmosis leaned forward, his face a few inches from mine. I saw the blood beat in his brow, the twist of his mouth. I was aware of the wine on his breath and the anger in his soul. I also noticed something else: just on the corner of his mouth, a fleck of his blood as if he had cut his lip or bitten his tongue.

'My father,' Tuthmosis swallowed hard as if fighting for breath, 'my father's dignity, the Magnificent One . . .' He coughed, holding a small napkin to his mouth; when he took it away I glimpsed the red stains. 'Sobeck should have been put in a cage with his whore,' he rasped, dabbing at his mouth.

'Sobeck is the guilty one,' Hotep said softly, 'not Mahu. He has simply come to plead for his friend. I have used my good offices to achieve two things.' He leaned forward, fingers splayed, as if counting for a child. 'Listen, Mahu. First Sobeck will not go to the Wood. He will be exiled to an oasis in the Western Desert. You know what that means?'

Oh I knew! A few palm trees, some figs, and water, but not enough to sustain a man for ever or give him the strength to try and break out across the desert. If he did, the Sand Dwellers or the Desert Wanderers, if not the Libyans, would catch him and flay him alive.

I closed my eyes and nodded in thanks. All I had achieved was to send Sobeck to a living death. Perhaps it would have been faster to have asked for a knife to the throat or sword-cut to the heart.

'Secondly Mahu,' Hotep's eyes glinted in amusement, 'you are to be given a commission in the Medjay. You are to go back to the Western Desert.' He paused. 'Finally,' his hand fell away, 'you are to leave now!'

I muttered my thanks and bowed, my face red with embarrassment. I rose and walked through the courtyard, ignoring Imri's shout, my heart seething with anger. Yet even as I did so, I recalled the blood on that napkin. What was it Aunt Isithia used to say?

Ah yes. *'He who coughs blood coughs life.'*

'He knotted veins to the Bones
Made in his workshop as his own creation.'

(*The Great Hymn to Khnum*)

Chapter 5

'Beyond the Far Horizon
Your beauty has dwelt for all eternity.
Incomparable in form!
Shrouded in mystery!
Yet beautiful in all your aspects.'

The Veiled One finished his prayer kneeling in the garden pavilion, face towards the rising sun. In one hand he held a water flower, in the other, swathed in a piece of linen, a pot of burning incense. His mother knelt beside him, her hands outstretched. I was not too sure to whom we were praying or why, yet I followed suit. The garden was empty, the air slightly cold, the mist tendrils still curling like white wraiths through the trees. The haze shrouding the sun had yet to part. Soon it would be New Year. Sirius the dog star would rise high in the eastern sky, the Ibis birds would flock back to the Black Lands and the Inundation would begin. Once again, the Nile would sweep from its mysterious source in the South to refresh the earth. Yet that day was my New Year's Day, a moment when my life changed.

The Veiled One finished his hymn, bowed and placed the incense bowl on the ground, the flower beside it. He leaned back, chatting softly to his mother. On the small table before us were three goblets of wine and soft bread smeared lightly with eating salt. A strange meal to begin the day but, there again, I was confused. In truth, I was only half awake. I had almost been kicked out of my bed by Imri when the dormitory was still dark and cold. I thought it was connected to the previous day's occurrence, that Hotep had changed his mind and I was to be arrested as Sobeck's accomplice. The Kushite, however, gestured at the jug of water, bowl and napkin he had brought.

'Come, Baboon,' he commanded, grinning over his shoulder at the other Kushites thronging in the doorway. 'Our master and the Great Queen want words with you.'

I had washed and dressed, carefully following the Veiled One's guard back through the dark garden and into the Silent Pavilion.

'Do you know who you are praying to?' Tiye broke into my reverie. 'Mahu, look at me.'

I went to bow again but she snapped her fingers. 'Look at me, man.'

'I gaze upon your face, Divine One.'

'I am sure you do,' she smiled wryly. 'But this is not the place for court niceties or polite pleasantries. God's Father Hotep has recommended that you join the Medjay and you are not happy with that.' She looked more closely at me. 'Your eyes are heavy. You drank deeply last night?'

148

'To the very dregs, Excellency.'

The Veiled One laughed quietly.

'No wonder. Out in the Western Desert,' Tiye continued, 'your skin will be burned black by the sun, you'll be blinded by the heat, eat sand and dust and live for the next stoup of water. You are not a happy man, Mahu.'

'Your Excellency is most perceptive.'

Tiye joined in her son's laughter. 'Well, you are not to go! I have made my will known. The Divine One supports me. You are to join my son's household.' She smiled at my surprise. 'My son has told me all about you, Mahu, Baboon of the South. You were born alone and grew alone, yet you have demonstrated your loyalty. My son owes his life to you whilst your assistance of Sobeck is praiseworthy.'

'*Did* you dream that night?' the Veiled One demanded. He was sitting between myself and his mother. Now he leaned forward, his cold, clawlike fingers squeezing the muscles on my face.

'I did not dream.'

'Good.' He kissed me gently on the cheek. 'You must never lie to me, Mahu.'

'Your father was a soldier,' Lady Tiye continued, 'a brave one. You shall be my son's soldier: his life and his health will be your sole concern.'

'Is his life under threat?'

'Good, good!' the Veiled One murmured. 'That's the way to begin, Mahu. Ask questions but keep the answers to yourself.' He glanced sideways at me and winked.

'Is my son's life threatened?' Tiye repeated the question. Her lower lip jutted out and she played with the simple veil which covered her rich black hair. Tiye's face was unpainted except for kohl rings around her eyes and a light layer of carmine on her lips. She'd piled her jewellery on a small garden table just near the door. 'Everyone who shelters in the shadow of the Divine One is threatened. Now, to my former question, to whom did we pray?'

'To Amun-Ra?'

She shook her head. 'To the Sun?' Her voice dropped to a whisper. 'To the Aten, the Sun Disc? Yes and no. More precisely, to the power which raises that sun and sets it, which sends forth the cooling breeze, allows the bud to flower, and the chick in the egg to stir.'

I remained impassive. Theology, the word of the gods, was of little concern to me. I was more intrigued by Queen Tiye's face in the vain hope that I might meet the Beautiful One again, rather than the strange events now occurring.

'Will you take the oath?' Tiye continued. 'By that power, by earth and sky, by fire and water, to be my son's man in peace and war? Will you?'

'Yes, Your Excellency.'

'Good.' She lifted the wine cup and thrust it into my hands. Picking up a piece of salted bread, she broke it into three and handed a piece to me and to her son. The rest she popped into her own mouth, chewing it quietly, her gaze never leaving me. The Veiled One and I followed suit. The bread was soft but the salt was hard and bitter and I had difficulty swallowing it. I then sipped the wine, full and strong, rich as blood.

'You have eaten the salt and drunk the wine,' Tiye declared. 'You have taken the oath. Life and death, Mahu.

Every time you eat bread and drink wine it will comme-
morate this occasion.'

Outside I heard a servant call. A horn wailed as a sign
that the day had officially begun. Tiye rose and left and so
it was that my life was woven into the life of the Veiled
One. I was his bodyguard, his manservant, sometimes his
friend and, when his moods shifted, even his opponent,
someone to argue with, as well as to lecture, warn and
instruct. I soon slipped into the regular routine of his
household. I'd rise in the morning and join the Veiled
One at his prayers, followed by meetings with different
officials and flunkies of the court. I was given my own
chambers in the far side of the Silent Pavilion, with
washed-green walls and a small storeroom beside it.

The daily routine of the household was soothing. Sometimes I thought about Sobeck and, now and again, wondered if the beautiful woman would return. Great Queen
Tiye and Prince Tuthmosis were frequent visitors and
sometimes, at least once a week, God's Father Hotep
came. The latter had accepted me. He'd smile and nod,
sometimes he'd draw me into superficial conversation
about affairs in Thebes or visitors from abroad. He'd
inform me how Horemheb and Rameses were now Captains in the Sacred Band, how Pentju and Meryre promised
their worth in the House of Life whilst Huy and Maya
were proving to be excellent scribes. Tuthmosis ignored
me as if I did not exist. On one occasion when he met his
brother alone in the small audience hall he asked that I
stand outside. The Veiled One shrugged and told me to
wait in the garden. For the rest, I was always close to
him. He would eat before noon, rest during the heat of

the day and then spend his time in a range of different studies, hobbies and pursuits.

Occasionally, mysterious visitors would arrive. They'd be garbed in striped robes, coarse garments and heavy sandals; they looked like Sand Dwellers with their long hair and beards though they lacked their shifty gaze and furtive ways. They were warriors with sharp-nosed, haughty faces who swaggered rather than walked and only reluctantly handed over their weapons to Imri's keeping. Why they came or what they discussed was kept secret. The Veiled One was very cunning. He always met such visitors at the far end of his audience hall or out in the garden pavilion where eavesdroppers would find it difficult to lurk. These men would come and squat before the Veiled One, talking softly, gesturing with their hands, always treating him with the greatest respect. Great Queen Tiye would often join such meetings and sometimes, at night, she and her son went out to meet these strange ones beyond the gates. I'd go with them, Tiye and the Veiled One shrouded in cloaks and hoods. The strangers would be waiting, hoods pulled over their own heads. They were always armed, one or two carrying pitch torches. They'd leave, slipping quietly through the darkness, both my master and his mother returning shortly after dawn. No one from the Silent Pavilion was ever allowed to accompany them. I'd established a good relationship with Imri and often practised with him on the drill ground. Over a beer jug I asked about these mysterious visitors. The Kushite pressed a calloused finger against my lips.

'You may ask, Mahu, but never expect an answer. I

know very little of them except that they are Apiru, a tribe of the Shemshu.'

'Apiru?'

'Hush!' Again the finger against my lips. He nudged me gently, got to his feet and strolled away.

The Apiru were no strangers to me. They were not desert people but nomadic tribes who'd wandered across Sinai following the Horus roads past the silver mines. They'd been allowed to enter Egypt and suckle at her fertile breasts. Some joined the army, others became craftsmen; they were Egyptian in everything but name. Others kept to themselves, living away from the cities, only visiting them to barter and haggle in the marketplace. I wondered what they would have in common with my master and with Egypt's Great Queen, yet Imri was correct. The danger of such a question lurked not so much in asking it, but in searching for the answers.

For the rest, the Veiled One immersed himself in his activities. He loved painting and sculpture, and two of Tiye's master craftsmen, the painter Bek and the sculptor Uti, were frequent visitors to the house. The Veiled One had taken over and converted a high-ceilinged storeroom, transforming this into what he called his 'House of Paintings'. I often joined him there. Sometimes Bek painted on screens, other times the walls, but only after the Veiled One had given his approval. Most of the paintings were similar to those found in temples, palaces or tombs, executed in vivid colours, light blues, dark greens, rich yellows: garden scenes, a hunter boating along the Nile, a hawk plunging on its quarry or an athlete about to throw a stick. The gods did not appear in them, however, nor did the Pharaoh or, indeed, the imperial court. Other paintings were more dramatic and vivid, different from any I had ever seen. Bek and Uti were related; in fact, they looked like twins, small men with round smiling faces, totally immersed in their art, ever ready to please. They were a little shamefaced about these new paintings, but listened patiently as the Veiled One enthused over their realism.

'We must live in the truth,' my master announced proudly, displaying the images of himself painted on the wall.

Bek and Uti had followed his instructions scrupulously and, rather than disguise his physical imperfections and deformities, they exaggerated them. The Veiled One was portrayed in a striped blue and gold head-dress, and a gloriously coloured kilt, with a sash round his waist, his face and jaw were portrayed as much longer than in real life, the sensuous lips more full, the eyes sharper and more elongated, his chest and belly more protuberant, his hips wider. 'The truth?' The Veiled One repeated, and gestured with his fingers. 'If life is truth and paintings reflect life, then they should be truthful. Well, Mahu, what do you think?'

'Has your father seen them?'

The question was a mistake. The Veiled One spun on his heel and strode out of the House of Paintings. Bek and Uti stood, heads down, as if they were war-prisoners.

'Never,' Bek whispered, 'ever mention his father again.' He raised his gentle face, eyes screwed up. 'You are most fortunate, Mahu. I have heard of others being struck with a sharp-edged cane for saying less.'

'*Does* his father know of these paintings?' I refused to be abashed. I had not intended to give offence and I was angry at being treated so unfairly.

'No one knows of them except us and Great Queen Tiye.' Bek laughed sharply. 'If we exhibited these in the temples and palaces we would be the laughing stock of Thebes.'

The Veiled One soon forgave me. He was always busy and, as Bek and Uti had once confided, passed from one thing to another like a butterfly in the garden. He would invite the two artists down, question them, work them like slaves, then reward them with banquets and a stack of gifts, only to forget them for a month. He'd become interested in shrubs, tending the herb plots or using plants to make stoppers for wine jars, chaff glued together or a parcel of young sycamore leaves. He would fashion candles and elaborate oil lamps. He would spend an entire afternoon making floral garlands out of the fibre of palm leaves, lotus petals and willow leaves. He'd experiment with the destruction of a snake's nest by leaving dried fish, lumps of natron or even an onion at its entrance. Occasionally he would call the housekeepers together and lecture them on the use of fleabane mixed with charcoal to drive away flies or the way to mix frankincense and myrrh, mingled with boiled honey, to give the kitchens and storerooms a pleasing fragrance. He was fascinated by animals, particularly the cats, which roamed through the storerooms ever vigilant against vermin. I once found him outside the kitchens dissecting a mouse's corpse, taking out the small organs and laying them on the paving. He glanced up as I approached.

'No, I didn't kill it, Mahu. I just wondered, is the life-force in a mouse the same as in a lion? Does the lion receive more? And, if that is the case, do we share the same life-force and express it in a different way?'

He never waited for an answer but returned to the task in hand. He was a generous master in many ways. One day he brought me a beautiful tame bird, a golden oriole. I was much taken with it.

'What will you call it?' the Veiled One enquired.

Again I replied before thinking. 'Why, Weni! He was our overseer at the House of Instruction.'

The Veiled One's face showed I had made a mistake. I flew the Oriole twice in the small meadow beyond the pavilion walls, but afterwards it disappeared and I never saw it again. My master did not replace it, and I never uttered the name Weni in his presence again.

He did not attend the Jubilee days or visit his father's court, nor did he observe the religious festivals. In none of the rooms did I see one statue or carving of a god. In a nearby market, I bought a small wooden statue of Anubis, a tawdry imitation of the great statue in the god's temple at Thebes, the one I had seen as a boy, the jaw of which moved so as to issue an oracle. I meant it as a gift for one of the servants who had been particularly kind to me. When the Veiled One saw it, he snatched it from my hand and ordered me to buy another. He later crouched on the ground like a little boy and pretended the two gods were talking to each other or fighting like quarrelsome curs. He was particularly fascinated by the moving jaw and used them as puppets.

'I am Anubis,' he would squeak, pushing one forward.

'No, *I* am Anubis,' the other one would reply. The Veiled One loved to use the two carvings to mock the great Lord of the Mortuary. Priests he hated, dismissing them as 'shaven heads' or 'soft pates'. At times he was mischievous and invited priests from a certain temple to a small feast in the cool of the evening, either in the audience hall or the garden pavilion. I was always beside him. The ritual was ever the same. The Veiled One would sit and ask them innocent questions. 'Where do the gods live? If they are spiritual, why do they have masks? If Seth killed his brother Osiris, how can he be a god? If the gods really live in the temples and are all-powerful, all-seeing and everywhere, how can they be locked up in a tabernacle? Why do they need food? And if the choicest meats are laid out for them, why don't they come and eat it or take it away to give to the poor?'

Of course the questions would change depending on the circumstances but the object was the same, a sneering ridicule. Invariably the priests left hot-eyed and sullen-faced. Afterwards the Veiled One would mimic them: despite his own disabilities, he had an eye for another's voice or look. He'd imitate their stoop, the sanctimonious way they walked or raised their eyes heavenwards. Sometimes, when he had drunk deeply, he'd deliver his famous lecture on how Isis had to hunt for her husband's penis.

'To sew it back on again?' he'd yell. 'When he's supposed to be a god? He doesn't *need* needle and thread! Can you imagine it, Mahu?' He'd stick out his own groin. 'Walking around with your penis sewn on?' He'd collapse in laughter or sing an obscene hymn he'd composed to Isis.

Soldiers he admired, and he talked to me volubly, excitedly, about history and the might of Egypt. He studied maps depicting the land routes into Kush, Punt and across Sinai. He knew the trade routes along the Great Green to Canaan. Once he joined me and Imri on the drill ground but he was too clumsy and slow, an easy opponent to overcome. Afterwards he took me aside, face laced with sweat, eyes agitated.

'I'm not very good, am I, Mahu?'

'In a chariot,' I replied tactfully, 'you'd excel the best.'

'You speak with true voice,' he smiled, slapped me roughly across the face but never returned there.

Every quarter an imperial physician would visit him. The Veiled One remained silent and passive as the man prodded him, staring into his mouth and ears or feeling his hands and feet. He and the physician never exchanged words. I was always present, armed with sword, dagger, a bow and a quiver of arrows.

'I feel like a horse at the stud farm,' the Veiled One described such examinations, yet he never resisted.

My master often visited the kitchens. He would just stand there, watching the cooks from under heavy-lidded eyes. Either I or Imri always tasted his food and wine. Never once did he tell us what he feared. Imri told me a few details about the Veiled One's early life. How he was not meant to live as a child. How the priests had recommended that he be placed in a reed basket and left to float in a crocodile pool. Tiye had been furious. The best physicians had been summoned but there was little they could do so the ugly child was banned from his father's presence. Only those with deformed faces, war veterans or criminals who had lost noses were allowed to serve him.

'You,' Imri tapped me drunkenly on the chest, 'are the first and only exception, though you are so ugly, you might as well be one of us!'

In many ways, it was a strangely halcyon existence, albeit tinged by danger. Nothing definite or precise but there were sometimes mysterious occurrences, with their own silent menace, which kept me nervous and wary. One incident took place during the second month of the Inundation in the thirty-fourth year of his father's reign, just after the Festival of Opet. Imri's men always escorted the stewards down to the city markets as the servants' disfigured faces might cause provocation and hostility. Amongst the provisions brought back was a basket of juicy figs, fresh and smeared with honey – the Veiled One's favourite delicacy, to be kept near him in his garden pavilion. I took the basket across. The smell from the figs was delicious: moving the lid, I was about to take one out when the figs moved like water rippling. I drew my dagger and knocked some of the fruit aside – a thin venomous rock adder, followed by another, coiled out. I killed both, took the basket and flung it away in a far part of the garden. I considered it an accident and told no one.

A few weeks later I was called down to the wine cellars, a long low cavernous room supervised by a wine steward, a former criminal who had lost both his nose and a slab of flesh on his right cheek. He was in the far corner already in his death throes, eyes glazed, legs and arms jerking, a white froth smearing his lips. Near him lay

an unstopped jar of wine from Absh, a favourite of the
Veiled One, always stored in a special jar protected by a
wadge of basketwork. I picked up the stopper; the docket
around it described the wine, the vineyard and the year the
grapes had been plucked. The cellarer had decided to help
himself and been most unfortunate: both the stopper and
the jar smelt so foul I whispered one of my aunt's spells
to repel venom.

The rest of the servants thought the man had suffered
some form of seizure or falling sickness. I had the body
removed and again informed no one. In the first month
of the Peret, the thirty-fifth year of the Magnificent One's
reign, the danger became more real. The Veiled One
often went down to the banks of the Nile, to watch
the boats and barges and the frenetic activity of the
riverside markets. He always sat in what I called his
tabernacle on a cart pulled by oxen, a veil across his
face. I always walked behind, and on either side strolled
the Kushites armed with spear and shield. Discipline was
lax; the guards often chatting amongst themselves, now
and again pushing away the curious. One of those shabby
individuals, a road wanderer, a travelling tinker or trader
came close to the cart, gathering his tattered rags about
him. He had a dark, pinched face, and his long hair and
beard were streaked with grey. In one hand he held a staff,
in another a sistrum which he clattered. Now and again he
broke into song. He reeked of sweat and other odours but
seemed harmless enough walking beside me, eyes on the
tail of the cart. I looked at him carefully; I remembered
the day Aunt Isithia took me into the temple and the
fortune-teller cursed her. Was it the same person?

'Have we met before?' I asked.

'No, great lord,' the beggar whined. 'I have only come to sing the praises' – pointing to the cart – 'of God's own son.' He broke into a chant, repeating almost word for word one of the hymns the Veiled One sang to the Sun Disc, the Aten:

'Oh gorgeous in every aspect are you!
Your power unseen
You fertilise the shoot
And stock the river with fish.
All creatures adore you . . .'

The man's voice grew stronger. He began to dance and cavort, singing his praises to the Aten. 'All glory to his son,' he warbled. 'All glory to him, Beloved of the Father.'

At the Veiled One's command the cart stopped. The Kushite driver came along the side and pulled back the curtains. The Veiled One sat there, his face now exposed. He snapped his fingers and pointed at the road-wanderer with his fan, indicating he should come closer.

As the fellow clambered into the cart and went to kneel at the Veiled One's feet to make obeisance, I noticed the bulge in the tunic on the man's right side; it moved even as the fellow twisted his shoulders slightly sideways. He was drawing a dagger. I drew mine and leaped into the cart. The Veiled One sat transfixed, eyes staring, mouth slightly open. The assassin made to leap forward but I knocked him in the back, sending him sprawling onto the bottom of the cart. He turned, dagger coming towards me. I thrust mine once, twice, deep into his exposed throat.

The cart was now surrounded by the Kushites, so the scuffle was hardly noticed by those passing on either side. I stared into the dying man's eyes, watching the light of life fade, a strange gargling sound echoing from the back of his throat. I looked at that face darkened by the sun, the lips opening and closing.

'No, we have not met before,' I whispered. The man's body jerked, his head fell to one side. I was content to drag the corpse off and leave it on the highway.

'No,' the Veiled One intervened. He spoke sharply to the Kushites. A rug kept in the cart was brought. The corpse was wrapped in this and we returned to the palace grounds. Once there, just before we entered the courtyard, the Veiled One ordered the cart to be stopped. He kicked the body with his foot off the tail of the cart and, grasping his cane, climbed down to examine it more carefully. The foul, dirty robes were removed. The Veiled One, unperturbed, studied the man's corpse carefully, noticing the criss-crossed scars on the muscular torso and thighs, the welt marks now faded on his back.

'A soldier,' he murmured, getting to his feet and prodding the man's belly with his cane. 'He does not look so dangerous now.'

The wound in the man's neck, a dark-red, jagged gash, still glistened with blood.

'Wrap him in sheepskin,' he ordered the Kushites. 'Give him the shroud of an accursed one. If there is a Hell, let him wander there for all eternity with my curse on him!'

The Veiled One grasped my arm and, leaning on his cane, hurried through the gates. I later discovered that the cart and tabernacle were also burned and the oxen which pulled it slaughtered, though the Veiled One never discussed the incident.

Once inside the house he retreated to his own chamber and stayed there until the following day. Just before dawn the Great Queen Tiye swept into the Silent Pavilion and was immediately closeted with her son. Later in the morning I was summoned to meet her in the audience hall. She asked me to describe what had happened, praised me for my vigilance and took from a napkin a beautiful amulet of blue faience depicting the sun rising between the twin horns of Hathor. The hall was deserted. All the servants had been dismissed, the window shutters closed. Tiye sat on the small daïs slouched on the cushions, though now and again she rose as gracefully as any temple dancer, to walk up and down. Sometimes she'd stop beside me, other times stand on the daïs. I kept kneeling on the cushion, my head down. She walked the length of the hall and came back, her slippered footsteps light and soft. Once again she sat down on the cushions on the other side of the table and gestured that I do likewise.

The Great Queen was calm though her eyes were bright and watchful, the skin of her face paler than usual. I did not know whether it was due to anxiety or the lack of any adornment. She was dressed very simply in a gauffered linen shawl across her shoulders, part of which served as a hood over her black hair gathered tightly at the back. She wore no jewellery, earrings or necklaces, only a simple copper bracelet on her left wrist. She kept playing with this as she studied me intently. I heard a sound and was about to turn.

'Yes, Mahu, someone is there.'

I recalled the escort, those strange visitors to the house, and knew one of them must be standing, deep in the shadows, an arrow notched to his bow.

'Mahu? Do you have anything to say?'

Those large dark eyes never wavered. I repressed a shiver and held her gaze. The Great Queen may have thanked and rewarded me but she did not trust me.

'Describe the incident again.'

I did so. Tiye listened intently, asking questions.

'It was planned.' She slid the bracelet on and off her wrist. 'Of course he will be dismissed as some madman with addled wits and disordered heart. However, I know and you know, Mahu, that it was planned. The dagger?'

'Burned with the rest,' I replied.

'But did you see it?'

'A long blade with an ebony handle.'

'Given to him,' Tiye declared. 'He carried no silver or gold? No precious objects?'

'A former soldier, I suspect,' I replied, 'to judge from the scars on his body and the welts on his back. I thought I had met him before.' I described Aunt Isithia taking me to see my father's corpse. Tiye dismissed this.

'A former soldier,' she mused, 'who was hired by someone who promises largesse and great bounty. My son was known to travel along the riverside. The guards are there but, as you say, lax. As for you, Mahu,' Tiye leaned forward and grasped my arm, her sharp nails digging deep, 'the assassin was taught a hymn.' She pressed her nails deeper. 'A hymn to the Aten which he knew would catch my son's attention. Anyone who sang, who knew the words of that hymn would rouse his curiosity. The cart is stopped and the assassin is given his chance.'

'Except that I killed the assassin, Excellency.'

'Yes, yes, you did.' She dug her nails in one last time then withdrew her hand. For a while she sat plucking on her lower lip, eyes half-closed as if about to fall asleep. She asked me if there was anything else. I said no and, fast as a pouncing cat, she leaned forward and slapped me viciously across the face.

'Aren't you forgetting, Mahu, you most worthless of Baboons, the attack on the camp by the Kushites?'

'But that was war!'

'Was it?' she demanded. 'When I ask you a question, answer it fully. What were those words the Kushite muttered as he died?'

I repeated them. Again the plucking of the lip. I stared round the hall. Now it did not seem so colourful or bright but a place where death lurked, where secret, silent assassination was plotted. Another sharp stinging slap made me jerk. I stared across at the Queen; her eyes were bright with fury.

'Is there anything else, Baboon? You must tell me the truth. For all I know . . .' She let her words hang in the air. I knew what she was going to say. Was I to be trusted? Was I involved in the attack on her son?

I replied honestly, describing the incident of the figs and wine: this time she did not slap me but just sat, tears filling her eyes.

'Whom do you suspect, Excellency?' I burst out.

She lifted her head. 'I could ask the same question of you, Baboon. You, with your clever eyes and ugly face.

My son chose well. Whom do you suspect? His father, the priests?'

I nodded. She leaned across and caressed my cheek. 'You've eaten the salt and drunk the wine,' she whispered. 'If I suspected you, Mahu, you'd die a choking death beneath the sands of the Red Lands. So listen carefully to what I am going to say. My son was born on an inauspicious day.' She drew back, staring at the table as if talking to herself. 'A difficult birth. I had sat in the child chair for an eternity. Pains, like flames of fire, coursed through my body. He was born just as the sun rose, and wrapped in swaddling clothes. I was weak, covered in sweat, the blood all about me. Even as the maids insisted that I retire to bed, I knew something was wrong. They kept him away from me, cared for by a wetnurse. Eventually I demanded the truth. The Divine One came down, my loving husband.' The words had a bitter twist to them. 'I went with him to the Royal Nursery. The physicians and priests were there, the air filled with their scent and babbling prayers. They showed me the child, my son with his strange, long head and misshapen skull. He was fully formed and strong, for he had been in my womb at least three weeks longer than he should have been. The physicians whispered, arguing amongst themselves. They did not tell me directly but I knew what they were saying. My son was cursed and should either be allowed to die or be exposed. I took off my shawl, wrapping it around that little body and plucked him up from the cot. I left that chamber and returned to my own quarters.'

She paused, staring down the hall, eyes narrowed, lips

tight. 'My husband came.' Her voice was no more than a hoarse whisper. 'He looked at the child and said that he was no son of his. I screamed at him – the most hideous threats, what I would do if the child was harmed. The Divine One truly loved me.' Her face relaxed into a smile. 'He agreed that nothing would happen, on one condition: he never saw him again. My husband, Mahu, is Amenhotep the Magnificent. He will not tolerate any imperfection or impurity, except in himself. Now I wonder, has he changed his mind? After all, the Crown Prince Tuthmosis will be his heir.'

I recalled that blood-stained napkin but remained silent.

'And what will happen to his younger brother,' she asked, 'when I am gone? Kept here,' she stared around, 'well away from the public gaze and prying eyes, will he demand to be treated as Pharaoh's blood brother? Go into the temples, Mahu, walk the streets of Thebes? You know the song as well as I do. "Pharaoh is Egypt, Egypt is Pharaoh, the beloved son of Ra." How can the gods love Egypt if the Divine One has a disabled son, distasteful to the public eye? A cripple, malformed?'

'He is none of those things, Your Excellency.'

'No he isn't, Mahu. In my eyes he is the Beautiful One.' She blinked away her tears. 'But it's his heart not his body the temple priests fear. He has no time either for them or their gods. Oh, I know about his dinner parties here and the way he mocks the shaven heads, the soft pates.' She turned her face sideways, studying me out of the corner of her eye. 'He has good reason to hate them. As a child he was moved from the nursery to the House of Life in the Temple of Isis. He was there two years before I discovered the cruelty and abuse to which he was subjected. They knew about his father's disapproval and they mocked him. I took him out but, even at court, I could not protect him all the time. This place was Hotep's idea.' She gestured around. 'I suppose he's happiest here. He asks for very little.'

'And Tuthmosis?'

'His brother feels guilty. I am not too sure if it's love or guilt.'

'Could there be a reconciliation?' I asked. Here was a Great Queen of Egypt confiding in a commoner, chatting about her son like some washerwoman down at the Nile.

'Never,' she replied. 'My husband believes his second son is accursed. When he heard about this place he issued a decree. No one was to serve my son but grotesques.' She smiled thinly. 'Except you and, as for that,' she sniffed, 'well, never mind!'

She rose to her feet and walked down the hall. Whoever was lurking there stepped out of the shadows. I heard a soft footfall but I dared not turn round. She came back arms wrapped across her chest.

'And the future?' She sat down on the cushions. 'And the future?' she repeated as if talking to herself. 'What will happen to my son when the Divine One goes into the Far West and I follow him? Will his brother protect him?' She shivered and rubbed her arms. 'And what happens,' she continued in a whisper, 'if Tuthmosis begets no heir but also goes into the Far West? Will the priests, the generals accept what they call a grotesque Pharaoh? Well, my Baboon, what do you think?'

'Excellency, I think nothing.' I was determined not to mention that I had seen the red-flecked napkin Tuthmosis had coughed into.

'Go on, clever Baboon,' she urged. 'You are thinking something.'

'May the Crown Prince Tuthmosis,' I declared, reciting the conventional phrase, 'live for a million years. May he enjoy jubilee after jubilee. May he see his children's children and may his power and glory be felt by the people of the Nine Bows.'

'So be it. So be it,' Tiye responded.

'But, if you have thought about the future,' I chose my words carefully, 'so has your husband, the Divine One.'

Tiye's mouth opened and closed.

'And?'

'Is there somewhere a papyrus document, sealed with the Divine One's cartouche, which gives instructions on what is to happen?'

Tiye closed her eyes. I had expected a blow, even an objection but we were past that. Tiye was chatting to me because, in truth, I was nothing: in the eyes of the Divine One, a mere fleck of dust, a few heartbeats away from total silence. But now I was voicing her own fear, like a priest in a chapel listening to the confessions of some devout pilgrims.

'Is there, Your Excellency?' I repeated.

'What do you think, Mother?'

This time I heard the footstep and turned. The Veiled One, dressed in a long white robe gathered at the waist, stood a few yards away, an arrow notched to the powerful

Syrian bow. He was standing slightly sideways, a calculating look on that long face. He was watching his mother, waiting for a signal.

'Should we kill the Baboon, Mother?'

'If you kill the Baboon, master,' I replied, staring at Queen Tiye, 'then you have lost a true friend and a lifelong ally.'

I heard the bow being pulled back but I couldn't move. I sat frozen. Queen Tiye was no longer staring at her son but at me. I heard a sharp intake of breath, the twang of the cord and the arrow whistled past over our heads to smack into the wall. Tiye's face creased into a smile.

'Baboon can be trusted. Come, my son.'

I heard the bow and quiver clatter to the ground. The Veiled One joined us on the daïs, plumping up the cushions, sitting down breathing quickly, eyes gleeful and bright.

'Did you really think, Mahu, I'd put an arrow into your back? Do you know what you are, Mahu? You are my baboon. When the Medjay go through the marketplace at Thebes their trained baboons go with them to catch felons and thieves. I am surrounded by felons and thieves, at least beyond these walls. You must have many questions but you never ask them.' He leaned forward. 'Where do my mother and I go at the dead of night? Who are those strange visitors? One day you'll know. In the meantime you are to catch the thieves and felons who want to take my life and send my soul into the darkness. He who ordains all things has ordained this.' He rubbed his hands together. 'I listened to what my mother has told you, it is the truth. I do not intend to die, Mahu, but to live for my true Father

Aten, the Beautiful One, who rides on the Far Horizon.'
His hand curled out. 'In whose eyes, a million years are as
yesterday, a brief watch in the night. Oh by the way, your
friend Sobeck . . .' He glanced sideways at his mother. 'I
am sure he was betrayed. My mother used her influence
to ensure that Sobeck does not die in the Red Lands.' He
stretched across and tugged my hair playfully. 'You have
won great favour, Mahu. Never forget that.' He leaned
back and rubbed his hands together. 'In the meantime,
let's have a party. We'll invite your friends from the
Kap – it would be good to see them all again, wouldn't
it, Mahu?'

His mouth smiled but his eyes were cold, devoid of
any feeling. Bowing my head, I realised that for better,
for worse, in this deadly game of plot and counter-plot,
I could not escape.

The hieroglyph for 'The Beloved' – *mri/merry* – combines the hoe and two flowering reeds.

Chapter 6

'Pressed in the lovely flesh of a woman
Any heart would run captive into such slim arms!
She lords it over the earth.
The neck of every male moves to watch her go.
He who held such a body tight would know, at last,
The supreme delight.
She would require the best of the bull boys,
First amongst lovers!
You men look at her splendid going,
Our lady of love to whom no rival can hold a light.'

The harpist plucked at the strings, sending out the bittersweet sound. His shaven head went down, even as we clapped and cheered at the beauty of his song about the glory of love. The Veiled One's hall had been transformed for this fcast, lit by scented candles and oil glowing in precious alabaster jars. We sat at our ebony-inlaid table which groaned under a splendid banquet: fish, fried and grilled in a sauce of olive oil, onions, hazelnuts, salt and freshly ground black pepper; white fish, their firm flesh coated with the sauce of pine nuts, almonds and garlic cloves; beef and lamb covered with chick peas and cumin; tajeens of beef and lamb in artichoke. Our goblets had been constantly filled with the finest wines.

The Veiled One had arranged the tables in a circle, seating me on his right hand, his brother Tuthmosis on his left. All the others were there. He had even arranged an empty cushion for Sobeck and had plates and goblets laid before it. Tuthmosis had vehemently objected but the Veiled One had laughed and insisted that even at a feast like this the ghosts were welcome. Each of us had a heset, a temple girl. Clad in thin, gauze-like gowns, their every movement was emphasised by the tinkling bracelets on their ankles and wrists; their long elegant fingers glittered with rings, their nails were painted a deep purple. They were there to entertain, to flatter, to soothe our hearts and satisfy our every whim.

At first the banquet had been difficult. This was the first time we had all met since Sobeck's banishment. Horemheb and Rameses were resplendent in their officers' uniforms, Captain and Lieutenant of the Sacred Band. They wore round their necks a collar proclaiming their membership of the most redoubtable regiments in all the hosts of Egypt. Huy looked more relaxed in his splendid robes. Pentju and Meryre hadn't changed much but sat together, whispering across the girl in between. Maya looked distinctly uncomfortable in a perfume-drenched wig, his face laced with sweat, although he was as charming and vivacious as ever. The Veiled One was a perfect host. The setting of a place for Sobeck, the hosting of such a party and the invitation to Tuthmosis to join them were all part of a studied insult to his own father. He'd whispered this to me as I helped him dress in the cool of the evening.

'I want my father to know, Mahu, that I will not remain silent, that I will not be kept for ever in the shadows and corners.'

The temple girls were trained courtesans but even they paused to study this strange-looking Prince. They would return to their temples, taking their stories with them: a message to the priests that the Divine One's second son was not content to hide like a mouse or pass like a shadow through the courts of Egypt. It had been four days since that meeting with his mother in this very hall. The Veiled One had not discussed the matter again but I knew what he plotted, what he wished me to do. He had placed the swollen-throated Uraeus, the spitting-cobra of Egypt around his forehead.

'The snake knows when to strike, Mahu.' He turned from the glittering piece of polished silver which served as a mirror. 'And so do you.'

For most of the meal my master had ignored me. Now and again he would whisper instructions and I would raise my hand for the steward of the feast or to summon Imri who guarded the entrance. The Veiled One became engaged in deep conversation with his brother. Only once did I catch fragments of their talk. Tuthmosis was urging his brother to be prudent, not to catch his father's eye or incur his anger.

'I already have.' The Veiled One picked up his goblet

and toasted his brother, then refused to answer the spate of insistent questions which followed.

I had mixed water with my wine but the heat and warmth, and the good food had made me sleepy. I was prodded awake by a sharp elbow thrust, and glanced quickly around. Maya was leaving the hall, alone. Horemheb and Rameses were showing off to their girls. Huy, cradling his wine cup, sat on the cushions, smiling beatifically to himself. Meryre was anxiously interrogating Pentju, probably questioning him about some ailment he suffered. Even as a boy Meryre, for all his confidence in the gods, had a secret dread of disease and infection. I waited my moment, excused myself, winked at Imri and followed Maya out into the darkness. I looked round. He was not in the courtyard so I went across through the half-open side gate. I paused and, from the sounds, I gathered Maya was relieving himself. I waited. He came stumbling back, stepped out onto the pathway and glanced up.

'Why, Mahu?'

'Why, Maya?' I smiled. 'I wish to have words with you.' I put my arm protectively across his shoulder, turned him round and walked back to the small, tile-edged pool where the lotus blossom floated gently in the moonlight. 'Sit down, sit down.'

He did so unwillingly, muscles tensed. 'What do you want, Mahu?'

'You are in the House of Scribes?' I asked.

'No, no.' He spread his feet, rubbed his hands together, shoulders hunched. 'I work in the House of Secrets.'

'Ah, the place of spies! What do you do there?'

'We gather reports from all over Egypt and beyond our

borders; from merchants, traders, sailors, our allies in Canaan, our servants in Kush, our envoys in Punt.'

'Very good. And you are doing well?'

'Look, Mahu, I don't need your sarcasm.'

'But you do need your life.' I took the dagger concealed beneath my robe and pushed the tip against his fleshy throat.

'You've drunk too much.' He made to rise.

I pressed the point harder. Maya yelped and sat back.

'Sobeck,' I insisted. 'Did you betray my friend's meetings with his loved one in the olive grove? You know I watched her die, or at least heard her screams. It was hideous! I visited Sobeck in the Chains. He was condemned to the Wood but the Divine One relented. Now my friend and companion Sobeck is being cooked like a piece of meat in the heat of the Western Desert.'

Maya's plump shoulders shook, and he trembled so much I thought he was having a fit. His face became contorted and he burst out crying.

'You are a contemptible bastard, Maya! You betrayed one of your companions. Why? Because he wouldn't lie with you? Because he wouldn't play with the thing you've got between your legs?'

Maya's sobs became uncontrollable. 'I am sorry,' he wailed, taking his hands away, the kohl round his eyes now running in long black streams down his cheeks. 'I'm sorry about the girl and Sobeck. But you have it wrong, Mahu. I loved Sobeck, I always have, I always will, even though I know it's wrong.'

Something about the petulant twist to his lips, the self-pity in that fat oiled face made me lose my temper.

The knife clattered to the ground. I tore off his wig. Maya
tried to resist but he was fat and never the best of soldiers;
I kept him seated and forced his head back. He shouted
and screamed. I put my hand across his mouth. He tried
to bite me so I punched him then pushed his face beneath
the water. He struggled and slid off. I stood in the pool
forcing his head beneath the water, watching the bubbles
break in the glorious moonlight, feeling his fat body thrash
like a juicy carp caught by a hunter. All my rage bubbled,
for Sobeck, for myself, for the insults I had suffered and,
above all, for the dangers this man posed. Suddenly his
body began to grow limp and I let go of his head. Gasping
and spluttering he staggered up and cast about. I caught
him by the front of his robe and pulled him up. We
stood, the water almost up to our waists. Maya's face
looked frightful. I wrenched the necklace from his neck
and threw it over my shoulder, hearing it clatter on the
ground behind me.

'I'm the Baboon Mahu. Do you remember why I was
called that?' I tightened my grip and pulled him closer.
'Baboons have strong arms and wrists.'

'You'll go to the Wood for this,' he spluttered.

'I doubt it,' I replied, 'and if I do I'll tell them you knew
all about Sobeck as well as your love for him. Does the
Master of the House of Secrets know about your private
life, Maya? Do you go to the temple forecourts or into the
marketplace to watch the pretty boys pass?'

Maya turned his head and spat some of the pool water
out of his mouth. I let go of him, pushing him away.

'You are right, Maya. I have no friends. But Sobeck was
the nearest I ever came to it. What did he do wrong but

love a girl? She was a Divine Ornament but the King of the Two Lands has more concubines than I have hairs on my head.'

'That's treason,' he spluttered.

He moved away but I followed.

'No, no, listen.' He held a hand up. 'I loved Sobeck, Mahu.'

There was something in his voice, the direct gaze – I knew he wasn't lying. On the one hand he was frightened but, on the other, my natural curiosity had also been stirred.

'Are you going to repeat the lie?' I swallowed hard. 'Are you going to repeat the lie that you didn't betray them?'

'I didn't.' He waded through the water. 'Mahu, this is freezing. You don't have to stick my head beneath the surface. I'll tell you what you want to know.'

I grabbed him by the arm and we climbed out of the pool. Picking up his drenched wig and necklace, I thrust them into his hands.

'I'll let you change.'

'I'm not going back there.' Maya wiped his mouth on the back of his hand. 'I don't like the way Horemheb and Rameses are staring at me, and I can't stand the smell of that girl.'

I began to laugh.

'Do I look so pathetic, Mahu?' He turned. 'Your knife is somewhere in the dark, isn't it? Or you can take me back to the pool.' He drew himself up. 'Yes, you have got strong arms and wrists. You've also got the brain of a baboon. I never betrayed Sobeck, can't you see that?' He walked forward glimpsing the uncertainty in my face.

'You stupid bastard!' His beringed hand slapped my face.
I didn't flinch or retaliate.

'You speak with true voice, Maya.'

I went and sat on the tiled edge of the pool.

'If I had betrayed Sobeck,' Maya followed me, clutching
his robe, teeth chattering, 'if I had betrayed Sobeck they
would have asked me how I knew. We would *all* have been
arrested. Have you got that through your thick skull?'

'But you were a spy,' I countered, 'in the Kap. You
discovered that I visited the Veiled One. You knew I had
been entertained by him.'

'What?' Maya drew back. 'Oh yes, I knew there was
something between you and that grotesque. Don't get
angry with me, Mahu, that's what he is. That's why
we had this party, isn't it? So you could bully me? So
he can show his face off and pretend he's not a recluse?
I never told anyone anything about you, Mahu. Who cares
anyway?'

'So the spy must be someone else?' I countered. Try as
I might, I couldn't keep the stammer out of my voice.

'Is that true, Mahu? Who will you have out next? Try
and push Horemheb's head beneath the water. He'll cut
your balls off. Or if he doesn't, his trained viper will.
Can't you see, nobody in the Kap would tell the Divine
One about Sobeck! I work in the House of Secrets, where
it has been known for a messenger to be killed for the
message he carries.'

I stared in disbelief. 'Then who was it? They even knew
exactly where Sobeck and the girl lay, the very part of the
grove. Perhaps Weni was the spy?'

'Weni?' Maya started to laugh. 'He didn't know his

crotch from his arse! Oh, in the early days he was good but in the end he couldn't roll out of bed without a beer jug being thrust under his nose. Sobeck told me about the way you visited the pool. Do you think you know everything, Baboon? We all know why Weni died. He didn't stumble or fall. He made fun of that grotesque and paid with his life.' Maya clambered to his feet and, gathering as much of his dignity as he could, walked down the path toward the postern gate. He paused, head down and even from where I sat in the poor light I could tell he was crying. He turned and came back. This time the tears were more dignified.

'Shall I tell you why I came here tonight? Do you think I *wanted* to be here? I came to see you, you stupid Baboon! We shared something in common – Sobeck. He liked you, even though he claimed you had no soul. I told him he was wrong, but in the end he was proved right. I came because I thought you might be my friend. I also came to thank you. Oh, the story is well-known. How you knelt at the feet of the Veiled One and begged for Sobeck's life. You stupid, monkey-faced bastard,' he spat out. 'I came to thank you!' He turned and walked away.

'Maya!'

I hurried after him. He paused but didn't look round.

'Maya, I was raised by a witch. I had no friends. I was brought to the Kap because my aunt couldn't stand me. You and the rest poked and bullied me. True, I gave as good as I got, but Sobeck was different. He was betrayed – don't doubt that. The lovers were caught red-handed going back to the palace. The guards knew where they met.'

'Oh, by the way,' Maya interrupted, speaking over his

shoulder, 'you mentioned Weni. He was dead long before Sobeck and his playmate used to meet in the grove.'

'I am sorry, Maya. For the first time in my life, I am apologising. I was wrong.'

I thought he'd ignore me but he sighed, turned round and came back, hand extended.

'Mahu.'

I clasped his hand.

'Mahu, I am still in your debt. I couldn't believe what I heard, that you pleaded for Sobeck's life. I couldn't do that nor could the rest. I won't forget that. I'll never be your friend but I will be your ally. Moreover, if you are looking for a spy then don't look amongst the children of the Kap.' He shook his wet robes. 'Give my apologies to your master and the rest. Tell them I feel slightly sick and wish to go home.'

He plodded away. I went through a side door up to my own chamber. My robe was dishevelled, the bracelet I had worn was now in the pool. I remembered the dagger and went down into the darkness to recover it.

'Is everything all right?'

I whirled round.

'Are you well, Mahu?'

Imri, sword drawn, stood under the outstretched branches of a sycamore tree.

'I'm well,' I called back. 'I shall be with you shortly.'

I returned to my chamber, stripped myself naked and cleaned myself with a cloth. I refused to wear a wig for such occasions. I dried my hair cropped close to my head, cleaned my face, dabbing fresh black kohl under my eyes, and put a pair of sandals on my feet to hide the dirt between my toes. I fumbled in my jewellery box to replace the bracelet.

When I rejoined the feast, nobody commented on how long I had been away or the whereabouts of Maya. Huy was now busy with a girl. Horemheb and Rameses had already exchanged their partners. The Veiled One was sipping at his cup. By the empty cushions on his left, and the look on his face, his brother had left, not on the best of terms. I eased myself onto the cushions, picked up a piece of grilled chicken and chewed it carefully.

'Maya won't be returning?' the Veiled One whispered.

'No.' I raised my cup to hide my face. 'Maya is an ally, not a spy.' The Veiled One stiffened.

I glanced quickly around. The soft plucking of the strings of the musicians and the noisy merriment hid our conversation.

'When we first met, Master, in the grove, whom did you tell?'

'Why, Mahu, no one except my mother. From that day you were marked.'

'Yet Hotep knew. He taunted me with the knowledge.'

The Veiled One drank greedily from his cup; his sallow face became flushed. 'Think, Mahu,' he urged.

I closed my eyes. I recalled sitting in the glade, the journey to the house, poor Sobeck slipping through the trees, hand in hand with his illicit love. Both the place where I had first met the Veiled One and the olive grove lay between the Silent Pavilion and the House of Residence. My mind teemed. The Great Queen Tiye would never betray her son. Was this some game by my own master – some devious ploy? But how had he learned about Sobeck? And I recalled his outrage, not because one of his father's concubines had betrayed him, but at the insult offered to the majesty of his office. Moreover, Sobeck's misalliance had taken place for a considerable period of time before the army marched into Kush. So was it a matter of betrayal? Perhaps Sobeck had been glimpsed and followed – but by whom? I recalled the basket of figs, the vipers lurking there, the poisoned jar of wine and that murderous assault down near the riverside.

'Master?' I dipped my finger into the wine and drew the first letter. 'I think I know the name of the spy.'

Three days later the Veiled One summoned me and Imri to a meeting out in the garden pavilion. My master was puce with rage. In his hand was a piece of papyrus which he waved in front of our faces. 'Envoys from the Hittite King are coming to the Divine One's court! They will be officially received by my father and my mother. Tuthmosis will be there, but I have not been invited.' He closed the door of the pavilion, his strange eyes bright with anger. I could tell by his jerky movements and slurred speech that he had been drinking. 'But I shall go.'

He ignored Imri's gasp of astonishment and gestured with his hand for silence.

'I shall go! It is but a simple walk away with my guard and household. I,' he struck his chest, 'am a Prince of Egypt. I have a right to wear the Uraeus. I have the sacred blood in my veins. I will *not* be challenged on this!' He made a cutting movement with his hand. 'I shall inform God's Father Hotep,' he spat the words out, 'and others at my father's court that I will make my presence known and show my face to the envoys of the Hittite King!' He shook his fist. 'I am not some pet monkey or a bird to be kept in a cage. My days in the shadows are over.'

A week later, on a balmy afternoon when the sun was setting slowly and the mountains to the west of Thebes were undergoing a dazzling change of colour, the Veiled One decided to go hunting. The Nile was full and lush, sweeping majestically, drenching the papyrus groves and bringing its richness to the Black Lands. A soft breeze cooled the sweat and refreshed the soul, and the eye was no longer blinded by the harsh heat and desert dust. The Veiled One decided he would hunt for birds amongst the papyrus reeds. Since his declaration a few days earlier about meeting the Hittite envoys, he had been strangely silent. Now he'd roused himself. He, Imri and I, armed with bow, arrows and throwing sticks would hunt marsh birds in the thickets along the Nile.

The Veiled One dressed simply for the occasion in a long white linen robe, tied round the middle with an embroidered sash, folded so it hung in a brilliant display of colour against the white robe. He wore a straw hat and carried his pet cat which always accompanied him on such trips. Imri advised keeping to the canals along the Nile but the Veiled One was insistent.

'No, we'll find more quarry on the river, particularly at this time of day. The birds are heavy and slow-moving.'

We went down. Imri had prepared an imperial skiff with seats in the stern and middle and a small throwing platform in the prow on which the hunter could stand. All three of us were expert with the pole. On this occasion the Veiled One did not immediately go along the jetty where the skiff was lashed but sat cross-legged on a rocky outcrop, face towards the sun, lips moving soundlessly, lost in his own world of prayer. I stared down at the river, still slightly swollen as it swirled by the thick groves of papyrus and overhanging willow trees. This stretch of the river was now fairly deserted, as it usually was just before evening.

'I am ready!' The Veiled One opened his eyes: he put on his hat, followed me down the path onto the jetty and into the skiff. As I clambered in after Imri, I noticed the Veiled One was carrying a leather bag which he placed carefully in the stern. I unloosed the rope, Imri grasped the pole and skilfully pushed the boat out into midstream. Occasionally, other craft passed us: fishermen, merchants, and an imperial barge full of soldiers and archers. These were followed by a flotilla of small craft, the statue of some god in the stern. Across the water drifted the smell of incense, the clap of hands and the faint music of the sistra and the lute.

'Probably taking their god for a swim,' the Veiled One laughed.

He issued instructions. We headed towards the far side of the Nile and a lush outcrop of water trees, bushes and papyrus groves. Imri looked askance at me. Such places were often the haunt of crocodiles, especially at this time of day, when they'd absorbed the heat of the sun and became more agile and aggressive in hunting their quarry. The Veiled One, however, insisted that Imri find a path through the papyrus groves. As we did so, birds burst from their cover in a brilliant display of plumage. I settled my feet on the shifting platform and loosened my throwing stick. The quarry were easy. Time and again I hit the mark and a plump body would fall in the water. Imri would pole skilfully towards it. I would scoop the bird out, make sure it was dead and place it in the basket. I heard splashes and glimpsed a crocodile, eyes and cruel snout jutting above the water.

'Master,' I knelt at the Veiled One's feet, 'this is dangerous. We have taken our tally. I think we should return.'

The Veiled One ignored me. 'Imri, pass me the pole. I'll show you how it can be done.' The Veiled One gestured at me to move aside. Imri, his face laced with sweat, handed over the pole. The Veiled One held it as a soldier would a spear, rolling the edge a few inches from Imri's chest. 'The Hittite envoys didn't come to Thebes.' He picked up the leather bag. 'Mother has written to me.'

The sweat on the back of my neck grew cold. An ominous silence quietened all sound in the papyrus grove: no more the squawk of birds or the flurry of wings. The barge swayed slightly. Imri the Kushite stood, muscular chest drenched in water, sweat and flecks of mud. He turned his head slightly, his good eye intent on the Veiled One.

'Master?' He spoke as if his throat and mouth were dry.

'They went to Memphis,' the Veiled One replied casually. 'Quite a flurry, messengers being sent hither and thither as if my father knew I intended to make a grand entrance. You told him, didn't you, Imri? You are my father's spy. Just like you told him when I first met my Baboon here, that morning in the grove when I worshipped the sun. You also discovered the truth about Sobeck. The only time you leave our pavilion is to walk in the gardens. Did you glimpse that stupid girl flitting through the trees with her lover? And what about the tainted wine and the figs with the vipers in it? Or that day down near the river when the madman attacked me? You were in charge of my guard – that's your duty! You weren't there that day, were you? If it hadn't been for the Baboon, I would be no more.'

The Kushite made to step forward but the Veiled One held the pole secure, moving it like a sword.

'You are a traitor, Imri. A spy. You are an assassin who does not know how my Father protects me.' The Veiled One's voice dropped to a whisper. 'My true Father. He has revealed the treachery of your heart, the evil you plot, the malice you nourish.'

'I . . . I . . .' the Kushite stammered.

'I . . . I what?' the Veiled One mimicked. 'What next, Imri? A knife in the dark?'

Something bumped into our barge, making it sway dangerously. I stared around. A crocodile, its eyes above the water, was floating like a log almost aware of what was happening though I knew he had been attracted by the cry of the birds and their corpses falling into the water.

'Oh Imri,' the Veiled One clicked his tongue. 'Go back to where you came from!'

The pole came down but then, with surprising speed, the Veiled One thrust it forward even as Imri's hand went to the dagger in his belt. He was too slow. The pole caught him a tremendous blow on the side of his head. He staggered, swayed and fell into the water. Immediately my master seized one of the birds we had caught, slit its twisted neck and threw it into the water even as he grasped the pole. I knelt terrified, gripping the seat as the Veiled One, feet apart, drove the pole into the water, moving the barge swiftly back through the reeds. Imri, half-stunned, flailed and screamed. The barge moved quickly but Imri recovered his wits and, aware of the danger, tried to swim, not to the bank but towards us, his dark, scarred face twisted, his one eye full of fear and fury.

The Veiled One had calculated well. Even as the barge raced away I could see the pool of blood forming on the water, the body of the duck half-submerged sending out the delicious tang of ripe meat and fresh blood. The papyrus groves seemed to heave as if some hideous beast was preparing to emerge. I glimpsed the tail of a crocodile, two, three heads emerging above the water. Imri was swimming towards us, no more than a yard away, face tight with determination. The water moved, a slight wave. Imri screamed, coming out of the water, chest well above it, then he was dragged down. Again he emerged as the crocodile seized him, turning and twisting under the water, dragging him beneath the surface. The creature was soon joined by others. The river beyond the papyrus grove was turning into a scene of frenzied activity, the water chopping, Imri's body spinning, the emerging snouts of other crocodiles. One last carrying, hideous scream, the water turning red – and then silence.

Chanting a hymn, the Veiled One poled us further and further away from that macabre scene. At last we were midstream. He kicked me gently in the ribs. I clambered to my feet and grasped the pole, while my master retook his seat in the stern. 'We have hunted and we have killed, Mahu,' he murmured. 'Now let us go home.'

Once back at the Silent Pavilion I announced the tragic death of Imri. Both my master and I adopted the usual rites of mourning, tearing our garments, throwing ashes on our heads, abstaining from food. We kept to our own quarters though we continued to meet secretly. My master betrayed no compunction or regret. 'I prayed, Mahu, to my Father, and he, who knows all things and sees all things, even the innermost secrets of the heart, told me that Imri must die.'

I bit my tongue and curbed my curiosity. The Veiled One sitting before me ran a finger through the ash which stained his cheek.

'You are going to ask why.' He tapped the side of his head. 'The answer came to me in prayer.'

I did not argue. In my view Imri was a traitor, an assassin. It was simply a matter of choice between his life and ours.

'But that is not the end, is it, Mahu? Come, don't sit there staring at me like a wise monkey on a branch! What does your teeming brain tell you?'

'That Imri was not alone.'

'Why do you say that?'

We were seated in the garden of the pavilion. I went out, gazed around and came back closing the door behind me.

'Imri never went very far. Therefore, in this group, there must be others who carried messages, who advised and counselled him.'

'Good. Good!'

'If one fig is rotten,' I continued, 'the rest of the basket is tainted.'

'And how many are in the basket, Mahu?'

'Eight guards, all Kushites. They have served you how long?'

The Veiled One pulled a face. 'Seven or eight years. They will continue to serve me.' He looked at me from under his eyebrows. 'Why, what are you saying, Mahu? If there are further problems, you must resolve them.' He flicked his fingers. 'Do whatever you have to.'

I mingled with the Kushite guard. They had their own barracks and lived their life separate from the rest of the household. Battle-hardened, scarred veterans, Imri's death had disturbed them. I joined them one night out in the courtyard where they held their own ceremony of remembrance, offering wine, fruits and meats before a crudely carved statue, chanting hymns in their own tongue. I felt uncomfortable. They demanded details on how Imri had died and, of course, I described it as a most unfortunate accident. How we had entered the papyrus grove and aroused the crocodiles. They shook their heads at this. 'But Imri was a skilled hunter,' one of them declared. 'He hunted along the river many a time. He knew its waters and the ways of such beasts.'

I could only shrug and say that even the most cunning of hunters make mistakes. I elaborated the story: how both I and my master had attempted to save him but the crocodiles, made ravenous by the birds we had brought down, had decided to attack – an event not unknown along the river. Nevertheless their suspicions were aroused. I could tell by the shifting eyes, the fleeting expressions.

Imri's death would not solve the problem. He would soon be replaced by another. I studied the Kushites and the rest of our household, absorbing every detail, observing habits and relationships. The Kushites not only kept to themselves but treated the rest of the servants, the Rhinoceri, the disfigured men and women who worked in the kitchens and elsewhere, with contempt. A deep antipathy existed between these two groups. The servants had all been chosen because of their disfigurement. The Kushites, however, saw themselves as warriors, their wounds as trophies of battle; they refused to be associated with common criminals and felons. The Rhinoceri lived in their own quarters. Some were married, others led a fairly lonely existence: unless they had the Kushites to guard them, they would not dare to enter the city or even the shabby markets which did thriving business along the riverside.

One of these Rhinoceri caught my attention: their undoubted leader, a young man of about my own age called Snefru, who acted as overseer of the stables. He was burly, with deepset eyes in a hard, disfigured face, a man quick with his fists though he still had a reputation for fairness amongst the others. He attempted to keep his own self-respect and dignity, shaving his head, being careful about his appearance as if to make up for the horrid scar which ran down the centre of his face where his nose and upper lip had been. He was very good with the horses, vigilant over their health and wellbeing. Their bedding, food and water were always rigorously checked, whilst he was skilled as any horse leech in dealing with colic or a myriad of the other minor ailments horses could suffer from.

Snefru would sit, eat and drink with the rest of the men in the cool of the evening, yet before doing so, he would always ensure he changed his leather kilt for a tattered but clean robe, scrupulously washing his hands and face in water mixed with salt. At first I studied him from afar but, with our common interest in horses, I soon learned his story. He had been a scribe of the stables in a military barracks on the far side of Thebes. His father, mother and sister had all died of the fever which often rages amongst the huddled tenements of those artisans in their mud-bricked houses beyond the walls.

'I could not afford the fees for the embalmers,' Snefru confided, brushing the flanks of a horse. 'And so I became desperate. I thought the stable would not miss a horse. One night I took one out and sold it to a party of Desert Wanderers. They, in turn, were stopped by the Medjay. The horse carried markings. They were killed and I was arrested. The only reason I escaped with my life,' he spread his strong, muscular arms, 'was because of my skill with horses.' He gestured at the scar. 'The executioner was clumsy. He removed my nose and part of my lip. I was banished to the village of the Rhinoceri. I stayed there for two years until royal heralds arrived. They were looking for skilled men to work here. I produced my record.' He shrugged. 'And I've been here ever since.'

'Are you a soldier, Snefru?' I found it hard not to look at that gruesome scar, almost as if his face was cut into two by a dark shadow. The 'wound' on his lip made him stumble over certain words.

'I have served in the levy,' he replied. 'On one occasion I even served as a driver in a chariot.'

'But not like the brave Kushites?' I lowered my voice.

'Oh, them.' Snefru came round the horse. Crouching down, he picked up its hind leg to scrutinise the hoof.

'Yes – what about them?' I squatted down with him.

'They are arrogant and cruel.' Snefru's eyes held mine. 'But so are you, sir. You are the master's shadow. Yet, over the last few days, you keep appearing here, offering me wine and bread, drawing me into conversation. You want something? I don't know what. You have no strange tastes. You are not fascinated by my disfigurement.' His tongue licked the corner of his mouth. 'And now we talk about the Kushites whose Captain, Imri, died so mysteriously in the crocodile pool. What is it you want?'

I got to my feet. 'I don't like stables,' I grinned, 'but the evening is cool, the stars are out.'

Snefru joined me outside. We walked and talked and I gained the measure of him. I had chosen correctly. This was a man to be trusted, but one with bounding ambition. We paused under a tamarisk tree and I gazed up at its branches.

'Wouldn't you like to change your life, Snefru? To receive a pardon for your crimes, the favour of our rulers? The opportunity to be valued and respected?'

'I hear your song,' Snefru replied, 'but the words are indistinct.'

'You like the tune?'

Snefru's face was hidden by the shadows. 'What we are talking about here,' he whispered, 'is a matter of life and death, isn't it?'

'Can your companions be trusted?' I remarked.

'The other Rhinoceri?' Snefru laughed softly. 'Of course they can.'

'They will do what you say?'

'That depends on what I offer.'

I drew him deeper into the shadows and, under a starlit sky, the cool breeze whispering, the trees shifting about us, I baited the trap.

Four days later the Veiled One ordered his chariot to be prepared, pulled by his fleetest horses. With myself as the driver, the Kushites armed and ready, my master swept out into the Eastern Red Lands to hunt the ostrich, the lion and the gazelle. We had done this before and the Veiled One always insisted that his chariot must be the most splendid, the panels of the side emblazoned with red, blue and gold, eye-catching designs. The gleaming black harness of the horses was decorated with silver and gold medallions 'bedecked like Montu', as my master put it. He was correct, for we were going to war not to hunt.

We reached the reserve and rested during the heat of the day. Evening fell, cool and fresh, but we did not thunder after the fleet-footed ostrich or the darting gazelle. The Veiled One remained in his tent, claiming he was unwell. He despatched some of the Kushites to hunt quail, hare, any fresh meat for our cooking fire. At first we followed the usual routine: four hunters were sent out, the other four remained as guards. The sun began to set, a cold breeze blew and the sky changed as it always did before the darkness came rushing in. We built a campfire and gathered round it. I shared out the supplies we'd brought whilst my master stayed in his tent. The food was palatable but highly salted, dried meat and some bread which had already lost its freshness during the day. The four remaining Kushites were nervous as their companions had not returned.

'They shouldn't have been sent,' one grumbled. 'We are soldiers, not hunters. It is our master's duty to provide the meat.'

I stared up at the night sky. We had camped in a small ravine, the rocks rising on either side of us. The Kushites were so nervous they were hardly aware of this break from the normal routine. We usually camped out in the open, our fires easy to see. I listened to their grumbles and poured the wine until they became more drowsy. I told them I'd be back and walked over to the Veiled One's pavilion. He was sitting moodily, sipping from a cup; his faraway gaze hardly recognised me. I heard the sounds, the crunch on gravel, the clash of weapons. When I left the tent the deed had been done. The Kushites had drunk deeply of the drugged wine. They now lay sprawled in pools of blood forming round their gashed throats. Around them stood Snefru and his companions, armed to the teeth with sword and dagger, bows and quivers slung over their backs. They were all dressed in those reed-battered hats, protection against the sun, leather kilts and marching boots, all supplied by the Veiled One from his small armoury. I walked over and glanced down at one corpse.

'And the other four?' I asked.

'Trapped and killed,' Snefru replied. 'It was easy enough. They divided into pairs. We heard them before they ever came into sight.'

I gazed round at the rest. All were Rhinoceri, each and every one hand-picked by Snefru, from my master's house-servants.

'You realise what has been done,' I declared, 'and you know there is no going back. These are Kushite warriors, veterans from the imperial regiments, selected by the Divine One himself to guard his son, but they could not be trusted and had to pay the price. You will take their place.' I paused. The silence of the night was rent by the coughing roar of the lion, followed by the yip of a hyena and the screech of another animal. 'You will replace them,' I continued. 'You will be my master's servants. The dust under his feet. There will be no sacred oaths, hands over the altar with fires burning and incense smouldering. You have taken the oath already in the blood of these men. Do not think the Divine One will pardon any of you who decide to betray the rest. Your death will be just as brutal as theirs: impalement on a stake.'

The hieroglyph for 'to be beautiful' – *nfr/nefer* – contains three depictions of the human heart.

Chapter 7

In the freezing cold dark of the desert we buried the stiffening corpses of the Kushites. Snefru informed me that the corpses of the others had been similarly concealed. We dug deep in the hot sand. Afterwards the Veiled One gathered us together.

'What you have done,' he declared gently, as if addressing a group of friends, 'has been ordained and is fitting punishment for traitors. No one lifts his hand against the Son of the Divine One. You are now to return.' He gazed round, peering at them through the dark as if memorising the faces of this group. 'Go back to the palace but return individually. Should anyone ask, you know nothing of this. Indeed, for time immemorial, you shall know nothing of this.'

Once they were gone, padding away through the night, the Veiled One took a brand from the fire and burned his pavilion. Then, taking his sword, he hacked at the chariot like a man possessed, denting its finery, shattering the decorations, splintering the javelin holder and damaging the quiver. The splendid Bow of Honour, his favourite weapon for the hunt, was also gouged and marked. Javelins and arrows were thrown onto the sand. Bereft of his cane, his ungainly movements assumed a menace all of their own. I was not invited to join him; he acted like a man demented. When he stopped, he stood, arms drooping, eyes glazed, chest heaving with exertion. He fell to his knees and threw sand over his face. Then, he drew his dagger, lurched to his feet and staggered towards me. He looked as if he was going to trip. I went forward to help but he moved quickly, his arm coming up, the knife slicing my upper arm and nicking my left wrist. I flinched in pain and drew away but he followed on, grasping my tunic and tearing it. I made to resist.

'Mahu, think! We have been attacked by Libyans, Desert Wanderers.' He fashioned makeshift bandages to staunch the wound then inflicted similar cuts on himself. All around us was darkness, in this haunted place with the roars of the night prowlers drawing closer and the biting wind turning our sweat cold, coating us in a fine dust which stung our eyes. I ached from head to toe. The wounds from the razor-edged knife smarted as if I had been burned with fiery coals. Once satisfied, the Veiled One took another brand from the fire and stared around. He looked eerie in the dancing flames with his long face and awkward body yet his eyes were steady. When he spoke, his voice was soft as if talking to himself or praying, I don't know which.

'Come, Baboon, we are finished here.'

We unhobbled the horses, the Veiled One patting them

reassuringly: the beasts could smell the blood, and the dark shapes of the night prowlers increased their alarm. We climbed into the chariot and were gone, out of that ghost-filled gully, hooves pounding, wheels rattling as we fled like birds of ill omen under a starlit sky back to our quarters in the Malkata Palace.

Snefru and the others acted as if nothing untoward had happened. Naturally, of course, the Veiled One's appearance without his Kushite guards, the state of both ourselves and the chariot raised uproar and alarm. Messengers were despatched to the palace. I assisted the Veiled One to his quarters, helped him strip, wash and don new robes. He did the same for me as if we were two boys desperate to escape the effects of our mischief. Royal physicians arrived. They questioned my master, scrupulously searched for any injury, then they turned on me. We both acted our roles and sang the same hymn: how we had gone out into the Eastern Desert to hunt and been ambushed by Libyan Desert Wanderers. The Veiled One acted all mournful, as did I. He described how his Kushite guard had put up a brave fight. Some were killed, others probably captured whilst, as the Veiled One hinted, the remainder may even have deserted.

Of course, no one could disprove our story. Great Queen Tiye, accompanied by the Crown Prince Tuthmosis, soon arrived. This time the Queen came in all her haughty beauty, garbed in costly robes, gold sandals with silver thongs, and a bejewelled head-dress. Crown Prince Tuthmosis looked more anxious than his mother. He was pale, rather thin from the loss of body fat. He ignored me and remained closeted with his mother and brother. At the end of their meeting Queen Tiye demanded to see me alone in the hall of audience. Tuthmosis had been sent to guard the door. The Queen acted her part, all anxious-eyed, a little nervous, solicitous and grateful that we had escaped – though I could tell from the amusement in her eyes that she knew what had truly happened.

'I am concerned,' her voice rose, eyes full of mockery, 'I am concerned at my son's security.'

'Excellency,' I replied, kneeling before her, 'I have already taken care of that. I have armed a number of the Rhinoceri servants. Many of them have seen military service. I believe your son, my master, thinks that security enough.'

We spoke one thing with our mouths and another with our eyes. Tuthmosis, however, was not so easily mollified. He came striding down the hall, coughing into his hands. When he stopped before me, I saw the piece of linen furtively thrust up the voluminous sleeve, pushed under a wrist strap which dangled rather loosely.

'Mother, guards should be brought from the palace!'

'Yes and no,' Tiye replied. 'My son is disturbed. I think it's best if he feels secure, for the moment at least.'

They left shortly afterwards. The Veiled One summoned me to his quarters. He was sitting cross-legged on his bed staring out of the open window and watching the sun set.

'All life comes from him, Mahu. He who dwells on all things and supports all things. The One who numbers our days and metes out judgement. I am his Beloved.' He looked over his shoulder at me and rubbed a finger up and down that long nose, his lower lip jutting out. 'All life is sacred, Mahu. Be it a bird on the wing or a fish in the river.'

'And the Kushites we slaughtered?' I asked.

'They died because their lives were not sacred any more.' He turned to gaze out of the window. 'What will happen to us, Mahu? We are like children, being chased by shadows. We can turn and hide and fight, but still the chase goes on. My father will send other soldiers or a gift, some tainted wine or poisoned food. What will happen, Mahu?'

I knelt down. It was the first time the Veiled One had ever really asked me a question. The tone of his voice revealed that he was waiting for an answer. I don't know what prompted my reply but the words came tumbling out before I could even reflect on them.

'He has commanded you, his son, to appear
rich and magnificent.
He has united with your beauty.
He will hand over to you his daily plans.
You are his eldest son who came into existence
through him.
Hail to you, the One who is splendid in skills!
You have come from the Horizon of the sky!
You are beautiful and young like the Aten.

'You will become,' I continued in a rush, 'Lord of the Two Lands, Holder of the Diadem, he who speaks with true voice, whose heel will rest on the neck of the People of the Nine Bows.'

The Veiled One lifted his hands. He was staring fixedly

at the setting sun. Then he clambered off the bed and came towards me. I kept my head bowed, staring at those strange feet with their elongated toes and bony ankles. He stopped, grasped me by the hand and pulled me to my feet, his face wreathed in smiles, his eyes bright with life. He placed a hand on each of my shoulders and stared at me as if he was seeing me for the first time. Then he clasped me to him. I could feel the bones of his pigeon chest, the strength of those long arms; I could smell the perfume on his flesh.

'Blessed are you, Mahu,' he whispered, 'least yet first amongst men. It is not flesh and blood which has revealed this to you but my Father who dwells beyond the Far Horizon and whose fingers have touched your heart so that you speak with true voice. Blessed are you, Mahu, son of Seostris, friend of Pharaoh.'

He released his grip and stood back. Hobbling over to a side table, he removed the cloth from a jug and filled two goblets of wine, serving me mine as if I was a priest in a temple.

'Do you know what you said? Do you recognise the truth of my reply?'

In fact, I didn't. On reflection what had prompted me was Tuthmosis, pale and narrow-faced, that blood-speckled napkin being thrust up his sleeve, and this enigmatic ungainly young man who could sing a song to a butterfly but kill like any panther from the South. We drank the wine and the Veiled One, drawing me close, whispered what I was to do. From that evening on I became responsible for his safety and security. Snefru, still nervous after the killing in the desert, became Captain of his guard.

The following morning a cart arrived, a gift from Queen Tiye, not food or drink or precious robes but the finest weapons and armour from the imperial storerooms. I gave Snefru two tasks: to train his men and recruit others who could be trusted, and to hire more servants from the village of the Rhinoceri. The Veiled One had a hand in this. He gave each of his new bodyguards an amulet, a scarab depicting the Aten, the Sun in Glory, rising between the Two Peaks in the East. He made them kneel in the dust of the courtyard, as he passed from one to another, gently asking their names, thrusting the insignia of office into their hands and softly caressing the head of each man. I was not so gentle but gave them a lecture Weni and Colonel Perra would have been proud of: their loyalty was to me and to their Prince. They were guarantors of each other's fidelity. The treachery of one was the treachery of all and the good of their Prince was the glory of all. I then distributed the weapons, the leather kilts, the shields and spears, organising a roster of duties, interviewing each new recruit, accepting some, rejecting others.

The walls and gates of the Silent Pavilion were now closely guarded. No one arrived or left without my knowing; even the servants who went down to the marketplace were watched carefully. To all appearances the Veiled One's household was depleted, disorganised. The Prince, our master, was sheltering in his chamber after the hideous incidents out in the Eastern Desert. The truth was very different. Security was the order of the day, the protection of the Prince our constant watchword. Food and wine were rigorously checked. A servant girl who could not explain why she had left the market in Thebes to visit the Temple of Isis quietly disappeared. At the same time the Prince opened his treasures. The Kushites had been paid from the House of Silver; now every one of his bodyguards was lavishly rewarded by the One they served. Of course God's Father Hotep came sauntering into my master's residence, walking through the gates, escorted by a gaggle of priests and officers from the Sacred Band. I quickly recognised the faces of Horemheb and Rameses: burned dark by the sun, garbed in their dress armour, they moved with all the swagger and arrogance of their kind. I met Hotep at the gates to the Prince's garden.

'I bring a request from my master,' I whispered, bowing low. 'He asks that your retainers' – I heard a gasp of anger from some of the officers – '*your retainers*,' I repeated, 'either stay in the courtyard,' I gestured round, 'where there is shade, and where food and wine will be brought, or perhaps beneath the trees beyond the gates.'

Hotep held my gaze, those bright, sardonic eyes studying me carefully.

'So you do not wish my companions to be wandering about?'

'Excellency,' I bowed again, 'you and yours are most welcome here. However, you must remember, the Prince has lost the Captain of his guard – that vile attack in the Eastern Red Lands . . .' I spread my hands. 'My master is not a warrior or soldier . . .' My voice faltered as if I, too, was nervous. Hotep turned, fanning his face, and gazed round, noting the guards at every doorway, spears at the ready, archers with their bows unslung. He grinned lazily at me and tapped me on the chest.

'Horemheb is right. You are a clever baboon.' He turned to his retainers. 'Gentlemen, you may stay here. I bear messages from the Divine One.'

And, brushing by me, he entered the garden where my master was waiting for him in the pavilion. His escort rather self-consciously broke up. Some drifted towards the gate or made for the shade of the trees. Horemheb and Rameses, gold collars gleaming in the sun, remained standing alone, tapping their staffs of office against their legs.

'My friends!' I exchanged the kiss of peace with each of them.

Rameses pinched my arm mischievously.

'You've climbed high, Baboon,' he whispered before letting me go, so I could clasp Horemheb's hand. The great soldier had filled out, muscular in his shoulders and arms, strong of grip, dark eyes in that hard, granite-like face. Both he and Rameses had their heads completely shaven. Horemheb had a scar high on his right cheekbone. He noted my gaze and rubbed this.

'A Libyan arrow.' His mouth smiled but his eyes didn't. 'Brother Rameses and I have been out in the Eastern Desert pursuing these marauders who attacked your master.'

'We found some javelins and arrows, bones whitening under the sun.' Horemheb squinted up at the sky. 'As mine will if we don't get into the shade and have some wine.'

I ushered them into the house, to the small tables

I had prepared in an alcove beneath a window which overlooked the garden. I served them sweet white wine and a dish of glazed walnuts smeared with honey on strips of flat bread. They both ate, noisily smacking their lips, dabbing their fingers in the water bowl and wiping them on the napkins as they stared around. Horemheb noticed the guards standing in the shadows and grinned.

'How good are they, Mahu?' he asked, nodding his head. 'As skilled as the Kushites?'

'They are loyal and they will kill.' I smiled and toasted him with my cup.

Rameses laughed behind his hand. 'Soldiers with no noses,' he taunted, 'and little military training. Have they been drilled by you, Mahu?'

'Tell me,' I replied, ignoring his question, 'what do men fight for the most? For money? Plunder? Women?'

'Glory,' Horemheb snapped. 'The glory of To-mery, the Kingdom of Egypt.'

'What about their own glory,' I retorted, 'as well as that of the One they serve?'

The smile faded from Horemheb's face. 'The Divine One could send the regiment here,' he whispered, 'and soon take care of these toy soldiers.'

'Attack his own son?' I replied. 'Queen Tiye's beloved? My friends, I shall tell you something: there are moments in life when you make choices. On these choices your life, your fame, your fortune depend.'

'What are you saying?' Rameses snarled, his lean face ugly with the anger seething within him.

'We are children of the Kap,' I replied. 'I am not threatening you, or describing the way things should be, just the way they are. I gave Sobeck good advice and he ignored it. I did what I could for him. Don't you expect me to do the same for you?'

Horemheb wiped his mouth on the back of his hand and got to his feet. Rameses followed. He was about to walk away when he came back and smiled down at me.

'I've got two new dwarves,' he said. 'I never forgot that night, Mahu,' his smile widened, 'and the horrors of the crocodile pool. You are right. You never know when you can be swept away.'

He and Rameses sauntered lazily to the door. They'd hardly gone when Hotep appeared. He gestured at me not to rise and sat down opposite.

'Well, well, well.' His furrowed face broke into a smile, eyes watchful, like a hawk on its perch. 'Quite a few changes here, Mahu.'

'It is important that the Prince feels secure.'

'He's under the care of the Divine One; we all rest in the shadow of his hands.'

'Of course,' I replied. 'Still, prudence and wisdom are gifts of the gods.'

Hotep picked up Horemheb's cup and sipped at it. 'Tell me again what happened in the Red Lands.'

I did so. Hotep sat nodding his head. 'And Imri?'

I gave him a description of our calamitous journey on the river. 'An unfortunate accident,' I concluded.

'And all of Imri's guard were killed out in the Red Lands?'

'So it would seem.'

'And you went hunting there?'

'We went hunting,' I replied, holding his gaze. 'Gazelle and ostrich, whatever crossed our path.'

'But you never took Saluki hounds?'

I hid my disquiet – a mistake we had overlooked.

Hotep put the cup down. 'Why didn't you take Saluki hounds? They are as fleet as any deer.'

'My master knows my dislike of Saluki hounds,' I replied quietly. 'My Aunt Isithia had one called Seth. He killed my pet monkey – I never forgot.'

'Ah yes, Isithia.' Hotep scratched his neck. 'I understand you don't visit her.'

'She is never far from my heart.'

Hotep smiled thinly. 'She said that your fates were intertwined.'

A prickle of fear curled along my back. 'Whose fates, Excellency?'

Hotep sipped from his cup to conceal his own disquiet.

'Why was I sent to the Kap?' I asked abruptly. 'My father was a brave soldier but Thebes is full of the sons of brave soldiers.'

'Your aunt petitioned me whilst your father's bravery was known to the Divine One, but that's in the past, Mahu.' Hotep smiled. 'The evils of one day are enough and we must look to the future. What will happen to your Prince when his brother succeeds?'

'May Pharaoh live for a million years,' I replied.

'Of course,' Hotep agreed, 'and enjoy a thousand jubilees. My question still stands. You talk of choices.'

'When did I talk of choices?'

Again the crooked smile.

'Don't you know, Mahu? Even the breeze can carry

words. You must make choices.' Hotep spread his hands. 'Which path you are going to follow? Whom will you truly serve? Ah well.' He brushed some crumbs from his robe and got to his feet. 'I don't want your answer now, but one day.' He plucked a fan from his sleeve to cool his face. 'You know where I am.' He turned away but then came back. 'Your master, he talks to you?'

'Like my aunt talked to her Saluki hound.'

Hotep smacked me across the face with his fan. 'What do you think of your master, Mahu?'

'I don't think at all about him, Excellency. I do meditate quite often, at the way things are and, perhaps, the way things should be. I remember the poet's words. You may know the line? "It is easier to hate than to love. It is better to love than to hate. But sometimes, you must hate to protect what you love".'

'A riddle?' Hotep stepped back.

'The solution is easy, Excellency. I could take an example from agriculture. They say that you are the son of a farmer?'

'And?'

'As the vine is planted,' I replied, 'so shall it grow.'

'Are you talking about yourself?' he queried.

'No, Excellency, I am talking about all of us.'

I have been asked where it really all started, when I became aware of the real cause. I have been asked to speak with true voice. I do find this difficult. It's like a fire in a house. You smell the smoke, you see the wisps but you are not certain where the fire is burning. So it is with the one they now call the Accursed, Akhenaten, the

Grotesque, the Ugly One, the Veiled One, the Beloved of the Aten, the Lord of the Diadems.

I suppose it all began the night after Hotep had left. They came for me when the darkness was deepest, sliding into my chamber, stifling my mouth, binding my hands and feet, wrapping me in a coarse blanket. I struggled, lashed out, but they carried me effortlessly, moving like shadows along the passageway down the stairs and across the courtyard. A cold breeze pierced the blanket and froze my sweat. A gate opened. The smell of wood, of flowers, of crushed grass; more voices talking swiftly, hoarsely indistinct. Orders were being issued.

I was thrown into a cart which moved; every jolt of its wheels felt like a blow. This time there were different smells, the sounds of the night, the screech of an animal in pain, the cry of a bird. The breeze grew colder; I heard the slop of water. I was being taken aboard a barge. My terrors increased. Images came and went of the Danga dwarf being swept towards the crocodile pool, of Imri fighting for his life. Who were my abductors? Had the Veiled One changed his mind? Had Hotep taken matters into his own hands? Or had the Magnificent One, tired of his wife's intervention, despatched his assassins?

I heard the scrape of the barge on the sandy shale and tried to relax, becoming more aware of the tight ropes round my wrist, the gag thrust in my mouth. Another cart-ride, jolting as before. I found myself sliding downwards, so the cart must be moving up a slight incline, probably into the Western Desert. The cold grew more intense. The sound of the night stalkers echoed ominously: a heart-wrenching roar, the full-throated hunting cry of lions, followed by the yips, snarls and barks of those who followed this ferocious hunting pack.

At last the cart stopped; I was lifted out. The blankets were pulled away, the gag released and the ropes binding my ankles were cut. I was aware of fire, light, icy winds, starlit skies, dark shapes around me. Then a shroud was placed across my head, sealing me once again in darkness. My breathing sounded for an eternity. I was forced to kneel; sharp pebbles cut my knees. I received a stinging blow across my back.

'Well, well, Mahu, Baboon of the South. We brought you out here to the desert where so many men's bones lie. Tell me, Mahu, what happened the night your master went hunting?'

'I have told you,' I spluttered. 'We were attacked by Desert Wanderers, Sand Dwellers, I don't know! They crept in, loosening shafts through the night. We tried to gather round the chariot. Some were killed, others were driven off.'

Again the stinging blow across my back.

'Lies!' the voice snarled. 'And what else, Mahu? Imri's death, a keen hunter, a man who knew the Nile and its dangers?'

'An accident!' I screamed.

'So many accidents,' the voice murmured. 'What does your master say to you, Mahu? Does he plot against the Divine One?'

'He tends his garden,' I retorted, 'and visits his House of Paintings.' For one eerie moment the image of that beautiful woman standing by the gate in the torchlight returned to haunt me.

'People visit him,' I spluttered. I felt a cut on my ankle, a knife slicing the skin. The cut was so unexpected, the knife so razor sharp, the blood was pouring out before a stab of pain coursed through my leg.

'We have only just begun, Mahu. We've drawn blood, we'll let it trickle then we'll bind your feet and leave you here.'

The questioning continued; about the fate of the Kushites, Imri's death, what my master did – who visited him? The questions came so fast I couldn't determine who was questioning me; in truth, I didn't care. My body shook. My legs trembled in a cold sweat. Sometimes I'd drift into sleep; dreams came, memories from the past. Weni lying in that pool, floating face down on the surface. On his back, my pet monkey Bes. In the trees beyond, Sobeck and his lover locked in a passionate embrace, her arms and legs around him, her long hair falling, unaware of the hunters racing towards them. The Veiled One sitting on cushions, his almond-shaped eyes staring at me intently. Queen Tiye slapping me across the face, Isithia dragging me by the hand. Cold water was thrown over me, another blow to my back and the questioning continued. At last I collapsed onto my side.

'Enough!' a voice cried.

The coarse-smelling blanket was taken from my head, the bonds on my hands were cut. I was half-dragged across to the roaring fire. A wineskin was forced between my lips, a platter of bread and soft delicious lamb thrust into my hand. I ate and drank.

'Mahu! Mahu?'

I raised my head. The Veiled One was sitting across

by the fire, dressed in a Sand Dweller's striped robe, the hood pulled back. At his side sat his mother Queen Tiye, similarly dressed, her hair falling down either side of her unpainted face. Beside them was a man who kept in the shadows, his face indistinct, although I could make out a sharp nose, glittering eyes and a bushy moustache and beard. I gazed around: a circle of men protected us, their drawn weapons glinting in the firelight – shields, spears and swords. Others were armed with bows, the arrows already notched. Beyond them another line of men held torches, keeping away the night prowlers, the beasts of the desert. I groaned and took a slurp from the wineskin.

'I am cold.' I grasped my ankle. The blood had stopped flowing, leaving an open, aching wound. 'Why this?' I protested. 'What games do you play?'

'Life and death,' Queen Tiye retorted, pushing her hands up the sleeves of her gown. 'You were visited today by God's Father Hotep, emissary of the Divine One. He sat with you in the hall of audience, didn't he?'

I nodded.

'He urged you to reflect about choices, what paths to follow.'

I nodded. The Veiled One sat gazing at me. In the light of the fire his face seemed more beautiful than grotesque, the eyes soft and liquid, the full pouting lips parted in a smile.

'Don't you trust me?' I asked. 'Is this what we have come to?'

'We had to make sure, Mahu.'

'Haven't I proved my loyalty already? What other evidence do you need?'

'It's not about the past,' Tiye interrupted, 'but now and the future.'

She spoke in a tongue I didn't understand to their companion who withdrew. Queen Tiye gestured at me to join them. They moved back from the fire so we could sit facing each other. Tiye urged me to eat and drink, holding the wineskin herself.

'You can sleep tomorrow, Mahu. Tonight you must listen. I have told you about my son's birth, the pain, the way he was abducted, kept by the priests and abused.'

The Veiled One snarled as if his mother's words pricked his memory and boiled the hatred seething within him.

'Ignored and abused,' Tiye continued. 'What the priests also knew, Mahu, were the dreams I had whilst I carried my son in the egg, whilst he danced in my womb. Dreams of grandeur, Mahu, of a Pharaoh who would rise high on the far horizon. Of course I was delighted! I chattered to my husband, the Divine One, who shared this knowledge with the priests. They cast their own horoscopes and Pharaoh became troubled. The priests did not share my joy but whispered about the Accursed, about a ruler who would mete out justice to the other gods of Egypt.'

I stared half-drunkenly back. I never cared for dreams or horoscopes. Aunt Isithia had cured me of all that.

'You don't believe us, do you, Mahu?' the Veiled One demanded.

I recalled my words to Hotep. 'I believe in the effects of love and hate. Of a child being alone and abused.'

The Veiled One laughed softly.

'Is that why you brought me out in the desert?'

'Look around you,' Tiye urged. 'Who are these men, Mahu?'

'Ruthless killers,' I replied. 'I ache from head to toe.'

Again the soft laugh.

'Desert Wanderers, Sand Dwellers,' I yawned, rubbing my arms.

'No, Mahu,' Queen Tiye smiled. 'They are my people.'

I caught my breath. In the Kap I had heard the stories and rumours, of how the Magnificent One had been captivated by this young woman from Akhmin. How he had broken with custom set from time immemorial that the Pharaoh always married a foreign princess. Tiye was the exception. Oh, how we had giggled behind our hands about her presumed expertise and prowess in bed. Now the laughter seemed sour and unworthy.

'My family come from Akhmin and soon you shall meet others from my tribe.'

The face of the Beautiful One returned.

'But for now,' Tiye continued, 'we are the Sheshnu, the Apiru, tribes who wandered across Sinai from Canaan many years ago, drawn by the wealth of Egypt, the black soil of the Nile, its fertile crops and the favour of Pharaoh. We have become one with Egypt. Well,' she shrugged quickly, 'at least some of us have. Others stay away from the cities, tending their flocks, serving their god. My family have followed other paths. Oh yes, Mahu, I am a Priestess of Min. I have danced and cavorted in his temple before his statue but that's only on the surface, like grass and bushes carried by the river. The customs of Egypt are like a garment I can put on and off whenever I wish.'

221

I sat impassive, no longer aware of my aches and pains, the soreness in my ankle, the cold wind, or the chilling sounds of the night.

'The Egyptian word for mankind is *Remeth*,' Tiye continued, 'which is the same word for *Egyptian*. In the beginning, Mahu' – she leaned forward – 'Egyptian, Libyan and Kushite were all one, serving the same, invisible omnipotent god. The Egyptians call him Aten, my people Elohim, or Adonai, the Lord. Different names for the same being. He dwells like the air we breathe. He is in us, works through us, sustaining all life yet he is also apart, all-loving, all-creative. That was in the beginning. Since then, mankind has gone its own way and fashioned gods for itself, making them in its own image, slicing the One God like you would a piece of fruit. A God of War, Montu; a God of the River, Hapi; a God of the Earth, Geb; the Sun God, Ra.' She gestured with her hand. 'Mahu, this is a time to put aside childish nonsense.'

'Mahu is not a priest,' the Veiled One broke in. 'He does not care for the gods, do you?'

I gazed unblinkingly back.

'You think I worship the Aten,' he continued, 'and so I do. But the glorious Sun Disc is only the symbol, the manifestation of my Father. My dream, Mahu, is to be Akhenaten, the Radiance of the Aten. It's not only my dream, it's my destiny.'

'One other god amongst many,' I argued back. 'Even the Divine One pays homage to the Aten.'

'Ah, yes.' The Veiled One raised a hand, like a teacher in a hall of learning. 'We worship the Aten and pay deference to the rest because that is the way things have to be, at least for a while.' He bowed his head. 'I know what you are thinking, Mahu.' His voice became muffled, mouth hidden behind the folds of the cloak. 'The Temple of Amun-Ra has thousands of priests. Its Houses of Silver are filled with precious stones, gold, silver, amethyst and jasper. The priests own estates and property from the Delta to beyond the Third Cataract. The temples have their own troops, chariot squadrons, scribes, a kingdom within a kingdom, Mahu. The priests determine the rituals and calendars of the year. They dominate every aspect of life. That is true of the temples of Karnak and Luxor. And what about the others – Anubis, Isis, and Ptah in the white-walled city of Memphis?' He gestured with his hand. 'Can you imagine, Mahu, what would happen if these temples united against the power of Pharaoh? Think of the wealth they conceal. Legions of priests with a finger in everyone's pot, feeding the populace from their granaries and stores, the bribes they offer, the people they can buy. They must be checked.' He glanced up at the sky. 'The night is passing,' he murmured. 'You have been given a glimpse of the future, Mahu, and that future will happen.' He grasped his cane, rose unsteadily to his feet and helped his mother up. 'That is why we brought you out to the desert, Mahu. To make certain of you, to bind you closer so you can participate in the sacrifice.'

They left me alone for a while. People came and went in the darkness. More food was brought. I fell asleep, slouching forward. I was shaken roughly awake; the sky was already lighter though the wind was still cold. On a small hillock not far away I glimpsed an altar, fashioned roughly out of stones heaped together, now ringed by those who had brought me here. Queen Tiye and the Veiled One were already before the altar, faces towards the rising sun. My guards gestured that I join them. I was allowed through the circle of men and climbed the hillock. A strange experience: it was unlike any sanctuary or temple court I had ever entered before. No coloured pillars or frescoes, just a sandy, pebble-strewn hill on the edge of the desert. The altar table was a slab of rock resting on others. At each end glowed pots of incense. In the middle stood bread, wine, and a flask of oil, next to a freshly slaughtered kid, its throat cut, the blood already crusted and dried around the gaping wound.

One of the Shemsou pulled the carcass into the centre of the altar. Queen Tiye crumbled incense over it. The Veiled One grasped the flask of oil and sprinkled it liberally, covering every inch. A firebrand was brought; Queen Tiye held it up. She and her son, eyes on the Far Horizon, watched the glow of pink turn a fiery red. The flame of the torch danced in the wind. For the first time in my life I felt I was in the presence, not of something holy, but eerie, strange. These two people standing so fixedly in that silent ring of men. The Sun Disc appeared, a brilliant red glow on the horizon, its light racing out over the desert. Tiye lowered the flame and the offering was consumed in a blaze of fire, smoke billowing towards the sky. The air turned rich with the smell of incense, oil and burning meat. Once the sacrifice was lit, Tiye broke into a paean of praise: her son joined in and the refrain was taken up by the circle of men. A powerful song, it seemed to follow the smoke and flames as they rose to the sky.

The sun was rising fast, turning the cold air warm; the

breeze, the breath of Amun blowing from the North, faded in the light and heat of the day. On the makeshift altar the fire began to die. The incense pot and what was left of the oil were poured over it. We stood back until nothing was left but charred, blackened remains, and the magic, the mystery, died with it. We were out on the edge of the desert under the strengthening sun about to face the searing heat of the day. I felt exhausted. Tiye was now issuing orders. The altar was dismantled, the stones being cast aside, the fires doused and, escorted by our retinue, cloaked and hooded, we made our way down to the rich pasturelands and back across the Nile.

On our journey home both the Queen and my master remained silent. We entered the palace grounds by a side gate. Our retinue with the carts disappeared, leaving the Queen, the Veiled One and myself to walk alone through the deserted gardens. We passed through guard posts; the Queen, armed with the imperial seal, was not checked or stopped, but given every deference. As we passed the House of Residence, the place where I had been raised, I paused in astonishment: the gates had now been removed from their hinges, the walls widened to allow the builders' carts in. Stacks of timber lay next to slabs of masonry and builder's tools. Already the masons, sleepy-eyed, were gathering. I hadn't been there for some time. I'd heard vague rumours about refurbishment and rebuilding.

'You are surprised, Mahu?' The Veiled One took off his striped robe, throwing it over his arm. He stood like a hunting dog sniffing the breeze.

'All things change, Mahu. This is going to form a new residence for me and my bride.'

'You are to marry, Master?'

'The bride is already chosen. My Cousin Nefertiti.'

'The Beautiful One!' The words slipped out of my mouth before I could bite my tongue.

'Yes, that's right.' The Veiled One stared at me, head to one side. 'That's what her name means: the Beautiful One has arrived. How did you know this?'

'I glimpsed her once.'

'Impossible.' He shook his head. 'But, there again, Mahu is the Baboon who hides amongst the trees. My Cousin Nefertiti is the daughter of Ay, my mother's brother.' He grasped my hand. 'You will meet her soon.'

Tiye was watching us strangely. The noise from beyond the walls grew: the shouts of masons, the creak of timber, the clatter of ropes and pulleys.

'You know nothing of her, do you, Mahu?' she asked, coming forward and pulling back her hood.

I noticed again how she wore no adornment, not one precious stone on her fingers, ears or around her neck. The same for her son, as if they had to enter the presence of their god purified, wearing nothing more than simple clothes.

'The Divine One wanted a marriage with a Mitanni Princess' – Tiye gave that twisted smile – 'but I convinced him otherwise.'

She was about to continue when I heard the sound of running feet and Snefru, breathless and wide-eyed, came running down the path. He fell to his knees trying to catch his breath and he touched the ground with his forehead.

'What is it?' the Veiled One snapped.

'My lord!'

'Kneel back, man.'

Snefru raised himself back on his heels, wiping the sweat from his disfigured face.

'A company of archers,' he gasped. 'The Strength of Khonsu are now encamped' – he gestured with his hands – 'not far from our pavilion.'

'Troops?' the Veiled One murmured, turning to his mother. 'The Divine One has sent troops!'

'Their officer,' Snefru panted, 'claims they are here to protect you against any further accidents or mishaps.'

The Veiled One's face suffused with anger. Tiye seized his arm. 'Let it be. Let it be,' she murmured, 'for the moment. Let us be like,' she smiled, 'yes, let us be like trees and bend before the wind.'

My master dismissed Snefru. He led me and his mother into a sunfilled glade. 'Whom do people say I am, Mahu?'

'You are Prince Amenhotep,' I stammered.

He raised his hand to slap me but let it fall.

'But who do men say I *am*, Mahu? What do they snigger behind their hands?'

'The Grotesque? The Ugly One? The Veiled One?'

My master nodded. 'You have spoken with true voice and so will I. I shall tell you my real name. I shall reveal it to you as I have to those who are close to me.' He stared through the trees at the sun. 'I am He-who-is-pleasing-to-the-Aten, my true Father, who knows my name. At the appointed time I shall reveal it to others but now to you, Mahu. I am He who is pleasing to the Aten. My name is Akhenaten.'

227

The hieroglyph for 'fragrance' – *idt/edit* – is a hand dripping with perfume, and a loaf of bread.

Chapter 8

Your love, dear woman, is as sacred to me as sweet
balmy oil is to the limbs of the restless.
Your love, dear woman, is as vital to me as the shade of
a cool tree in the blazing midday heat.
Your love, dear woman, is as alluring to me as the fire
in the freezing night wind.
Your love, dear woman, is as precious to me as the
gurgling spring to my thirsty throat.
Your love, dear woman, is as delicious to me as sweet
soft bread to a starving man.

So says the poet, so says Mahu when he first met Nefertiti!
'She of Pure Heart and Pure Hands, Beloved of his Flesh,
Great King's Wife whom he loves beyond all others. Lady
of the Two Lands, Mistress of the Diadem, Wearer of the
Two Plumes, Mistress of the House! Nefertiti, may she
live forever! Beloved of the Great High Sun Disc who
dwells in eternal jubilee.'

I still sing her praises. The very thought of Nefertiti sets my heart dancing in its own dark chamber. The faintest whiff of her fragrance is like the sound of gushing water in a stone-dry desert. She is the warmth on the coldest night, that wide-eyed girl whose memory calls across the years as clear as the song of a swallow on a quiet spring morning. Nefertiti's touch is still with me; her smile warms my soul and sends the memories whirling like birds from a thicket. She comes to me on the wings of an eagle in the dead of night wrapped in storms, Nefertiti, my pearl of great price. My witch queen with her face of dazzling beauty. Nefertiti, the beautiful woman who has arrived!

Nefertiti arrived during the hot season in the thirty-third year of the Magnificent One's reign. She and her entourage swept into the courtyard to be met by Akhenaten, his mother, God's Father Hotep and myself standing behind them. Oh, how shall I describe her? How do you describe the sun? The cool North wind? The beauty of a million dazzling flowers? Oh, of course, I shall try. She was about medium height dressed in embroidered robes. She shimmered and dazzled in jewellery: a pair of bracelets of copper, gold-studded with turquoise, cornelian and lapis lazuli were fastened to her wrists by a golden clasp. A necklace of unique pendants decorated her exquisite neck: it was made of balls of turquoise, lapis lazuli and cornelian, all set in gold cages, and, in the centre an amulet with the inscription: *All Life and Protection*. Against her lovely chest rested a falcon pectoral displaying the sun disc; it was inlaid with precious stones of blue glass. Anklets of amethyst and gold beads glittered above silver sandals with thongs of pure gold. She was most graceful of form, long-legged and narrow-waisted; the front of her white gown was pulled tightly back to tease us with her full white breasts and elegant throat. People have asked me to describe her face. Perfection in every sense! Oval-shaped with high cheekbones, a short narrow nose above full red lips. Her skin was like dusty gold framed by dark-red hair which cascaded down to her shoulders. Finally, those eyes! Dark blue, eerily beautiful beneath the heavy painted lids. Yet Nefertiti's beauty was more than that. The way she walked, languorous but purposeful, head slightly back, the imperious gaze belied by the laughing mouth and sparkling eyes.

On that day, Nefertiti came and stopped before Akhenaten and crossed her arms, coy though seductive, her lovely fingers splayed out against her shoulders. She bowed her head. Even as she did so, she winked at Akhenaten, and, in a soft but carrying voice, spoke the formal words of greeting. Akhenaten took her hands. From where I stood behind him I sensed the joy which flooded his entire being. He replied formally, their faces met then parted. After this we processed into the audience hall, rich with the smell of cooking and the aroma from pots of perfume and countless baskets of sweet-smelling flowers. Eventually I was introduced. I did not make the obeisance: I just stood and stared at this woman whom I had loved at first sight and will love to my last breath. Akhenaten coughed. Nefertiti smiled, one eyebrow slightly raised, the tip of her tongue between those delicious lips. She laughed, came forward, hands touching my arms, those dazzling blue eyes dancing with mischief.

'You are Mahu.' She spoke as if I was a close friend, a brother. 'You are Mahu,' she repeated, 'the Prince's childhood friend. I have longed to meet you.' She paused and glanced in mock anger at Akhenaten. 'You are more handsome than they said,' she added impishly.

I made the obeisance. She withdrew her hand, the tip of her fingers caressed my skin.

We were ushered to our seats. Hotep and Tiye sat at one end of the small table, Akhenaten and Nefertiti at the other. I sat facing the other person who was to play such an important role in my life though, to be honest, at first I hardly noticed his smiling face. My heart was still singing, my blood thrilling, I was in the Field of the Blessed. Oh, of course, Nefertiti was Akhenaten's betrothed. She would become the Nebet Per, the mistress of the house, the Ankhet Ennuit, his married woman, the Hebsut, his wife. Yet that did not concern me. She was so beautiful. Who cared how many might stare, touch, possess her, as long as I could?

The food was served, the goblets filled. I sipped and ate absentmindedly, almost unaware of the diced meat mixed with rice and nuts, the cauliflower and anchovies, the fish in lemon, the lamb and beef in their savoury sauces. Nefertiti was my food and drink. I studied her out of the corner of my eye. Her moods were as changeable as the moon, shy but coquettish. She flirted outrageously with Akhenaten, fluttering her eyelashes, their hands brushing, touching and teasing beneath the table. At times she broke off talking to him and turned to the servants. She ignored the disfigurement of the Rhinoceri but chattered pleasantly to them, asking for their names and how long they had served. Snefru, acting as steward, was specially singled out and complimented. Nefertiti in those first few hours captivated everyone, with her charm and tact. Eventually I had to look away. Her gaze would catch mine, the smile would fade, her eyes becoming more searching as if she was weighing me in the balance like the Goddess Ma'at, sifting for the truth. Only then did Ay sitting opposite me make his presence felt.

Ay, father of Nefertiti, handsome and dangerous as a panther. A man in his mid-thirties who had seized the cup of life and meant to drink it to the dregs. He was comely of face with a hard, muscular body, every inch the professional soldier. He wore a short, oiled and perfumed wig over his reddish, cropped hair, those sharp, ever-seeing eyes heavily lined with kohl, his handsome, highcheeked face delicately painted. I could see the likeness between father and daughter though Ay possessed an obvious sharpness, carefully hidden beneath effete movements, exquisite manners and precious speech. He had intelligent eyes, a smiling mouth, smooth cheeks and an even smoother tongue. Even then, fascinated as I was by Nefertiti, I recognised a dangerous man, who rejoiced and exulted in his own talents as well as those of his beautiful daughter.

Oh yes, Ay was a joy to behold and a terror to be with. From the very beginning it was so. A mongoose of a man, of cunning heart and keenest wits. He was dressed in embroidered robes, silver rings on his fingers, and a collar of gold around his neck. He ate and drank sparsely, more intent on studying me. When I noticed him, he grinned boyishly and extended his hand across the table. I clasped it. He then gently led me into conversation about the hunting along the river, the price of wheat, and the details of his own journey down the Nile. At the end of the meal Hotep and Queen Tiye withdrew, as did Akhenaten and Nefertiti, hands clasped together, whispering endearments. I watched them go, such a strange contrast. Akhenaten with his ungainly body and strange face, the jerky movements, the tap of his cane; Nefertiti almost gliding beside him. Yet it was not so much a contrast. They complemented each other: Akhenaten with his sharp, haunting features next to the glorious beauty of his companion. It was almost as if they were no longer man and woman but merged to become one flesh, one being.

Once they'd gone, I felt as if the sunlight had left the room. For a while I sat sadly cradling my wine cup. Ay plucked a grape and coughed. I looked up, the servants had gone. Only Snefru guarded the door.

'You are fascinated by my daughter?'

'Any man would be.'

Ay smiled, his eyes half-closed as if he was tired and had drunk too much. He began a desultory conversation but, as he talked, I became aware of how crafty he was. Oh, he mentioned the gossip of the court, once again the weather and the crops. He also used such items to let slip how much he knew, as well as details of his own life: his two marriages, his career as a scribe, his war service as a commander of a chariot squadron. In any other situation he would have been a bore. He kept filling my wine cup, at the same time watching me intently.

'Life changes, Mahu.' He put the wine jug down, his hands going beneath the table, a deliberate movement; with any other man I'd suspect he was searching for a knife. Then his right hand came up. 'I am your friend, Mahu. I have watched you. I know all about you. I am one with you.'

This time the offer of a hand was more formal. He curled back his fingers to reveal an amber and jasper amulet depicting the Aten in the palm of his hand. 'I am your friend, Mahu, your ally.'

'Under the sun,' I replied, 'no trust will last, neither in brother nor in friend. Don't they tell us, the Wise Ones, not even to put our trust in Pharaoh or our confidence in the war-chariots of Egypt?'

'But a true friend is powerful protection,' he retorted. 'It is dangerous to walk alone under the sun.'

I clasped the hand. Ay gripped my fingers and tightly squeezed, then let me withdraw, pushing the amulet into my hand.

'Come,' he drained his cup. 'We have eaten and drunk enough.'

We left the hall of audience arm-in-arm as if we were blood brothers or father and son, Ay talking, gesticulating with his fingers, saying how pleased he was to see the marvels of the Malkata Palace. How he, his family and entourage would be moving into the House of Residence. Once we were through the gate and into the olive groves he dropped such pretence. He clasped my arm, asking me sharp, short questions. Where did I come from? What about my years in the House of the Kap? My experience in war? The campaign against the Kushites? My friendship with Sobeck? He asked such questions though he already seemed to know the answers. Exasperated, I paused. I wanted to go back to the house and feast my eyes on Nefertiti.

'You said you knew everything about me,' I confronted him. He was the same height as me. Ay clicked his tongue and glanced away.

'I wanted to hear you talk, Mahu. Yes, I know everything about you – and more. I knew your mother.' He smiled at my astonishment. 'She was beautiful. Did you know that she was distant kin?'

I shook my head in amazement.

'Oh yes' – he made that airy gesture again – 'third or fourth cousin. I forget now. However, her mother came from the town of Akhmin.' His grin widened and he punched me playfully on the shoulder. 'So it's good to meet you, kinsman.'

'I never knew this.'

'Of course you didn't.' He cleaned his mouth with his tongue. 'Your father was besotted with her. A happy couple.' He glanced over my shoulder as if studying something behind me. 'Aunt Isithia, however,' he smiled grimly, 'she was different, wasn't she? Your father's half-sister. A sour vessel, Isithia. Crooked of speech and crooked of soul. Did you know she was married twice?'

Ay enjoyed my amazement. 'Oh yes, a young priest in the service of Amun-Ra at Luxor. He died of a fever, or so they say. Some people whispered that he had been given a little help across the Far Horizon.'

'Aunt Isithia?'

'In her days she was a temple girl and more. She dabbled in the black arts, became skilled in potions and poisons. Some said she was a witch, others a necromancer who cast horoscopes.'

He walked round me, as if to ensure that no one lurked in the trees, no spy eavesdropped. He stopped beside me, his mouth only a few inches from my ear.

'When the Prince was born, the priests of Amun-Ra went to Aunt Isithia and asked her to cast a horoscope, to draw back the veil of time and glimpse the future.'

My heart skipped a beat. Ay's touch on my shoulder was cold, his voice hoarse yet powerful, as if speaking across the years and rousing nightmares in my adult soul.

'So you see, Mahu' – it was as if he could read my mind – 'accidents do not happen. You were not included in the Kap because of your father but because of your aunt. In her younger days she was a beauty and she offered services as a widow to other priests. They say she even had a cure for impotence; a strict mistress, Isithia.'

I recalled those cries in the night, those mysterious cowled visitors.

'Did Isithia cast the horoscope for the Prince?'

'Of course.' Ay kept his mouth close to my ear. 'She predicted the Prince would deal out justice and judgement to the other gods of Egypt. If the priests had had their way, the Prince would have been drowned at birth. The Magnificent One almost agreed, had it not been for my sister Tiye and the protection of He who sees and hears all that is done in secret.'

'And she cast my horoscope?'

'Yes. You were born at about the same time as the Prince. You know how it's done? The horoscope of a commoner against that of a Prince of the blood. The priests demanded this. They were astonished when Isithia declared that your life and that of the newborn Prince – the Grotesque,' he pronounced the name slowly, 'were inextricably linked.'

'And they demanded my death?' I felt the sudden rush of blood to my face.

'Of course,' Ay whispered, 'but the Magnificent One was most reluctant. Your father was a great soldier and Queen Tiye – well . . .' he sniggered. 'The priests may have had Pharaoh's ear but she had access, how can I say, to other parts of his body? You were always destined for the Kap, Mahu. Brought here and watched and then allowed to serve the Grotesque. The Magnificent One is fascinated. He wishes to see if the horoscope cast unfolds, if your aunt spoke with true voice.' He patted me on the shoulder and came to stand squarely in front of me. 'The Magnificent One allowed both of you to live but your aunt, under pain of death, was forbidden to cast a horoscope ever again. You were too young to remember this: she was taken away in the dead of night by men from the House of Secrets. They kept her in a chamber, polluted by the corpses of slaughtered animals.' He screwed up his eyes. 'Oh, it must have been six or seven days on hard bread and brackish water. A stinking pit, a warning to her of what might happen if she ever violated the Decree of the Divine One.'

'The flies?' I whispered. 'Aunt Isthia always hated flies.'

'So would you,' Ay laughed, 'if you had been locked in a pit with swarms all about you, crawling over your flesh.'

'So, this is all ordained?'

He caught the sarcasm in my voice.

'We don't believe in that, do we, Mahu?'

I shook my head. Ay took my hands in his, head slightly to one side.

'I do like you, Mahu. So, tell me the truth.'

'I don't believe Aunt Isithia could see the future,' I replied.

'But?' Ay let go of my hands.

'Aunt Isithia was first married to a soldier, then to a priest of Amun-Ra,' I explained. 'As a widow she served other priests who came to drink from her cup of pleasure. From the moment . . .'

'From the moment Akhenaten was born,' Ay finished the sentence.

'From the moment Akhenaten was born,' I continued, 'the priests were against him. They saw him as a curse from God, ungraceful of face and not fair of form. Isn't that how they put it? How could such a Prince be presented to the people? How could such a Prince embody the glory of Egypt? How could such a Prince with his ugly face and deformed body enter the Holy of Holies to make sacrifice? They wanted him dead and Aunt Isithia simply complied with their wishes.'

'Very good,' Ay nodded. 'And yourself, Mahu?'

'My mother died giving birth. Isithia hated her. My father was a soldier, often absent on military service. Aunt Isithia was saddled with an unwanted brat. She wished me dead but tried to pass the responsibility onto others. She sowed the seeds.' I shrugged. 'And we all know the harvest. Akhenaten was cursed and I must live with that curse. So, when my father died, the Divine One felt guilty. He recalled the oracle and so I joined the Kap.'

Ay stood back and clapped his hands softly.

'Very clever, Mahu.'

'There were no oracles,' I declared. I turned, hawked and spat. 'Just a wicked woman and her accomplices. That's why she was arrested, wasn't she, and taken to the Place of Chains, the House of Secrets? The Divine One wanted to make sure she spoke with true voice.' I laughed abruptly. 'Of course Aunt Isithia saw the future then. If she confessed that she'd told a lie, she would have stayed in that pit, whatever the gaolers promised her. It was better for her to stick to her story and hope for the best.'

'And that, my dear Mahu, is how legends begin.'

'But do you believe,' I asked, 'that Akhenaten will dispense judgement and justice to the other gods of Egypt?'

Ay bent down, picked up a rotting fig from the ground and squashed it between his fingers. 'That's how much I feel about the gods of Egypt, Mahu. What I do believe in,' he stared at me, a gleam of fanaticism in his eyes, 'is the glory of Egypt, the power and majesty of Pharaoh. The rattle and charge of her war-chariots and the tramp of her regiments.' He gestured with his hand. 'But in Thebes, in Memphis, in all the great cities of the Nile, Egypt harbours a viper in her bosom: the power of the priests. The power of the temples, their wealth, their hunger for more.' He drew closer again. 'The real threat to Egypt does not lie in the barbarians who throng our borders or the Libyan Desert Wanderers, jealous of our cities, eager for our gold. It's the enemy within, Mahu. They must be curbed.' He spread his hands. 'Look at the Divine One,' he whispered, 'the Glorious One. How does he spend his time, Mahu? By building more temples and glorifying the priests! He has let the raging lion in the door, and thinks by throwing meat at it he will satisfy its hunger.' He shook his head. 'The lion must be either driven out or killed. Politics, Mahu,' he grinned, 'that's what I believe. My politics are my religion. My religion is my politics. And what are politics but the pursuit of glory and power of our House and the Kingdom of Egypt?' He rubbed his hands together. 'Now you could ask why I have spoken to you so frankly, so openly. Because, Mahu, you and I are kindred souls. I need you, you need me. And where can you go? To the priests of Amun-Ra? To the Divine One? To God's Father Hotep? They'd simply torture you for everything you knew and later bury you out in the hot sands. They'd forget you even before the dirt began to fill your mouth and nostrils. You are with us, Mahu, because you want to be but, more importantly, because you have to be.' He grasped me by the shoulder. 'Now tell me – these troops that are camped around our master's house: are they there to spy, protect, or do both?'

And chatting like two lifelong friends, we continued our walk through the sunfilled grove and into the bloody intricate politics of the imperial court.

It's remarkable how people can draw a line under events, then look back and say, 'That's when it happened, that's when it changed.' Sometimes it's an easy task: the crucial point is marked by the death of a ruler or a relative. Sometimes the change is so gradual that only on reflection do you realise that things were never the same again after a certain point. The arrival of Nefertiti and her entourage marked such a change. Imperceptible at first, their influence grew like ivy round the vine, higher and tighter, spreading out its creepers.

After our little talk, Ay became a firm ally, a tactful but forceful adviser. He was at least fifteen summers older than me, yet I had to shake myself to realise he had not been with me in the Kap. Nefertiti, of course, I always regarded as a dream who dwelt in my soul since the moment of conception; I recognised and loved her immediately. I accepted the others of her retinue because of her. The principal of these was Ay's half-brother, Nakhtimin. He had resigned his colonelcy of a regiment to join his relatives at the Malkata. A slender, dour man of few words, Nakhtimin served as Ay's Chamberlain and Principal Steward, constantly in the background organising and managing, seeing to the small things of life. He was particularly interested in Snefru and Akhenaten's personal guard. Despite the difference in status, he and Snefru became friends. Nakhtimin turned those whom Horemheb had contemptuously dismissed as 'toy soldiers' into a professional fighting force. He, Snefru and I often went out into the wastelands to recruit similar men who had either lost their souls or were prepared to sell them. We were like a wall which ringed a garden. Akhenaten lay at the heart of this garden and he flowered as if a fire blazed in his soul. Of course, within weeks he and Nefertiti were married. The simple ceremony was followed by a sumptuous feast, supervised by Ay and witnessed by Tiye, Crown Prince Tuthmosis, Nakhtimin and myself. I gave them gifts, an alabaster jar of the most expensive Kiphye perfume for Nefertiti and a glorious bow of honour to my master.

When Nefertiti moved into Akhenaten's quarters, I felt a stab of jealousy though this was soon soothed by her very presence, my closeness to her. She and Akhenaten were absorbed with each other, living in a paradise of their own creation. Akhenaten lost his fretful energy, that occasional vindictiveness, and became calmer, more harmonious. The physical changes were equally notice-able; the furrowed lines disappeared around his brow and cheeks. Nefertiti also taught him how to move more easily, to exude a certain majesty in his bearing, a bravery in accepting his disabilities whilst turning them into something special.

The weeks passed. Ay was busy in the House of Resi-dence. Akhenaten and Nefertiti, hand-in-hand, would tour what they now called their Palace of the Aten, be closeted in their chamber or, surrounded by their guards, go out into the gardens and grounds. At first Akhenaten was so besotted with Nefertiti, I hardly spoke to him. One day I was sitting in the pavilion when I heard his footsteps and there he stood in the doorway resting on his cane, clutching his gauze-like robe tightly. I could tell from the dirt on his knees and the specks of mud on his robe that at such an early hour, just after dawn, he and Nefertiti had been out worshipping their god. Once the Beautiful Woman had arrived, there were no more nightly forays into the desert or cloaked strangers gathering at the gates.

This was not only due to Nefertiti but the arrival of imperial troops and the accompanying spies who watched us every second of the day. On that morning Akhenaten's face was solemn. I would have slipped to my knees on a cushion but he gestured that I sit back and he knelt before me. He stared earnestly up at me.

'I never knew, Mahu,' he began, 'there could be so much happiness. I have been in the Land of Incense. I have flown on eagle wings beyond the Far Horizon.' He leaned closer, pride blazing in his eyes. 'I am a Prince of the Blood, Mahu. I am Akhenaten but, first and foremost, I am a man. In that, there is no difference' – he gestured with his hand – 'between myself and those around me.'

It was the first and only time my master Akhenaten, beloved of the One, ever compared himself to another man, ever claimed to possess that ordinary humanity, ever boasted of our common heritage. He touched me gently on the forehead, rose and left. I knew what he meant. On occasions, both he and Tiye had hinted that, because of his disability, Akhenaten was a eunuch, impotent, incapable of the most sacred act, unable to beget an heir. It was one of those cruelties thrust into his soul by the malicious-minded priests and the detractors surrounding him. Nefertiti, with her consummate skill, potions and powders, soon changed all that.

My own relationship with Nefertiti developed; there was no more teasing and sometimes I would catch her studying me.

'You are not a baboon, Mahu,' she once remarked as I helped her supervise the gardens, 'you are a cat, that's what you are. You sit and watch us, don't you, with those dark brooding eyes and heavy face? The Beloved,' her constant description of Akhenaten, 'always talks of you. How you have played, feasted and even fought together.' I never contradicted her. In his fevered brain, Akhenaten apparently depicted me as a brother, the real blood-brother he wished he had.

Within a year Nefertiti's influence over Akhenaten was complete. He wouldn't do anything without her, constantly seeking her advice and, by implication, Ay's. Sometimes he would rise late, heavy-eyed and drowsy, but always content, at peace. The most constant visitor was Ay, walking with his daughter or briefing the Prince on the gossip of the palace and what was happening in the great city of Thebes. Akhenaten, Nefertiti beside him, would listen carefully. Both of them would question Ay and later discuss what had been said. If my master changed, Nefertiti did not. She remained serene yet vivacious, a goddess in splendour, be it in her tight sheath-like dresses on formal occasions or in an elegant loose-fitting robe, flowers in her glorious hair as she moved around the palace. Never once was she, her father or the Prince invited into the imperial presence but this did not seem to bother them. In fact, they seemed quite content, as if lulling the suspicions of those they knew were watching them.

Nefertiti truly became mistress of the house. She would question Snefru and the servants, study the accounts, check the stores or go into the kitchens, supervising the cooks, winning them over with her charm and wit. She was fascinated by the gardens and proved herself a skilled herbalist, becoming in all but name, the palace leech and apothecary. She knew the properties of mountain celery

– how, mixed with juniper berries and other ingredients it would calm pains in the belly; how birthwort in red wine would ease cramps and bring about sleep; how melon leaves could treat blood ailments whilst maringa oil mixed with figs would reduce inflammation in the gums. She was greatly interested in medicine and kept her own stores of potions and powders. She treated her own husband and, yes, the rumours were true – she was skilled in aphrodisiacs and in more exotic remedies for illnesses of the soul.

Ay was the only one who left the Residence, often journeying down to Thebes to the temples or to walk in the marketplace. He and Nakhtimin his half-brother would visit acquaintances, officials and officers and bring back all the gossip and rumour. Nakhtimin would often be the only guest at dinner, with food especially cooked by the Princess herself, delicious and savoury. The wine would flow and we would discuss, till the early hours, the affairs of Egypt, the growing might of the Hittites, the Magnificent One's alliance with Tusharatta, King of the Mitanni, the disturbances in Canaan and how these problems must be resolved. On one occasion Ay announced that the Divine One, concerned that Ay was not receiving the help and support he needed, had despatched a high-ranking scribe to assist. The chosen scribe, Ineti, was from the House of Life in the Temple of Amun-Ra; he was lean-visaged and bony-framed. Ay had no choice but to accept him, but we all knew Ineti was really there to spy.

Queen Tiye also visited, but not as often as she used to: she had aged somewhat, seemed troubled and perhaps was a little jealous of Nefertiti's closeness with her son. On rare occasions, Crown Prince Tuthmosis also arrived with his entourage. He looked better, though still thin, slightly weary with a racking cough. He, too, fell under the spell of Nefertiti and his envy of his younger brother was almost palpable.

If a distance had grown up between myself and Akhenaten, Nefertiti compensated for this. She would often single me out for discussion about this or that, her beautiful face always smiling, always serene but those striking blue eyes curious as if she hadn't decided who I truly was. Sometimes she'd talk about her early childhood, her days in Akhmin, how her father had educated her and how, like her Aunt Tiye, she had entered the service of the God Min in the local temple. She could pull a bow, knew how to handle a sword or dagger and often asked me to accompany her to watch the Prince's bodyguard be drilled on the parade ground. On occasion she'd even ask me to join her inspecting the Khonsu, the company camped beyond the walls. Naturally, she was a welcome guest there, being shown every honour. At first I thought she wanted to flirt with the officers, which she certainly did, but she was more interested in their knowledge, their experience in war, their handling of weapons, particularly the use of massed archers and the effectiveness of a chariot squadron. We went along the river, chatting to the marines, recalling the deeds of the great Pharaoh Ahmose who used barges to drive the Hyksos from the Delta. I revelled in such occasions. Nefertiti would often hold my hand, clutch my arm or whisper in my ear. She was not embarrassed about describing this to Akhenaten, remarking 'how she and Mahu had been here or there, seen this or done that'.

About fourteen months after her arrival, in the Season of Peret, I suffered from stomach pains. Nefertiti learned about this and sought me out. I was surprised because, in the woods beyond the Residence I had found a small grove, a private place where I would go by myself with a jug of wine and some food to sit and think. I'd recall Dedi and her kindness, my days with Aunt Isithia, and I'd wonder why my father had been so cold. I tried to imagine my mother and, time and again, I would reflect on what Ay had told me. I'd go back along the years: my experience in the Kap, my friendship with Sobeck. Above all, I'd often wonder where the path I was treading would lead. At the time all seemed calm and quiet; Akhenaten and his wife, the ever-present Ay, the feeling of watchful calmness. Yet I also felt as if we were being prepared – but for what?

On that particular day the cramps in my belly were so harsh and painful I was glad to be alone. I took no food or wine but sat against the tree enjoying the green coolness of the glade. I heard a sound and looked up. Nefertiti stood there, a small basket in one hand, a cushion under her arm. She was dressed in a gauze-like robe, an embroidered sash round her slender waist. Usually she would have her hair bound or tied up. Now it was parted down the middle, tumbling freely to her shoulders. She wore no jewellery except for a silver Aten on a gold chain round her neck.

'My lady.'

Before I could scramble to my feet, she placed the cushion on the ground and knelt before me.

'Mahu, I understand you are ill.' She gazed sadly at me. 'Why didn't you see me?'

'I . . .'

'Were you embarrassed?' She must have noticed my cheeks flush.

I rubbed my stomach. 'It will go soon enough. Must be something I ate.'

She opened the basket, took out a cup, poured in a few drops of liquid and handed it to me. I sniffed at the rim.

'Juniper berries?' I asked. Again I sniffed, this time more playfully. 'And crushed almonds?'

'And something else,' she smiled. 'Mahu, drink. It will calm the pains.'

I did so. No more than a mouthful, bittersweet to the taste, before those soft fingers took the cup from my hand. Nefertiti sat and watched.

'Do you have such pains often?'

'No, most glorious physician,' I teased. 'In fact, I am truly a baboon. I am very rarely ill.'

'Aren't you?' She moved the basket so as to rest her hand just below my knee. 'There are illnesses and illnesses, Mahu.'

'My lady?'

'Those of the soul,' she retorted. 'Why do you come here, Mahu?'

'I thought I'd be alone. I thought no one could find me, so how did you?'

Nefertiti smiled, moving her head slightly from side to side.

'I have a care for you, Mahu. I want to know where you go. The Beloved has told me about your bravery in the Kushite attack. How you have helped him,' her voice grew hard, 'with the traitors within.'

'I am my master's servant,' I replied, reciting the diplomatic courtesy. 'A mere footstool under his feet.'

She dug her nails into my leg until I winced.

'If the Beloved heard that, he'd be angry. You are his friend, Mahu, his brother.'

'He already has a brother.'

'No, Mahu, he has a keeper. A young man who feels guilty about him.'

'Could you not help the Crown Prince Tuthmosis?' The words came spilling out before I could stop them.

'Help?' she queried. 'How could I be of help to the Crown Prince?'

'He has a racking cough.'

'Dust,' Nefertiti replied. 'Our fates, Mahu, are written on the palm of God's hand. What will be will be.'

'You don't believe that,' I accused. 'Neither you nor your father believe that.'

Nefertiti's eyes were no longer sparkling, but cold, vigilant. I thought I had gone too far, given insult. She moved the basket and made herself more comfortable.

'No, you are right.' She paused, as if distracted by the cry of the birds. 'Is that a hawk?'

'No, my lady, a heron hunting over the river.'

'No, Mahu,' she continued. 'Our fates are written on the palm of God's hand but they are also written on our own. We do have a part to play. The Crown Prince Tuthmosis,' she shrugged prettily, 'he has his own physicians. If he asks for my help . . .' She let the words hang. 'Are you lonely, Mahu? Is that your sickness?'

I couldn't stop myself. I began to tell her, haltingly at first, about my days with Aunt Isithia and my studies in the Kap. I am sure she knew this already but she wanted to hear it from my own lips. She seemed genuinely interested. Now and again she asked a question, particularly about my colleagues: Horemheb, Rameses, the friendship between Maya and Sobeck. I enjoyed it, sitting there in the silence, the Beautiful One before me. I was fully aware of her scent, her touch, her look: her very presence seemed like a cloud around me cutting me off from the rest of the world. I thought she would go but she stayed, telling me further details about her life. How she had a sister, Mutnodjmet, who loved pet baboons and dwarves.

'You should introduce her to Horemheb,' I teased. 'They would have something in common.'

'Perhaps I will. Tell me, how is your stomach now?'

Only then did I become aware of how the discomfort had completely disappeared. I felt calmer, more refreshed.

'Have you ever flown, Mahu?'

I stared speechless.

'Have you ever wished to fly like a bird?' Nefertiti's face was serious. 'Or have you ever wished to feel the very essence of things?'

I recalled different dreams, the sensation of floating, of how I had once felt like a bird above the Nile, watching the boats, barges and punts below.

'In my dreams,' I agreed, 'or when the wine has been drunk.'

'And have you ever loved, Mahu?'

'Once,' I replied.

Again the sad gaze. 'And what happened?'

'Nothing,' I replied, embarrassed and confused.

She opened the basket and took out a clay jug, modelled in the form of a poppy turned upside down.

'From the Islands far out in the Great Green,' Nefertiti explained, 'a fragrant drink. Come, Mahu, don't be suspicious. It will soothe your belly, your heart and your soul.'

She emptied this potion into the cup and I drank it greedily. I would have done anything she said. The drink was almost tasteless except for a slight sweetness. Nefertiti sat watching me all the time: her face seemed more beautiful, if that was possible, her eyes larger. She seemed to be closer, her breath upon my face. I was also aware of how the glade had changed. The trees took on a life of their own, the branches stretching down to caress me, the small wild flowers changing in colour, growing and receding as if the days and seasons had speeded up: their entire growth, flowering and dying caught in one exquisite moment. The sweetest music filled my ear. I felt so happy, I didn't want to break from the moment. Memories came and went. Sobeck smiling down at me. My master leaning across the table and feeding me. The temple girls I had lain with were there, moving against a curtain of brilliant colour and, above all, Nefertiti. She was beside me, arms around me, her robes of glory slipping down her shoulder, her hands on my chest, moving down to my groin, the most delicious sensation of pleasure. We embraced. I could feel her cloying sweetness, her body sinuous, gorgeous in touch and smell. She was sitting astride me, hands on my chest, her beautiful face framed by hair which seemed to glow like fire, those blue eyes like sapphires catching the sun. I heard her voice deeper and sweeter. Other people were there. Ay kneeling beside us, also sharing her embrace. I was being lifted up, going towards the sky, which changed in colour from dark blue to a fiery red, dominated by the sign of the Aten. Then I was falling, dropping gently into a velvet darkness.

When I awoke I was alone. The sun was beginning to dip, the day was drawing on. I was lying on the grass, the pillow Nefertiti had brought me beneath my head. I recalled the dream and scrambled to my feet but the glade was empty, silent except for the cooing of a pigeon and a faint rustling in the undergrowth. I felt tired but refreshed. I glanced down. My robe was tied, the sandals I had left beneath the trees undisturbed. No sign of Nefertiti, no trace she had even been there. I sniffed my hands and arms, smelled nothing but my own sweat and the fragrance of sweet oil. For a while I just stood trying to recall what had happened. Nefertiti had given me a potion. Poppy seed? Something to relax, to make me sleep. And yet those dreams . . . I clutched the cushion and walked back to my quarters.

I left the cushion in my chamber and went down to the hall of audience. Nefertiti and Ay were seated at the far end, heads close together, discussing something in low voices. Both raised their head at my approach. Nefertiti now had her hair dressed, caught up in a beautiful pearl-edged net, an embroidered shawl across her shoulders.

'Why, Mahu, so you have returned? You fell asleep, which is what I intended. Your stomach?'

'No pain at all, my lady. Indeed I am ravenously hungry.'

'And you slept well?'

'I dreamed,' I replied.

'We all dream dreams, Mahu. They can point us to the way things should be.' She held my gaze like a fellow conspirator. 'I have cooked something special,' she added. 'It's best if you prepare yourself.'

A courteous, tactful dismissal. I bowed and withdrew. In my own chamber I stripped and washed, examining my body carefully for any cut or mark, any trace of what had happened out in the glade. I felt my crotch, took my hand away and sniffed at my fingers, and I caught it, something I had never anointed myself with: the smell of the acacia plant, the juice used by temple girls to lower the potency of a man's seed.

The hieroglyph for 'festival' – *hb/hebd* – is a square bowl above an oval one.

Chapter 9

The Khonsu corps were replaced with a company of the Sacred Band, war veterans taken from their duties in the temples of Karnak and Luxor. This particular corps, their shields depicting the insignia of Amun-Ra, were under the direct command of Rahimere, Mayor of Waset, the city of the Sceptre, Thebes the Splendid. Rahimere came to the Palace of the Aten gloriously bedecked in his chains and necklaces of office. My master, Ay, Nefertiti, myself and Snefru met him in the hall of audience. Rahimere processed in, surrounded by his officials, scribes and shaven-headed priests. There was little love lost between Akhenaten and this pompous Mayor. My master and his entourage remained seated. Rahimere stood, one foot forward, one hand clutching his robe as if he was lecturing, as Ay later described it, the dung-collectors of Thebes. He was a pompous little man with bulbous eyes, a snub nose and a strident voice.

'I am here . . .'

'How dare you!' Ay's voice cut across the room like a whiplash. He got slowly to his feet. 'Are you not, sir, in the presence of a Prince of the Blood? You come into this hall and show no courtesies. You bring no gifts. You offer no salutation.'

Rahimere's chin quivered, eyes darting to the left and right.

'You may withdraw,' my master coolly declared. 'If you wish, Your Excellency, you may withdraw and perhaps visit another time,' he raised a hand, 'when you remember the courtesies and protocol befitting a Prince of the Blood, Beloved Son of the Body of the Divine One.'

Rahimere reached his decision. Gasping and muttering, he fell to his knees: the rest of the retinue had no choice but to follow suit. He did not nose the ground but bent his head. Rahimere quivered in fury. I caught the angry glances of his entourage whilst I am sure they heard my master counting slowly under his breath. He kept them waiting until he had reached twenty, then he clapped his hands.

'You may rise,' he declared sweetly.

The Mayor and his company did so. Some of them were old men in snow-white pleated robes and glowing collars of office. They represented the priests of Amun, Akhenaten's sworn enemies: so overcome with malice, they had forgotten the courtesies. They shuffled their sandalled feet.

'If I had known you were coming,' Ay declared, 'we would have prepared some wine, bread and meat befitting the occasion, but you arrive like bailiffs.'

'I apologise,' Rahimere mopped his face with the sleeve

of his gown, 'but this matter is urgent. A courier should have been despatched.' He looked angrily over his shoulder.

'Why, what is the matter?' Ay asked. 'Has war been declared? Are the Libyans marching on Thebes?'

'No, the archers will be withdrawn,' Rahimere gabbled, 'as will be the marines from the river.'

'Is that all?' Ay sat down on Akhenaten's right. 'Is that the urgency of this meeting? To invade our presence because a corps of archers has been withdrawn together with barges of marines berthed at the quayside, a mile from the Nose of the Gazelle?' Ay turned his head and stared back in mock disbelief at Akhenaten, who just clicked his tongue noisily. Nefertiti did not help matters by starting to arrange the wild flowers in her red hair, singing a song beneath her breath.

'I . . . er,' Rahimere had totally misjudged the situation. 'I bring you news: they are to be replaced by a corps of the Sacred Band.' Akhenaten laughed. Nefertiti giggled. Now it was Ay's turn to click his tongue and shake his head in disapproval. Rahimere's dark eyes glowed with anger, yet he could do nothing except make empty gestures.

'Ah,' he added spitefully, 'this is important. The officers in charge,' now Rahimere's eyes slid to me, 'will be commanded by former children of the Kap. I believe you know them?'

'Ah, our good friends.' Akhenaten clapped his hands like a child. 'Horemheb and Rameses.'

'Huy will be their scribe,' Rahimere continued, 'Pentju their physician and Meryre their chaplain.' He smiled falsely. 'We thought it best if your former friends . . .' he let the words hang in the air.

'Guard me!' Akhenaten called out harshly. 'Are they here to guard me, protect me or to spy on me?'

'Your Excellency,' Rahimere blustered. 'The Divine One . . .'

'May he live for evermore,' Akhenaten's voice thrilled with sarcasm.

'The Divine One wishes you to be protected and safe, to keep you close to his heart as he does your elder brother.'

Rahimere had made his point. Akhenaten could claim whatever he wished but Tuthmosis, the Crown Prince, the Divine One's heir was the true power in the land.

'Anything else?' Akhenaten leaned forward and plucked a grape from the table before him. He didn't wait for a reply but popped the grape into his mouth and turned, plumping the cushions as if they were not comfortable enough. 'Anything else?' he called out, his back still turned to Rahimere.

My master looked up, caught my gaze and winked.

'The Divine One sends his salutation and blessing.'

'And do give him mine in grateful return.' Akhenaten turned back, picked up a bowl of grapes and passed them to Nefertiti, then to Ay. He glanced up, 'Oh, you are still here? Excellency, it was most kind of you to come.' He raised a finger. 'You may now withdraw.'

The Mayor, the priests and officials did so, faces mottled with anger, eyes blazing with hatred. Ay went to speak, but Akhenaten raised his hand. Suddenly from the courtyard came the sound of furious barking, screams and cries, the lash of whips, the shouts of servants and the braying of a horn. Akhenaten burst out laughing and turned to Snefru standing beside him.

'What are my hunting dogs doing there? You know they are full of energy.'

'You told me to bring them down, Master.' Snefru fell to his knees, hands to his face.

'Oh yes, so I did.' Akhenaten grinned. 'Poor Rahimere! To walk straight into a pack of dogs ready for the chase and full of energy. I understand he doesn't like dogs.'

Nefertiti and Ay joined in the laughter. Snefru was dismissed and I was ordered to kneel before them. Akhenaten, one hand raised, head slightly turned, listened to the sounds in the courtyard recede as order was restored.

'Rahimere will not forget his visit here.' His smile faded. 'So they are sending Horemheb, Rameses and the rest, eh? Guards and spies.'

'Spies!' Nefertiti spat the word out, no laughter in her eyes and face. 'They are here,' she commented, 'to act as our friends, to be entertained, to be able to come and go as they wish; to listen to the chatter and gossip of the servants.' She laid her head on Akhenaten's shoulder, rolling back her beautiful eyes. 'But we'll see,' she added impishly.

Five days later the Sacred Band arrived: three hundred men under the command of Horemheb, now a Major, and his ever-present faithful Lieutenant, Rameses. Nefertiti immediately issued invitations to both of them and others, including Maya from the House of Secrets, to a splendid banquet in the Hall of Audience. She personally arranged the menu, supervised the cooking, and selected the wines. Any delicacy the palace could offer was served: the tenderest goose, rich spiced lamb, dishes of vegetables, sweetmeats and savouries to be served at the end of the meal. On the evening of the banquet, she appeared as the very embodiment of grace and beauty, garbed in a sheathlike dress from head to toe in the purest white linen, with gold, a shawl of shimmering jewels across her shoulders. She wore no wig; her magnificent hair flared out like a brilliant cloud, fastened with miniature brooches and clasps studded with gems and other precious stones. Earrings glinted in her lobes. A silver gorget circled her throat and a pectoral of shimmering cornelian, carved in the form of flower petals, rested against her chest. Armlets and bracelets covered with precious stones dazzled in an almost spiritual glowing light. Beside her Akhenaten was dressed in a robe of glory, a thick braided wig on his head. He wore no jewellery, as if not to rival his wife's magnificence. We were all welcomed into the Hall of Audience. Its walls had been freshly painted and bedecked with streamers of blue and white, and polished tables inlaid with ebony were arranged along the centre, surrounded by cushions of costly fabrics.

The food was served on precious dishes which caught the glow of the countless alabaster oil jars. No musicians, dancers, conjurers or temple girls were present. Nefertiti did not wish any distraction in her seduction of these new arrivals. Horemheb delivered the official salutation, Akhenaten made the speech of reply. We sat down on the cushions, Horemheb and Rameses either side of Akhenaten and Nefertiti at the top. Everyone was there. Huy, resplendent in his robe of office, was now thickset and square-jawed. Pentju, very much the learned physician, carried a small staff, its end carved in the shape of a ram; an amulet round his neck bore the emblem of the Wadjet, the ever-seeing eye of Horus. Meryre was in his priest's robes, a stole about his neck. He reeked, as Huy wryly observed, of incense, slaughtered flesh and sanctimony. Opposite me sat Maya, his plump face and round eyes heavily painted like a woman's – even his fingernails and toenails were carmined a deep red. He greeted me cordially enough and immediately launched into a torrent of whispered pithy comments about Horemheb and Rameses.

We all acted as if we met frequently, yet there was no hiding our self-consciousness and the almost tangible wariness of each other. Of course, Nefertiti transformed the event. All of us were fascinated by her. She sat like the minx she was, a Queen in every sense, gracious and kind, charming yet haughty so when she did smile the recipient rejoiced at his good fortune. Even Maya, driven more by envy than lust, did not take his eyes off her. Beside her Akhenaten revelled in his wife's beauty, proud yet amused by my companions' reaction. During the banquet Nefertiti made an innocent, pretty speech of welcome. To all intents and appearances she was mouthing empty phrases – but in fact she was suborning them. She began by complimenting them all on their careers.

'If I were a Queen of Egypt,' she laughed mockingly, 'you, companions of my Beloved since his early days,' her eyes danced with mischief, 'loyal friends, boon companions – oh yes, if I were Great Queen you would sit in the Sacred Circle, be our counsellors, advisers, chamberlains and Generals.' She paused, just for a while, until the merriment and laughter faded. 'More importantly,' she continued, 'you would be his friends, *my* friends. Of course, you will be, you shall be.' On and on she talked, emphasising her points with those lovely hands, moving her head to take each and every one of us into her gaze. She finished with toasts of loyalty, but her words had sowed the seeds and her charm would nurture them. Ay joined us later in the meal, sitting down at the end between myself and Maya. He, too, acted his part. Innocent, wide-eyed questions about Maya's service in the House of Secrets deliberately made my companion uncomfortable. I wasn't surprised when he announced that he would like to withdraw to savour the cool night air. Ay winked at me to follow and, as I left, Ay moved further up the table to his next quarry – Pentju, Meryre and Huy.

Outside the door Maya clapped me on the shoulder. 'I hoped you'd join me.'

We walked across the courtyard into the garden. The perfume of the flowers was cloyingly sweet under a starlit sky. Maya took out his fan and wafted it. I noticed he carried a little pouch strapped to his left wrist. He didn't walk in his thick-soled sandals but rather swayed like a woman, moving slowly, swinging his hips as he fanned himself prettily.

'"Beauty has its own face. It is she".' Maya brought the fan up to his face, staring coldly at me over the rim as he quoted the poem. '"Loveliness has its own form. It is hers." A remarkable woman.' He simpered.

'Do you say that yourself,' I asked, 'or is it what you have learned from others in the House of Secrets?'

Maya snapped the fan closed and put it back into its

little pouch. He nodded towards the lotus-covered Pool of Purity shimmering in the moonlight. 'You have your bodyguard here, Mahu?' he asked archly. 'Am I to go for a swim again?'

'No.' I patted him on the shoulder, gesturing that we walk on. 'Were Imri and his Kushite spies working for the House of Secrets?'

'I don't know,' Maya whispered. 'They could have been spies, but not for the House of Secrets. They did not report to God's Father Hotep.' He paused and chuckled at my surprise. 'Oh yes, clever Baboon. Imri and his companions may have been spies, but for whom?' He hunched his shoulders prettily. 'I don't know. Were they murdered, Mahu?'

'They were spies.'

'I don't deny that. What you've got to ask yourself though, is for whom?'

I curbed the panic seething within me.

'And Aunt Isithia?' I asked. 'You received my message?'

'Oh yes. Aunt Isithia,' Maya purred back, 'is a most interesting case. A former caster of horoscopes though now she is forbidden to meddle any further. You do have an interesting relative, Mahu. She may not cast horoscopes but she is a keen hand with the whip,' he blinked, 'an expert in inflicting delicious pain.'

'What do you mean?'

Maya laughed behind his hand. 'You know what I mean. Do you think you were taken into the Kap for your looks and your breeding? Oh, I've been through your records *and* hers. Isithia wanted you out of the way for many reasons. She still enjoys the protection of the Divine One. She instructs some of the lesser concubines, the Royal Ornaments, in certain arts of love: techniques, perhaps, which may come as a surprise to them but certainly not to her.'

'Could she have learned about Sobeck?'

'Possibly.'

I scratched my cheek. 'So, Aunt Isithia wanted me out of the way because she hated my mother, she hated me, she saw me as a burden and she had other interests?'

'Correct,' Maya simpered.

'Which would become difficult to pursue as I grew older?'

'You speak with true voice, Mahu.'

'And now?'

Maya started as a bird of the night swooped low: a black, fast-moving shadow under the starlit sky.

'And now?' I repeated.

'Your aunt is well-protected. She has highranking friends amongst the priests of Amun-Ra. Why, Mahu,' he mocked, 'don't you visit her?'

'You know the reason I don't, as you know why she doesn't visit me. Well, not for years.' I chucked Maya under the chin. 'Come, lovely one,' I whispered, 'did Imri ever visit her?'

'Perhaps,' Maya smiled, 'but he also visited the Crown Prince Tuthmosis.'

'So it was Tuthmosis,' I stated.

Maya stepped back as if to hide his face. 'Now you have it, Mahu. Your Prince's brother is very frightened.'

'Of what?'

'Of the stories.' Maya squinted up at the night sky. 'That his brother, this Grotesque, has been touched by the gods, chosen for some special task. His marriage to that beauty will not help. She is unique,' Maya mused, 'with that reddish hair and light blue eyes. Such strange colouring. I heard rumours that they are not true Egyptians but descendants of Wanderers . . .'

'Who *is* a true Egyptian?' I asked. 'And what does the House of Secrets know about Princess Nefertiti and her father?'

Maya pulled a face. 'Very little. They have been concealed like arrows in a quiver.'

'Who by?'

'The great Queen Tiye.'

'For what purpose?'

'Well,' he sighed, 'it's now evident. About the Princess,' he continued, 'we know nothing. Ay has a record as a capable administrator, a skilled commander of chariotry.' Maya tapped his sandalled foot and turned as if to go back. I caught his arm.

'Why do you still watch Aunt Isithia? Oh, I know about the horoscopes, and her stay in the Chains in the House of Secrets.'

Maya stepped so close I could smell his perfume.

'She's linked to something more sinister,' he whispered. 'Sometimes the Divine One suspects that the Grotesque, your master, is not his son.' He lifted his fingers for silence. 'He cannot bring himself to believe he is the father of such a man.'

'What? But . . . ?'

'Shush.' Maya pressed his fingers against his lips. 'Listen, Mahu. Have you ever heard of the prophet Ipurer? He lived about five hundred years ago. He prophesied a violent revolution, of everything being turned on its head, of a Messiah who would come to shepherd his people and whose presence would be,' Maya squinted, 'what is the line? – "cooling to the flame".' He swung the little pouch on his wrist. 'The prophecy finishes with these lines: "Truly he shall smite evil. Where is he to stay? Has he come or does he already sleep and walk amongst you?"'

'Legends! Superstition!'

'The Magnificent One *is* superstitious, Mahu. And his fears are shared by the priests of Amun. Can't you see how it goes? The Divine One is confronted with a sickly and ungainly grotesque about whom dark things are uttered. Fertile ground for our priests who also want him gone, who can hint that perhaps he is the Messiah, prophesied by Ipurer. Isithia may still have her uses in concocting a poison to solve the problem. Ah well, so much for the great ones, eh?'

'So, Aunt Isithia still distils her potions?'

'And offers instructions to others.'

'She's an old bitch!'

'A true murderess,' Maya replied. 'The blood of her own kin stains her hands.'

'*What?*'

'I came across a police report. A few scribbles. Isithia truly hated your mother. She may not have supplied the best medicine for her, when she was recovering from your birth.'

'I . . .'

'Can't you speak, Mahu?'

In truth I felt a hideous coldness, a clenching in my stomach.

'But, but my father would have . . . ?'

'Your father never suspected. Many women don't survive childbirth. When Aunt Isithia was in the cells she was baited with this.'

'Why wasn't the matter pursued?'

'It was nothing much. Information laid anonymously to the House of Secrets, the tittle-tattle of servants, studied and filed away.'

I recalled Dedi and her whispered hoarse comments in that darkened garden so many years ago.

'Well, well, Mahu, will you take revenge? If you do,' he urged, 'do not take it now.'

I had drunk many goblets of wine yet I felt sober. I wanted to run away, leave the palace and go out to Aunt Isithia's house, clutch her scrawny throat and confront her.

'Not now, Mahu.' Maya clutched my wrist. 'You have learned well. Hide your face, hide your feelings, hide your hand. Strike when you must. Wait for your day. Stay now,' he urged, 'and I'll tell you more.'

'About what?'

'Tell Ay to be careful.'

'Of whom? Spies?'

'No, assassins.' Maya peered up at me. 'Ay is seen as Queen Tiye's principal adviser and now as your master's.'

'Who are they?'

'Oh, Mahu,' Maya smiled, 'assassins don't wear proclamations round their necks. They don't send you pretty little letters telling you they are coming.'

I grasped him by the shoulders and pulled him close.

'Why are you telling me this, Maya? How do I know you are not just dirtying the pool? You have a talent for mischief.'

'Sobeck.'

'Oh come!' I snarled, pressing more heavily on his shoulders.

'Sobeck's gone.'

'No.' I withdrew my hands.

'He escaped.' Maya looked quickly to the left and right. 'You know how it is, Mahu, out in those prison cages. They are chained, they exist on water, food that's grown there, anything their guards may hunt as well as the charity of Sand Dwellers and Desert Wanderers. If they can escape, what can they take with them? Anyway, Sobeck took his chances. He went out in the Red Lands. They found his corpse, the skeleton picked dry. They only recognised him by the manacles still round his wrists and the clay tablet lying nearby. He had stolen a knife and a water bottle; both were gone. The back of his head was stoved in.'

I groaned and turned away. 'Poor Sobeck!'

'Nonsense.' Maya came up behind me. I whirled round. 'Think, Mahu, Sobeck was a warrior. He'd escape with a dagger and a water bottle. Libyans don't creep up and smash you on the back of the head. They stand far away and pick you off with a barbed arrow. No such arrow was found nearby. Don't you see, Mahu? Sobeck killed someone, took his clothing, the water bottle and knife, then put the manacles round his victim, together with the prison clay tablet. He's escaped.'

I heard a bird screech. I walked over to a bush, plucked the flower growing there and sniffed its fragrance. My mind teemed with thoughts, images and memories.

'Sobeck will return to Thebes,' Maya continued, following me across. 'You know he will, Mahu. He'll come back to the city. He'll look for his friends: the only one he can trust is you. If he survives the desert he will contact you. He will ask for your help. This is the price you pay for what I have told you. Say to Sobeck that Maya had nothing to do with this treachery, that Maya loved him, still does and always will.' He clasped my wrist and sauntered off into the night.

I went and sat by the Pool of Purity: the blue lotus blossoms were now open, the air sweet with their perfume. I couldn't believe what Maya had said about Aunt Isithia, Sobeck, and Tuthmosis. I wanted to make sense of it, put it all together. I heard a footfall, but didn't turn.

'You learned a lot, Mahu?' Ay squatted down beside me.

'A great deal.' I told him about everything except Sobeck. Ay, of course, was not fooled.

'Why should that little bag of secrets confide in you?'

'We once had a friend in common.'

'I didn't know you were that way inclined, Mahu.'

'I am not but he is.'

'What will you do about Isithia?' Ay asked.

'What do you advise?'

'Wait!' Ay got up and gestured at me to follow. 'Wait, Mahu, as I will. So our enemies have turned to murder:

do you know who the assassin could be?' I shook my head. 'I do.' Ay grinned in the darkness. 'But he, too, will have to wait.'

He looped his arm through mine. 'I love going down to the Nile, and watching the black and white kingfishers dive and swoop. They move so fast, you have to concentrate. Sometimes I don't see any at all and I wonder where they have gone. So, when they return, I am even more curious.'

'Have you come,' I asked, 'to talk about kingfishers in the dead of night?'

'The party is ending.' Ay turned towards where the light could be glimpsed pouring through the windows of the palace. 'Your friends have eaten and drunk more than they should. They are being helped out by their servants. Horemheb, however, marched off as if he was on the parade ground. We will have to watch him, Mahu, him and Rameses. Two hearts that beat as one, and cunning hearts at that.'

'The kingfisher?' I queried.

'Ah, yes.' Ay whistled under his breath. 'The great scribe Huy brought an invitation. In a few days' time, as you know, the Divine One celebrates the Festival of Opet where he moves from the Temple of Amun-Ra at Karnak down to Luxor. A glorious, triumphant procession as Pharaoh communes with the gods.'

'The Kingfisher?' I asked again, though I half-expected Ay's reply.

'The Divine One has moved as swiftly. He has graciously invited his second son to take part in the official festivities.'

'And has our master accepted?'

Ay clapped me on the shoulder.

'He has no choice, Mahu, and neither do we.'

The great sweeping avenue, lined either side by golden-headed sphinxes, marked the great processional route linking the temples of Karnak and Luxor. On that particular occasion, the last day of Opet, it was flanked by a living, thick hedge of people. Thebes had emptied itself of its inhabitants and the crowds were swollen by visitors from every city in the kingdom as well as beyond on this glorious, sunfilled day when Pharaoh showed his face to his subjects who revelled in the glory and might of Egypt.

The royal procession was led by the principal War-Chariot Squadron: the electrum silver and gold of their carriages dazzling in the light. The horses, milk-white Syrians, handpicked from the royal stables, were gorgeously apparelled: dark blue plumes nodded between their ears, their black harness embossed with glittering silver and gold medallions vied with the blue, red and silver of the javelin sheaths and arrow quivers strapped to the chariots. The horses moved slowly, almost like dancers, their drivers, the most skilled in Egypt, guiding them carefully, all moving in harmony with each other. Between the chariots marched the Standard Bearers holding the insignia of that particular squadron, the lustrous jewel-encrusted ram's head of Amun-Ra. Behind the chariots, in solemn march, came the high officials of the army and court; garbed in white robes, they wore plaited wigs on their heads to which ostrich feathers, dyed a myriad of colours, had been attached. Each of these highranking notables carried their symbol of office: a gold-embossed fan. Ranks of infantry followed these, veterans from every part of the Empire marching in unison dressed in blue and gold head-dresses and white waistcloths. They carried spears and ceremonial shields also emblazoned with the insignia of Amun and were flanked by lines of archers, quivers on their backs, bows in their hands.

The sound of that massed march almost deafened the music of the pipes, the rattling of the long war drums, the clash of cymbals and the blast from the trumpets and conch horns of the military band. Clouds of fragrance billowed up as the shaven heads, the priests of every rank, garbed in their white robes, shoulders draped with jaguar and leopard skins, walked slowly backwards, faces toward the royal palanquins bearing Pharaoh Amenhotep the Magnificent and his Great Queen and Wife Tiye. Hundreds of these priests scented the air with gusts of pure incense as the temple girls, visions of beauty in their long, voluptuous wigs and diaphanous robes, danced to the rattle of the sistra whilst others sent thousands of scented flower petals whirling through the air.

In the most gorgeous of palanquins, its curtain pulled aside, slouched the Magnificent One on a throne of gold made more beautiful by the inlaid jewels along its arms and sides. Amenhotep was garbed in the robes of glory: these still couldn't hide his corpulent body with its sagging breasts and paunch. He wore the Red and White Crowns of Upper and Lower Egypt, the flail and rod in his hands held against the Nenes, the precious holy tunic beneath his Robe of Glory. He sat, one elbow on the arm of the throne, glaring sternly before him as his subjects cheered, the more devout falling to their knees to press their foreheads against the ground. Pharaoh was moving in all his glory. Around his brow was coiled the Uraeus, the lunging cobra, the protector of Egypt and the defender of Pharaoh; the snake symbolised the fire and force Egypt might loose against any who troubled her. On either side of the imperial palanquin walked the high-ranking officers – those who were allowed into the private chambers of Pharaoh. Each carried a huge, pink-dyed ostrich plume drenched in cassia, myrrh and frankincense to keep the air sweet as well as to waft away the dust and flies, not to mention the sweat and smells of the massed cheering crowds kept in line by stern-faced foot soldiers.

Slightly behind Amenhotep came Queen Tiye in her palanquin, her perfumed body drenched with sweat between the robe of feathers which covered her from head to toe. The robe was fashioned from the glowing plumage of exotic birds. Beneath the heavy crown displaying the horns and plumes of Hathor, Tiye's face was smiling and sweet. Unlike her husband, the Queen turned every so often to the left and right to acknowledge the cheering crowds. Next walked Crown Prince Tuthmosis, Akhenaten slightly behind him. Both wore crown-like rounded hats, jewel-studded with silver tassels hanging down the back. They were dressed alike in pleated linen robes, resplendent in glorious necklaces, pendants, bracelets and rings, their faces painted, eyes ringed with dark green kohl. Each Prince was ringed by fan-bearers, flunkies and incense-waving priests. Tuthmosis carried a staff, its gilded top carved in the shape of a falcon. Akhenaten rested on a cane inlaid with ebony and silver, a personal gift from Ay. They both walked barefoot, imperial sandal-carriers trotting behind, holding their footwear for whenever they needed it.

Tuthmosis was greeted with fresh bursts of cheering but, as I walked, well behind the legion of shaven heads, I caught the murmur of the crowds as they noticed Akhenaten, the King's other son, paraded for the first time in front of Pharaoh's people. Exclamations of surprise, cries of wonderment, as well as mocking laughter were audible across the avenue. Whoever had arranged the procession had been very clever. Tuthmosis walked so Akhenaten, too, had to overcome his disability and process under the blazing sun with as much dignity as he could muster. Nefertiti had not been invited – a subtle insult. She would have certainly distracted and pleased the crowds, but the invitation, carrying the personal cartouche of Amenhotep, had made no mention of her so she was compelled to stay at the Palace of the Aten. She'd disguised her anger behind smiles whilst she carefully instructed Akhenaten on how he was to walk and bear himself.

'The sun will be hot,' she had warned, 'try not to wear sandals. Shift your weight to the cane Ay will give you. Neither look to the left nor the right. But be careful – do not react.'

'To what?' Akhenaten asked softly.

Nefertiti glanced away. 'To whatever happens,' she murmured.

She had taken me aside out in the gardens, walking up and down, that beautiful body tense with fury. She reminded me of the Goddess Bastet, the Cat Goddess who walks alone. Nefertiti strode backwards and forwards; now and again she would unfold her arms, fingers moving, the hennaed nails glittering like the claws of an angry cheetah. I could tell from her breathing how the anger seethed within her. At last she calmed herself and stood over me as I sat by the edge of a pool. She pressed a perfumed finger against my lips, moving it up so the nail dug into the end of my nose, blue eyes ice-cold.

'Take great care, Mahu. My Beloved is in your hands.'

I had done my best or at least tried to. The Festival of Opet had been a long exhausting procession of public festivities as the God Amun-Ra, his wife Mut and their son Khonsu were taken from their darkened shrines at Karnak and carried the one and a half miles to the riverside Temple of Luxor and back. Processions by road, processions by river. The imperial barges, resplendent in their paintwork, prows carved in the shape of hawks' heads, moved slowly up and down the river surrounded by a myriad of craft. At night banquets and receptions by torchlight and oil lamps took place, sacrifices offered amidst clouds of incense. The array of troops and the solemn parade of priests and officials seemed endless. It was a feast of colour, song, music, dancing, eating and drinking, which exhausted even the most experienced courtier.

If Akhenaten was meant to tire, to appear gauche or clumsy, he'd survived the test well. He always walked carefully, his ungainly body poised, his face set in a permanent smile. Nefertiti had taught him well. Both Ay and myself were always nearby. Court officials and flunkies, their rudeness hidden under cold politeness, tried to separate us whenever they could. During the evening feasts, Akhenaten was placed close to his father – but the Magnificent One seemed to be unaware of his existence, not even exchanging glances, never mind a word. Tuthmosis and his sisters, however, were fussed, touched and even anointed by their father, particularly the dark-eyed, pretty-faced Sitamun, Amenhotep's fourteen-year-old daughter, a luscious little thing in her tight-fitting sheath dress and braided perfumed wig. During one feast she was even allowed to sit on her father's lap, head resting against his chest as he fed her sweetmeats from the table.

Akhenaten never complained. In fact, he hardly spoke either to us or anyone else, but accepted his lot with a faint smile and a twist of his lips. At night we often tried to draw him into conversation but again the smile, the shake of the head. Only once did he reveal his feelings with a quotation from a poem:

'Why sit morose amidst the doom and dark?
As you drink life's bitter dregs,
Smile across the cup.'

Akhenaten had drunk the dregs, now the festival was ending with that solemn procession from Luxor to Karnak. Eventually we left the avenue with its long line of impenetrable sphinxes and went into the temple concourse.

We passed the glittering lakes and crossed a courtyard with its hundreds of black granite statues of Sekhmet, the lion-headed goddess who had devoured the first men. We were now about to enter the heart of the great Temple of

Karnak. Trumpets and horns sounded, the blue, white and gold pennants tied on flagpoles above the gates danced and fluttered like pinioned birds. More trumpets and horns brayed and the huge bronze-coloured doors of Lebanese cedar swung slowly open on their brass pivots. We entered the sacred precincts of Amun-Ra, a vast forest of granite and stone, comprising temples, colonnades, statues and columns. More crowds were gathered here: notables and diplomats were given preferential treatment and so it was in the different squares and courtyards we passed.

In the central courtyard the procession came to a halt. The imperial palanquin was lowered amidst a swarm of shaven heads. The priests of Amun-Ra, divine fathers, priests of the secrets, lectors, stewards, chapel priests and their host of helpers clustered about. Trumpets sounded, drums were beaten and flower petals whirled through the air, mixing with the clouds of incense and the fragrance from the myriad baskets of flowers placed around the courtyard. A group of musicians and dancers came down the steps leading from the temple proper, a moving mass of music and revelry to greet the Divine One's arrival. Amenhotep remained in his palanquin, as did Queen Tiye, whilst the lead singer of the choir intoned a paean of glory to him:

'The gods rejoice because you have increased their
offerings.
The children rejoice for you have set up their
boundaries.
All of Egypt rejoices for you have protected their
ancient rites.'

The rest of the hymn was taken up by the chorus.

'How great is the Lord in his city.
Alone he leads millions:
Other men are small!
He is shade and spring,
A cold bath in summer.
He is the One who saves the fearful man from his
enemies.
He has come to us.
He has given life to Egypt and done away with her
sufferings.
He has given life to men and made the
throats of the dead to breathe.
He has allowed us to raise our children and bury
our dead.
You have crushed those who are in the lands of
Mitanni,
They tremble under thy terror.
Your Majesty is like a young bull,
Strong of heart with sharp horns,
Whom none can withstand.
Your Majesty is like a crocodile,
The Lord of Terrors in the midst of the water,
Whom none can approach.
Your Majesty is like a glaring lion.
The corpses of your enemy litter the valley.
You are the Hawk Lord on the wing.
You are the Jackal of the South.
You are the Lord of Quickness, who runs over the Two
Lands.'

Once the hymn was ended Amenhotep was to make the formal reply. Only this time he turned and whispered to a fan-bearer, his herald. The man stepped forward. I heard a low hum and, glancing back at the steps, saw Shishnak the High Priest of Amun come slowly down and process across the courtyard. A thin, angular man with bloodless lips and dark penetrating eyes, Shishnak was used to the drama of the temple liturgy and able to exploit it for his own purposes. Either side of him walked two acolyte priests swinging golden censers and, behind them, a Standard Bearer. The latter carried a large ornamental fan, shaped like a half-moon at the top of a long golden pole, displaying the insignia of the temple – a ram's head with golden horns, jewels as its eyes, the face and muzzle of cobalt blue.

Shishnak stopped in front of the imperial palanquin and gave the sketchiest of bows. Amenhotep returned this, a slight movement of the head but a gesture which spoke eloquently of the power and wealth of this High Priest, this supreme arbiter of religious affairs. Both priest and Pharaoh remained motionless. The herald was about to turn when I heard a gasp and looked up. Three black crows, birds of ill-omen, circled the courtyard. One came down to perch on the head of a statue, the other two joined it on the ground nearby, malevolent-looking with their cruel beaks and raucous cawing. A priest ran up waving a fan and the birds flew off, splitting the air with their hideous squawking. Ay, beside me, was all tense. He muttered something under his breath. The herald, however, unperturbed by what had happened, loudly proclaimed, 'His Majesty is pleased to enter the sacred precincts of his

Father's temple. His speech of thanks will be delivered by his dearest son Prince Amenhotep.'

That was the only time my master's name had been proclaimed officially. The herald's declaration was greeted with gasps of surprise. Ay was cursing under his breath: 'First the birds of ill-omen and now this. He is unprepared – he will stutter, falter.'

I made to go forward but Ay seized my arm. 'Don't be a fool; we are only here by grace and favour,' he hissed.

The Magnificent One had plotted and trapped his son. He had been paraded in public, his entry to the temple arranged to coincide with those birds of ill-omen and now, untrained and inexperienced, either in public office or public speaking, he had to deliver a speech in the presence of Pharaoh and all the might of Egypt. Akhenaten leaned on his cane. I could tell from his posture how tense he had become but then he turned and looked up at the sun. His face was calm and he smiled, that dazzling smile which could captivate and disarm you.

'We are waiting.' The High Priest's voice carried like a drumroll across the courtyard. 'We are waiting for the son of the Magnificent One. All ears listen! All hearts rejoice at the great favour shown this son of Pharaoh!'

He had hardly finished when my master's voice answered, clear and carrying, thrilling like a trumpet through the air.

'Oh Father, Eternal One,
All the lands are under your sway
Your name is high, mighty and strong.
The Euphrates and the ocean of the Great Green

Tremble before you.
Your power rules the region
From here to the ends of the earth!
The people of Punt adore you
And in the East Land, where the spice trees grow,
the trees are fresh for the love of you!
You bring their perfumes to make the air sweet
in their temples on feast days!
The birds of the air fly because of you!
The creatures on the ground
Eat and live because of you!
All creatures visible and invisible
Stand in awe before you,
Oh glorious Father,
Eternal Aten!

My master paused and, completely oblivious to the gasps
and exclamations this had caused, continued his paean of
praise.

'Magnificent is thy name!
You bind the lotus and the papyrus!
You are true of voice,
Your eye is all-seeing!
What is done in secret is clear to you.
What is whispered is heard by you.
You have established your majesty upon the mountains.
How beautiful is your coming.
My Father, I give you thanks for this day!'

My master fell silent. The priests of Amun were a joy

to behold, mouths gaping in sagging faces, hands flailing. Even Shishnak stood as if stricken. A hurried conversation took place between the Pharaoh and the herald. Trumpets blared and Pharaoh, helped by two of his assistants, left the throne. Accompanied by Queen Tiye and the High Priest, Amenhotep the Magnificent marched across the courtyard and up the steps into the sacred place. Only then, in private, could he commune with his gods and vent his rage at the impudence of his son, the Grotesque, who, in the very heart of Amun-Ra's Temple, had dared to intone a paean of praise to his strange god Aten. The rest of the Assembly had to wait patiently.

I glanced quickly at Ay; his face was impassive but his eyes were bright with amusement. Other officials started talking amongst themselves whilst my master stood leaning on his cane, smiling beatifically up at the sun.

Seth, the red-haired God of Chaos, was often depicted with a beak, horns and forked tail.

Chapter 10

'Of course our Prince was magnificent.' Ay bit into a succulent piece of spiced meat. He smiled wonderingly to himself, relishing both the memory and the food. We were sitting out at the Nose of the Gazelle, a craggy promontory overlooking the Nile, Ay, myself, Snefru and the scribe Ineti. A splendid day! Down by the waterside fowlers were busy. They'd spread their nets over a collapsible frame and placed it in clear water between clumps of reeds. The frame was fixed by stakes driven into the mud, then the hunters lurked behind a bush, ropes in their hands, ready to close the net trap on its hinges. The lure was baited with juicy crumbs and seeds. The birds came clustering in, fighting and squabbling over the bait. A fowler appeared, startling the birds; he shouted an order and the net snapped closed, trapping the birds inside. For a while all was confusion. The nets bulged as the birds, packed together, fought vainly to escape. Once they were exhausted the fowlers opened the net, quickly removing the young whilst they slaughtered the rest, necks were wrung, heads chopped off, blood drawn and feathers plucked, then the birds were tossed into pots of salted water.

'Our Prince,' I observed, 'was meant to be trapped but he escaped the net of the fowlers.'

The smell of blood and salt wafted towards us. We sat in a semi-circle around the napkins opened to reveal spiced goose, fresh bread and sliced fruit. Our clay goblets brimmed with the best wine, poured by Ay himself, who had arranged the outing after our return from Karnak. Snefru seemed intent on the fowler, whispering under his breath the different types of bird caught: wild goose, lapwings, sparrows, green-ribbed ducks, grey doves with black collars, quail, hoopoes, red-back shrikes and pigeons.

'They should be careful.' Ay pointed to the reed-filled pools along the riverside. 'Eels, pike and lampreys thrive there and, where they do, the crocodiles gather.'

Snefru refused to meet my eye as he began again to list the different fish which could be caught as if, by simple repetition, he could allay the tension and fear. Despite the meat and wine, that glorious, sunfilled afternoon, Ineti sat cradling his cup, gaze unwavering: if they could, his ugly juglike ears would have flapped because Ay was on the verge of treason. I bit into the fruit and bread and wondered where Ay was leading. Akhenaten had stayed behind with Nefertiti. In fact, he had been constantly with her since our return. No banquets, no feasts, just an ominous silence. Nefertiti had been as angry as a raging cat. She'd clawed my face, twisted my cheek: her beauty made her anger all the more terrifying.

'My Beloved was baited,' she snapped. 'Taken like some tame goose to be paraded before the people. What was he meant to do? Stumble and fall? Either physically or in his words?'

'Excellency,' I protested, 'your Beloved, my master, excelled himself.'

'He shouldn't have sung the hymn to the Aten,' she retorted.

Ay disagreed. When Akhenaten joined them, I was dismissed so they could continue their quarrel in private.

Ay drained his wine and pointed to the hosts of birds flying above the marshes.

'They remind me of those crows, the ones which flew over the Temple of Amun. A clever trick, that! The shaven heads undoubtedly caught them, starved them, then had them released as soon as we entered the central court. The crows would be noisy, raucous and eager to fly under the sun. Birdseed was scattered round that statue, strewn on the ground, to draw them down. Yet our Prince proved to be master of the occasion.'

Snefru's scarred face was now all alarmed.

'And what a speech our young Prince made,' Ay continued. 'Such wit, such tact. The shaven heads of Amun must be seething with rage. Ah well.' He sighed and refilled our goblets. 'The Magnificent One's grand design faltered and was replaced with ours.' He breathed in. 'It's good to be here. I love the smell of the river, the sweet and the sour, the ripeness and the dross, the rotting vegetation. Life and death, eh? I hope Shishnak rots in his temple.'

Ineti coughed; his face was ashen, eyes full of fear at what he was hearing.

'One day,' Ay murmured, 'the Aten, the Unseen, Everseeing God will come into his own and be worshipped everywhere. The clever tricks of Amun, the charades in his temple, will be over. I'd love to go into the Holy of Holies.' Ay chattered as if he was talking to himself. 'They pick up this ridiculous statue on its so-called sacred barque and Pharaoh asks it a question. If the barque moves forwards the answer is Yes. If No, it goes back. I mean,' he laughed, 'it's carried by the shaven heads! They will give Pharaoh the answer he wants. But, of course, he is growing stupid, isn't he?'

Snefru moaned. I felt a chill of fear. Ay was now staring at Ineti.

'You can't believe those juglike ears can you, Master Scribe? Are you taking careful note of what I have said?' Ay leaned forward. 'Are you going to run back to your masters in Thebes and tell them about the treason you have heard? Well, you won't be running anywhere. Ineti, the wine you have drunk is poisoned. You can't taste it. It contains a special potion distilled by my daughter: snake venom mingled with a few deadly powders.'

Snefru jumped to his feet, throwing his cup away.

'Oh, not yours,' Ay snapped, his eyes never leaving Ineti, 'just the scribe's.'

Ineti tried to move but he couldn't. His sallow face had turned grey, eyes large in his face, a strange colour about his lips. White froth bubbled at the corners of his mouth.

'The symptoms are quite swift. Death does not take long. You can't move, can you, Ineti?'

The scribe sat as if carved out of stone; only the throbbing in a vein in his neck showed that the death struggle had begun. It was eerie, frightening, blotting out any other image: the cry of the birds, the faint shouts of the fowlers, the breeze picking up along the river, the buzz of bees, the incessant whirl of the myriad insects. I put my goblet down. Ay stretched across and touched Ineti's face. The scribe was now fighting for breath like a man whose lungs have filled with water. The sounds from his mouth grew more hideous; he was straining and gagging as if he was going to be sick, eyes rolling back in his head. At last, he collapsed to one side, face hitting the sharp rocky ground so hard that flecks of blood appeared, then he lay still.

'Why?' Snefru murmured.

Ay grabbed dirt from the ground, and threw it over Ineti's corpse, then picked up his goblet and toasted the river.

'Get back.' He recited a spell from *The Book of the Dead*. 'Retreat! Get back, you dangerous one! Do not come against me! Do not live by my magic! Get back, you crocodile from the East! The destination of you is in my belly. May you live in fiery darkness forever. Well, Snefru,' he rubbed his hands together and pointed further along to a clump of bushes. 'Drag the corpse over there. No one will see it.'

Snefru, however, was already on his feet looking round.

'Horemheb and Rameses will send spies.'

'I doubt it,' Ay murmured. 'It's the Prince they watch and my daughter. Even if they do find out, we'll all take an oath, won't we? Ineti must have eaten something which disagreed with him.' He laughed merrily. 'Go on, Snefru, drag the corpse into the bushes. Cut deep into his chest, pluck out his heart and throw it away for the birds and jackals to feast on. Cursed in life, Ineti will be cursed in death. His *Ka* can wander the cold arid halls of the Underworld. Let him never know peace. Go on, man!'

Ay dug into the food basket, pulled out a long knife and thrust it into Snefru's hand.

'Cut out his heart. As you do so, recite a curse! Go on now!'

Snefru grasped the knife and pulled Ineti's corpse away as if it was a bucket of filthy rubbish. He dragged it across the ground, keeping low so the fowlers from the riverside could not see him. The scribe's sandalled feet scraped the ground, arms and legs jerking like those of a broken doll.

'Well, Snefru's got his work cut out!' Ay laughed at the pun.

I looked towards the river. The fowlers were now moving away. Like Ay, they were happy at a good day's hunting.

'He was the assassin, Mahu.'

Ay filled my cup, grinned at my uncertainty and exchanged his cup for mine. His grin widened as I changed them back.

'Trust me, Mahu! Trust our master! Ineti was an assassin, a spy. We all know that. Like a viper hidden under a rock he was waiting for his moment. You don't mourn him, do you?'

'I don't give him a second thought.'

'Good! I used to take Ineti down to the markets in Thebes to buy provisions. He wasn't a very good spy. He'd always wander off down the same street and enter a beer-shop where he'd give the owner a small scroll of papyrus. I persuaded the owner to give it to me. Well, the last scroll at least. I cut the rogue's dirty throat just in case.'

'And the papyrus?'

'Oh, it told Ineti's master, whoever he is, what I did, where I went, no more than a hint that if I was to die, perhaps it could be some sudden city accident or a fight at a wine-booth. Now, that's not the place for me to die, is it, Mahu? But I didn't just kill Ineti for that.'

He picked up a piece of well-cooked goose and bit into it carefully. 'You saw what happened at Karnak. We are at war, Mahu! In war you strike as much terror into the hearts of your opponent as you can. Oh, our enemies will realise we killed Ineti but they won't be able to prove it. They'll never find his corpse. Snefru will come back after dark and toss it into a crocodile pool. We are sending a message, Mahu. We are as ruthless as they are.'

'Who are they?'

'To be perfectly honest, boy, I don't know.'

'I am not your boy.'

'No you are not, Mahu, you're my scholar. Anyway, this is the way things are done. They attack us, we attack back.'

'They will seek revenge for Ineti's death.'

'Let them and they'll pay a price, but before they do, they'll think carefully.'

'Who do you think they are?'

'Everybody, Mahu! The Crown Prince, the Divine One, Shishnak, High Priest of Amun, Rahimere the Mayor of Thebes. Either one, two or all of them. You have been involved in a battle. The enemy deploy, hidden by a screen of dust or a rise in the ground. You have to wait, spy out their true strength, let them show their standards. The same applies here.' He paused.

Snefru's grunts as he hacked at Ineti's body carried clearly back to us.

'Wash your hands!' Ay shouted. He paused, ears straining. I caught the words of the curse Snefru was chanting as he cut out Ineti's heart.

'Can we trust Snefru?'

'Oh yes. Especially now.' Ay wiped the sweat from his forehead with the tips of his fingers. 'I once told Snefru how Ineti worked for the courts. He was a Scribe of Wounds, supervising the mutilations carried out against convicted criminals. Snefru may be surprised by the speed of Ineti's death, but I suspect he's enjoying his work.'

When Snefru came out of the bushes he was dressed only in a white kilt; his stomach, chest, hands and arms were covered in blood.

'Is it done?'

'The birds already feast on his heart.' Snefru's face broke into a smile.

Ay glanced down at the river. 'And the fowlers have gone. Snefru, go down there and wash.'

We watched him go. Snefru cleaned himself quickly,

stripping naked, staying on the edge of the river, fearful of what the smell of blood might arouse. Ay repacked the baskets except for Ineti's cup which he flung down the rocks and, with Snefru trailing behind us, we returned to the Palace of the Aten. Akhenaten and Nefertiti were in the garden sitting beneath the outstretched branches of a sycamore tree fashioning a floral collarette of flowers. They both looked up as we approached; Akhenaten's face brooding, his dark eyes watchful, Nefertiti as serene as any well-fed cat.

'It is done,' Ay declared.

'Good!' Nefertiti murmured. 'Now, my Beloved, never put blue and green so close.' She glanced up and smiled. 'Mahu, we have to pack. Queen Tiye has sent us a message. An imperial barge will be here for us in two days.'

Ay took me by the arm and we withdrew.

'Where are we going?' I asked.

'To the birthplace of the Aten,' he replied. 'Tell Snefru to select ten of his best men. Have provisions ready to take down to the quayside.'

Two days later the Queen's barge arrived: a splendid ship with jutting prow and stern, both carved in the shape of a snarling golden lioness. The rest of the imperial barge was a glittering blue, black and red with the wadjet eye on each side of the prow, and lunging, lifelike cobras beneath the stern. Elaborately painted kiosks stood on either end, with a doubled roofed deckhouse in the middle; this was painted a dark blue with a golden Horus head on each side. A huge blue and white mast stretched up to the sky, its great sail reefed.

Of course the arrival of the *Dazzling Aten* caused

consternation amongst the officers of the Sacred Band who had not been warned of its coming. Horemheb and Rameses came hurrying up to the house, half-dressed in ceremonial armour, and demanded to see the Prince. Ay met them in the entrance portico and insisted on serving cool beer and slices of rich walnut cake. Horemheb and Rameses had no choice but to observe the courtesies. They squatted on the cushions, nibbled some of the cake and sipped at the beer.

'Is the Prince on board?' Rameses asked.

'No,' Ay replied.

'Why is it here?'

'We are going on a journey.'

Horemheb opened his mouth to ask at whose command but Rameses nudged him.

'We are not prisoners,' Ay continued evenly. 'Our master is a Prince of the Blood. He may come and go where he wishes.'

'Where are you going?' Rameses demanded.

'Why, Captain, a pleasure cruise along the river. The weather is beautiful. The Nile runs thick and fast. Flowers and trees bloom. We may do some hunting amongst the papyrus groves or even out in the Eastern or Western Desert.'

'We have to accompany you.'

'Why?'

'Orders,' Horemheb retorted. 'The Prince, of course, is not a prisoner, but he is the beloved son of the Divine One.'

'Ah, yes,' Ay interrupted sarcastically.

'Our commission,' Rameses' voice was strident, 'our

commission is to defend and protect the Prince! Where the *Dazzling Aten* goes we will follow.'

'Then, my dear soldier, you had best go back into Thebes and talk to the Chief Scribe of the Marines. You have a war-barge, you'll need provisions. We can't possibly feed you.'

'Our chariots?' Rameses complained.

'Your chariots are your concern,' Ay shrugged. 'They will have to be left here.'

'There's another matter.' Rameses' voice became more measured. 'The scribe you reported missing, Ineti? We found some bones, the flesh picked clean, down near the shallows.'

'Poor Ineti.' Ay shook his head. 'I told him not to go along the river. However, some people can't be told, can they?' He got to his feet and brushed the crumbs from his robe. 'And now we are busy. We are leaving tomorrow evening.'

Horemheb and Rameses hurried off. For a while all was confusion in the small military camp which lay between ourselves and the quayside. However, by the time we left, Horemheb and Rameses were organised. A powerful, black-painted war-barge, with hollowed, broad hull, slipped in behind ours: it was manned by a small squadron of marines and joined by Horemheb and Rameses and several of their company. We left just before darkness, moving out into midriver, Ay himself leading the paean of praise as the oarsmen bent and pulled back. Our craft leaped forward in a burst of speed, a well-planned taunt for Horemheb and Rameses who hastily followed in pursuit.

Akhenaten and Nefertiti occupied the central cabin, Ay the kiosk on the stern. I stayed with the crew wrapped in warm blankets, close enough to the glowing braziers to receive some warmth as well as a little protection against the night flies. We made good progress, now and again calling into some small village to fill water jars or barter for supplies. Nefertiti and her Beloved acted like a royal couple. During the day the sides of the cabin were taken down and they would sit under the awning, fan-bearers about them, enjoying the gorgeous pageant of colours on either bank: the bright green maize, the softish yellow hue of oats, the blazing gold of corn. They'd comment on the fishing smacks and other craft plying the river: boats packed full with mercenaries moving down to the forts, barges of supplies – wine, beer, cedarwood, bronze and copper as well as livestock. As the day drew on, we would comment on the shifting colours of the sands and marshlands on either bank as they turned from red-gold to deep purple.

On the second night out Nefertiti graciously invited Horemheb and Rameses to a supper on the imperial barge. Horemheb brought his two new dwarves; they looked like identical twins with their bald heads, bushy beards and small thickset bodies. Rameses had a baby giraffe which had followed the hunters after they had killed its mother the previous evening; it was the only time I ever saw him show affection to anything or anyone except Horemheb. A pity he was so clumsy; the next day the giraffe fell overboard and drowned. Anyway, that was a beautiful evening, the river supplying its own entertainment. A barge taking pilgrims from the shrine of Hathor, Lady of Drunkenness, came alongside ours. The men and women on board were drunk, merry and loud, unable to discern whom they were shouting at or who the women flirted with by baring their breasts or lifting their skirts.

Horemheb and Rameses were not the ideal guests; they acted in a surly manner throughout and not even the pilgrims of Hathor could raise a smile. They glowered at me and seized this opportunity to take me aside and remonstrate about what had happened.

'I am not your spy,' I protested.

'I just wish you hadn't left so quickly,' Rameses whined.

We were standing in the stern of the ship warming our hands over a small dish of glowing charcoal, carefully protected in its copper bucket. I noticed Rameses' hand was shaking slightly and the truth dawned on me.

'Of course.' I leaned over and tapped him on the face like he used to do to me in the Kap. 'You don't like water, do you, Rameses?'

'I become sick,' he confessed, not lifting his head. 'I asked that idle bastard Pentju if he could give me something.'

'Never mind,' I soothed. 'I am sure the journey won't be long!'

We passed cities and towns but no orders were issued to put in at Abydos, the holy city of Osiris, or even Akhmin, where Tiye and Ay had family and kin. It was as if they did not wish to converse or be tainted by anything. We moved majestically up the Nile, a journey of over two hundred miles: restful days, peaceful nights. No one ever mentioned where we were going or the reason for our journey. Akhenaten and Nefertiti were at peace. On one occasion, just after sunset, they organised some of the best voices amongst the marines to sing the most beautiful haunting hymn which stirred the heart and provoked bittersweet memories. A song about a lost time, a dazzling time, free from the taint of death or sickness. Akhenaten and Nefertiti sang together, hands clasped, voices ringing out across the water. Fishermen on their boats plying their nets before darkness fell, stopped to listen. The chorus was taken up by the deep-throated marines, a rhythmic chant. Even now, many years later, at dusk, as the sun sets, I close my eyes and recall that singing.

One afternoon about eight days after we'd left Thebes, Akhenaten fell strangely quiet, and flanked by Nefertiti and Ay, stood by the taffrail staring out at the eastern bank of the Nile. I stood behind him and watched as the lush vegetation and palm trees gave way to a stretch of desert land. Ay shouted an order. The sails were furled, the rowers were told to tread water. Slightly behind us the war-galley also slowed. Akhenaten and Nefertiti never moved. They stood, fascinated by a sunbaked cove of desert, about eight miles broad which stretched from the Nile to towering limestone cliffs dominated by two soaring crags with a half-moon-shaped cleft between. This was the Holy Ground! It was the first time I saw it: lonely, washed by the Nile and dominated by those brooding cliffs which changed in colour as they caught and reflected the setting sun. An empty place with its own aura: the more I stared, the more it seemed to drift across the water towards me, drawing me into its haunting empty loneliness.

Late in the afternoon we prepared to go ashore, our barge threading its way through the sandbanks where water melons grew. Ay had a quiet word with the Captain. Only he, Akhenaten, Nefertiti and myself were to disembark. Once we had, the Prince knelt and nosed the ground as if adoring the two distant peaks. Nefertiti and Ay followed suit whilst I stood staring around, trying to shake off my wariness. I wanted some sound to break the stillness. Akhenaten whispered a prayer, rose and walked across that sacred soil with the sun slipping behind us sending shadows racing along the cove and up those limestone cliffs. The evening breeze whipped our faces like some muffled voice trying to communicate a secret. My sandals crunched on the hard ground. I knelt down and sifted amongst the stones, picking up the sea shells like pieces of fine glass or alabaster. These lay strewn amongst the pebbles and glinted in the light of the setting sun.

'Once,' Akhenaten murmured, staring down at the shells I held in my hand, 'the Great Green covered this land until my Father drove it back to its boundaries.'

I squinted up. Akhenaten was gazing hungrily at the cleft between the two crags.

'Once my Father walked here in the cool of the evening, enjoying its lush greens, rejoicing in the company of the Sons of Men – that was his delight.' He blinked and squatted down beside me, eyes bright with excitement. 'That was in the Dazzling Time, Mahu, when the Sons of Men walked with God and all was harmony, before the Thief of the Underworld made his presence felt. Can't you feel them, Mahu, the ghosts of the Dazzling Ones all about us? The breeze carries their faded words and hymns.'

He tapped the soil. 'The roots still lie here, embedded deep. The desert will bloom and the jonquil flourish amongst the rocks. Once our vision is realised, my Father will, once again, walk amongst men.'

I stared disbelievingly at him, but he never noticed my mood.

I knew nothing about his strange theology. Even when I reflected on what Tiye had told me, what did it amount to? The worship of an Unseen God who manifested his power in the symbol of the Sun Disc? Akhenaten plucked up some sand, pebbles and shells, letting them fall through his fingers. He rose and, with Nefertiti beside him, walked further inland. The shouts from the war-barge carried ashore. Akhenaten abruptly turned and went striding back, his walking cane rapping on the ground, robes fluttering about him, long arms gesticulating.

'Go back!' he shouted. 'Stay on board! Do not pollute this holy ground for my Father has blessed me. He has blessed me and will bless me again.' He climbed onto a boulder, his body ungainly-looking against the darkening sky, face bathed in the light of the setting sun.

'Go away,' he repeated. 'Do not trespass on holy ground.'

Ay went down to the riverside and repeated the orders not to land, his voice carrying like a herald across the water. The consternation on the war-barge was audible but Ay was insistent. Only a few servants from the *Dazzling Aten* came ashore. They erected pavilions and tents, gathered brushwood and lit a fire, bringing supplies of meat, wine and bread. The sun set and the plain darkened, broken only by the light from our campfire. Akhenaten sat, arms linked with Nefertiti, eyes half-closed as if drinking in the very smell, taste and sounds of this place. They retired early. Ay and myself shared a smaller pavilion. I lay listening to Akhenaten and Nefertiti singing, followed by the clink of cups and the sound of their lovemaking before I drifted into sleep.

Akhenaten woke us long before dawn. I felt cold. Outside the air was chilly. Only a faint burst of light beyond the mountain range showed day was imminent. Akhenaten acted like an excited child, pacing up and down as Ay and Nefertiti laid out blankets and cushions. At last Akhenaten knelt down, Ay and Nefertiti on his left and right. I crouched on my cushion. Nefertiti rose, returned to her pavilion and brought out three glowing bowls of incense. She placed one in front of Ay, Akhenaten and herself. The incense smelt bittersweet in the morning air. The glow in the East strengthened as if a ball of fire was about to surface behind the dark mass of the mountains. A bird flew overhead, its song piercing the freezing air. The land fell silent. Stars disappeared and the Sun Disc appeared directly between the two peaks at the centre of the cleft, rising with all the majesty of dawn, shattering the darkness, lighting the mountains, its rays spreading over the plain as if hungry to reach the river. Akhenaten moaned in ecstasy, head going backwards and forwards. He intoned:

'How beautiful are you,
How visible your glory!
Visible power of the invisible!
Glory of the dawn!
More brilliant than the Morning Star!
Your hidden power sustains all creatures!
Above the earth, on the earth, below the earth.
All beings take life and power from you.
All creation waits to do your will.
Oh Father, bless your son as he blesses you.
Oh Father, make yourself known as I will make you
known
And honour your name and glorify your being in this
holy place.'

Akhenaten's voice thrilled stronger and stronger like a trumpet blast shattering the silence, heard even by our companions on the barges.

'I shall do a beautiful thing for you!' Akhenaten continued.

'To all the boundaries of this earth.
I shall do a beautiful thing for you
To the North, to the South,
To the West and to the East.'

Akhenaten bowed, followed by Nefertiti and Ay, pressing their heads against the ground. The Sun Disc broke free, clear of the mountains, and rose against the sky, transforming the earth and the air in a blaze of light and glory. Then Akhenaten stood, a beatific smile on his face.

'Go down to the waterside, Mahu,' he urged. 'Tell the others they can now come ashore.'

I did so. The crew of the *Dazzling Aten*, followed by Horemheb, Rameses and their soldiers clambered ashore. My two companions were angry but their anger was tinged with a sharp curiosity. They had witnessed the drama of the sunrise and bothered me with questions. Why was this place sacred?

'I don't know,' I told them.

'Are you sure?' Rameses persisted. 'There must be few places in the Eastern Desert where the sun rises so dramatically.'

I shook my head and walked away.

'They are curious, aren't they?' Ay came up, still hunched against the cold, a shawl across his shoulders.

'Never mind them,' I snapped. '*I'm* curious.'

'This is a sacred place.' Ay stared at me from under heavy-lidded eyes.

'I know that. I'm not a child – the sunrise is most dramatic.'

'When our people first came to Egypt,' Ay stroked his reddish hair, 'they assembled here and built their altars to the Unseen God.'

'Why here?'

'Because, according to legend, this was once the dazzling garden, the place where God and Man met.'

'And now it's just a desert,' I replied.

'Look for yourself, Mahu.'

I did so, wandering across the plain, and soon realised

that its aridity was only superficial. In clefts and gullies, I discovered underground water streams and untapped wells, their presence only visible in the quickly drying water as the day progressed. Behind me servants were carrying up stores and setting up tents. Hunters were sent out to bring fresh meat; two of these returned at a run shouting and waving their arms.

Horemheb was sitting by the campfire deep in conversation with the two dwarves. Rameses was testing water from one of the barrels. Akhenaten and Nefertiti had withdrawn to their pavilion. Ay was aboard the *Dazzling Aten*. The way the hunters hastened towards us proclaimed that something extraordinary had happened. If it was an attack by Desert Wanderers and Sand Dwellers they would have raised the alarm. These two stopped, fighting for breath, bodies drenched in sweat.

'You must come,' they gasped, pointing back towards the rocky escarpment, ravines and gullies which marked the beginning of the limestone cliffs. 'You must come silently.'

Ay came ashore, scratching his jaw. Akhenaten and Nefertiti left their pavilion, wrapping their robes about them. Horemheb had already slung his bow, Rameses was shouting for the marines.

'It's not like that,' one of the hunters said.

'Well, what is it?' Ay demanded.

'No, I cannot describe it,' the other replied. 'Master, you must come!'

Akhenaten and Nefertiti put on their sandals. Horemheb and Rameses, followed by Ay and myself, left the camp with the hunters. The day was blazing hot, and a stiff breeze from the river wafted gusts of sand and dirt, toasting our eyes and coating our lips. By the time we had reached the line of boulders, all of us were drenched in sweat. The hunters gestured to us to be silent as we climbed the shale, sandalled feet slipping. We reached the top, more boulders; the ground fell away between two rocky outcrops. It led to what looked like a dried-out water hollow, ringed by straggly bushes and brambles clinging to the thin soil. The hunters moved slowly. We passed the corpses of quails slain earlier. They led us up to a barrier of rock and rubble. We peered over this down to the hollow.

At first I could see nothing but then, beneath a large bramble bush, I glimpsed movement. A lioness lay there, a great tawny-skinned beast, body stretched out, tail moving, her great forepaws spread out before her. Between them lay a baby gazelle which rose, stumbling, yet it kept its feet. The gazelle moved round the lioness; it cropped at a tuft of grass, then came back and settled down as if it was the lioness's cub. The lioness did not kill or menace it but treated it gently, nuzzling and licking it carefully. I gazed in astonishment. The lioness was a powerful beast, yet she treated that gazelle as tenderly as any cub. Great cats play with their victims, like a house cat with a mouse, but this was not the case.

We all, even Horemheb and Rameses, gazed speechlessly at the scene. Nefertiti's face had never looked more beautiful; she was radiant, her eyes glowing. The walk and climb had made her hot – I could smell her perfume. I watched the delicious drops of sweat snake down the golden skin of her face. Akhenaten crouched as if beholding a vision. Even the cynical Ay was speechless.

All the time I waited, tense, for the lioness to spring, deal that baby gazelle a killing blow or inflict a savage bite to the nape of its neck, but both animals remained content together. At one point the lioness turned, ears twitching, and glanced towards us as if she could see us and gave a threatening growl deep in her throat.

We were about to withdraw when the hunters crouching behind us hissed a warning. Further down the hollow, in the break between the two rocks, a splendidly-maned lion had emerged, walking softly, tail out. The breeze ruffled his powerful mane; muscles rippled along his body as he padded gently down the incline towards the lioness. At first she didn't notice but then, in a rapid movement which made me jump, she sprang up and turned, belly low to the ground, ears flat, against her head, face transformed into a snarling mask. The lion came on threateningly. The lioness refused to give way, moving towards him, her whole body arched and ready for battle. The lion paused, head going from side to side. The lioness, likewise, and for a while she sat glaring at the newcomer. Then the lion threw back his head and gave a low, coughing roar. The lioness inched forward, ready to spring, while the gazelle crouched gracefully on the ground, unperturbed by the growing menace. At last the confrontation ended. The lion hurriedly backed off, tail twitching and, with as much dignity as he could muster, returned the way he came. The lioness, however, remained crouched until satisfied the threat was gone. She then drew herself up and, jaws open, emitted the most ferocious roar. Tail whisking from side to side, she glared up at the escarpment as if considering what to do with the threat which menaced her from above.

'We must leave,' the hunters insisted. 'She knows of our presence and will tolerate us no further.'

The lioness returned to the baby gazelle, standing over it, licking it, gently reassuring it. Then she lifted her head, those great amber eyes glaring up at us. The hunters were now pleading.

'We have seen enough,' Ay whispered and we withdrew.

Akhenaten revelled in what he had seen, striding ahead with Nefertiti almost as if he had forgotten his ungainliness, swinging his cane like a soldier would a sword, one arm round her shoulders, his mouth only a few inches from her ear. Ay, however, questioned the hunters as did Horemheb and Rameses, yet this was no trickery.

'Have you ever seen that before?'

The elder hunter, a grizzled veteran, shook his head.

'Never, my lord,' he replied.

'You are a Kushite, aren't you?' Ay demanded.

'My mother was. My father was a farmer in the Black Lands.'

'Have you ever heard of such a story?' Rameses insisted.

'I have heard tales about the great cats treating a gazelle like a cub, but until this day I never believed it.'

'Perhaps it's true.' The other hunter gazed round. 'Perhaps it can be explained. The lioness may have lost her own cubs. She may even have killed the gazelle's mother and dragged her body away. I have known the young to follow the killer which has taken its mother.' The hunter hoisted his bow over his shoulder. 'I forgot to bring the sand quails,' he smiled. 'We'll leave them for the lioness. It was worth the price.'

*　　*　　*

311

Later that afternoon we left that strange deserted cove along the Nile. Akhenaten stood in the prow of our barge staring until it disappeared behind rocky outcrops and the thick hedges of palm trees. Once it had disappeared he stood, head bowed, tears trickling down his long furrowed cheeks: he grasped Nefertiti by the hand and they both returned to the cabin amidships.

The news of what we had seen soon spread amongst the crew, only increasing their curiosity about the journey and its destination. Some declared they had seen similar signs. Horemheb and Rameses looked genuinely perplexed. Ay could only shake his head.

'Some things can be explained,' he confided, 'some things cannot. The Prince believes it was a sign and it's best if we leave it at that.'

Our journey back to Thebes was uneventful. We were distracted by the different sights on both shores as well as the varied life along the river. At dawn and sunset there were the undecked fishing boats with their huge nets; fowlers in their punts, busy along the reedfilled banks. In the cool hours came the pleasure boats bright with their gilding and blue, red and yellow paints which cast vivid reflections on the surface of the shimmering water. We passed Dendera, following the river down past the desert mountain ranges giving way to wide swathes of cultivated land where palm, acacia, fig tree and sycamore thrived. Eventually we glimpsed the silver- and gold-plated tops of the pylons, obelisks, temple cornices and rooftops of Luxor, Thebes and Karnak. We made our way carefully through the different flotillas going up and down the Nile or across to the Necropolis. At last we slipped along our own quayside thronged with servants waiting to greet us.

It seemed strange to be back in the Palace of the Aten. Later that day Akhenaten and Nefertiti invited both Ay and myself to a splendid but private banquet held on the daïs behind thick gauze curtains at the end of the hall of audience. Snefru kept guard and brought the food himself: plates of freshly cooked meat and bread, dishes of vegetables, small pots of sauce, a welcome relief from the hardened bread and dry salted flesh we had eaten on board during most of our journey.

Akhenaten was fascinated by what we had seen. Time and again he returned to the lioness and the gazelle as a sign from his Father that all was well and all would be well. He began to question Ay about the place itself: the building of quaysides, the exploration of wells, how canals could be dug. Akhenaten's face became flushed, eyes bright as he talked of plans to found a new city, build temples open to the sun. I wondered if Tiye had arranged the journey to distract her son. Or was it what she and her husband intended for this rebel at the imperial court? Was Akhenaten to be banished from the Malkata and the City of the Sceptre to some lonely outpost where he could indulge his own private beliefs? Nefertiti seemed just as enthusiastic. I found it difficult to imagine a woman like herself, not to mention her father Ay, being expelled from the centre of influence and power. The meal was coming to an end when an imperial herald arrived. He was dressed in white, a gold fillet around his head, a white wand in his left hand, a scroll of papyrus in the other. Snefru brought him to the hall of audience. The man knelt before the daïs and handed over the scroll. Ay unfolded this: it bore the crest of the imperial cartouche, Pharaoh's own seal. Ay studied the contents and looked anxiously at Akhenaten. 'A summons from your father. Tomorrow afternoon you are to join your brother, the Crown Prince Tuthmosis, in the Holy of Holies in the Temple of Amun-Ra at Karnak.'

All pleasure faded from Akhenaten's face. 'The vigil,' he whispered under his breath. 'We are to spend four days before the tabernacle of that hideous demon and pledge our loyalty to the God of Thebes.' He sat, head back against the wall, eyes glaring, his strange chest rising and falling as if he had been running fast.

Ay ordered the herald to withdraw. Akhenaten's face grew ghastly, liverish, eyes starting in his head, lips moving but no sound, not a word. Nefertiti tried to calm him but he brushed her hand away. He made to rise but slumped back. He grasped his cane and with one sweep sent the platters and plates, cups and goblets, alabaster oil jars flying from the tables. He rose to a half-crouch, the cane rising and falling, smashing into the acacia wood, cutting deep as if it was a sword, whilst the anger raged in his face; his lips white-flecked, eyes popping, chest heaving. The oiled, perfumed wig he wore became dislodged. Akhenaten threw it at me and, with both hands, smashed the cane up and down, curses tumbling from his lips. Ay stood and watched. Nefertiti flattened herself against the wall, fearful and watchful. At last Akhenaten let go of the cane and, turning sideways, placed his head in his wife's lap, drawing his knees up like a child, fingers going to his mouth. Nefertiti stroked the side of his face, talking in a language I could not understand, soft gentle words to match the rhythmic movement of her hands. She glanced at Ay and gestured with her head. Ay left the hall and returned, a small goblet of wine in his hands. Snefru still stood by the doorway, transfixed by what he had seen. Ay handed the wine over to Nefertiti who coaxed her husband to drink, making him sit up, holding the cup for him until he grasped it with two hands, drinking greedily, face now slack, a terrifying look in his eyes.

'Leave,' Ay whispered to me. 'Leave and never repeat what you have seen. Take Snefru with you.'

I did so at once, pushing Snefru out into the cold night air, closing the doors behind me.

'What was that?' Snefru asked.

'The rage of a god,' I replied.

Snefru was about to walk away when he came back. 'Master, I apologise, but on the night you returned, a message came for you.'

'A message?' I asked. 'No one sends messages to Mahu. It cannot be Aunt Isithia.' I spread my hands. 'Snefru, where is this message?'

'It was brought by one of those amulet-sellers. Only a few lines: "Let's live and love".' Snefru rubbed the scar where his nose had been. 'Yes, that's it. "Let's live and love. Suns set and suns rise".' He shrugged and spread his hands.

My heart quickened. 'Anything else?'

'The amulet-seller said he came from the small-wine booth which stands at the mouth of the Street of Jars. Do you understand what it means, Master?'

I shook my head and walked away. Of course I did! Sobeck had returned. He was in Thebes and wished to see me.

The hieroglyph for 'enemy' – *hfty/hefty* – is a placenta, a horned snake, a bread loaf and plural strokes.

Chapter 11

Pale-faced and anxious-eyed, Akhenaten left the palace the following afternoon. He was surrounded by shaven heads from the Temple of Amun and escorted by guards displaying the golden ram's head of their god. My master had quietened down. Nefertiti had attended to him and Pentju had also been summoned in the dead of night to give him a soothing draught and check that all was well. Nobody was allowed to accompany him; even Horemheb and Rameses were ordered to stand aside as my master was taken down to the waiting barge: a black-painted, sombre craft with the ram's head on the prow and an ugly carved jackal face on the stern. Once Akhenaten was gone, our house seemed to lose its soul. A chilling silence drove Ay, Nefertiti and myself out into the garden to sit under the shade of date palm trees. Snefru, sword drawn, circled us like a hunting dog, alert for any eavesdropper, brusque in dismissing servants who came our way. Ay's confidence had been shaken. He conceded the priests of Amun had acted more quickly and ruthlessly than he had ever imagined.

'An imperial summons,' he shook his head, 'cannot be ignored.'

'He could have feigned sickness.'

'Daughter, they would still have taken him.'

'Why?'

'Ostensibly,' Ay sighed, 'to acquaint himself with the God.'

'And the truth?'

Ay glanced at me. 'Mahu, you are so quiet. Can the pupil inform the master?'

'Yes.' Nefertiti moved closer, her breath on my face, her perfume tickling my nostrils, hands against mine.

'For one or two reasons,' I replied.

'Yes?' Ay demanded.

'To break his will.'

'Never.' Nefertiti's eyes widened.

'Or to kill him.'

Nefertiti's head went down; she gave a low moan, a heartwrenching sound. When she glanced up, her eyes were mad with anger. Her hand lunged out, nails ready to rake my cheeks, but her father seized her wrist.

'You are sure, Mahu?' he asked.

'I am certain. The Prince will not be cowed. He asserts himself. He worships a new god.'

'Whom his father also worships,' Ay declared.

'Only as a ploy,' I replied. 'A political balance against the host of Amun and only then at the insistence of Queen Tiye. Egypt has many gods,' I continued. 'Amun does not object as long as its supremacy, its monopoly of wealth and power is not challenged.'

'But our Prince is not the heir.'

'He could be,' I replied. 'He might be.'

The garden fell silent except for the call of a dove to its mate. 'What makes you say that?' Ay plucked at a blade of grass.

'Tuthmosis is a blood-cougher.'

'Not necessarily the mark of death.'

'In one so young?' I challenged. 'Even if he lives and enjoys a million jubilees – may the gods so grant,' I added mockingly, 'so might our Prince.'

'And?'

'Our journey to the North is now well-known. What if, in the future, during the reign of an ailing Pharaoh, Akhenaten withdraws from Thebes, journeys to his holy site and sets up a rival court, a new temple of religion?'

'Very good,' Ay whispered. 'A master pupil. You do think, Mahu.'

'He just doesn't talk, do you, Mahu?' Nefertiti's anger had cooled. She was staring curiously at me. 'Go on,' she urged.

'If our Prince dies there's no threat of schism, no challenge . . .'

'But if Tuthmosis dies as well?' Ay asked.

'The Magnificent One has daughters,' I smiled. 'Shishnak or someone else might marry one of these. It would not be the first time there has been a change of dynasty in Egypt.' I stared across the garden. 'And if that happens, we would join our master across the Far Horizon. No one here would be allowed to survive.'

'Queen Tiye would resist,' Nefertiti declared.

'Bereft of her husband and her sons? Don't you think the priests of Amun know Queen Tiye is the true source of her second son's waywardness?'

'So, what can be done?'

'Nothing,' I replied. 'This is the eye of the storm. Our Prince is in the hands of his god.'

'How could they explain away his death?' Nefertiti asked.

'You know full well: an unfortunate accident. Do you remember those crows flying over the Temple of Amun, the Prince's so-called blasphemous hymn to the Aten in such sacred precincts! The shaven heads of Amun would claim that Akhenaten's death was a just punishment from their god as well as a vindication of Amun's supremacy. They do not intend to nip the bud, or cut the branch, but hack at the roots.'

'We must have time,' Nefertiti whispered, rubbing her stomach. 'Mahu, I am pregnant.'

I went to congratulate her. She held up a hand.

'Pentju has confirmed it.' Her face creased into a smile. 'I have asked Meryre to become my chapel priest. Both are sworn to silence. Why?' she teased, head slightly to one side. 'Do you think, Mahu, that you are the only child of the Kap who swears loyalty to us?'

'Excellency,' I replied formally, trying to overcome my own embarrassment. 'All men swear allegiance to you.'

'Very good, Mahu.' She tweaked the tip of my nose and lifted her shift to reveal a slightly distended stomach. I am perhaps two months gone. Pentju has even whispered that I may have twins. The divine seed has been planted, it must be allowed to grow.'

'Oh, how?' Ay plucked at his lower lip, still lost in his thoughts. 'How can these matters be turned?'

'You've fought in a battle, sir,' I mocked, recalling his words. 'There is always a moment, perhaps even only a few heartbeats, when chance or luck . . .'

'No such thing,' Nefertiti snapped.

'The hand of God,' Ay whispered, 'can change things. We have our spies at Karnak.'

Nefertiti glanced away. 'And what will you do, Mahu?'

I thought of Sobeck, smiled and didn't reply.

Later in the day I slipped into Thebes, taking a circuitous route to elude any pursuer. So strange to be in the city! The walls of the houses facing the street were dingy, windowless and silent; their doors hung open to reveal shadowy passages or the first steps of a staircase leading up into the darkness. Voices spoke, shouts, a child's cry. Now and again I had to stand aside for a donkey, laden with burdens, trotting nimbly by under its driver's stick. Occasionally houses would jut out, their upper storeys meeting to form dark suffocating tunnels. I walked quickly along these into some sunfilled square grateful for the light, noises and smells. The traders, as always, were busy. Sheep, geese, goats and large horned oxen were being herded and paraded for sale. Fishermen and peasants, squatting before their great reed baskets, offered vegetables, meat, dried fish, and pastries for sale. People haggled noisily, bringing their own goods, necklaces, beads, fans, sandals and fish hooks to trade.

A farmer was shouting at a buyer, eager to purchase a slumbering ox.

'No less! No less,' the fellow shouted, 'than five measures of honey, eleven measures of oil and . . .'

I paused as if interested and glanced quickly around. No one was following me.

'What do you think, sir?' the buyer bellowed.

'At least half an *ouŋou* in gold,' I replied.

The haggling started again. I slipped away, concealing my face beneath the folds of my robe as if trying to fend off the stench of sweat, salt, spices, cooked meat and dried fish.

The odour was too much, as was the stinking, flea-infested reek of the alleyways. I went deeper into the city, across the open markets with their stalls and shops. I stopped to admire Hittite jewellery, Phoenician perfume, Syrian cordage, gold, silver and other metals. Feeling hungry I bought a small reed basket of dried dates covered in a syrup of honey and spices, dotted with pistachio and shredded almonds. I took this across to watch a goose being roasted over an open spit. When I had finished eating, I sat under a palm tree so a barber could shave and oil me. All the time I watched for that familiar face, a fleeting glimpse of someone trying to hide. I kept well away from processional routes, the temples and other outbuildings. I acted like a steward of some great mansion out on a day's shopping. I paused before a jeweller's stall; he was arguing with a customer over the alloys for electrum.

'Forty measures silver and sixty gold!' the customer declared.

I stared down at the precious stones, emeralds, jasper, garnets and rubies.

'I have others in a chest at the back,' the jeweller broke off from his quarrel, 'away from thieving eyes and hands. This man,' he grinned at the customer, 'he's got it wrong, hasn't he?'

'Yes,' I agreed. 'An *ouηou* of electrum is twenty measures silver and eighty gold.' The customer glared at me and shuffled off. I opened my own purse and measured out half an *ouηou* of silver into the small dangling scales. The jeweller's eyes widened.

'It's yours,' I declared softly, 'if you just let me stand here. Tell me, is someone following me?'

The jeweller played with the scales, head going from side to side. 'No, no, there's no one. Ah, I am wrong. There is someone. He has just gone behind the stall. He's dark-skinned, a desert man, dressed in a leather war-kilt, a belt across his chest. Ah, he's turned and is going elsewhere.'

I left the silver, walked away and gazed round. I could not see 'Leather Kilt' amongst the crowd, only Nubians with their skins of smoked bronze, long-robed Desert Wanderers, Libyans with their feathered head-dresses, and fair-skinned Shardanah mercenaries. I crossed a needle-thin canal into the poorer quarter of the city which ran along the old quayside, down the narrow, crooked paths reeking of filth between houses of unbaked brick covered with a layer of mud and a roof of palm leaves. Between these, a few ragged acacia and sycamore trees shaded muddy pools for cattle to drink from. The inhabitants spent most of their time out on stools or rush mats, protected with sharp prickles to guard against scorpions and other vermin. They sat, engaged in tasks or eating a dish of onion and flat cakes baked over the ashes of their fires, little pots of oil beside them to soften the hard bread which broke their teeth and chapped their gums. They were garbed in filthy rags, their faces ash-stained. Children, almost naked, played in the mud, running and screaming, the din made all the more hideous by the yip and snarl of narrow-faced, yellow-skinned mongrels. The poverty was disgusting. In people's faces I saw hollow eyes red and swollen, sunken cheeks and toothless mouths; smoke curled everywhere. I coughed and retched, wary of the rubbish strewn about. The beggars were legion, but my strength, not to mention the dagger I carried, kept them back.

I stopped at a corner and gave a scribe a *deben* of copper. He had set up a stall under a tree to write out temple-petitions for the illiterate. Taking the copper, he directed me to the waterfront where I found the Street of Jars, a thin strip of a lane full of beer-houses and winebooths. I glanced round. No dark-skinned man in a leather kilt followed me. I went into the cleanest-looking beer-house. The reception room was freshly limed, with mats, stools and piles of stained cushions for its customers. The place was half-empty except for a few tradesmen drinking jugs of beer and taking sips of palm brandy, and perfumed liqueurs cooked slowly in a pot. A grey fog of smoke curled from the kitchen and cheap oil lamps. I sat in a corner and ordered some beer. As I did so, 'Leather Kilt' sat down opposite me. He was burned black by the sun, shaven-headed, an earring in one lobe, copper-studded armlets and wrist-guards along his arms, a belt of similar colour and texture across his chest, military sandals on his feet. He leaned over, took my jug, drained it and pushed it at the pot boy, indicating we needed two more. I stared at that face, eyes crinkled by the sun, the leathery skin, the ugly scar which marked the left cheek, dead eyes in a dead face, a grim mouth.

'Sobeck!'

'Sobeck!' His lips hardly moved. 'I don't know what you are talking about. My name is Kheore – that means being. For that's what I am – I simply *am*.' He smiled at the riddle.

The boy returned with the beer jugs. Sobeck indicated that I was not to talk. We drank the beer and left, going down to the riverside. The quays were busy with their shabby markets through which soldiers, marines and sailors paraded, trying to catch the eye of the pleasure girls. Tumblers, tinkers, traders and scorpion men, the sellers of amulets and scarabs, bawled for trade. Storytellers announced what they had seen in their wondrous travels. Sobeck pushed his way through these and led me down an alleyway. At the bottom lay a derelict warehouse, its brick walls collapsed due to flooding. Inside, beneath the sodden palm-leafed roof mingled a pile of mud and bricks.

'Everything collapses around here.'

Sobeck sat down on a part of the outside wall, indicating I sit on a nearby plinth.

'Only the gods know what this was once. A temple? A warehouse? A brothel? A beer-shop? Anyway, it's a good place to talk. There is only one lane leading to it, so I can see if anyone comes.'

I stretched out my hand. Sobeck hawked, spat, then grasped it.

'I owe you my life.' He stretched as if to catch the breeze coming in from the river. 'I escaped,' Sobeck declared. 'I wandered for days. A Sand Dweller attacked me. He must have been a scout and not a very good one. The fortune of the gods, eh Mahu? He loosed an arrow but it hit the clay tablet round my neck. I pretended to be dead. He came in to see what plunder he could take.'

'And you killed him? You broke the back of his head?' For the first time Sobeck showed surprise.

'Maya told me. He works in the House of Secrets.'

'That plump piece of shit!'

'He didn't betray you,' I declared.

'Then who did?'

I spread my feet and gazed on the ground: I was intent on my revenge. 'You will not believe this.' I glanced up. 'My Aunt Isithia.'

A knife suddenly appeared in Sobeck's hand, its blade only a few inches from my face.

'It's a long story,' I lied. 'I won't give you the details. My Aunt Isithia was, is, a courtesan, well-known to the priests of Amun and the courts of the Divine One. She trains the Royal Ornaments in certain pleasures and practices.'

The knife was lowered. I sat listening to the whirr of insects and the faint sounds from the quayside.

'I know all about the Divine One's pleasures,' Sobeck murmured, 'but I never told anyone outside the Kap.'

'Aunt Isithia's suspicions were roused,' I continued. 'Do you remember Imri?'

'The Captain of the Kushite guard,' Sobeck retorted. 'He guarded the Grotesque, or as you termed him, the Veiled One.'

'Aunt Isithia heard some chatter about your dalliance with a Royal Ornament, the challenge to steal the Statue of Ishtar and so on.' I paused. 'She informed the authorities who instructed Imri, already their spy on the Veiled One, to keep this particular grove under close guard. He saw you both and reported back.'

'I'll kill him!'

'He's already dead,' I replied. 'Drowned in a crocodile pool.'

Sobeck put the knife away. 'Your work, Mahu? You never did anything for anyone.'

'Except plead for your life, Sobeck, and risk coming here.'

'So Imri is dead.' Sobeck tapped his sandalled foot. 'I thought he killed Weni for insulting the Grotesque!'

'Weni,' I retorted, 'died for mocking a Prince of the Blood. The Divine Ones will only tolerate this if it's done at their command.'

Sobeck moved and saw me flinch, my nose wrinkle at his sour odour.

'Yes, you'd notice it, Mahu, coming from your perfumed quarters. Do you know what I do now? How I make a few *deben* of copper? I am a dog-killer. I slaughter mongrels both here and in the Necropolis. I skin and mummify them so they can be sold to pilgrims as offerings.' He half-smiled. 'It's an exciting profession, Mahu. You meet some interesting people.' His smile faded. 'It stops me from starving.'

'Why did you follow me?' I asked.

'I've been following you since you left the palace. If you'd come straight to the Street of Jars I would have suspected that you'd allowed yourself to be deliberately followed, but the route you took,' he shrugged, 'the stalls you stopped at . . . There's a price on my head, Mahu. A very good one. I am not some common criminal but someone who squeezed between the thighs of a royal concubine. The House of Secrets has as many spies as flies on a dog turd.'

'So why did you send the message?'

'Ah, the love poem?' Sobeck whistled softly under his breath. 'I wanted to find out if I could trust you. I need money, Mahu, silver and gold, precious stones. You always were a hoarder.'

'And if I say no?'

'Then, Mahu, you are no longer my friend. You can go, but you'll never see me again.'

'And why do I need your friendship?'

Sobeck crouched down and poked me hard in the chest. 'In this land of tribulation, Mahu, never make an enemy when you can make a friend. The imperial court is not unique, it's the same here. You fight, you struggle, you kill or die, either of starvation, a club to the back of the head or a knife under the ribs.'

'I have already helped you.'

He got to his feet. 'Ah yes, Aunt Isithia. I'll reflect on what you said, Mahu. You want her dead?'

'She's nothing to me, Sobeck. She's a witch: a woman with no heart or soul.' I recalled Dedi, Ay's secret whisperings. I rose to my feet. 'She owes me a life. It's time the debt was paid.'

I walked to the crumbled doorway.

'Do you remember that jeweller I stopped at? Do you think he can be trusted?'

'If he can't be,' Sobeck quipped, 'he'll die.'

'I will leave you something there,' I held up my hand, fingers splayed, 'five nights from now.'

Sobeck walked across and clasped my hand. 'You could inform the Divine One or Hotep? Even your own master?'

'In this land of pain,' I grinned, 'this place of tribulation, you need every friend you can get, Sobeck. Anyway, you have been punished enough. No child of the Kap should end his life gibbering and screaming on a stake.' I held up my hand. 'Five nights from now.'

'Let him go!' Sobeck hissed out into the fading light.

I paused. A dark shape appeared in the doorway, a small thickset man, tufts of black hair framing a monkey-face. In one hand he carried a knife, in the other a club.

'I see you have friends already, Sobeck.'

'Ah, this is the Devourer,' Sobeck laughed, 'a demon from the Underworld, a man who can help us both. By the way, Mahu, I leave it to you whether you tell Maya about me. So go in peace, friend!'

Monkey-face stood aside and I went out into the night.

The Palace of Aten lay eerily silent during Akhenaten's visit to the Temple of Amun-Ra. A soul-wrenching tension affected us all as we waited for news. On the fifth day, as promised, just before the ninth hour, I went back to the jeweller's with a sealed casket. I'd kept my own treasures, gold, silver and jewels collected over the years. Akhenaten was a generous master. Monkey-face was waiting to take it. He grasped the casket, lips snickered into a grin and disappeared into the crowd. I dallied in the beer-house then visited a palace of delight where two Syrian girls in their thick perfumed wigs, bangles and anklets jangling, gorgets of silver round their throats, entertained and pleasured me. I returned along the river, past the picket guards set by Horemheb, to find Snefru waiting for me at the gate.

'You are needed, Master.'

He almost pushed me into the hall of audience. Inside, three figures gathered round a glowing brazier; their muffled cloaks, shadows dancing against the painted wall, made them look like spectres, ghosts out of the West.

'Come, Mahu.' Queen Tiye pushed back her hood. Her face was drawn, her eyes red-rimmed with weeping.

'Where have you been?' Ay snapped.

'We have waited for you,' Nefertiti whispered.

'At my pleasures.' I bowed and made to kneel.

Tiye grasped my wrist. 'This is no time for obeisances or courtly courtesies,' she said sadly. 'Tuthmosis my son is dying.'

'What!'

'Your lord has taken sanctuary in the Temple of Amun-Ra.'

'How do you know?' I gasped.

Tiye looked over her shoulder into the darkness. 'Come!'

A shape emerged from the entrance leading down to the kitchen. One of the oil lamps flared, revealing the round, painted face of Maya. He was swathed in a shawl, which concealed neither his exotic perfume nor the jingle of his jewellery. He reminded me of the Syrian girls I had just left.

'Well met, Mahu.' He minced into the circle of light.

Tiye patted him affectionately on the shoulder. I realised only then how this powerful group were intent on winning over all the children of the Kap. They had planned, they had intrigued, they had plotted from the start to isolate, educate and train young men to serve the Grotesque, the Veiled One, Akhenaten.

'Was it always meant to be like this?' I asked the question without thinking. 'Were we always supposed to be servants for him?'

'Yes,' Tiye replied. 'But the Divine One, at the last moment, refused to let my son join you. This house was the nearest he got. Everything else including' – Tiye gestured at Ay and Nefertiti – 'was to be hidden in the shadows.'

I pointed at Maya. 'What have you learned?'

'I have two spies in the Temple of Amun,' Maya drawled, eyes smiling. 'A lector priest and an acolyte responsible for their laundry.'

Ay laughed sourly. Maya ignored him.

'Early this evening they informed me that Tuthmosis was found seriously ill in his chamber.'

'Where was . . . ?'

'Your master?' Maya's eyes rounded. 'He stayed near the Holy of Holies. Apparently Tuthmosis had returned to his chamber beyond the central courtyard where he became seriously ill. The alarm was raised by a servant. A priest tried to tell Akhenaten, as he now calls himself, what was wrong but he refused to leave the Holy of Holies.

333

Akhenaten fears for his life – he believes there's a plot to kill him and he refuses to leave the sanctuary.'

I thought of Akhenaten, long-faced, cowering in those dark aisles, his enemies surrounding him like a band of dogs.

'Excellency,' I gestured at Ay, 'why not send your brother Nakhtimin to inform the Divine One?'

'My husband is befuddled! As yet no one else knows.' Tiye's eyes filled with tears. 'If they did, they might decide to strike . . .'

'At the roots,' Ay finished the sentence.

'If the Divine One is informed,' Maya jibed, 'he might decide to cut both root and branch.'

'What do you advise?' I asked.

Maya gazed blankly back. The rest stood in silence. I recalled my conversation with Sobeck about Aunt Isithia. We were snakes coiling in the darkness. Everything we did was cloaked in secrecy. My journey to Thebes, those long sombre alleyways with the burst of sunlight at the end. I had run through them so quickly.

'Surely,' I began.

'Surely,' Ay mimicked my words.

'Strike now,' I urged. 'This is the moment, that heart-beat in the battle, when all hangs in the balance.'

'How?' Nefertiti asked.

I threw all caution aside. 'Let me go to the Temple of Amun. Horemheb and Rameses can be my guards. The shaven heads don't know them. They'll see what they expect to see, officers from the Sacred Band. Huy is a royal scribe, Meryre a chapel priest,' I pointed to Nefertiti, 'whilst Pentju is her physician, a scholar in the imperial

House of Life. That's it.' I clapped my hands. 'We will all be emissaries from the Great Queen. Horemheb and the rest were all sent to spy on us; let's turn their weapon against them.'

Nefertiti clapped her hands, her beautiful face bright with life.

'I'll seal the document,' Tiye intervened. 'Despatched under my own seal.' Her eyes glowed with excitement. 'No, on second thoughts, I will go with you.'

'Impossible!' Ay objected. 'They would suspect something's wrong. Why should the Great Queen accompany her envoys at the dead of night?'

'True,' Tiye conceded. 'I hold my own cartouche. I'll sign passes, issue a demand, saying I wish emissaries to see my son.'

'*Both* your sons,' I urged.

'Agreed.' Tiye nodded absentmindedly.

'And if they refuse?' Ay asked. 'If the shaven heads object?'

'Sooner or later,' I replied, 'the news of Tuthmosis' sickness and my master's sanctuary will become known.'

I paused and walked away. Something was wrong. Crown Prince Tuthmosis was seriously ill in the Temple of Amun yet Tiye and the rest were not concerned about him. It was Akhenaten.

'Tuthmosis,' I declared. 'He's dead already!'

'I know what you are thinking.' Tiye's voice carried across the room. She came up close. 'I love my two sons, Mahu, but Tuthmosis is doomed. I know that, we all know that. I recognised the symptoms, his hideous secret for the last seven years. He coughs blood.

No physician can save him. Indeed, this is what could have happened now: an attack, the bursting of blood within. However, I must, I can if God is good, rescue my surviving son. He has a destiny.' Her voice faltered. 'Please,' she whispered; the imperious Queen of Egypt was pleading with me. She stretched out and grasped my hand. 'Please, Baboon of the South, you have the cunning.'

'What about the rest?' Ay demanded. 'Horemheb and Rameses? They might refuse.'

'Let's invite them to a meeting,' I retorted, still holding Tiye's hand, 'and see if they'll agree.'

My proposal was accepted. Ay was a little truculent, his jealousy of me apparent, but Nefertiti had forgotten her fears and took him aside, whispering, stroking his arm. By the time Snefru returned with Horemheb and Rameses, Huy and Pentju, Ay was in full agreement. Maya, of course, had disappeared, murmuring that it was best if his comrades did not see him.

Any protests at being disturbed at such a late hour died on their lips as Horemheb and the rest came into the hall of audience and greeted Queen Tiye. They silently made obeisance and waited until Snefru had arranged cushions on the floor and withdrew. We all squatted down, staring at each other over the glowing light of the alabaster jars. Queen Tiye was flanked by Nefertiti and Ay, whilst I sat with the rest facing them.

'This is no idle summons,' Tiye began. 'Mahu will explain.'

My blood was still running hot. Despite the night I was not tired but eager to press on. I told my comrades in short, pithy sentences what had occurred and what was planned. When I finished there was silence.

'It means we force our way,' Ay began, 'into the Temple of Amun accompanied by only two soldiers.'

'And the Great Queen's warrant,' I replied.

'And if we refuse?' Huy asked.

'Then we can all go to bed,' I replied.

'If you refuse,' Horemheb grated, '*you* can go back to bed, Huy.' He glanced along the line. 'Answer the question, Mahu.'

He was sitting next to me, so I turned and held his gaze.

'Go back to bed, Comrade, but you and I, we shall be finished. We shall never be comrades or friends again. The next time we meet will be as sworn enemies.'

'And if we try to stop you?' Rameses whispered.

'That is not your duty,' Ay snapped. 'You are supposed to be here to protect us.'

'I am only asking,' Rameses cheekily replied. 'We are officers in the Sacred Band. Tonight's work could finish us.'

'And if you don't co-operate,' Tiye spoke up quietly, 'you are finished anyway.'

'Can't you see?' I urged. 'One way or the other, this very discussion will be made public.'

'We are trapped,' Meryre shrugged. 'Either way we are trapped.'

'No, you are not.' I breathed in deeply. 'The Fields of the Blessed have called Crown Prince Tuthmosis. He is dying.'

'How do you know?' Rameses demanded.

'Shut up!' I snarled. 'Tuthmosis is dying all right, otherwise we wouldn't be here. The Divine One,' I gestured with my hand, 'grows old. His younger son's destiny is to be Pharaoh, Owner of the Great House, Lord of the Two Lands. Akhenaten will wear the Diadem and Uraeus. He will hold the Flail and the Rod. He will make the People of the Nine Bows tremble under his feet. Tonight could be your great moment of glory.'

'I agree.' Huy waved his hand. 'I wish to be part of this.'

Pentju and Meryre followed suit. They both asked why they were needed. I dismissed their questions.

'A royal priest and physician from the House of Life? Your presence,' I declared, 'is vital in a formal delegation from the Great Queen.'

The circle fell silent. Everyone waited for Horemheb and Rameses. The latter made to speak but Horemheb covered his friend's hand with his own.

'We are with you,' Horemheb announced softly, 'and, if it's to be done' – his craggy face broke into a faint smile – 'it's best done quickly. There's not a moment to lose.'

The meeting broke up. Ay brought a writing tray with the finest papyrus as well as black and red ink and a sheath of pens. Passes were issued, a warrant drawn up, all sealed with the imperial cartouche of Great Queen Tiye. Horemheb and Rameses borrowed swords, I placed a dagger beneath my robes and, gathering our cloaks, we went out into the courtyard. Rameses was there with a small escort, all armed and bearing torches. We were about to leave when Nefertiti came out on the steps and called my name. I went back and looked at this vision of beauty, lovely as the night. She pressed two of her fingers against my lips.

'I swear, by heaven and earth, we shall never forget this, Mahu.' Then she was gone.

We hurried down to the river and clambered into the war-barges for the short journey up the Nile. We kept close to the reed-covered banks. I was not aware of the roar of the hippopotami, the breeze gently shaking the tree branches or the disturbances of the water, the cackle of birds in the undergrowth or the lights far out on the Nile as fishing boats returned to shore. We sat, a silent group lost in our own thoughts. Soon we reached the Sanctuary of Boats, the Mooring Place of the Golden Ram, the quayside of the Temple of Amun-Ra. Torches lashed to poles illuminated the steps as we clambered up. The dark mass of the temple soared above us. Guards carrying the sacred shields, ram's masks on their faces, stopped us: in muffled voices, they demanded we show passes and warrants and explain our presence.

Horemheb now took charge. On our way down to the quayside he and Rameses had stopped at their camp to decorate themselves with all the insignia of their rank: Collars of Gold and pendants displaying the Silver Bees of Bravery. The guards let us through. We entered a side gate and crossed the different courtyards of the Temple of Karnak. The forbidding faces of statues glared down at us in the moonlight. Cresset torches glowed against the night, flames dancing in the breeze. We heard the cries of the sacred flocks of geese and herds of rams and bulls which roamed free in the fields and meadows of the temple. Now and again gaps of pale light displayed the relief on the walls, revealing mysterious beasts and royal processions leading to a bizarre world where gods and exotic animal creatures lorded over all. We passed through heavy doors cut in black granite, along narrow alleyways, past colossal statues of Osiris, Isis, Horus and the other gods of the temple pantheon. Every so often a group of guards would challenge us then let us through copper-lined doors, deeper and deeper into a labyrinth of cold, sombre passageways where the gods were supposed to walk and the veil between our world and the next grew exceedingly thin. Occasionally we'd hear the chant of a hymn or smell the fragrance of the incense and flower baskets.

At last we reached the Great Central Court leading up to the hypostyle hall where Akhenaten had sung his hymn. The Power of Amun was waiting for us at the foot of the steps: row upon row of temple guards, some wearing striped head-dresses, others the jackal or ram's masks of Anubis and Amun-Ra. Torches flared, censers were swung. In front of the serried ranks stood clusters of priests and acolytes. I smelt the dried blood of sacrifices offered in reparation for ancient sins. Pentju moaned with fear. It all formed an awesome sight! The soaring columns of the temple, the black granite, the grotesque statues, the glint of spear and sword, those hideous masks and the silent concord of priests in their white robes and stoles. Shishnak stood in front of them all, grasping his staff of office. Meryre began to panic but Horemheb scratched his nose, an unconscious gesture when he was about to lose his temper.

'One thing I hate are temple guards,' he murmured. 'Do they think we are frightened by children's masks?'

He strode across, sandalled feet echoing on the paving stones, gathering speed as he walked. I and the rest had to run to keep up, past the statues, the obelisks, the stele proclaiming the triumphs of previous Pharaohs. Horemheb paused a few inches in front of Shishnak and handed over his commission from Queen Tiye. The High Priest unrolled it and my heart leaped. Shishnak's hand was shaking whilst a bead of sweat raced down the side of his forehead. He kissed the seal and handed it back.

'I . . . I don't know.' His humble words belied his haughty, lined face. Those glittering eyes didn't seem so hard or imperious now.

'What is the matter?' Rameses demanded, almost pushing me aside. 'My lord, the message from the Great Queen is most simple. She requires the presence of her sons now. We are their escort.'

Shishnak glanced at his acolytes. 'You'd best come,' he whispered and, spinning on his heel, he led us through the throng of priests and serried ranks of soldiers up the steps.

The Hall of Columns was a funereal forest of stone, lit here and there by shafts of light. This mournful place reeked of blood, and of sinister mystery, which the dancing flames did little to dispel. The columns soared up into the darkness. I couldn't even glimpse the roof. A ghostly coldness hung, an unseen mist which chilled the sweat on our bodies. Shishnak, escorted by his acolytes and officers, led us down a passageway; they stopped before a chamber guarded by two sentries. Horemheb dismissed these and ordered the rest of Shishnak's escort to withdraw. Shishnak put his hands to his face as if to intone a prayer; his two forefingers running down the deep furrows in either cheek.

'I must tell you,' he stammered, 'I learned this just before you arrived: the Crown Prince, the Lord Tuthmosis, is dead! May Osiris welcome him into the Undying Fields! May Horus shower him with light!'

'I want to see his body!' Horemheb abruptly declared.

Shishnak unlocked the door. The chamber within was lit by oil lamps; torches glowed either side of a high window. A comfortable room with its gleaming furniture and painted walls, it was now dominated by the lifeless form sprawled on the bed hidden by gauze-like curtains. Without being invited, Horemheb pulled these aside. Some attempt had been made to dress the corpse. At first sight it looked as if Tuthmosis was asleep, though I noticed the blood tinge on the right corner of his mouth, his strange pallor, the half-open eyes, the feeling of complete stillness. Horemheb turned; he almost dragged Pentju to the bedside.

'Our own physicians from the House of Life . . .' Shishnak said nervously.

'Never mind them,' Horemheb snapped. 'We have our own.'

Pentju quickly scrutinised the corpse, turning the face, looking at the chest and stomach, pulling aside the robes.

'A seizure,' he declared. 'Death by natural causes. At least, that's what I think. The skin is cold, the muscles are stiff.'

'And the blood?' I asked.

'Part of the seizure,' Pentju explained. 'A vessel may have burst.'

'How did this happen?' Horemheb demanded.

Shishnak coughed. 'Both the Crown Prince and his brother had gone into the Holy Place to pray before the naos. For some unknown reason, Tuthmosis came back here. He left the door ajar. I had heard that he had left and came down to see what had happened. Crown Prince Tuthmosis was lying on the floor; he was trembling, blood dripped from his mouth. He complained of pains in his chest and stomach, of violent headaches, weakness in his limbs. I helped him to the bed. The physicians were called, but they could do nothing.'

'Don't you think you should have alerted the Divine One?' Horemheb asked, playing the role of the outraged officer. 'Sent messages to his mother?'

'Of course, of course,' Shishnak apologised, the fear obvious in his eyes, 'but matters were complicated. I sent a priest to alert his brother but the Prince hid behind the naos, screaming insults, saying we had murdered his brother and that we intended to kill him. I went to reason with him but he was hysterical. He picked up incense pots, flower baskets, even a figurine and hurled them at us. The platters of food we had laid before the shrine were also thrown. I thought it best if we placated him, persuaded him to withdraw before we alerted the Great House. I will see to the corpse,' he continued hurriedly. 'He will be transported with every honour to the House of Death.'

'The dead do not concern me,' Horemheb said, walking to the door.

'My Lord Shishnak,' I intervened, 'where is my master's chamber?'

'Across the passageway,' the High Priest replied.

I walked out, Horemheb following me. The door to Akhenaten's room was unlocked. It turned out to be a chamber very similar to that of Tuthmosis. The bed was undisturbed, shrouded in its gauze-like sheets. Candles and oil glowed, a small capped brazier sparkled in the corner.

'I must see my master,' I declared.

'You cannot go in there.' Shishnak's old arrogance asserted itself. 'You are not purified.'

A stoup of holy water rested in a niche in the chamber wall. I took off my sandals, went across and bathed my hands, face and feet with the salt-laced water; it stung my eyes and a small cut on my face. I shook myself dry, using the edge of my robe.

'Now I am purified.'

'But you can't.'

Horemheb drew his sword.

'What other way is there to convince the Prince?' I hissed, my voice echoing along the cavernous passageway. 'I am his servant – he will trust me.'

Shishnak closed his eyes, fighting with himself.

'It's the only way,' Horemheb repeated.

Shishnak opened his eyes, then, grasping me by the arm and telling Horemheb to stay, he led me back into the Hall of Columns. Two acolytes escorted us through the gloomy hall past statues and carvings, shrines and chapels to the great gold-plated doors of the Holy of Holies which shimmered in the light of torches held by the officers gathered there. One of the acolytes whispered instructions. The doors opened. I ignored the exclamations and cries of the guards and priests clustered behind me and strode straight into that cold, empty tomb of a room. The great tabernacle stood on its stone daïs, the open doors displaying the gold-plated figure of Amun, the Silent One, the God Who-Watches-All. Before it were small slabs of stone on which the offerings and flower baskets were placed: these had been violently disturbed. The floor was strewn with gold plate, goblets and jugs, slabs of meat, loaves of bread, fruit of every kind. I walked slowly, almost slipping as my foot crushed a bunch of juicy grapes. The air reeked with sweet and sour smells of natron, incense, cassia and the cloying smell of myrrh. A haunted place of shifting shadows. One of these moved from behind a pillar. My master entered the ring of torchlight, his robes stained, cut and torn, but he had regained his composure.

'Mahu. It's good to see you.'

I stretched out my hands. 'Master, we are to escort you home. You are safe.'

Akhenaten strode towards me, his cane rapping the ground.

He kicked aside platters and grasped my hand. 'Mahu, let us go. Let's leave this abode of demons.'

'Rouse yourself, turn yourself over, O King!'

(Utterance 664: *Pyramid Text*)

Chapter 12

'It springs for thee,
The rising of the Nile.
The water of life.
It grows for thee,
That which comes from the water,
The rich black lands of Egypt.
The sky burns for thee,
The land trembles for thee,
Thy feet are nosed by pure water.
The King is prosperous!
The palace flourishes!
The month is born!
The land is covered.
The barley grows!'

Meryre's sonorous voice carried the hymn throughout the chamber. Dressed in white drapery, he acted the role of lector priest before the Royal Circle in the great Council

Chamber next to the Banqueting Hall at the heart of the Malkata Palace. I was there, forced to listen to his nonsense. I kept my face straight as I tried not to recall Meryre, arse naked, being chased like a squirrel by the rest of the children of the Kap across the marshy shallows of the Nile.

It was supposed to be a sacred occasion. Akhenaten sat on a daïs shaped like a shrine with a stucco pillar on either side painted blue and green with golden ivy clinging to it. The top of these columns were blood-red acanthus leaves, their base yellow palm fronds rimmed with silver. Along the top of the daïs was a serried row of cobras, gilded green-gold and black with sparkling angry ruby eyes, glaring threateningly out at us. The rest of the chamber was painted a cobalt blue, the Magnificent One's favourite colour, except for the pillars, carved in the shape of thick papyrus stems, which glowed a vibrant green and yellow.

The stone floor of light blue was smooth and polished as water. At either end of the chamber, rectangular Pools of Purity edged with red tiles glistened in the glow of oil lamps. On the surface of these pools floated blue and white lotus, their sweetness mingling with the sponges soaked in perfume placed in pots in shadowy corners and niches. The windows were unshuttered and, like the doors, their lintels were of precious wood, lapis lazuli and glittering stones. Outside stretched the gardens, the paradise of the palace, lush and verdant. From where I stood behind my master, I could hear the braying and bleating of the sacred flocks.

Akhenaten was dressed in state costume: short drawers

of pleated gauze ornamented at the back with a jackal's tail and, in the front, a stiffened apron of gold and coloured enamel; a large robe of the purest linen draped his shoulders. On his feet were peaked sandals and over his head a beautiful cloth of gold striped white and red. A pectoral of the purest jewels carved in the shape of the Vulture Goddess Nekhbet hung round his neck, rings of office decorated his fingers and in his hand was a golden *ankh*, the sign of life. I had watched his face being painted and embellished before the Royal Circle met; the dark kohl rings round his eyes contrasted with the flesh-coloured paint on his face and his carmine-daubed lips. Across the Royal Circle sat Hotep in his white robes and gleaming chains of office. The Magnificent One's close friend and First Minister kept his face impassive though when he stared at me, cynical amusement glinted in his eyes. Great Queen Tiye sat on Akhenaten's right, Nefertiti on his left, her abdomen now bulging out, straining against the loose thin robe. Ay, holder of the Divine seal, sat next to her.

Everyone was lost in their own thoughts as Meryre's voice rose and fell. In the ninety days following Tuthmosis' death, matters had moved as swiftly as a swallow racing against the sky. The Divine One, stricken by the death of his firstborn, had sunk deeper into a stupor of drugged pleasure, or so Ay had informed me. Great Queen Tiye had also aged: grey-faced, shoulders slightly stooped even though her beloved son had now not only been recognised by the Palace but proclaimed as the Magnificent One's Co-regent, joint ruler, Beloved of Amun, Horus in the South.

My master had certainly changed. The events in the

Temple of Amun-Ra remained hidden. The few details I had gleaned were that he and Tuthmosis had been worshipping in the Holy of Holies when Akhenaten had started to ridicule what he termed 'the empty charade of the priests'. Tuthmosis, angry at such blasphemy, had clashed with him and withdrawn.

'He left me to laugh,' Akhenaten declared as he squatted in the garden pavilion dressed in his robes of mourning, ash staining his head and brow. 'Mahu, I was laughing at the little statue in its cupboard. I told him I'd pick it up and walk away.' Akhenaten squinted at the lotus he held. 'Then the shaven heads came back. They said my brother had fallen seriously ill. I stopped laughing. I thought it was a plot to draw me out so I refused to leave' – he smiled – 'until you came. How did you learn about it? Mother is as enigmatic as ever.'

I told him about Maya. He nodded, thrust the lotus in my hand, rose and left. I never had time to voice my own suspicions. The time was not ripe. I had no proof but there was something about those two chambers in the Temple of Amun-Ra which jarred my memory; something amiss, out of place. It was like trying to recall a dream, the details always evading me. Oh, of course, everyone was thanked. Horemheb and Rameses were promoted to the Maryannou, members of the crack royal corps known as the 'Braves of the King'. Huy became Chief Scribe in the House of Envoys, Pentju, Royal Physician with the right to wear the panther skin and the Ring of Light as well as carry the Staff of Life. Meryre was confirmed as Principal Chapel Priest, Chaplain to the Royal Household and Lector Priest to the Imperial Royal

Circle. Ay had really come into his own: he was given, amongst others, the titles of Pharaoh's Close Friend, God's Father, Principal Councillor, Chief of Scribes, Keeper of the Seals. Maya, of course, would have to wait. And for Mahu? Ah well, Mahu received nothing but caskets of precious stones and a close embrace from both Akhenaten and Nefertiti, reward enough, together with the title of Keeper of the Keys. In other words, I was Akhenaten's personal bodyguard.

Crown Prince Tuthmosis' corpse had been taken across to the Necropolis to be dressed and moved to his father's royal mausoleum where the Keeper of the Secrets of Anubis had bathed his young body in natron, packed it with perfume and adorned it with exquisite jewels. The Hope of Egypt had been wrapped in the purest linen, gently placed in his nest of gold coffins and laid to rest. Egypt had mourned, observing the seventy days' ritual when the young Prince's Ka travelled into the Eternal West. Courtiers and officials rent their robes, strewed ash on their heads and faces, wailed and keened in mourning.

At last the funeral obsequies were over. Life in the city and in the palace along the Nile continued though Great Queen Tiye had been busy. Ten days after Crown Prince Tuthmosis had been sealed in his coffins, my master, under his first name Amenhotep, was proclaimed Co-regent in the Hall of the Great Feast of the Royal Diadem at Karnak. Nefertiti had given him the strictest lectures so he behaved himself beautifully. He had allowed the priests to sprinkle him with holy water, consecrate him with the sacred oils and clothe him in the royal robes which clung around him like some beautiful mist.

This time there was no murmured laughter or mockery at Akhenaten's ungainly body and awkward gait. The crook, the flail and the *ankh* were pressed into his hands. Priests wearing the masks of hawks, rams, greyhounds and jackals clustered about anointing him, blessing him with incense as the great Double Crown, with its Uraeus head-band, was lowered on his head. Shishnak himself, scowling in the Royal Circle, had to proclaim the words on behalf of his god, the great Amun-Ra.

'I have established thy dignity as the King of the North and as the King of the South.
Oh my Son, Lord of the Two Crowns,
I bind the lotus and the papyrus for thee.'

Afterwards Akhenaten had processed solemnly to the Great Room of the Royal Rising and Divine Embrace. He had broken the holy clay seals of the naos and adored the sacred statue surmounted with its ostrich feathers and enamel eyes glowing fiercely out at this new Pharaoh of Egypt who, as he secretly confessed later to me, would have liked to have smashed it to dust with a mallet.

Akhenaten was now Master of Egypt. He sensed it, he felt it and so he had changed. He brimmed with quiet confidence, a slumbering majesty which pervaded all his movements and gestures, voice and words. He watched everything with amused eyes and a cynical smile, yet remained tactful and discreet. Nefertiti was the same. She had not been proclaimed as Queen, not yet, but her hour had come. She was the Great Wife, mother-to-be of

Pharaoh's children, Mistress of the House, Lady of the Palace. If her hour had come, so had Ay's. The only obstacle, a counter-balance to the influence of his son, was the confirmation by the Magnificent One of his close friend, Hotep, as First Minister. All matters had to be decided jointly with him. Queen Tiye had urged her son to co-operate fully with this powerful courtier as well as with the other dignitaries, generals, priests and nobles, the 'Sheneiu, People of the Royal Circle', or the 'Quenbetiu, the Royal Corner'. All these men bore the title of 'Sole Friends of the King', 'Lords of the Secrets of the Royal House', 'Lords of the Secrets of all the Royal Sayings', 'Lords of the Secrets of Heaven'. Fan-bearers and dignitaries rejoicing in their glorious titles, these represented the real power of Egypt.

In the middle of the council chamber squatted scribes from the Purple Chamber of the House of Secrets, writing trays across their laps, ready to catch the words of Pharaoh's friends. Each member of the Royal Circle was allowed one retainer in the chamber. I was Akhenaten's and Nefertiti's. I was amused that Hotep had chosen Maya, who seemed discomfited, shuffling now and again, moving from one foot to the other. At last Meryre's boring chant died away. Akhenaten immediately moved to establish his authority.

'I wish,' he intoned, face all solemn, 'to quarry stone at Silsila to build a temple to Re-Herakhty, the Aten. As you know,' he warmed to his lecture, 'Re-Herakhty is a manifestation of the Sun God: a man with a falcon's head crowned with the Disc of the Sun and encircled by the Uraeus.'

Shishnak coughed, a gesture of quiet contempt for this lecture. Akhenaten ignored him.

'My Father,' he continued, 'my *Father*,' he emphasised, 'has revealed to me a new manifestation – no longer the symbol of a man with the hawk's head, only the Sun Disc itself encircled by the Uraeus with a pendant *ankh* sending forth rays of light. I saw this in a dream. At the end of each ray of light was a hand which blessed me and mine! My Father is determined on this. I have shared my dream with the Overseer of Works: stone will be quarried and my temple to the Sun Disc, the Glorious Aten, will be built at Karnak. This is my wish, my will shall be done!'

Shishnak's face betrayed a seething fury. Akhenaten's first official gesture had been to recognise a different god and insist that a temple to that god be built in the sacred precincts of Amun at Karnak.

'My Lord Shishnak,' Hotep's voice carried softly, 'you have heard the words of the One.'

'I have heard,' Shishnak replied through gritted teeth, 'and the One's will shall be done. I have a question.'

Hotep nodded. Shishnak turned his face to Akhenaten.

'When did your Father, the Divine One, the Magnificent One, reveal this to you?'

'Are we here,' Akhenaten retorted, 'to discuss the love between Father and son? I am the will of my Father. He who does my will, does the will of my Father and pleases him.'

The matter was closed. I stared at the back of Nefertiti's head; her resplendent hair was gathered up beneath a jewelled head-dress. Despite her pregnancy she sat majestically, back straight, eyes staring assuredly out, quietly baiting the likes of Shishnak and the rest. I recalled my own bravery in the Temple of Amun. I had not been publicly rewarded yet her smile, her loving gestures, had been satisfaction enough. She glanced round as Hotep raised other business. I caught her impish smile even as Queen Tiye leaned over and whispered to her son.

'You have offered grave insult to Shishnak. Retaliation must follow.'

The Royal Circle moved from one item of business to another. The despatch of heralds and messengers, the strengthening of troops beyond the Third Cataract, the incursion of desert raiders against merchants, the despatch of chariots along the Horus Road to protect the diamond mines of Sinai. Routine business. My mind drifted to Sobeck, Aunt Isithia, other matters, only to be drawn back to Nefertiti's hair. As the murmured conversation continued, I composed a poem:

> Glorious as the Rising Morning Star,
> Sopet at the beginning of the New Year!
> Jubilee upon Jubilee!
> Shining light, fair of skin.
> Lovely the glance from her eye!
> Sweet the speech of her lips!
> Gracefully she treads the earth!
> My heart is captured by her movements.
> All men say her embrace is beatitude,
> Honey-sweet her kiss.
> Her beloved must be first amongst men.

My reverie was broken by Shishnak's grating voice. He

was talking about Tushratta, the King of Mitanni, and a scribe was distributing tablets of hardened polished clay – letters from the Mitanni court in the birdlike Akkadian script. Shishnak talked swiftly, about the importance of Egypt's alliance with the Mitanni, how those who lived between the Upper Tigris and the Euphrates were a vital element in this alliance.

'Princess Tadukhiya,' Shishnak stared round the Royal Circle, 'of Narahin is a most comely young woman. Fellow councillors, you may recall how she was sent into Egypt to marry the Crown Prince Tuthmosis, who has now gone into the Glorious West.' Shishnak gestured at Akhenaten. 'The Mitanni still expect us to honour our treaty's obligations: their Princess must marry the Son of Egypt, its Pharaoh.' Shishnak had loosed his bolt at the obvious love between Akhenaten and Nefertiti. The silence was palpable but the shift in Nefertiti's shoulders, the way Akhenaten's head came back, spoke eloquently of their anger.

'I have a wife.' Akhenaten's voice was harsh. He gestured to Nefertiti. 'I have a wife,' he repeated. 'The heiress, Fair of Form, Lady of Graciousness, Worthy of Love, Beloved of the Aten, Mistress of Upper and Lower Egypt, Great Wife of the King.' His voice rose to a shout of defiance. 'She Whom He loves, Lady of the Two Lands, May she live for ever and ever!'

'Quite so. Quite so,' Hotep replied, bowing to Nefertiti. 'But now, my lord, you are joint ruler of the Two Lands. We have allies to please, treaties to keep, obligations to meet . . .'

* * *

Later at the Palace of the Aten, I was part of the heated exchanges between Akenhaten, Nefertiti and Ay about the marriage proposal made by Hotep and Shishnak. Oh, they had accepted Akhenaten's speech, they had offered no insult. They had pointed out how the Divine One's harem was full of princesses from every corner of the empire and beyond. So, for the sake of Egypt, Akhenaten would have to follow his father's example. At last Queen Tiye had intervened and, in a worldweary voice, declared that her son must reflect on the advice offered and make his reply. The meeting of the Royal Circle ended. Akhenaten and Nefertiti had not even let Meryre finish gabbling the prayers before they rose, gave the most perfunctory of bows, and swept out of the Council Chamber. Nefertiti had controlled her anger, not so much at the marriage alliance but at Shishnak's impudence. Now, in the shadows of the hall of audience, she gave vent to her fury.

'I will take Shishnak's head,' she swore, 'pluck out those venomous eyes and pickle them in salt. I'll take those lips and sew them together with twine.' Hands resting on her swollen abdomen, she stared solemnly at me then burst out laughing. 'Ah well,' she sighed, 'it will have to be done.'

Akhenaten nodded.

'It will have to be done,' Ay confirmed, 'and the sooner the better. My lord, they hope you will refuse. They will invoke your father's will' – he caught Akhenaten's glance – 'I mean the Magnificent One.'

'Where is she now,' Akhenaten asked, 'this Mitanni princess?'

'In the white-walled city,' Ay replied, 'in a mansion outside Memphis.'

'She is to be brought South,' Akhenaten replied. Leaning over, he caressed his wife's swollen stomach, kissing her on the shoulder, neck and face.

'Every soul has its song,' he whispered, 'and you are mine. Only you, Heiress of Egypt, Woman of the Sacred Line and the Holy Blood, will bear my child. Only the issue of our bodies and souls will wear the crowns of Egypt. You are my Princess and my altar.'

Ay grasped my hand and gestured with his head to leave. We rose, bowed and left Akhenaten and Nefertiti lost in each other.

The decision had been made. Both myself and Ay were left to supervise the practical details. Akhenaten's decision to marry the Mitanni Princess was proclaimed later that day. Ay was distracted, being more concerned with implementing more changes in the great palace. Nakhtimin, with his bland eyes and secretive face, was promoted to Standard Bearer of the Royal Household with direct command over the imperial bodyguard. Another kinsman of Queen Tiye, Anen, was given high office in the priesthood of Amun. Those who could not be trusted were also dealt with. Certain Generals were despatched North to the Delta, chief scribes were found fresh employment in other cities along the Nile or sent on so-called urgent business to the provinces. Leading citizens of Thebes, not to mention the Keepers of the Secrets, were constantly entertained and regaled at the Palace of the Aten. Akhenaten and Nefertiti didn't seem to care about such details. They were more concerned with their own whispered conversations, visiting the House of Paintings or supervising the construction of a small altar to the Aten. Real power rested with Ay. He met with notables, supervised the construction of more buildings, linking Akhenaten's palace to my old House of Instruction where the children of the Kap had been raised. Warehouses, storerooms, and granaries were built to house Akhenaten's newfound wealth and status: the Per Hagu, the House of Foodstuffs, the Per Nuble, the House of Gold, the Per Ehu, the House of Oxen, the Per Asheu, the House of Fruits and, above all, the Per Ahuu, the House of War, with its armouries stocked full of spears, shields, swords and daggers. Ay gave responsibility for the House of War to me as he did the construction of more barracks and the selection of mercenaries to swell Akhenaten's personal military retinue.

My master only became interested in these new buildings once they had been completed and were ready for decoration. Then he'd become feverishly involved, insisting the halls be flooded with light, that the carved columns of wood were to be painted in different colours, the doors festooned in gold and silver and the lintels decorated with flashing lapis lazuli and malachite. He personally supervised the paintings on the walls and the layout of the new gardens. He'd go out as the ground was broken up and shout instructions at the workers, where to plant, how to sow grass, how to cast seed, plant bushes and shrubs so as to catch both the sun and the rain.

Days passed one into the other. Ay received reports from Thebes and the rest of the palace: he discussed these with me before moving into council with Akhenaten and Nefertiti. One morning Snefru, now Captain of my personal guard, interrupted a meeting to say we had a visitor. I hardly recognised the old man leaning against the courtyard wall with his snow-white hair, wrinkled face and watery eyes.

'Master Mahu.' I certainly recognised the voice.

'Why, it's Api! What brings you here?'

'Your Aunt Isithia has died.'

'How unfortunate!'

'I thought I should come to inform you. She fell one night . . .' Api's mouth opened and closed. 'She fell. She was on the roof terrace,' he gabbled on, 'and we heard a scream. She must have slipped.'

'Yes,' I agreed, 'she must have slipped.'

'But she hadn't drunk much. She must have leaned over.'

I recalled the roof with its couches and its tables, the trelliswork fence. Isithia cradling her wine cup. Sobeck's dark shadow creeping up the outside staircase. He always could move like a cat.

'Death swoops like a falcon,' I murmured.

Api was staring at me. 'It's a pity you never saw her before . . .'

'It's a pity I ever met her,' I snarled.

Api recoiled. He fell to his knees, shuffling back, the toes of his sandals scraping the paving stones. 'I meant to give no . . .'

'None taken. Who inherits the old bitch's house and goods?'

'The priests of Amun: the house, the chattels, the land. They all go to the House of Silver at Karnak.'

'And you?' I asked.

'Nothing! After years of service, nothing!'

I walked round him. Servants crossed the courtyard staring curiously at us.

'And neither do I have anything to give you.'

'Master, I thought you could help. You are soon to be Chief of Police in Thebes.'

'What?' I clutched the man by the front of his robe and dragged him to his feet. He was nothing more than a bag of bones. 'What did you say? How do you know?'

'Your aunt was talking about it just before she died. She was laughing. "Fancy Mahu," she declared, "Baboon of the South becoming Chief of Police." Master, I have nothing!' he wailed again. I recalled Api trailing round after Aunt Isithia, no better than a dog.

'I was never cruel to you,' he moaned.

'Did she kill my mother?'

Api stared at the ground.

'Did she kill my mother?' I insisted, loosening my grip.

'In a way, yes. When your father was absent, it was one cruelty heaped upon another. After you were born,' he hurried on, 'your mother had a fever.'

'Aunt Isithia's potions!' I stared up at the sky. I could have howled like a dog. 'Because of that bitch I am what I am. Where's her corpse?'

'In the Necropolis, the House of Death belonging to the Guild of Falcons. The priests of Amun sent it there.'

'I am sure they did. They'll take her money and put her corpse into the nearest hole in the ground. She's not to be buried with my parents. As for you . . .'

Api fell to his knees, hands outstretched. As Snefru came through the doorway, cudgel raised, I waved him back. I returned to my own quarters and brought back five small ingots, an *ounou* of silver and three precious stones. I pushed these into Api's hands.

'Goodbye, Api. You are a fortunate man.'

He drew his brows together.

'I thought of killing you as well,' I whispered.

His jaw dropped in horror and awe.

'What did I say?' I smiled. 'I have forgotten already – so have you, haven't you Api?'

I watched him go stumbling across the courtyard and immediately sent a message to Sobeck that I wished to meet him. In the days following I received no reply whilst I was soon taken up with the arrangements for the arrival of Princess Tadukhiya at the Palace of the Aten. She arrived on the appropriate day with a small retinue of giggling maids, carts full of treasure and a group of Hittite slaves. Akhenaten met her in the courtyard. The Princess herself sat hidden behind a veiled canopy. Akhenaten exchanged pleasantries with the notables who had escorted his new wife then dismissed them. Nefertiti, standing in cloth of gold, shimmering with gorgeous diamonds and precious stones, stood like a statue under the shade of a parasol held by Ay. Akhenaten inspected the gifts then turned to the Hittites, strange-looking men with the front part of their heads completely shaved, parrot-like faces and bizarre tattoos in dark blues and reds across their chests and arms. Akhenaten was fascinated by them even though they looked a sorry lot. He ordered them to sing a song of their own country and, whilst they did so, joined his wife under the parasol, tapping his foot on the ground, head slightly turned. The song was the most mournful dirge, more like the cackling of birds than the song of a choir. Nefertiti giggled. Akhenaten, however, acted as if something petty had distracted him. Once the song had ended, he asked them what they did in their own country. They replied that they were musicians captured in a raid.

'Were you really?' Akhenaten snapped his fingers.

I hurried across with another parasol and he walked round the slaves, touching their skin.

'What do you think, Mahu?'

'If they had to sing for their living,' I replied, 'they'd soon starve.'

Akhenaten grimaced. He continued his inspection. I noticed at the back of the group were two Medjay, scouts who accompanied the procession to make sure light fingers went nowhere near the treasure wagon. Whilst Akhenaten hummed a song under his breath and perused the carts full of treasure, I recalled what Api had told me. *Was* I to be made Chief of Police of Thebes? How had my aunt known? Why hadn't Akhenaten discussed the matter with me?

'I know what we'll do.' Akhenaten stood on top of the cart, his fine robes spilling out about him. 'Mahu, I want these Hittites to wear women's wigs and dress in female attire. I am going to call them my Orchestra of the Sun. I will educate them myself.'

'Why women's attire?'

'Their days as warriors are finished.' Akhenaten clambered out of the cart. 'They will be a symbol of the everlasting peace which my reign will bring, when swords are hammered into ploughshares and the chariots of war become carriages of pleasure.'

I could see the Princess's arrival had interrupted Akhenaten's thinking so I kept silent. I was always nervous about talking to my master in public lest the name Akhenaten might slip from my lips. The Prince had made me swear a great oath, my hand over the Sun Disc, that his sacred name would remain hidden until his Father gave him a sign to publish it, as Akhenaten said, to the ends of the earth and beyond.

The retinue was becoming restless. Akhenaten had not been discourteous. It was customary for such a period of waiting to be observed before a prince met his new wife. The poor Hittites looked totally bemused, shuffling their feet and muttering to each other in their clicking tongue. Akhenaten went and stood by Nefertiti. At last the sweating palanquin-holders were ordered to release their precious burden. They did so gently, the curtains were pulled back and Tadukhiya emerged. She was small and dark, no more than fourteen summers old, her black hair bound up under a rather exotic head-dress. She was garbed in gaudy but costly robes. She tripped gracefully toward Akhenaten, who grasped her hands and kissed her on each cheek, staring down at her affectionately. The contrast between the two women was startling. The Mitanni was perfectly formed but rather small, with slanted eyes in a dark-skinned face, a pouting mouth, pointed ears, and her plump cheeks glistening with oil. Nefertiti visibly relaxed; this new wife would be no rival.

'She looks like a monkey,' she whispered to me. 'That's what we will call her.'

And so her name became Khiya. No cruelty was intended. Khiya was a term of endearment, no more insulting than Akhenaten's greeting in which he described Nefertiti as 'Ta-Shepses, the Favourite'. He welcomed her to the palace, staring down at her, grasping her hands whilst she gazed shyly back, raising a hand to her mouth to hide a smile, a gesture she repeated when taken across to meet Nefertiti. At the time I thought Khiya was stupid. I was wrong: she learned quickly and wanted to survive. I noticed how she did not need further introduction to my master's retinue: Ay she knew by name and reputation, the same for other members of the household, myself included. Horemheb and Rameses were praised as great warriors and I realised, as she was taken through the group, that someone had explained to her in great detail her new husband's household as well as the power and status of his notables. Khiya was given her own quarters in new chambers Ay had ordered to be built and soon came to be accepted more as Nefertiti's principal lady-in-waiting than a wife in her own right. Indeed, Khiya trailed Nefertiti like a pet monkey, giggling and chattering a stream of innocent questions. Nefertiti was more than content.

'She is pretty and rather empty-headed,' Nefertiti confided in me when we walked in the orchard to take the breeze wafting in from the river. Nefertiti often insisted on this, walking slowly, holding her stomach whilst discussing the doings of the day. Pregnancy had given her a fullness, a contentment which enhanced her beauty, a gracefulness both alluring and majestic. I had not forgotten that day in the orchard, the strange drink and even stranger dreams which followed. Nefertiti made no reference to this but treated me as a brother, asking my advice or questioning me about my first meeting with her husband. Khiya never joined us on such walks.

'She can certainly talk,' Nefertiti confided. 'She chatters like a monkey, Mahu. Does she ever confide in you?'

I shook my head. I never said what I really knew or felt, at least not until I was certain. I would have loved to have questioned Nefertiti about Api's strange remark about being appointed Chief of Police at Thebes. The honour intrigued me yet I was wary; such an office could mean my removal from the Royal Household and, above all, from her presence.

'Do you think Khiya stupid, Mahu?'

'No one is stupid.'

Nefertiti clapped her hands and laughed. 'There speaks the bodyguard.' She narrowed her eyes. 'The Chief of Police.'

'Chief of police?' I queried.

'We'll, that's what you are, isn't it, Mahu? Searching out those who wish to hurt my beloved? Protecting us?'

'You have Horemheb and Rameses, not to mention your Uncle Nakhtimin.'

'Put not your trust, Mahu, in the power of Pharaoh nor your confidence in the war-chariots of Egypt.' She shivered and rubbed her arms. 'Years ago in Akhmin I visited one of those soothsayers. She said my death would be at the hands of a great friend.'

'My aunt was a soothsayer. I don't believe in such things.'

'You don't believe in anything, do you, Mahu?' She came closer. 'What is Amun to you, or the power of the Aten? Well?'

'I find it difficult to believe,' I replied, 'as my master does, that the gods wander the heavens like the massed priests of Amun. Go down to Thebes, Excellency, watch the seething mass of people. Do you really think the gods are interested in them?'

'But the Aten?' she insisted. 'The One? The Invisible and Undivided?'

'I wish him well, Excellency. And, when he introduces himself to me, I'll return the courtesy.'

Nefertiti tweaked my cheek, grasped my arm and walked on down the pebbled path between the trellised fence of the vine groves. 'We were talking about Khiya, an empty-head, a mere child. But,' Nefertiti paused. 'Sometimes, you watch me, Mahu. Why?'

'You know the reason,' I replied softly.

Again the laugh, this time self-conscious.

'Khiya is different. She watches me like a monkey, as if learning my movements, wanting to imitate them.'

'She's in awe of you,' I replied. 'She wishes to please.'

'A willing student in the arts of love,' Nefertiti replied mischievously, 'very astute, very active and eager. I have watched her closely. I had to tell her that squatting on all fours is not the only pose for a Princess of Egypt. She is also very noisy. Squeals like a cat. Akhenaten is much taken with her.'

In fact Akhenaten treated Khiya with great affection as

if she was some newly bought toy. She often joined us at meals and, when he decided to walk in the cool of the evening, she would always be invited along. Nefertiti, of course, watched her like a bird of prey would its next meal.

'She'll never breed,' she confided hotly. 'No child of hers will wear the Double Crown of Egypt.'

Of course, as the weeks passed, Khiya became accustomed to the routine of the court. Ay was now often absent or closeted in his own chamber, poring over maps as well as reports from his myriad spies in Thebes. But he did not distance himself from me; we met every day for at least an hour. Ay had delineated my duties most carefully.

'You, Mahu,' he would sit squatting on a cushion, hands extended, 'you are to watch and guard the Palace of the Aten. I will take care of affairs beyond its walls.'

And then he would deal with business: describing the affairs of Egypt, the deployment of his regiments, the rumours and gossip from the temples, the quality of the harvest, the bartering in the marketplace. He pursued one aim – to keep everything in order to sustain harmony.

'Let the days merge into each other,' he remarked. 'Let people not realise' – he gave that crooked smile – 'at least not now, that there is a new power in Egypt.'

I was tempted to raise the question of the post of Chief of Police in Thebes, but I decided against it. Ay himself was responsible for this. The city had two Police Chiefs, one for the East and one for the West of Thebes; they reported directly to Rahimere, the Mayor. Any change in this would have disturbed the harmony, the peace Ay so zealously pursued.

'Keep close to Khiya,' he also advised. 'She's new to the palace.'

'But one day, surely,' I mused, 'our master will have his own harem, his House of Love? We can't watch them all.'

'One day, some day,' Ay retorted caustically. 'That does not matter. For the moment you have your orders.'

I didn't need to watch Khiya. She watched me. I never really understood the attraction. She had learned about her nickname and accepted it with her usual good-natured charm. Perhaps it was mine, Baboon of the South, or the fact that she had seen Akhenaten and Nefertiti confide in me and thought that whatever was good for the Great Royal Wife was good for her. At table she would always single me out for comment or just sit and stare, those black eyes studying me curiously. As Nefertiti became more confined to her own quarters, surrounded by physicians under Pentju and the ever-chattering midwives, Khiya would search me out. We'd walk hand-in-hand like brother and sister through the palace grounds. Sometimes, when we were well away from public view, she'd sit at my feet like a scholar in the House of Instruction and gaze up at me. In some ways she was like Nefertiti, asking me question after question about her new husband, his early days. On occasion we could hear him training his orchestra, and Khiya would laugh.

'So strange,' she mused, 'how he is interested in so many minor matters. He showed me his House of Paintings. The Prince explained how all art must speak the truth.

But what *is* the truth, Mahu? Why is he attracted to the Aten? In my country we have many gods – they live in the trees and rocks.'

I'd answer like a teacher or an absentminded father would his daughter. On one occasion she looked away, then glanced back. I saw it, just for a moment, a knowing look, eyes a thousand years old in a mere child's face. Oh, we all underestimated Khiya – and that includes myself. Yes, there was the usual feeling of unease but nothing alarming, just a glance, the pitch of her voice but we constantly misread the signs. If we met a jackal skulking through the narrow streets of the Necropolis, an ibis wading through the Nile or an ape grinning behind some palm fronds, we reckoned it must be the visitation of a god, a sign of things to come. We ignored Khiya at our cost and the price we paid was terrible. Ay confessed she was his real mistake and, if that cobra of a man could be deceived, why not me?

More pressing matters claimed our attention. Nefertiti eventually gave birth. Pentju withdrew and the midwives gathered with the silver and ebony birthing-chair, pots of the shepen plant and the corpses of skinned mice, should things go awry. The shaven heads of Amun-Ra sent five priestesses to represent the Goddess Isis and the rest. Akhenaten sent them packing but superstition still had its day. Charms were fashioned out of fishbone, prayers were offered to ward off 'Him', the Thief of the Underworld, who prowled the cot beds of infants ready to suck their life out. Akhenaten prayed to his strange god, demanding his blessings. In the end, the gods, or Chance, arranged things smoothly. Nefertiti gave birth to twin daughters, lusty girls who made the right cry and were born on an auspicious day. Two more human souls, destined to be caught up in the giddy whirl of Akhenaten's dreams.

My master was pleased and proud. There was feasting and rejoicing in the brilliant, colonnaded halls where the babes were praised and fussed. Presents were showered on them, jewels and trinkets, robes and foodstuffs. Akhenaten preened himself, comparing his prowess to other Pharaohs, though I knew his soul too well, or thought I did. I caught his disappointment that he had no son. Suddenly, my days of festival were harshly interrupted. I kept thinking about Api's strange remarks and wondered why Sobeck had not replied. In the end he did. A peddler came to the kitchens and Snefru brought me the message: a friend wished to meet me and buy me a present of the most exquisite jewellery.

'I am a crocodile immersed in dread.
I am a crocodile who takes by robbery.'

(Spell 88: *The Book of the Dead*)

Chapter 13

Dressed in one of Snefru's garish cloaks and carrying my sealed jar in a leather pannier slung across my shoulder, I went across the Nile to the Necropolis: a journey which always reminded me that, as in the palace, life and death sat cheek by jowl. At the quayside a beggarman, squirming through the crowds, seized my wrist, going down on his knees to show his peaceful intent.

'The jeweller,' he whispered through sore gums, 'his stall is closed. However, your host will welcome you at the Sign of the Ankh in the Street of the Caskets near the Basketmakers' Quarter in the City of the Dead. Do you understand?'

'I understand.' I tried to shake off his grip.

'Go in peace, pilgrim,' he smiled. He leaned forward in a gust of stale sweat and cheap oil. 'And be careful you are not followed.'

A boatman took me across the Nile. The sun was dipping and the fishing boats were out, the men on board shouting at each other, eager to find the best stretch to catch lampreys, skit, grey mullet and the pale-backed dark-bellied batisoida which always swam upside down. Henbirds, alarmed by the noise, rustled the branches of trees and brought the papyrus groves to life with their squawking and nesting. A screech owl hunted over the mudflats. Higher up, against the blood-red sky, vultures and buzzards patrolled; when one plunged, it was the sign for others to join the feasting.

The river was so busy it was impossible to see if anyone was following me. Matters worsened when the river guards, in their war-barge, manoeuvred along the edge of the reeds and shouted at us to move away. The alarm had been raised by some fishermen still waving their pitch torches as a sign of danger. Apparently a group of harpooners in their skiffs had cornered a young hippopotamus in the shallows only to find another, a cow, ready to give birth. This, in turn, had attracted the attention of crocodiles. The bull, summoned to his mate's distress call, also returned to enter the fray.

The harpooners had withdrawn but the hippopotami were now so agitated they were likely to attack anything which caught their attention. I used the confusion to stare across at the dappled river bright in the dying rays of the sun and the dancing torches of the fishermen. I was looking for a boat, a punt or a barge with one passenger, someone who seemed out of place, but I could detect nothing.

Having landed safely at the Quayside of the Dead with its brooding, ill-carved statue of the green-skinned Osiris, I made my way across the Place of Scavengers and into the warren of streets in the lower part of the City of the

Dead. It was a sombre place, suitable only for those who wished to shelter from the law and needed the darkness to cloak their activities. Sailors and marines staggered about, beer jugs in hand. Ladies from a House of Delight drifted through them trying to entice them in a cloud of cheap perfume, clattering jewellery and sloe-eyed glances, their rouged mouths in a permanent pout. Elsewhere, beggars, scorpion men, confidence tricksters, Rhinoceri, outlaws from the Red Lands, the grotesque and the crippled rubbed shoulders with grey-robed Desert Wanderers.

The lanes and streets were arrow-thin funnels lit by the occasional blaze from an oil lamp or the dancing fire of a cresset torch. The air was bittersweet with the stench of corruption from the cheap embalmers' shops where the corpses of the poor were over-dried in baths of natron, hung on hooks to dry, pickled, stuffed with dirty rags, then doused in cheap perfumed oil before being handed back to their relatives. Casketmakers, shabti-sellers and coffin-polishers touted for business. Women of every nation, skimpily dressed or clothed mysteriously in hoods and robes, offered their bodies for sale. Tale-tellers and minstrels offered their wares, while professional travellers shouted how they had stories for sale about a land of frozen whiteness, yellow-skinned men who lived in palaces or roaming hordes of barbarians who killed and plundered and drank from the skulls of their enemies. A sideshow in front of a shop, covered with a patched tapestry of faded animal skins, offered a chance to view a Syrian 'strong as a ram, pleasure three women at once'. Another show invited the curious to view a woman with three breasts, a dwarf with two heads or a bird which could talk like a man. Soothsayers and fortune-tellers vied with dancing troupes to catch my attention. A gang of pimps shrieked at a group of white-garbed priests, dancing madly in the name of their foreign god, to leave them and their customers alone. Stalls and shops spilled out rubbish. Bakers and meat-sellers offered platters of freshly cooked lamb, beef, goose and fish, grilled above spluttering charcoal and spiced hot to the tongue to satisfy any taste as well as to hide any putrefaction. Such a mêlée made it impossible to see if I was being followed. I felt uneasy because I was left alone, as if protected by some invisible presence, yet I could see nothing, except for a shaggy-headed dwarf, dressed in a striped robe, who always seemed to be either beside me or in front.

I reached the Sign of the Ankh, a pleasure-house and beer-shop which catered for the casket-, coffin- and basket-makers. On that particular evening it was deserted inside, although its small courtyard was full of bully-boys in their leather kilts, baldrics and thick marching sandals, lounging round a cracked fountain. They looked up as I entered but no one rose to challenge me. The entrance to the shop was also guarded. Inside, the low-ceilinged room, reeking of sawdust and burned oil, was brightly lit. A row of barrels and baskets were stacked at one end. Sobeck sat on a pile of cushions under a shuttered window. Others of his gang stood or squatted, deliberately shrouded by the shifting shadows. Sobeck smiled as I entered, put down the puppy he was playing with and rose to greet me. His eyes, however, were still on the door.

'You did well, my friend,' he said, then called: 'Was he followed?'

The dwarf replied in a guttural tongue I could not understand.

'Apparently you were,' Sobeck clasped my hand, 'but we lost him.' He sat down and gestured at the cushions piled at the base of a wooden column. I took the dagger from my sash and squatted down. A jar of beer was thrust into my hand. Sobeck cleared the platters from the small table which separated us. The puppy, unsteady on its legs, stumbled over, licked my knee, sniffed at the basket and curled up beside me. Sobeck raised his goblet in a toast. I replied but didn't sip.

'It's not poisoned,' Sobeck laughed.

He picked up my cup, took a generous sip and handed it back. He looked better than the last time; his face was not so lean, though fresh scars marked his cheeks and upper right arm. His kilt was of good quality, as was the shawl which draped his shoulders and the sandals on his feet. Rings and bracelets glittered on his fingers, wrists and arms flashed like fire. His head and face were cleanly shaved, gleaming with oil; his eyes were the same, like those of a hungry hunting cat. He kept his dagger close by.

'You are well, Mahu, Chief of Police?'

'I am not Ch—'

'You soon will be. I heard your aunt laughing about it, that's how I know.'

'The night you visited her?'

Sobeck grinned behind his hand. He ordered dishes of catfish with plump, fresh lettuce and slices of lush pomegranate. A beggar girl served us. Sobeck took the dishes and divided the food between us.

'Well?' He chewed noisily. 'What do you want?'

I finished my food, opened the basket and took out the sealed alabaster jar full of flies buzzing over a lump of honey. I placed it on the table before him. Sobeck stopped chewing. 'Is this a gift?'

'Yes, it is.'

'For killing your aunt?' Sobeck pulled a face. 'It was easy enough. She was arrogant, and thought the soldiers camped in the gardens outside her house would be protection enough. She apparently liked to be alone. Anyway, her neck snapped like a twig. Now you bring me a jar of honey and some buzzing flies?'

I opened my wallet and placed three precious stones on the table.

'I want you to take the jar of flies to the embalmers and ask them to place it next to the head of Isithia's corpse. She never could stand flies.'

Sobeck smiled. 'And? There are three stones here.'

'You are to bribe the embalmers to remove her heart and its protective scarab before they wrap the corpse in its bandages. I want my aunt's soul to wander the Underworld.'

'I didn't think you believed in it?'

'I am a calculating man, Sobeck. Just in case.'

Sobeck tapped the third diamond. 'And?'

'Isithia's house will be deserted. I want it burned to the ground, it and everything in it – but do not harm the willow tree in the orchard beyond.'

'A fire?' Sobeck glanced up at the ceiling. 'That will take oil, not to mention desperate men.'

I placed a fourth diamond on the table.

Sobeck swept it up in his hand. 'You must have hated her.'

'She made me what I am.'

'And what are you, Mahu?'

'As the tree is planted, so it grows.'

'So what do you want?' Sobeck's voice was barely above a whisper. 'What do you really want, Mahu, friend of princes, confidant and counsellor, soon to be Chief of Police?'

For a moment he looked like the boy I used to play with in the Kap, running wild through the trees or hiding from Weni. I felt tearful but the tears didn't come. 'What about this Chief of Police thing?' I asked.

'Your aunt told me as I came up the steps. She thought I was her manservant. She kept repeating it as if savouring a joke. "My little Mahu," she laughed. "The ugly Baboon, Chief of Police. Well, I never!"'

'How did she know?'

'I never stopped to ask. In fact, it was only afterwards I reflected on what she had said.'

'You saw no letter on the table, no documents?'

'I was there to exact my revenge, not to steal things. I'll do that before I burn the house down.' Sobeck pushed a piece of fish into his mouth. His eyes were no longer so hard. 'Oh, you'll become Chief of Police, Mahu, don't worry about that. We are in the time of waiting, aren't we? The old Pharaoh is dying and the Grotesque waits like a cat hiding in the bushes ready to pounce: he and his two red-haired relatives, the Akhmin gang. They are already making their presence felt.' He leaned over and filled my cup. 'It's our business, Mahu, to watch things: to keep our ear close to the door and listen to the rumours and whispers. Who has been sent here? Who has been sent there? Which officer is in charge of that district? Why are certain regiments despatched upriver, and others brought closer to the city? Why is Ay so insistent on hiring mercenaries?' He caught my surprise and smiled. 'Oh yes, he's supposed to be strengthening the garrison of Akhmin: the numbers have grown so large you'd think the Hyksos had returned. Sooner or later, perhaps sooner than later, Ay will appoint a certain General,' he waved his hand, 'the next Mayor of Thebes.'

'And the new post?' I added. 'Chief of Police?'

'That's my clever Baboon, Mahu! Ay can't do it all in one sweep. It's like drawing a picture: a brush-stroke here, a brush-stroke there, not yet completed, not even formed, but the artist knows what he intends. So, Mahu, Baboon of the South, my question still stands. What do you really want? Is it power? Do you like being close to Ay and his gang?'

'I want to be part of something,' I replied, 'to please and be pleased.'

'To love and be loved?'

'Sobeck, sarcasm doesn't suit you.'

'But the Princess Nefertiti does you. Is that the real reason, Mahu? Is that why you love the palace?'

'Why are you *here*?' I retorted brusquely.

'I'll come to that by and by. Do you know,' Sobeck picked up the dagger and moved it from hand to hand, 'I really do like you, Mahu, more than anyone. I'll never forget I owe you my life. If you hadn't sent me that message, I would have sent you one. When you are Chief of Police, you and I can do business together.'

'You already seem to have a lot of partners.' I gazed

around at the men half-concealed in the shadows. 'Business partners?' I queried. 'Where is the Ape?'

Sobeck shouted into the darkness for a basket to be brought. It was dirty and stained with blood which had seeped through the meshes. The little puppy beside me stirred so I stroked it gently. Sobeck placed the gruesome basket on the table, took off the lid and drew out the severed head with its half-closed eyes, jutting mouth and jaw, the neck of fraying black flesh. He placed it gently back. 'The Ape or what's left of him. He tried to betray me. You've heard of the Hyenas, Mahu?'

Of course I had. The Hyenas were the violent gangs who swarmed through the slums of Thebes and the squalid streets of the Necropolis. Sobeck ordered the basket to be taken away and traced the scar on his face.

'I also owe you for the treasure you sent me. It has helped me to make a few adjustments to my life.'

'You control the gangs?' I asked.

'Almost,' he replied. 'But by next year I will be able to say yes. I learned a lot at that prison oasis, even more on the journey back. Pharaoh has order in his kingdom, I shall have order in mine. The tomb-robbers, the pimps, the smugglers, the traders in flesh, the scorpion men, the unemployed, the mercenaries and discharged soldiers will all know their places in my little world, and if they don't – well, they don't deserve to be here. I'll have my House of Silver and my troops. Whatever you ask, Mahu, from my kingdom you shall have.' He snapped his fingers. 'As simple as that.'

'But you couldn't find the man who followed me?' I taunted.

'No.' Sobeck smiled thinly. 'We still make mistakes, Mahu. It's just like being in the House of Instruction. Learning doesn't come like a meal on a platter. So,' he lifted his cup again, 'let's toast the past and the future.'

'Have you met Maya?' I asked.

Sobeck shook his head. 'He's the only one I leave alone. I don't know why, but one day I will renew my acquaintance. He doesn't know I am alive.'

I didn't answer.

'I know all about the rest. Pentju's in love, you know – a lady called Tenbra. He's infatuated with her, they will be married within the year. I hope she keeps him away from the House of Delight here in the Necropolis, otherwise he will need all his medical skill to cure the ailments he'll catch.'

'And Horemheb and Rameses?'

'Ah, two cheeks of the same arse! Two dirty nostrils in the same nose. My prize bully-boys. Horemheb is a puritan. He looks at a woman and immediately thinks of breeding rather than pleasure. Rameses is the one I watch. Venomous as a viper – he likes inflicting pain. Oh yes, he's a visitor here, well-known in the House of Delight for his use of the whip, the stick and other petty cruelties. I often wonder if his old friend Horemheb knows about his private pastimes.' Sobeck straightened his shoulders and stuck his chest out, such a clever imitation of Horemheb that I laughed.

'Horemheb wants to be a great General, the new Ahmose.' Sobeck breathed in. 'He's of peasant stock from the Delta, born of a young girl who caught the Magnificent One's eye.'

'He's the Divine One's son?'

'Might be. Or of one of his courtiers. The Divine One,' Sobeck's face turned ugly, 'could be generous with his Royal Ornaments, only that he had to give, you never took, as I found to my cost. Does he still drink the juice of the poppy?' Sobeck scratched at his chin.

'They say,' he continued, chatting quickly to show off his knowledge, 'the Magnificent One is more interested in his eldest daughter Sitamun than he is in his wife. But, one day soon, he will die. They will bury him out in that great mausoleum he has built, guarded by those Colossi of red quartzite.' He leaned across the table. 'Now that's one tomb, Mahu, I intend to visit.'

'You were talking of our companions?'

'Meryre . . .' Sobeck shook his head. 'Such a pure priest, such a naughty boy: he loves Kushite girls, the fatter the better. He doesn't pray so much when he's squealing between mounds of perfumed oiled flesh.' Sobeck rocked backwards and forwards. 'Huy is different. Oh, he likes the ladies but it's wealth he wants, and power! To become a Great One of Pharaoh and rise high in the tree.'

'You know so much.'

'Of course I do, Mahu. Where do you think these people hire servants? They come to the marketplace or the Necropolis, this young man, that young woman. These people go home to chatter and gossip. It's surprising how many people talk as if servants don't exist. Oh, by the way, you should tell your master to be careful. The great ones of Thebes, not to forget our shaven heads in the Temple of Amun, hate him beyond all understanding.'

'And what do you know of the Akhmin gang?'

'Oh, you mean God's Father Ay and Nefertiti the Great Wife?' Sobeck whistled through his teeth. 'They are very close, very close indeed! Ah well.' He picked up the diamonds he had placed beneath the cushion, took the pouch from his belt and poured them in. 'Watch the night sky, Mahu, and you'll see the fire.'

He helped me to my feet.

The puppy also rose, yelping. Sobeck leaned down, grasped it by the nape of the neck and pulled it up.

'I am still in the dog-skinning business, Mahu! This will be good for the child of some pilgrim.' The dog yelped again, little legs flailing in the air. 'An orphan.' Sobeck placed it back. 'No one will miss it.'

I leaned down and scooped it up; the puppy licked my hand. 'I'll take it.'

'What?' Sobeck laughed. 'Mahu, have you gone sentimental? But you have made a good choice.'

'I know,' I replied. 'It's a greyhound, isn't it? They make good watchdogs.' I held Sobeck's gaze. 'And if treated affectionately, will give the utmost loyalty. I don't give a fig about a puppy. What I am anxious about, Sobeck, is taking a goblet of wine on the roof of my house whilst some silent shadow comes creeping up the stairs.'

Sobeck put his arm round my shoulder, pushing me towards the door. 'Keep your dog, Mahu. You are going to need all the protection you can get.'

I paused. Again he gave me a squeeze, nails pressing into the fleshy part of my arm.

'We talked about what we want,' he whispered. 'Horemheb's ambition, Huy's lust for wealth and power, but your master, the Grotesque, he's the dangerous one. He wants to be a god.'

'So does every Pharaoh.'

'Ah yes, Mahu, but the Grotesque is different. He really thinks he is a god, the only god, the God Incarnate. Mark my words, those who look for god in everything end up looking for god in themselves – and usually find it.' He released his grip and patted me on the shoulder. 'You are safe to go. No one will trouble you.'

Still wearing Snefru's coat, I reached the quayside. Ferries were few as darkness had fallen. The river people were reluctant to ply their trade, fearful of pirates and smugglers, not to mention hungry crocodiles or angry hippopotami. However, as soon as I arrived the punt appeared, broad and squat, low in the water. A young man stood in the stern, pole resting against his shoulder. An old man, whom I took to be his father, sat just before the prow carved in the shape of a panther's head: above this a pitch torch flared whilst a quilted hide of sheepskin covered the rear benches.

'Fruit,' the old man called, gesturing, 'but if you want . . . ?'

I climbed in, handed over some copper *debens* and sat in front of the old man. He crouched, red-rimmed eyes smiling, chomping on his gums. From a card round his neck hung an amulet, a jackal's head. The old man was singing softly under his breath, rocking backwards and forwards. I wondered how much beer he had drunk. The puntsman was skilled enough and the craft moved away, out from the dangers lurking along the reed-filled banks.

I clasped the puppy, warm under my cloak, my mind full of thoughts about Sobeck and the hidden threat of his words. The old man chattered, but I didn't really listen. The dancing torch flame caught my gaze. My eyes grew heavy. I was stupid, I relaxed. The strengthening cold breeze awoke me. When I stirred and glanced up, the old man didn't look so cheery or welcoming; his was an evil face full of ancient sin. He was staring at me as if I was a bull for the slaughter, squinting to see if I had a pendant beneath my cloak or bracelets on my wrist. I glanced to my left. The punt was now in midriver, further from the bank than it should have been; we were too far out in the blackness, the river running strong. The puppy stirred as it caught my alarm.

'This is not—!'

I felt the blade touch the back of my head.

'Now, traveller, be at peace.' The old man rocked backwards and forwards, chortling with laughter. The boat was moving swiftly; the puntsman must still be at his post so the blade was being held by an assassin – that's what the sheepskins had concealed. They'd been waiting for me and I had walked into the trap like some brainless hare caught in a hunter's net.

'Here?' the harsh voice grated behind me. 'One stab, one slash!'

'Oh no.' The old man wiped his nose on the back of his hand. 'Not here, near the crocodile pools: no sign, no trace.'

'Whatever you were offered,' I declared, 'I'll give you more.'

The old man squinted at me, leaned over and patted me

gently on the wrist. 'It's not like that,' he replied sadly. 'It's not like that at all.'

'Who?' I asked.

'Ask the Lord Anubis when you meet him.'

'Why?'

'Ask him that as well.'

The puppy was now squealing. I gazed across the night-shrouded water. The banks were distant, their fading pricks of light mocked me. Was this Sobeck's work? No, I reasoned he would have killed me as soon as we met. I made to move, the knife pricked my neck and I winced. A screech owl called, a soul-chilling cry echoed by the roar of a hippopotamus. The water slapped against the boat, the night air was freezing cold. I wanted to be sick but my throat was too dry even to swallow or beg for my life: those cruel old eyes showed no pity. These assassins had been hired for the task and they'd complete it.

'We will take everything you have.' Again the pat on my wrist. 'And if you behave we'll cut your throat before the crocodiles even know you are in the water. Good,' the old man sniffed. 'You are going to be quiet, no crying and weeping, bawling and begging. Listen, I have a poem.' He hawked and spat. 'I recite it to all my guests.' He poked my cloak where the puppy squirmed. 'You have a dog there?' He pulled back my robe with the tip of the dagger concealed in his hand. 'A puppy, how sweet! Well, we'll kill that, too, as an offering to the River God, to keep us safe. Look at the mist. You have only got one journey,' he sniggered. 'We have to make two.'

A bank of mist was drifting across the water, wafted and shifted by the breeze.

'Now keep that little cur silent.' The old man preened himself. 'My poem is important, it's your death lament.' He intoned: 'In the end, 'all things break down, All flesh drains. All blood dries . . .'

'Ahoy there!'

I gazed into the night. A skiff, a torch lashed to the pole on the front, was aiming straight towards us.

'Ahoy there! May the God Hapi be with us! May his name—!'

'What do you want?' the old man screeched.

'I am lost.' The light concealed the speaker.

'Where do you want to be?' the assassin behind me bellowed.

'In the Fields of the Blessed,' the cheery voice rang out. The skiff turned abruptly to the left, coming up behind us. The assassin behind me dared not turn, nor could the puntsman. The old man was staring by me, trying to make out the newcomer. A sound like that of swift fluttering wings carried across the water, the music of an arrow. The man behind me holding the knife crashed into me, hands scrabbling at my back even as he coughed up life's hot blood. Another whirr, a shriek followed by a splash as the puntsman collapsed into the water. The punt rocked dangerously but its broad flatness held it secure. The old man reacted too slowly. I lashed out with my fist as he rose. He staggered to the side, tried to regain his balance but tumbled into the water. The puppy jumped down between my feet. I pushed it away as I lurched to the side. The assassin behind me had now fallen over backwards. The arrow had taken him in the back of the neck and its barbed point jutted out under his chin. The old man was desperately trying to clamber aboard.

'Please!'

I struck his vein-streaked, bald head. The punt was rocking from side to side. I clawed his face, pushing him under the water.

'Finish your poem!' I screamed. 'Let the river beasts hear it!' My nails dug into his face, one finger jabbed an eye. He lashed out at my hands. The water swirled, then he was gone. I sat back catching my breath. The corpse of the assassin who had pricked my throat followed his master into the water. The puppy was mewling softly. I snatched it up and looked for my rescuer. The skiff came alongside. The young man sitting so calmly within it smiled at me: a powerful Syrian bow across his lap, a quiver of arrows beside him. And that's where I met him! Djarka, at the dead of night with the cold freezing my skin and my heart and belly lurching with fear. He just smiled at me, his smooth, olive-skinned face unmarked even by a bead of sweat, those dark thick-lashed eyes staring curiously. He played with his black oiled hair, ringlets tumbling down each side of his face. At the time he looked more like a young woman than a man. I watched his hands. I could see no dagger.

'Mahu.' He spread his arms. 'Mahu, come!' His voice was tinged with an accent. 'I am Djarka of the Sheshnu.'

'So?'

'I am one of the Silent Ones who serve Great Queen Tiye. I am to be your servant.'

'I don't need one.'

'Oh yes, you certainly do,' he sighed. 'Come, we can

393

talk on the way. The Great Queen wishes to speak to you. Let's be gone before the river guards pass.'

I gripped the soaked puppy and jumped into the skiff. Djarka grabbed the paddle and we moved swiftly away, leaving the barge rocking in the river, its fiery cresset torch fading to a distant blur of light.

'You were following me?'

'Of course.'

'Sobeck's men never caught you?'

Djarka shrugged the robe off his shoulders and passed it back to me: it was quartered in four colours, red, blue, black and bright yellow.

'People always look for the same,' Djarka declared over his shoulder. 'I try never to be the same. Sometimes I wear a hood. Sometimes I remove my sandals. I watched you leave the Sign of the Ankh. You went down to the quayside and acted very stupidly. They were waiting for you.'

'But how did they know? Sobeck must have betrayed me.'

'No.' Djarka turned back and concentrated on his paddling. We were now approaching the Karnak side of the river and I could glimpse the lights along the quayside. 'Sobeck would have killed you and buried your body out in the Red Lands.'

'Then who?'

'Someone wants you dead but, there again, someone wants me dead. We kill each other in our thoughts.'

By now my stomach had quietened, my heart beat not so fast. 'You are a priest, a philosopher?'

Djarka laughed merrily like a boy and my heart warmed

to him. 'No, I am a hunter,' he replied. 'No, that's wrong.
I am an actor who mimes. Wrong again,' he mused. 'I am
merely the Great Queen's servant. I met you years ago,
Mahu, out in the desert but I was a boy. You wouldn't
remember. Ah well, we are here.'

Djarka nosed the craft along the quayside steps which
served one of the smaller courts of the Malkata Palace. He picked up a rope, lashed it to the metal ring
driven into the wall and helped me out onto the slip-
pery steps.

'Can't you get rid of that?' He pointed at the puppy.
He plucked it from my hands as he led me up the steps.
We hurried across the courtyard, then Djarka stopped at
a storeroom, pulled open a door and threw in the bow and
arrows, followed by the little puppy, slamming the door
shut on its whining and yelping.

'It will be safe and warm there and will soon go to sleep.
What are you going to call it?'

'Karnak.'

Djarka gave a twisted smile. 'The shaven heads of Amun
will love that.' He led me into the palace proper: guards
in their blue and gold head-dresses, ceremonial shields
displaying the ram's head of Amun, stopped us. Djarka
produced a clay tablet pass which silenced all questions
and we were ushered on.

Queen Tiye was waiting for us in a downstairs chamber
overlooking a small enclosed garden. The air was sweet
with fragrance and through the open window I could see
braziers glowing, their light shimmering on the ornamental lakes and pools. The room itself was bright, its walls
painted blue and yellow with an oakwood border along

the top and bottom. Queen Tiye was sitting on a small divan, the cushions plumped about her, poring over rolls of papyrus. She was dressed in a simple white tunic with an embroidered shawl studded with precious stones about her shoulders. As we came in, she glanced up. Her eyes were tired; the furrows on either side of her mouth were deeper, more marked than before.

'You are safe, Mahu?'

I went to kneel but she waved at the cushions before the divan.

'Sit down! Sit down! You too, Djarka.'

'You had me followed, Excellency?'

'Of course I did.' Queen Tiye's head went to one side. 'Do you think you can go to Thebes, Mahu, and not be noticed? I know all about Sobeck and the jeweller. He's dead, you know. I tried to suborn him and, poor fellow, he paid the price. You are wondering why I didn't have Sobeck arrested?' She shrugged. 'Why should I? For stealing a royal concubine? He can have the lot! Moreover, what threat does he pose?'

I remained silent.

'He wasn't safe.' Djarka spoke up. 'He was attacked on the river by the Jackal Heads.'

'Jackal Heads?' I recalled the amulet slung round the old man's neck.

'A family of assassins,' Djarka cheerily replied. 'In fact, a clan who hire themselves out for murder.'

'Your Aunt Isithia knew them,' Tiye added. She smiled at my surprise. 'Oh yes, she knew such assassins for a long time.'

I recalled the day going into the Temple of Anubis to

view my father's corpse: that strange beggarman at the quayside as well as the day my master was attacked.

'Sometimes they guarded her,' Queen Tiye declared, 'and that intrigues me. Did you murder your Aunt Isithia, Mahu? At first I thought you did but you were in the palace when she died.' She picked up a small cup from the table and sipped at it.

'I didn't kill her, Excellency, but I danced when I heard the news.'

'I am sure you did.'

'Who hired the Jackal Heads?' I asked.

'I don't know. Perhaps I am not the only person who thinks you killed your aunt; it could be a blood feud. One day,' she pursed her lips, 'one day we'll find the truth to all this and pull up the roots. Until then, you are my son's protector and Djarka will be yours.'

'I have Snefru!'

'Djarka will be yours!' she repeated flatly. 'He is of good family and well suited.' She narrowed her eyes. 'You have very dangerous friends, Mahu. Sobeck, or whatever he calls himself now, is well-known to the police but he might be an ally.'

'You wished to see me, Excellency?' I was cold and tired.

'Come!' Tiye rose and crossed to a water clock standing in the corner. She glanced at it then picked up a cloak and swung it round her shoulders. 'You'd best see this.'

We left the chamber, going along a maze of glorious corridors, across courtyards, penetrating deeper into the palace. Guards stood hidden in shadowy enclaves.

Servants hurried by; fine robes billowing, bare feet slapping on the shiny floor. Halfway down one corridor Tiye paused, opened a door and led us into a chamber which smelt musty. No lights glowed. She stumbled about, whispering at us to be silent. Then she moved to the far wall, fumbled, and removed a small flap: a ray of light beamed into the room. She gestured me over. Djarka stayed leaning against the door. I crouched down, peered through and caught my breath.

'The House of Love,' Tiye whispered.

I was staring into the central chamber of the Magnificent One's harem. The room was shadowy, though its centre was ringed with light. It was a beautiful place with water basins, lightly coloured pillars and a myriad of glowing oil lamps in pure alabaster jars. In the centre of the pool of light the Divine One sprawled naked in a thronelike chair. I could see every inch of his corpulent body, the heavy paunch and plump thighs glistening with oil, his powerful face, chin against his chest. All around him concubines fluttered, their slim naked bodies carefully shaved, lips painted, eyes lined with kohl, fingernails and toenails deeply carmined. Some anointed him with precious perfumes whilst others brought freshly plucked lotus for him to smell or sweet iced melon to quench his thirst. Beside him stood a small table bearing a game board, on which enamelled, terracotta pieces with dogs' heads and hawks' heads waited to be moved. The Magnificent One sniffed at the lotus or chewed a piece of melon. Now and again he'd grab the hand of one of the concubines and push it between his legs, even as he turned to throw the knuckle-bones to determine the next move upon the board. Against the far wall ranged a line of alcoves, above them the flashing gold of the Royal Vulture, its wings spread out. In one of the shadow-filled alcoves stood a divan, its cushions of many colours piled high. The Magnificent One rose and, taking two of the girls, entered the alcove and lay on the divan. The rest of the concubines patiently waited until he returned.

I wondered why Great Queen Tiye had brought us here: I was about to ask when a eunuch appeared, resplendent in white robes and insignia of office, body glistening, his sweaty, plump face painted like a woman's. He came into the pool of light. Two of the concubines acted as fan-bearers on either side of him. The eunuch clapped his jewelled hands and shooed the women out from the Magnificent One's presence. Pharaoh himself had returned to his thronelike chair. He picked up the knuckle-bones and threw them on the board, became angry at what he saw and turned away, flicking one of the pieces over with his finger. The chamber was now deserted.

'Watch!' Tiye hissed.

I heard a door open. The effect on the Magnificent One was startling. He pulled himself up in the chair, hands going between his legs. A shadowy form appeared, a young woman. She stepped into the light and I caught my breath. She was tall and slim; a thick braided perfumed wig framed her beautiful face. She was naked except for the jewellery which flashed at ear, throat, wrists and ankles. When she moved in her high-heeled sandals to stand before Pharaoh, I realised why the room had been emptied. I had only glimpsed her on a number of occasions but the young woman was Sitamun, Pharaoh's eldest daughter. She crouched at her father's feet, hands brushing his thighs, fingers moving towards his crotch. Then she rose and sat on his lap, legs dangling down either side as she moved further and further up, putting her hands about his neck. Pharaoh was now squirming with pleasure. I glanced at Queen Tiye: her face was like that of some ghost out of the West. Even in the poor light I glimpsed the grey pallor, the tear-rimmed eyes.

'That,' she whispered, 'is the price I have to pay.' She closed the flap very carefully and pressed the side of her head against the cold wall. 'The Co-regency,' she whispered. 'Sitamun is playing the Great Queen, the Great Wife. Our daughter! His own flesh and blood!'

'Why, Excellency?' I whispered. 'Why have you shown me this?'

Tiye remained silent, a hand to her eyes as she sobbed quietly, a heartrending sight. She brushed her eyes with her fingers.

'Look on the magnificence of Egypt, Mahu, and despair.'

I thought she'd moved away but she turned and pressed both hands against the wall as if she wished to claw through the stone and plaster. My fingers searched for the flap. I felt the small handle, pulled it down and stared back at the House of Love. Sitamun had gone. Amenhotep sat crouched on his throne. I was about to lift the flap back when I saw a movement in the shadows. Someone else was in the room, a woman shrouded in a cloak.

'Excellency,' I whispered.

Queen Tiye ignored me. I peered through again. Amenhotep had risen and, grasping a cane, he waddled out of the pool of light, a ridiculous figure with his fat, vein-streaked legs, the drooping cheeks of his bottom, the creases of fat along his back. He moved into the shadows. The woman who was there offered her cloak which he placed round his shoulders. I could hear whispering but Amenhotep's body blocked any view – yet I was sure I knew who the woman was: the Princess Khiya. What was she doing here, watching the Magnificent One make love to his own daughter? I felt Tiye's nails in my cheek, forcing me away. I stood back, the flap was closed and Tiye led us out into the passageway. She only talked when we returned to the chamber, Djarka and I kneeling before her as she paced up and down. She looked grief-stricken though more composed.

'What have you seen tonight, Mahu? Well,' she sighed, 'what you have seen is the rottenness in the blood; the way dreams can slip into nightmares. The Magnificent One, the brave-eyed lion, Horus in the South, being pawed by his own daughter. If Sitamun bears a child,' Tiye stopped pacing and glared down at me, her eyes as fierce as any cat's, 'you are to kill her and the child.'

'Excellency,' I protested.

She brought her hand back and slapped me across the face. 'There can be no more sons of Egypt!' She crouched down before me. 'You have seen my nightmare, Mahu. I now ask myself: is that rottenness also in my son? Will he surrender his destiny for passing pleasures? That's why I chose Nefertiti for him.' She stood up. 'That's why you are his protector.'

I kept kneeling, head down. I didn't know why I had been taken to see what I had. Was it Queen Tiye's way of warning me? Or was she preparing to murder her own daughter and grandchild? Perhaps she was trying to purge her own soul for allowing her husband full rein in his decadence?

Tiye gently touched me under the chin and forced my head back. 'What else did you see, Mahu, when you looked again?'

I held her gaze. 'Nothing, Excellency. I was just intrigued.'

'Good!' She stroked my cheek. 'Remain intrigued, Mahu, and you will remain alive.'

'*Enk Shweer Neb-ef*—
I am cursed by his Lord.'

Chapter 14

I was appointed Chief of Police over the entire city of Thebes and the surrounding area shortly after I recovered from a fever in the thirty-seventh year of the Magnificent One's reign. I received my Gold Collar and Seals of Office at an official ceremony before the Window of Appearances from Akhenaten and Nefertiti, God's Father Hotep looking on smugly. I was to work in the new buildings of the Palace of the Aten, my chambers standing next to Ay's; the latter had also received further honours, including the title of the Commander of the Chariots of Min. My master never told me why I had been chosen or why there had been a delay over the publication of such a great office. Ay did that at the subsequent banquet as we dined on a range of delicacies cooked in the Canaan fashion over herb-strewn charcoal, the dishes being served by Syrian girls dressed in the guise of Hathor, the Lady of Mirth.

'You are, Mahu,' Ay spoke over his cup, 'a cunning soul

and you accept that what our Prince wishes has force of law, and that convinced me.'

So he had delayed my appointment! I was too drunk to respond, whilst the Gold Collar weighed heavily round my neck. The other children in the Kap were busy toasting me. Horemheb and Rameses, resplendent in their Guard Officers' uniforms, were both looking lean and fit after a season out in the Red Lands hunting down and killing outlaws who preyed on caravans. Huy was absent, being despatched as an envoy across Sinai. As professional soldiers, Horemheb and Rameses were most interested in this. They grumbled about the creeping inaction of Egypt's border troops to counter the unrest amongst her client states across Sinai, especially in the face of the growing power of the Hittites. Maya also attended as Hotep's retainer. He looked plump and comely in his perfumed robes.

'Ringed and bangled,' Rameses hissed, 'as any whore.'

Maya kept his distance as well he might: he had yet to decide which path he would tread. Pentju and Meryre lorded it over all, two wise fools full of wine and their own importance. Pentju was gabbling about the light of his life, the Lady Tenbra whom he had impressed with his wealth and status, so hoped to make a good marriage.

Of course, there were distractions enough at the banquet. All of us had to applaud Akhenaten as he directed his Hittite Orchestra of the Sun, now trained in the lute, the oboe, the harp and cymbal. The members of this singular group had their own quarters and no longer looked so strange in their heavy wigs and female robes, faces gaudily painted. They had soon reconciled themselves to their fate as consecrated to the god whilst seeing their eccentric ruler as God's incarnate representative. We cheered as if they had been inspired by Hathor herself. They played passably well. Nefertiti, sprawled against the cushions, her babies lying swaddled next to her, kept up a playful commentary that whatever happened, the Hittites must not sing.

The banquet ended, as all such occasions did, in drunken toasts and bouts of false bonhomie. Nevertheless, we all knew it was a time of waiting, though waiting for what, had not yet been revealed. For the Magnificent One to journey to the Far Horizon? For Akhenaten to reveal his face publicly to the people? To confront those forces so implacably opposed to him in both court and temple? It was a busy time for me as I took my new duties seriously. Unrest and uncertainty seethed beneath the surface of the elegant colourful life of the court.

My alliance with Sobeck was formalised and strengthened. He now proclaimed himself as Lord of the Am-Duat, King of the Underworld, that hidden Thebes, a city of thieves, pickpockets, charlatans, vicious gangs, assassins, pimps and prostitutes. I would not interfere with him but he would help me whilst taking care not to cross the boundaries I had drawn.

I inherited two deputies in East and West Thebes, but soon replaced these with merchants, friends of Sobeck, bitter opponents of Rahimere the Mayor of Thebes and High Priest Shishnak. They reported to me constantly, a flood of petty information from servants, peddlers, workers in the Necropolis, merchants and spies, as well as the Medjay, the desert scouts and river guards. All the chatter and gossip of Thebes came into my office. Sobeck supplemented this and I soon won a reputation for ruthless efficiency. Visitors coming in from the Eastern and Western Deserts were greeted by a line of stakes bearing the impaled corpses of outlaws, bandits, river pirates and tomb-robbers. House-breakers, burglars and market thieves received swift justice in the courts, and brandings, floggings and executions were carried out in public, usually at the scene of the crime. Stolen goods were quickly recovered. Sobeck received a reward for these as well as the bounty posted on the heads of such malefactors. He celebrated my appointment by telling me to drink wine on a certain evening on the highest roof of the palace overlooking the city. I did so and sipped the richest wine from my cellar as I watched the fire flare and Aunt Isithia's house go up in flames. I toasted and cheered the fierce red glow in the sky. Sobeck also sent information about the temple priests, that gaggle of hypocrites of whitewashed sepulchres. The shaven heads, led by Shishnak, were buying weapons and armour, increasing their guards and hiring mercenaries from as far afield as the Islands in the Great Green. Of course, they kept these out of Thebes and quartered them on their extensive estates along the Nile. I warned Ay. He just shrugged – 'Mahu, the race hasn't yet begun' – and returned to the reports from his spies detailing the great wealth of Amun.

In the palace Akhenaten proved to be a doting father and loving husband. A certain distance, even coolness, had grown up between us but that was due to Ay's influence as well as the distraction of his wives and family. At first

Ay, as he'd confessed, had been opposed to me securing the post of Chief of Police. He'd wanted the office to go to another member of the Akhmin gang.

'It wasn't personal, dear boy,' Ay whispered, 'but in life, blood always comes first.'

In other areas Ay didn't fail. Members of the far-flung Akhmin gang were appointed to posts whenever they fell vacant; if the Magnificent One tried to object, Queen Tiye always smoothed things over.

Nonetheless, I was not completely ignored. Akhenaten would sometimes go walking with me. He talked volubly or, indeed, lectured me about the Aten, his closeness to the Godhead and the truth of his destiny. I sensed he was holding back, due to the influence of Ay and Nefertiti, though sometimes the truth came out. He'd talk of dreams and visions of being visited by the Aten, or how he had flown on eagle's wings beyond the Far Horizon.

'I soared above the Eternal Green, Mahu.' Akhenaten would stand, hands clasped, eyes half-closed. 'I have looked on the face of the everlasting vision.'

At other times he'd not be so forthcoming, curt in his speech, stumbling in his walk, slow of thought, even indecisive in all his movements. I wondered how much of his mystical experiences, as well as his bouts of depression, were the result of Nefertiti's potions and powders. In the two years following my appointment as Chief of Police, Nefertiti became pregnant twice again – a matter on which Akhenaten preened himself, hoping desperately for a son but hiding his disappointment at the birth of a third and fourth daughter.

Nefertiti became caught up in her role as wife and

mother though she would also be constantly closeted with Akhenaten and her father as they dreamed and talked about change and revolution in Egypt. Oh, she was, and remained, always lovely, ever alluring, fair of form, gracious and good. Nevertheless, she did change, imperceptibly at first, this change expressing itself in a certain haughtiness in look, gesture and speech. She could be openly dismissive of Great Queen Tiye while the Magnificent One's growing obsession with his eldest daughter became a constant subject for her mockery and salacious jokes. On state occasions the tables were now turned. There was no longer any laughter or giggling whispers about the Grotesque but bold mockery of Sitamun, who revelled in her status as the Great Wife of her own father. Tiye seemed to have given up any attempt to oppose her, being more content to hide in the shadows and wield what secret power she could. Sometimes, when Sitamun's name was mentioned at a banquet or a meeting of the Royal Circle, Tiye would catch my eye, invoking memories of the night I'd peered into the House of Love whilst listening to her hissed instructions of what was to happen if Sitamun ever conceived a child. I would stare coldly back, quietly hoping that Tiye would, with her potions and powers, do her part to ensure her eldest daughter's womb remained barren.

Of course neither Nefertiti nor Akhenaten had forgotten Shishnak, the High Priest; their support for the Aten was growing more visible. The Chapel of the Aten continued to be built at Karnak and both Akhenaten and Nefertiti often visited it, parading majestically past the shaven heads, stopping to comment how inscriptions to the Aten could be inscribed on that doorway, this pillar, that wall or pylon. It was all a mockery. Akhenaten had his own sun altar within his palace grounds. He also went out into the Western Red Lands to a place called the Valley of the Shadows in order to worship his god. Sometimes I accompanied him there. I always felt uneasy, as if what was about to happen there somehow stretched back from the future to touch my soul and warn my heart. The valley itself was narrow and sombre, steep-sided, its flank strewn with boulders, rough gorse, brambles and shifting shale. It had only one entrance, a narrow pass which fell steeply down to a snake-like track which curved and twisted, ending in an impasse of sheer rocks over which the Sun Disc would rise.

I always considered the valley to be a haunt of ghosts with its many caves and hollows on either side. Akhenaten saw it as a sacred place. He built a small altar at the far end, at the foot of the sheer cliffs, in order to sacrifice bread and wine to the Aten. He'd go out in his chariot, a few palace guards with Snefru's retinue trotting behind him. They'd seal the entrance whilst Akhenaten went ahead with myself, Nefertiti, and sometimes Ay, along the floor of the valley to what he called 'his sanctuary before the Sun Disc'. Such visits were a sinister experience conducted in that ghostly light which separates night from day. The bushes and boulders became skulking monsters or the hiding-place of some secret enemy. I had the entire valley investigated. The Medjay reported how witches and warlocks often met in its caves to practise their midnight rites. I could well believe it. One morning I smelt smoke and later that day I despatched Snefru to investigate and report back with true voice. Snefru confessed he was frightened, not so much by the human remains they had found in one cave, as they must have been years old. He claimed the hidden menace of the valley could be sensed even in the bright light of day. I advised Akhenaten to find a different place. He lost his temper, screaming at me that I was thick-headed and dull-witted. Later he apologised sweetly, saying how was I to know where the veil between him and his god became so thin?

Khiya was never taken on such pilgrimages even though she was deeply curious about her new husband's religion. She'd often come tripping along the garden path, eyes all innocent in her round pretty face, a litany of questions about the gods and temples of Egypt.

'Who is Mut?' she'd ask. 'What is her relationship with Amun, and is Khonsu their son? Do they rank higher than the Earth God Geb? Is the Sun Disc a god or just a symbol?'

Despite her puzzled looks and open eagerness to learn I was wary of her, yet Khiya stayed close to me, sending me gifts at New Year and on festival days. She always singled Karnak out for fussing as he grew from a mewling pup into a muscular, brown-haired hunting dog with swift legs, a strong jaw and fierce eyes. He followed me everywhere.

Khiya also developed a special fondness for Djarka, 'my second shadow' as Snefru jealously described him. Djarka's added attraction to Khiya was a profound knowledge about herbs and a love of gardens as intense as Nefertiti's. Khiya and her maid would insist that Djarka lecture them on the names and properties of different flowers and herbs. Khiya remained ever-smiling even though Nefertiti grew more haughty and distant, keen to emphasise her status and rights as Great Queen. Khiya submitted to all this, accepting the snubs, more concerned with her herbs or improving her knowledge of the Egyptian tongue. She was deeply interested in love poetry which she liked to declaim as the Orchestra of the Sun played softly in the background. Nefertiti resented such occasions for then Khiya, who had a beautiful voice, would come into her own. I can still recall certain lines which always charmed my heart.

What a heaven it might be
If our heart's true wishes became real
To care only for you,
An eternal jubilee!

Sometimes Khiya's mask slipped and she suffered the consequences. She once showed me angry bruises on her arms and shoulders, results of Nefertiti's violent outbursts which intensified as her pregnancies advanced. On another occasion Khiya came and sat on a small stool watching me draft a proclamation.

'What's that?' She pointed to the hieroglyphs of waving grass.

'That's *seket* – it stands for field.'

'And *heb*?'

'An alabaster bowl to drink from.'

'Would you get me something to drink, Mahu?' She placed soft fingers on my wrist. 'No, not wine,' she smiled. 'Not now. The juice of the poppy which comes from the island of the daydream so I, too, can fly on eagle's wings.'

I withdrew my hand. I recalled the Magnificent One with his stodgy thighs, dropping arse and fat-caked back, lumbering to meet that mysterious woman in the shadows. Was that Khiya? Had she come seeking the precious opiate which the Magnificent One loved so much?

'Your Excellency,' I replied formally, 'if I had such a juice I, too, would have eagle's wings.'

Khiya never referred to the matter again. I asked Djarka what he thought.

'Like you, my lord,' the title was always tinged with mockery, 'Khiya is a spectator caught up in the whirl of this frenetic dance.'

'Don't talk riddles.'

'I am not, my lord Mahu. Haven't you ever wished to be a gentleman of ease living the simple but good life with a wife and family?'

'I don't know if I could. As the tree is planted,' I quoted the proverb I had used with Sobeck, 'so it grows.'

'We are not trees, Lord Mahu, but souls who make choices, decisions.'

'In which case I have made mine. Or had them made for me. I cannot, I will not, leave the dance.'

'Never?'

'No, no, no. Never.'

I often thought of that reply but Djarka spoke the truth. Despite my best efforts I was a spectator, a watcher, as when I peered through that secret flap into the Magnificent One's House of Love. Would I spend my life peering out at the likes of Akhenaten and Nefertiti? Or be part of their lives even as I watched? I concluded both were true and often discussed this with Djarka. He soon proved his worth, a good companion who warmed my heart and eased the bitter cold in my soul: he was the younger brother I would have loved or the son I might have had. Oh, he was ruthless too, of course, and could kill in the blink of an eye. My gratitude to him for rescuing me from the assassin on the Nile was boundless yet there was more to Djarka than being a good soldier, a good retainer with a truthful heart and clever wits. He became my body servant, a trusted steward, faithful envoy and the nearest thing I ever had to a family. Djarka had a dry sense of humour, a wry attitude to the world. He trusted no one, not even himself, yet he was honest about it. Unlike me, he believed in an afterlife and an ever-seeing, ever-present God, a concept I never understood or accepted. He soon learned that theology bored me and would turn swiftly to other matters, being a superb archer and skilled slinger though he was hopeless with horses.

Akhenaten would sometimes journey up the Nile on the barge *The Glory of Aten* to visit the sacred place as he had done years earlier. I was never invited along. Only Ay, Nefertiti and their children, protected by Nakhtimin's palace guards who were never allowed to land, accompanied them. During such absences I'd take a chariot out with Djarka as my companion. We'd gallop across the fringes of the desert, Karnak bounding behind us, trying to keep up and not be lost in a cloud of dust. I would put the chariot into a furious war charge, wheels rattling, carriage swaying, horses galloping full out. We'd hurtle across the hard ground until the horses became exhausted. Afterwards we'd eat and drink and discuss the affairs of the court. On other occasions we'd hunt gazelle or antelope, me guiding the chariot, Djarka standing beside me, feet apart, his great Syrian bow strung, Karnak loping alongside ready to bring down our wounded quarry. I loved the hunt for the sake of the chase but we could also talk, well away from walls and windows, free of servants and the lurking eavesdropper. Djarka was full of praise for Great Queen Tiye whom he worshipped. On Akhenaten he would not comment except to make an observation very similar to Sobeck's.

'He has a destiny. Our Prince has a vision for Egypt better than what has gone before but he must remember he is not that vision, only its prophet.'

As our friendship grew Djarka became more scathing about Ay and Nefertiti. He was aware of my infatuation with the Princess but trusted me, not hesitating to dismiss them both as 'thieves from the Underworld'. I'd argue back but I could never change his mind.

'They are opportunists,' he told me, 'infatuated with power along with the whole Akhmin gang.'

'You are prejudiced.'

'And you are infatuated, Mahu – a dangerous thing for a Chief of Police. Little Khiya knows the truth,' he added, 'that's why she stares so empty-headed. Why do you think they trust you? Because they know they control you; you are their property, body and soul.'

Such arguments would become intense, but in the end Djarka would just laugh.

'When all is said and done,' he'd conclude, 'it will be Akhenaten who decides.'

On other occasions we'd discuss the growing tensions

in Thebes, a dull ache which never went away. Djarka was always solemn about that. 'I agree with Queen Tiye,' he'd murmur. 'Whatever we do, it will end in blood.'

Month had followed month, season had followed season, year had followed year, full of rumour and gossip. I had become accustomed to it. When the bloodletting finally came, it began so softly, indistinct, like the rains do when a mere cloud, the size of a man's hand, appears in the brilliant blue sky. In the second month of Peret, in the Season of the Sowing, our cloud appeared. A message came from Sobeck to meet him out at the Oasis of Strangers in the Western Red Lands. He was waiting for me and Djarka, his scorpion men all about him, armed to the teeth, guarding the oasis, its palm trees dying as the well which once served it slowly dried up. Sobeck escorted me deeper into the oasis while Djarka unhitched the horses and led them into the shade. Sobeck's scorpion men drifted across to chat as well as to admire our harness and carriage.

'Listen to this, Mahu.' Sobeck put an arm across my shoulder. 'One of my acquaintances, a merchant, trades in animal skins with the Libyans. He brought me a strange rumour that one of their most powerful tribes is moving South.'

'The Libyans are always doing that, probing for a weakness.'

Sobeck held up a hand. 'These are buying up weapons, chariots and warhorses and they are not using animal skins to barter with, but this.' He opened his left hand; the small six-sided ingot of gold winked in the sunlight. I plucked it up and weighed it in my hand.

'Pure gold,' Sobeck confirmed. 'Freshly minted, un-marked. The Libyans are using that to buy arms from mercenaries along the coast of the Great Green.'

'This comes from Egypt. Is it possible,' I replied, 'that only a few are being used?'

'My merchant friend says the Libyans have plenty – and there is more.' Sobeck gestured to the distant heat haze. 'My friend became very curious, even more so, when this tribe or clan – well, at least its warriors, about five hundred in all – completely disappeared from their usual hunting grounds. Well now!' He played with the ring in his earlobe. 'My spies eventually learned from the womenfolk that, ten days ago, these warriors moved across into the Eastern Desert. They are still out there, a war-party with weapons and provisions.'

'What about our scouts and patrols?'

'How far do they go, Mahu – twenty, thirty miles at the most? The Libyans are further out.'

'The Eastern Desert Lands are quiet.'

'Precisely. You don't expect to find a Libyan army across the Nile.' Sobeck grinned. 'Moreover, they've probably broken up into small cohorts. Oh well.' He patted his flat stomach, brushing away the sweat. 'I have also brought you a present – two, in fact.'

He called across the oasis. A scorpion man hurried over, placed two leather buckets at Sobeck's feet and threw back the flaps. I flinched at the stench of corruption from the two severed heads; flies, whirling black dots, came buzzing out.

'I think you have been introduced.' Sobeck lifted the face of the old man, the Jackal's assassin. I had told

Sobeck the tale and ordered him to wipe out the entire clan.

'Oh yes, he survived.' Sobeck tapped one of the sunken yellowing teeth. 'I caught up with him sheltering in a village to the south of Thebes. He's the last so there will be no blood feud.' He threw the head like a ball onto the sand and plucked out the second, a Libyan with long hair, swarthy skin, peaked nose and full lips, a calm composed face bereft of the horror which had masked that of the old assassin. 'My merchant friend was so intrigued I became curious. I hired some of my Sand Wanderers to search well beyond the area patrolled by the chariot squadrons. They caught three scouts. Two were killed but this one,' he threw the head after the other, 'was brought in. I questioned him, with the help of a little fire.'

'Won't they be missed?' I asked.

Sobeck shook his head. 'Libyans are travelling across a terrain unknown to them; it's quite common for scouts and guides to become lost. Anyway, he spoke before he died. His war-party had been bribed to cross with gold, silver, precious stones and whatever plunder they could take.'

'By whom?'

'I don't know. It would have to be someone very power-ful.' Sobeck continued, 'Think, Mahu, five hundred war-riors crossing the Nile. They would need barges, someone to look the other way.'

'And the prisoner told you?'

'They crossed just above the First Cataract.'

'A deserted place,' I declared. 'No black lands or greenery.'

'That's where the scouts were found, in an area where

there are no mines and very few patrols – an arid, deserted place. Someone must have provided the barges, a deserted mooring place, as well as maps of the wells and springs. Anyway, now I was truly intrigued. I took my body-guard down the Nile and found the barges still moored there.'

'So the Libyans have a way back?'

'Five hundred fighters, Mahu, warriors: very well-armed, bribed with gold, and furnished with barges and maps, hiding in a place no one would think of searching. What are they going to attack?'

'It can't be Thebes, it's too powerful.'

'The Malkata lies on the east bank,' Sobeck whispered, 'so does the Palace of the Aten.'

'All are well-guarded.'

'Against a sudden assault?'

A coldness pricked the nape of my neck, sending a shiver across my shoulders. I stared at the severed head, embedded in the sand. The vultures were already circling above us.

'It's not the Malkata,' I replied. 'It's the Valley of the Shadows out in the Eastern Red Lands.' I explained Akhenaten's pilgrimages to what he termed his 'sacred shrine'.

'Ah well.' Sobeck pulled his dagger in and out of its embroidered leather sheath. 'Now we come to something else.' He gestured across the oasis. 'Do you trust Djarka?'

'With my life.'

'Why, what do you know of him?'

'He's a member of the Sheshnu,' I declared. 'One of

their tribe. A good hunter, faithful and loyal to Great Queen Tiye.'

'But you trust him with your life? Why?'

'He reminds me of you, Sobeck.'

'As I am?'

'As you were.'

Sobeck glanced away. 'Good, good,' he muttered. 'But don't trust Snefru.'

'No!' I shouted and stepped back. 'No, not Snefru?'

Djarka, talking to the scorpion men, turned in alarm, his hand going to the quiver at his feet. I gestured all was well.

'Yes, Snefru.' Sobeck was enjoying himself. 'He has been with the shaven heads of Amun.'

I glanced at the severed head of the Jackal leader. I couldn't make out his features, as the eyes and nose were buried in the sand but, for a moment, I thought its mouth was laughing.

'What's the matter, Mahu?'

I recalled stepping into the assassin's punt.

'I'd always wondered,' I replied, 'how they recognised me. Of course I was wearing Snefru's cloak, garish, like that of a Desert Wanderer.'

'Well, now you know.' Sobeck lifted his hands in a gesture of peace. 'You'll remember me, Mahu.'

I stepped closer. 'Why did you remember *me*, Sobeck? Why are you doing this?'

'Because of what I was, because of what I am.' He smiled thinly. 'If you go into the dark, Mahu, then so do I. Peace, friend.' He backed away. 'I'll watch with interest what happens.'

*   *   *

Djarka and I took Snefru that same day after darkness had fallen. Fighting hard to control my fury, I asked him to come for a walk, out of the palace grounds into the trees, not far from where Ay had poisoned the scribe Ineti. I chattered about what we were going to do on the morrow, certain items to be bought in Thebes. When the opportunity presented itself I stepped back and knocked him senseless with a blow from the club I'd hidden beneath my robes. Djarka soon had the unconscious man's hands and feet lashed to pegs driven into the ground, a filthy rag thrust into his mouth. He squatted beside him while I returned to the palace and searched Snefru's chamber. I found what I was looking for in a wall cavity hidden by the bed: a leather bag full of the same ingots Sobeck had showed me, as well as a pass allowing Snefru into the inner precincts of the Temple of Amun.

By the time I returned, Snefru had regained consciousness and Djarka had placed a small alabaster jar of oil next to his head. I felt a twinge of pity at those fear-filled eyes, that grotesque, scarred face twisted in pain. Djarka had already been busy cutting his cheeks, arms and legs with a razor-sharp dagger. The blood seeped out. I removed the gag.

'You can scream, Snefru, but if you do, someone may hear and I'll have to put the gag back. Shall I tell you where we are going? Out to the Red Lands, the hole has already been dug. I will bury you alive. You're bleeding so the lions and hyenas will come and sniff you and . . .'

'Master, Master,' Snefru gabbled.

'Don't Master me,' I replied, crouching next to him. 'I've found both the pass and the gold. I know about the Libyans and your meetings with the shaven heads. All you have to decide, Snefru, is whether you are to die quickly and quietly here or out in the Red Lands. You'll scream and yell as the hot sand fills your mouth and nostrils. The prowlers will sniff your blood and dig you out, like a warthog hiding in its den.'

'I know nothing!' Snefru screamed, body buckling against the thongs as Djarka, squatting on the other side, sliced his arm.

'Why, Snefru?' I asked. 'I trusted you.'

'You used to.' Snefru glared at Djarka.

'Oh, it's more than that,' I retorted.

'The shaven pates.' Snefru gave a sigh. 'A quick death, Master?'

'Very quick, no more than a heartbeat.'

'Two months ago,' Snefru confessed, 'one of their acolytes approached me in the marketplace at Thebes. He took me into a beer-house and told me they knew everything about Imri and how he and the others had died. One day I would be punished, he swore; they'd crucify me on the walls of Thebes. They said the Grotesque,' Snefru coughed, 'was a heretic, who would soon be sent into the Underworld to meet his just deserts. They offered me a farm, gold, the protection of Amun.'

'What – just for information?' I scoffed. 'Snefru, you knew so little. Tell me about the Libyans,' I persisted.

'All I was told is that one day soon, Akhenaten would go into the Valley of the Shadows.'

'And you'd go with him,' I interrupted. 'You and the rest would seal the valley entrance.'

'The Libyans would attack,' Snefru went on. 'I was to wear a blue rag round my left arm and hide.'

'And the Libyans would sweep in, kill your companions, murder the Prince and anyone with him.'

'There was more.' Snefru cleared his throat and Djarka withdrew the knife. 'If possible, they were to attack this place.'

'The Palace of the Aten?'

'A night raid to kill and burn as much as they could before retreating downriver.'

I struck Snefru across the face.

'Of course,' I whispered. 'And the chariot squadrons would search the Eastern Desert but the Libyans would be back across the Nile.'

'If any chariot squadrons *were* sent out,' Djarka added. 'If our Prince were dead, and Ay and Nefertiti, not to mention ourselves, there would be a delay, caused by the confusion and chaos.'

'Who's behind this?' I asked.

'I met the same priest,' Snefru yelped as Djarka cut his arm again. 'He brought me messages, gold. They've chosen the day; it's very soon.'

'I know which day they'd choose,' I snarled. 'Our Prince is famous for deliberately ignoring the decrees of the Temple. On an inauspicious day when everyone stays at home, he insists on going out long before dawn to worship his god.'

Snefru nodded.

'The rest?' Djarka asked. 'Your companions?'

'They know nothing.' He winced as Djarka cut again. 'They are innocent.' Then he began to cry, the tears coursing down his scarred cheeks.

I got to my feet, wiping the sweat from my neck.

'And me, Snefru?' I glared down at him. 'You gave me your cloak – the sign for the assassins hired by Amun – me, your friend – your master.'

'I had no choice', he mumbled. 'The shaven heads wanted you out of the way, as well as to frighten the Grotesque. They knew of your secret journeys to Thebes, they told me to lend you one of my cloaks . . .' He began to sob.

'Does he know more, my lord?' Djarka asked.

'No,' I replied. 'He would only be told the time and place. Everything else was left to others.'

I walked to where Karnak sprawled obediently under a tree quietly watching what was happening. He got to his feet so I crouched down and stroked his muzzle.

'Kill him, Djarka!' I shouted.

My servant sang a few lines of a hymn I couldn't understand. When he had finished, Snefru gargled and choked as his throat was slashed.

'Get rid of the corpse.' I got to my feet gesturing at Karnak to follow. 'Oh, and Djarka,' I peered through the darkness, 'tell the others in Snefru's company that their leader has been sent on an important errand, and that he will be away for at least a month.'

'And?' Djarka asked, coming forward, resheathing his dagger.

'They can't be trusted,' I replied heavily. 'Whatever happens, they too must die.'

*   *   *

The following afternoon, as the heat of the day faded, I met Maya at my request in a House of Delights managed by one of Sobeck's Lieutenants. It was an exquisite place with a tinkling fountain in a white stone courtyard. Inside was a brilliantly painted hall of columns with beautiful eyecatching scenes on the wall depicting young men in a number of poses. I met Maya in one of the love chambers which led off from this hall. It had a cool tiled floor, its walls were painted a soothing green, and the ceiling was a dark blue decorated with silver stars and a golden moon. In the centre stood a great bed of state, its feet carved in the shape of lions' heads.

'Why, Mahu!' Maya gazed admiringly around. 'I didn't think we shared such tastes.'

'We don't,' I replied, gesturing at a corner where cushions were piled around a table. 'But this is as good a place as any to talk. I think it's best if you relaxed.'

We took our seats, to be served mouthwatering dishes of goose and quail, pots of fish grilled over charcoal fires, wine from the best vineyards. Pretty boys, with sidelocks falling down their faces, dressed in nothing but the scantiest of loincloths, pearl drops in their earlobes with matching necklaces and bangles, tended to our every wish. Maya enjoyed himself. He had grown plumper and even more astute. He ate and drank well, pawed the boys, then leaned back, patting his stomach, staring up at the ceiling.

'If you want to know something, Mahu, the answer is I don't know. And now I'd like to sample this House's other delicacies but I'd prefer to do it by myself, or do you like watching?'

'Do you know who owns this house?' I asked.

Maya loosened the band round his waist, splaying his fingers, admiring the paint on his nails.

'No, you tell me.'

'Kheferu. Have you ever heard of him?'

'Yes, he's some thief from the Underworld, a pimp, a bully boy.' Maya gestured. 'Who cares?'

'Sobeck,' I replied.

Maya dropped his hand and stared open-mouthed. 'Kheferu?' he replied.

'Kheferu is Sobeck,' I whispered. 'He came back, Maya, and carved out his own fortune, his own career.'

'Is he here?' Maya would have sprung to his feet but I pressed his plump shoulder back.

'I can arrange for Sobeck to meet you but he's changed.'

'In my heart, never.'

'He's not what you think, Maya.'

'I don't give a fig what you say, Mahu.'

'Don't you?'

'You are lying.' Maya pulled away. 'This is a story you have made up to make me talk.'

'Is it? It's not just a question of talking, Maya. You work at the House of Secrets. You, like Sobeck, like myself, know what's happening in Thebes. One day a bloody confrontation will take place between my master and the priests of Amun. You will have to decide which party you support.'

'The House of Secrets,' Maya gabbled, 'belongs to no party.'

'Nonsense!' I replied. 'And you know it. The time of blood is upon us, Maya. Sobeck is with me. I am with the Prince, the legitimate Lord of the Two Lands.'

'Only Co-regent,' Maya snapped.

'Nonsense,' I repeated. 'The Magnificent One might as well be in the Far West. He spends his days in a drunken, drugged frenzy, obsessed with his eldest daughter.'

Maya blinked kohl-ringed eyes.

'Moreover,' I persisted, 'you have already chosen. You are having dinner with me.'

'I can explain that.'

'Can you?' I replied. 'You are a child of the Kap, Maya. If the priests of Amun win, do you think they'll allow any of us to survive?'

'Who are they?'

'That's what I want to find out. Now, let me tell you a story.'

I told him about meeting Sobeck, the Valley of the Shadows, the gold, the Libyan war-party and Snefru's confession. Maya's face grew ashen; he was gulping at his wine, hands shaking. When I had finished, he sat staring moodily at the state bed.

'I can't tell you anything.'

'When this is all over,' I edged closer, whispering in his ear, 'friends and allies will be promoted, enemies punished.'

Maya was hooked. I knew he was but he had to make the decision himself.

'Such things are kept secret.' He looked out of the corner of his eye at me. 'You know that, Mahu.'

'The gold,' I asked. 'Where did it come from?'

'Oh, that's easy enough,' he replied. 'The House of Silver at the Temple of Amun. They have their own Mint.'

'And how would it be transported to the Libyans?'

Maya's fat face creased into a smile. 'Again, easy enough. A year ago the Temple of Amun sent an important delegation to the Libyans to demonstrate the favour of their god and advance their own interests.'

'Of course,' I agreed. 'And the shaven heads of Amun are sacred, their pack donkeys can carry whatever they want. No guards would dream of searching their chests or panniers – but how about the barges?'

Maya clicked his tongue. 'That's what you want to know, is it? You want me to search amongst the files and records. It's quite customary for orders to be issued for barges to be collected.'

'That's right, and I want to know who ordered those barges.'

'You know that already,' Maya countered.

'Yes, but I want proof. Who gave the order?' I gestured at the wine jug. 'I am going to sit here and finish that while you go and find out. I'll wait for your return.'

Maya made to protest.

'I'll wait for your return!' I snapped.

He left a short while later. I lay down on the cushions and slept for a while. I was woken by a loud knocking; one of the servant boys came in to announce that my friend had returned. Maya came bustling through the door. He had changed his robes and looked more alert. He smacked the boy's bottom, closed the door behind him, then leaned against it.

'May the gods help us, Mahu, but we are in this together.'

'The barges?' I persisted.

'God's Father Hotep,' Maya replied. 'He ordered the

barges to be assembled on different quaysides and transported to a point just above the First Cataract.'

'And the reason?'

'Army manoeuvres.'

'Of course, there are always army manoeuvres and the order would soon be forgotten.'

Maya nodded. I got to my feet.

'So it's Shishnak and Hotep. Possibly that fat fool Rahimere, Mayor of Thebes.' I stretched out my hand. Maya grasped it and suddenly brought his other hand up, the point of the dagger only inches from my face.

'No, don't be troubled.' He moved the dagger away and wiped the sweat from his brow. 'Mahu, if you've lied, I'll kill you!'

'If I have lied,' I replied, 'you won't have to. If we lose this, we'll lose everything. There's something else, Maya. You were there in the Temple of Amun when Tuthmosis died. You must suspect something was wrong. I could tell that.'

'I learned something but I kept it to myself.' He spoke quickly, hoarsely. 'My spy is a lector priest who supervises the temple's laundry. On the night Tuthmosis died he was told to burn some expensive linen sheets. He never asked why but inspected them. They were covered in a sort of bloody vomit.' He put the knife away. 'You know what that means, Mahu?'

I recalled the dead Prince's chamber.

'The sheets were unmarked,' I whispered. 'And the same was true of Akhenaten's. Tuthmosis didn't die in his own chamber.' My heart skipped a beat. 'I know what happened, Maya. Tuthmosis went to his brother's chamber to await him. Whilst there he must have drunk poisoned wine intended for Akhenaten. The alarm was raised. They moved Tuthmosis back to his own room, cleaned Akhenaten's, replacing the sheet which had been stained. The priests of Amun made a hideous mistake. They poisoned the wrong brother.'

Maya, ashen-faced, moaned quietly under his breath.

'What will you do, Mahu?'

'I have no choice,' I replied. 'But I tell you this, Maya. Report to the House of Secrets today and tomorrow but, on the third day, keep well away. Hide yourself against the coming storm.'

'O you who cut off heads and sever necks.'

(Spell 90: *The Book of the Dead*)

Chapter 15

'May you sit on your throne of bronze!
Your forepart being that of a lion,
And your hindpart being that of a falcon.
May you devour the haunch from the
Slaughter-block of Osiris
And entrails from the slaughter-block of Seth.'

I sat back on my heels and stared at Akhenaten. He was enthroned in the centre of the garden, Nefertiti on his right, Ay on his left. Nakhtimin's guards kept all approaches secure. Akhenaten's twin daughters played at his feet, their younger sisters were sleeping in the nursery. The girls looked like little worms, heads shaven, bodies naked except for jewelled anklets. They sat facing each other, hands clapping as they cooed and cried.

'O King,' I intoned, continuing the formal protocol. 'Mighty in waking, great in sleeping, for whom sweetness is sweet. Rouse yourself, O King.'

I had asked for this formal audience and invoked the usual liturgical rite by intoning a hymn to the power of the King. Only by doing this did I convey the seriousness of the situation and the dangers which confronted us. I wouldn't dare raise such matters in the Royal Circle where the advice of friends and allies would be listened to most carefully by sworn enemies and foes.

Akhenaten sat rigid, staring at me; for a moment, fear flared in his eyes. Nefertiti, her hair hanging undressed down to her shoulders, had also shooed away her maids. They had been squatting around her discussing the different perfumes and creams: how terebinth gum, mixed with moringa oil and nutmeg, removed wrinkles, whilst the juice of lotus, pink lily, papyrus and isis, with a dash of myrrh and frankincense, provided the most fragrant perfume. They had been laughing at how a concentration of cow's blood, gazelle horn and putrefying ass's liver might halt greying. Akhenaten and Ay had been standing near a Pool of Purity deep in discussion. My entrance had ended all that.

I had knelt on the cushions, pressed my forehead against the ground as Akhenaten returned to his thronelike chair. Nefertiti and Ay had joined him whilst the servants were dismissed. Now all was quiet, the silence broken only by the chatter of the children. Ay sat, agitated, plucking at his lower lip, head slightly turned as if fearful of what I was going to say. I told them all everything, though Sobeck's name was never mentioned. I talked directly and quickly. Nefertiti hid her mouth behind her hand; Ay's fingers went to his face. Akhenaten went ashen, eyes blazing with fury. Furrows appeared round his eyes and mouth, a nest of wrinkles, and a vein high in his head bulged and pulsed. When I had finished, he breathed out noisily.

'Do you not nose the ground before the Lord of the Two Lands, before the living image of the One!'

Down I went, back bent, forehead flat against the ground. Akhenaten rose to his feet, almost pushing his children aside. He walked over to me and I could see his sandals, thonged with gold and silver; an anklet round his left ankle depicted the Sun Disc. He walked past, came back and kicked me viciously in the ribs. I rolled on my side, hand going for one of my daggers. Akhenaten kicked me again, face mottled, froth bubbling at his lips. His eyes seemed like glowing coals. He stood at a half-crouch, hands hanging down, his breathing laboured. He'd wrenched off his head-dress and his robe hung askew. I remember his loincloth being stained at the front, the vein streaks high in his legs. The pain in my stomach and side were intense. For a few seconds, I couldn't breathe; bile gathered at the back of my throat.

'I did better than anyone!' I shouted back, tearing the collar of office from my neck and throwing it at his feet. 'I am not your dog! Go, ask your ministers why *they* didn't know! Where was Ay? *Where?*' I scrambled to my knees and pulled myself up, holding my bruised side. 'Get yourself another dog, Pharaoh. Cut me loose and I'll run.'

Akhenaten started towards me. The babies were shrieking; Ay remained seated in his chair, petrified by fear. Nefertiti was the one who came between us. Running over, she knelt down and put her soft arm round my neck and pulled my face towards her, pressing herself against me. My nose was full of her perfume. My pain was forgotten as her warm softness seemed to envelop me, her breath hot upon my cheek.

'Mahu, Mahu,' she whispered. 'Haven't you heard? Sometimes it's difficult to distinguish between the message and the messenger.' She turned to her husband, her voice high above the cries of the children. She spoke fiercely, I think it was in Sheshnu. Akhenaten's eyes still gleamed with madness.

'Go, Mahu!' she ordered. 'Wait outside!'

She pulled me to my feet and pushed me towards the gate out of the enclosed garden. In the courtyard beyond, Nakhtimin and his men, alarmed by the shouting had drawn their swords. I waved them away and slumped against the gate-post nursing my bruised ribs. From the garden rose shouting and screams. Nakhtimin was called in, then he hurried out. I noticed the collar had been pulled from his neck, the side of his face was blood-red. The shouting continued, then there was silence.

At least an hour must have passed before the gate opened. Akhenaten came out, grasped my hand and raised me up. He was calm, his eyes clear, his mouth smiling. In front of the guards he clasped me close and kissed me full on the mouth, on each cheek, finally on the forehead.

'Don't leave me, Mahu,' he murmured hoarsely, 'because my just rage and divine anger spill out! Come.'

He led me back into the garden. Nefertiti and Ay, all composed, standing hand-in-hand, smiled at me. Akhenaten made me sit in his thronelike chair. He refastened the gold collar round my neck, took the Aten ring off his finger and slipped it on one of mine. Then he patted my shoulder, staring down at me, smiling before squatting on the cushions, gathering his children on his lap.

'I am sorry, Mahu,' he said. 'I truly am.' He kissed the head of one of his daughters. 'You are not a dog but my close friend, my brother. But to learn that I am to die within three days?' He pursed his lips, his strange eyes sad. He kissed his children absentmindedly, stroking their little bodies. I felt embarrassed to be on the throne. Akhenaten's mood had so profoundly changed.

'For what you discovered today,' he continued in a half-whisper, 'you shall always be Pharaoh's special friend.'

Nefertiti gripped my right hand, her sensuous fingers thrusting into my palm. Ay took my left hand, clasping it by the wrist. Akhenaten continued cuddling his children, asked a few questions, nodding vigorously at my replies. He dismissed my warnings.

'I shall go into the Valley of the Shadows.' He raised a hand, fingers splayed. 'My Father and I are one. He is with me. All who are against me are against him. You are my Father's messenger, Mahu. You are part of me as I am part of you. When the Revelation comes, he shall show his face to you and smile on you.' Akhenaten grew solemn, traces of the anger returning. 'These assassins will not know peace either in life or after death. You shall protect me, Mahu. You are my Father's messenger, you shall be with me. You shall be the instrument of our justice and our vengeance.' He pointed his hand at the sky. 'My Father will direct me.' He picked up one of the twins, cuddling her close, turning to kiss her cheek and head. All the time those dark, brooding eyes, unblinking in their gaze, watched me.

'Kill them, Mahu.' He leaned forward. 'Kill them all and send their souls into eternal night.'

Akhenaten was determined to confront the danger, to prove that his Father had not deserted him, but the details of the grand design were left to me. Nefertiti and Ay urged that I tell as few as possible and only let them know what I had to. I became feverishly involved in the preparations. Horemheb, Rameses and Nakhtimin were ordered into the Palace and given temporary command of the chariot squadrons of Hathor, Anubis and Horus, troops whom I reckoned to be the most loyal to us in the Egyptian army. Ostensibly they were to engage in manoeuvres, to be despatched North on training exercises. Secretly they were each given confidential instructions about where to gather, at what hour and what signals they should expect. Mercenaries were brought in by night. They, and trusted units of the Imperial Guard, were ordered into full battle-dress, provided with cold rations and water. Late in the evening, before the day of the expected attack, they were moved secretly into the Valley of the Shadows, to remain hidden in the caves, gullies and hollows. Each man was to be instructed that if he left, or betrayed his position, he would face instant execution. Snefru's comrades were also prepared. They were brusquely informed how Snefru had been sent on a secret errand: they would join him soon, but until then they would be under the direct command of Djarka. I looked at their scarred faces, men who might have served me well. I could not save them. They were tainted and therefore dangerous.

On that fatal day we left in the early hours. I had guessed it was that day: it was inauspicious, but Akhenaten would ignore this and go into the valley whilst the next such day was not for another six weeks, too long for a Libyan war-party to survive on their own in the Eastern Desert. I drove Akhenaten's chariot; small leather cases at my feet carried his war-kilt and armour. The dark was bitterly cold. The stars pressed down close whilst the yawning desert, cloaked in shadows, appeared sinister in its unspoken threats. We entered the valley in that grey light before day; the stars were dimming, the sky turning a strange colour as the creatures of the night roared their hymns and slunk away from the heat of dawn.

I left Djarka and Snefru's retinue armed with shield and spear at the mouth of the valley. Djarka had his instructions. Akhenaten and I went ahead. Our horses, the fastest in the royal stables, were snorting and shaking their heads, the gold dyed plumes between their ears nodding in the early morning breeze. We reached the foot of the sheer cliffs at the end of the valley. Akhenaten thrust the fire-making instruments at me. I set fire to the dry brushwood piled on the steps of the makeshift altar, lit the oil lamps and placed the smoking incense bowls on the grey granite altar slab. Akhenaten serenely offered bread and wine to the Sun Disc now rising in glory, a majestic fiery glow. The God emerged from his Underworld, the Glory of Egypt rising to feast on the hideous banquet of death and destruction which would shatter that day. Akhenaten sang his hymn, an awesome sound in that sombre, ghost-filled valley. His voice rang true and strong, echoing up into the skies.

Once the sacrifice was completed I grasped a fire-brand and made the signal to either side of the valley. The escarpment became alive with men pouring out of the caves, gullies and hollows. Mercenaries led by handpicked officers from the Nakhtu-aa, all armed with heavy shields, spears, war-clubs and curved swords formed serried ranks facing up the valley, shields locked, spears out, swords in their belts or between their feet. Each rank was separated by a line of archers, quivers full, heavy bows ready. Akhenaten armed himself in a coat of polished leather reinforced with metal scales. The war-crown of Egypt was formally fastened to his head with its gold-green straps. He stood like the God Montu in his chariot, javelins in their pouches, a long curved sword in his hand. I donned my armour and stood beside him in the chariot. I had hardly grasped the reins when further down the valley a conch horn wailed, shattering the silence. Our ranks moved to the murmur of men, the creak of leather, the rattle of weapons then that heart-catching silence which always precedes a battle.

Heart pounding, mouth dry, I watched the trackway. Djarka came racing out of the darkness, following the sliver of sunlight racing across the valley floor. The ranks parted. He came running through, bow slung over his shoulders; his quiver was gone but the war-club in his right hand was thick with gore. He knelt before the chariot.

'They are here,' he gasped. 'More than we thought.'

A dull roar rang through the valley, followed by silence. I looked over the heads of our soldiers, along that valley, now brightening under the rising sun. At first I thought a shadow was spreading towards us; it was a horde of men racing like ants, spears and swords glinting. I glimpsed poles bearing the severed, bloody heads of Snefru's men. The enemy poured towards us. They were running blind, dazzled by the light of the rising sun; they had not yet realised what lay before them. Behind the horde rose clouds of dust as their officers followed in a squadron of chariots. The war-cries of the Libyans rose, a bloodcurdling shriek echoing along that narrow trackway. 'Now, Djarka,' I shouted. 'The sign!'

Djarka was ready with a new quiver of arrows and a pot of fire he had taken from the altar. He strung one arrow, dipped its point coated in resin into the flame. One, two, three streaks of red flared up into the sky then the horde was upon us. In the face of the dazzling sun, they realised, too late, our strength and preparations. The impetus of their charge could not be checked whilst their own chariots, moving so fast, clinging close to their rear, made any pause for deployment impossible.

The first wave of Libyans impaled themselves on our spears. Those who slipped and fell were quickly clubbed, trampled underfoot as our first rank stepped forward. Orders rang out. Our foot soldiers knelt as the archers, bows strung, poured volley after volley into the air, loosing a death-bearing hail of cruel barbs to wreck bloody damage amongst the massed ranks of the Libyans. The enemy milled about, their chariots withdrawing clumsily to create more space. Our archers loosed more volleys as we slowly advanced, a wall of razor-sharp death pushing the Libyans back. They desperately tried to break through, only to fall back and regroup. They had glimpsed

Akhenaten in his chariot. I now displayed, at his order, the great silver fan, carved in half-moon shape, bearing the golden emblem of the Sun Disc. The Libyans tried to bring their archers up but the press was too great. We moved, trampling men beneath us, their bodies gashed with arrow and spear, heads a bloody mess from blows inflicted by our powerful war-clubs. Akhenaten stood like a statue, not even wincing as arrows sang by his head and face. He softly sang a hymn to the Aten. I moved the chariot forward; Nakhtu-aa on either side guarded our flanks, cutting the throats of the wounded. The fighting became intense. The Libyans threw themselves on our ranks, trying to scale the valley sides to outflank us. A few did, inflicting terrible damage. I desperately wondered when Horemheb and Rameses would arrive. The Libyans, clad in animal skins, shaven faces covered in war-paint, now concentrated on Akhenaten. Here and there our line buckled. The enemy captains, aware now of our true strength, searched for a weakness. So far I was not part of the fighting, just guiding the chariot; the horses, becoming increasingly frantic, crossed a carpet of tangled bloody corpses. Djarka, moving just ahead of these, slightly stooped, arrow notched, searched for a target. More and more Libyans appeared on our flanks.

'Where is Horemheb?' I screamed.

A group of Libyans came charging down the valley side, desperate to break the Nakhtu-aa. Our archers cut them down. The hideous din of battle filled our world as we hacked, clawed and clubbed. Sometimes it was hard to distinguish between friend and foe as clouds of dust rose, covering us from head to toe in a fine white powder. Once again the Libyans hurled themselves forward. I heard the war-trumpets, braying strongly through the clamour, followed by the thunder of chariots, and new clouds of dust appeared behind the Libyan horde. The Anubis squadrons of war-chariots had finally arrived, each carrying three soldiers. The Libyans were now hemmed in. The battle was won and the massacre began. Streams of blood curled along the valley floor. The Libyans were caught in a trap, a vice slowly closing. They were unable to break through either to the front or the rear. The two valley sides were too steep to scale. Those who tried it stumbled and came rolling down in a cloud of dust and a rain of shale and pebbles. Our men were waiting and cut their throats. We killed and killed until exhausted. I say 'we' though I never struck a blow, guiding the chariot whilst Akhenaten loosed javelin after javelin into the dwindling Libyan mass.

At last the enemy threw down their weapons and knelt in the dust, hands stretched out for mercy – but the bloodlust was up. Those who surrendered had their heads pulled back, their throats slashed. Some mercenaries even forced the young Libyans to lie face down against the hard ground to urinate on them and inflict other indignities before they finished them off. At last Akhenaten issued an order and all fighting came to an end. He climbed down from his chariot to receive the plaudits and cheers from his troops. The Libyan captives were hustled forward, no more than two dozen. An avenue was formed leading up to the imperial chariot, its wheels, the blue and gold electrum, coated in drying blood. One Libyan chieftain tried to bargain for his life. Akhenaten shook his head, gripped his war-club and issued an order. Each prisoner was bound, arms behind him, hustled up and made to kneel. Akhenaten grasped his victim's hair and swung the war-club, cracking skulls, dashing out the victims' brains as easily as he would shatter a nut. The pile of corpses grew. The valley was silent except for the groans of the prisoners and the sound of Akhenaten's bone-crunching war-club. He stood, a fearsome figure, spattered with gore, blood swilling in pools around his ankles. At last all the prisoners were dead. Then Akhenaten lifted the war-club like a priest would an Asperges rod.

'Aten is glorious!' he screamed. 'Our victory is his!'

His voice echoed round the valley like a peal of thunder: again and again he repeated it. His troops replied, going down on their knees, roaring the paean of praise.

'Aten is glorious! Our victory is his!'

Chest heaving, face stained with blood, Akhenaten finally climbed back in the chariot. I gathered the reins as his commanders clustered round. My master congratulated and thanked them.

'Aten is glorious.' He gestured at the carpet of bodies stretching on either side. 'Let the enemy dead rot,' he commanded, 'their bellies swell and burst. Let them stink in the air. They have polluted my Father's holy place. Let their bones whiten as a warning!'

I felt my hand touched. Horemheb, covered in dust and sweat, grinned up at me.

'You delayed.' I leaned down. 'You should have come sooner.'

'The chariots carried more men.' Horemheb wiped the

dust from his lips. 'We were slower than intended but we saved you.'

'And yourself!' I whispered hoarsely, pointing to the mercenaries whom the squadrons had brought in. 'I gave the Captain orders: if you didn't move, they were to kill you.'

Horemheb's eyes smiled. 'I shall remember that, Mahu.'

'And I shall never forget.'

Escorted by his troops, still singing his praises and removing the bodies from the path of his horses, Akhenaten left that valley never to return. At the mouth of the gulley I looked back. Our men were reforming. The sky above them was growing dark now, the vultures sweeping in. They were already busy on the corpses of Snefru's retinue which sprawled headless in bloody pools. I murmured a prayer for them and passed on.

Akhenaten gripped the rails of the chariot, eyes closed, lips moving silently. I don't know whether he was praying or issuing silent threats. However, once we returned to the palace, the terror began. News of the sudden, unexpected battle in the Valley of the Shadows had swept through both the palace and the city. My men had already been prepared. A wave of arrests took place, all land and river routes were sealed. Powerful merchants, notables, and army officers were rounded up and hustled through the streets to be questioned in the palace. Some of the guilty ones had either fled or tried to. A few took poison and those who had fallen under Akhenaten's displeasure were invited to take the same honourable path. Ay set himself up as Pharaoh's supreme judge. Terror was his weapon. Solemn oaths of loyalty, underwritten with generous donations of gold and precious stones, were the acceptable guarantee of good behaviour. Those who kept their nerve and stayed survived. Those who panicked and fled were banished, their estates confiscated. A few were singled out for punishment, being offered exile or a cup of poison. In the army and different Houses of State a number of important posts became vacant, all immediately filled by Ay's nominees. The same happened in the great temples. The priests submitted, the sign of the Aten was publicly displayed and, most importantly, temple granaries and treasures were placed at Akhenaten's disposal. Wealth and foodstuffs from these were distributed amongst the poor, the petty traders and, of course, what Sobeck called 'his own starving flock'.

Sobeck and I met soon after and we agreed on well-organised but very noisy demonstrations in favour of Akhenaten and against the temple aristocracy in both Thebes and the Necropolis. These took place, spoiled by a little rioting and arson, but the effect was pleasing. The doors to the sacred granaries and treasuries were opened even wider. Temple guards and mercenaries were absorbed into Nakhtimin's palace guard. All officers in the army were invited to take oaths of loyalty. Very few refused. Rameses and Horemheb were promoted to full Colonels, Scribes of the Army, responsible for the Seth and Anubis regiments, now deployed around Thebes. Changes were also published in provincial towns. The Magnificent One, now a recluse in the House of Love, could do nothing. Our persecution of the Amun cult and its supporters proved unexpectedly easy. In Thebes and elsewhere a deep resentment surfaced at the arrogance, wealth and growing power of Karnak and Luxor. Other temples, both in Thebes and elsewhere, rejoiced at the news of their disgrace and Akhenaten received congratulations and assurances of loyalty from the temples of Horus in the Delta, Ra at Heliopolis, Ptah at Memphis, Osiris at Abydos and elsewhere.

Queen Tiye assumed responsibility for the House of Envoys, dealing with matters beyond Egypt's borders. Pentju became Supervisor of the Royal House of Life. Maya, Overseer of the Royal House of Silver. I was given the House of Secrets. I visited its well-guarded precincts to assume the seals of office, and enjoyed wandering through its courtyards and gardens, visiting the small houses and mansions where the scribes worked. I inspected the dungeons, which were surprisingly empty, and then solemnly processed across a central courtyard to meet its School of Scribes in the hall of columns – a low, dark building shot with rays of light. Flanked by Djarka and three burly mercenary Captains, I displayed my commission and informed them that I was to be Overseer of the House of Secrets with immediate effect. They would take an oath of loyalty to me and would be lavishly rewarded for faithful service. If they found such an oath distasteful they must resign, receive a temple pension and be invited to finish their days farming as far away from me as possible. They were to be given the afternoon to reflect upon my offer and gather again at the ninth hour to take the oath.

'However,' I warned, walking down between them, 'if you take the oath and later betray me, or my masters, you will be impaled, your families sold into slavery and your estates confiscated.'

They sat in silence and heard me out, not that they had much choice. Moreover, like the administrators, they were still stunned by the news of the battle in the Valley of the Shadows a few days earlier. They were also shocked, their loyalty to their own masters severely shaken. Court intrigue and political confrontation were part of their life. However, for high-ranking servants of Pharaoh to invite enemies of Egypt onto her sacred soil, to kill her Prince and ravage his city was a heinous blasphemy. I left them to their thoughts and asked the Chief Scribe to open the Chamber of Secrets where the most confidential and valuable records were kept. He took me down and unlocked the heavy cedar door studded with bronze clasps and ushered me into a windowless room with dark-red walls; countless alabaster oil jars placed in niches provided light. I demanded the records for Akhenaten and the children of the Kap. The Chief Scribe, now sweating and trembling, spread his hands, saw the look on my face and fell to his knees with a moan. 'I am sorry, my lord,' he gabbled. 'God's Father Hotep removed them two days ago.'

I replied that I did not wish to see him again. I added that there were good farms to be bought in the Delta and, if I found him in Thebes the day after next, I would have him impaled in the courtyard outside. I left the fellow to his trembling and met the other scribes, all of whom took the oath. Ay had already given me a list of supporters in the House of Secrets. I chose a lean, youngish-looking Canaanite called Tutu, blunt of speech, sharp of wit and shrewd-eyed. He also had a dry sense of humour, promising to be the most loyal and true Chief of Scribes.

'After all,' he added, 'the worst thing after impalement would be to become a farmer.'

I inspected the House of Secrets but Hotep had done his task well. Many valuable records and manuscripts had simply disappeared. Ay had ordered that, for the moment, neither Hotep nor Shishnak be touched. Nevertheless, I ringed God's Father Hotep's opulent mansion with mercenaries as 'protection during this emergency' and did the same for the Priests' Quarter at Karnak. I became very busy exploiting the growing feeling of outrage in Thebes and throughout the cities along the Nile, at the attempted assassination of Pharaoh's beloved Coregent. Ay's agents were also busy. The chorus of support for Akhenaten swelled into a hymn to be heard on everyone's lips. Foreign envoys visited the Palace of Aten with assurances of support. Mayors and high priests flocked to Akhenaten's splendid receptions in the opulent halls or gorgeous gardens of the Malkata Palace. The immense House of Silver was opened. The treasure of the temples became a river, an unending source of gifts and bribes.

In the month following the Battle in the Valley of the Shadows, Ay and I worked tirelessly, silencing all opposition and encouraging the stream of flattery and praise for our master. Hotep stayed in his mansion tending his garden and composing poetry. Everyone at court realised he had been involved in treason and conspiracy yet he was still the Magnificent One's closest friend, the architect of the glory of the old Pharaoh's reign. Karnak was different. Our spies amongst the priests reported growing divisions and feuds, open muttering which eventually spilt into fierce resentment and revolt at the way Shishnak had managed temple affairs. Bereft of support in either Karnak or Luxor, Shishnak did what I prayed he would. He tried to flee, dressed as a woman, accompanied by a few acolytes. He took a barge North looking for sanctuary. I was waiting for him, with four war-barges full of mercenaries and marines. We intercepted Shishnak's craft, sank it and all aboard, except for Shishnak whom a boarding party plucked screaming from the stern before I gave the order for the Karnak barge to be rammed. Shishnak was bereft of all dignity, a comical figure in his rather gaudy wig, fringed shawl and gauffered linen robe. I insisted that he wear them even as I bound his arms, ignoring his pleas for mercy. I took him to the Palace of the Aten for summary trial before Akhenaten, Nefertiti, and Ay. He was greeted with mocking laughter followed by punches and kicks. Nefertiti, resplendent in her robes, clawed his cheek and spat into his face. Akhenaten punched him in the stomach whilst Ay lounged in his chair and roared with laughter. Shishnak did not face death courageously. He begged and bawled. He tried to plead and bargain. When this was rejected he fell sullenly quiet, refusing to answer the charges of treason and murder.

'You killed my brother!' Akhenaten bellowed. 'You intended to murder me! You have always wanted my death. You used the temple gold to bribe the Libyans. You suborned Snefru. You attacked,' he gestured at me, 'my friend.' He punched Shishnak in the face, splitting his upper lip and drawing blood from his nose. 'You, a priest of Amun, who wipes the arse of a wooden idol and plots the murder and destruction of God's Holy One.'

'No!' Shishnak wailed, his painted face now splattered

with blood, tears and sweat, the ridiculous wig hanging askew. 'It was not me but God's Father . . .'

'God's Father?' Nefertiti yelled, her beautiful face contorted with rage. 'God's Father! How dare you give that viper of a traitor such a title!' She lunged from her chair, a pointed hair-clasp in her hand and gouged the side of Shishnak's neck. The man screamed, turning on his knees as he tried to hobble towards me.

'Mahu,' he whined, 'for pity's sake!'

I knelt beside him and removed that ridiculous wig and wiped his face with a damp cloth. I held a cup of wine laced with myrrh to his lips.

'Drink,' I urged.

Shishnak did so even as Nefertiti screamed at me. Akhenaten protested at the cup being sullied while Ay sat smug and pleased as a cat revelling in the scene.

'Drink,' I repeated. 'Shishnak, you are going to die. All you must do is decide how.'

'Confess,' Ay drawled. He played with the bowl of iced melon in his lap. He sucked on a piece, then offered the bowl to Akhenaten.

'Confess,' I urged. 'Shishnak, you plotted our deaths – the Holy One, his Great Wife, God's Father Ay and myself. Would you have shown me pity, would you have laughed as I was impaled or buried alive in the Red Lands?'

Shishnak drank greedily from the cup.

'You are like a soldier,' I continued. 'You chose to go to war and you lost. Go into the night like a man.'

I recalled the Jackal leader chuckling at me, the ice-cold terror I felt on that nightmare river journey. 'I can do no more.'

I let him drain the cup. Djarka joined us in the hall of columns. He fastened a cord round Shishnak's forehead, looped in a small rod and began to turn. Shishnak's screams were hideous. Akhenaten called for a halt. The Hittite Orchestra of the Sun was summoned, gathering at the far end of the hall, and ordered to play as loudly as possible. Djarka returned to his task. Shishnak's eyes bulged, face turning a purple-red, veins standing out. Every so often Akhenaten would crouch before him.

'Yes, Shishnak?' he would ask.

Nefertiti became interested in a floral design she was painting. Ay returned to the reed basket of documents on the floor beside him. They only became interested when Shishnak broke. He talked in exchange for a speedy death and honourable burial. In the end he simply confirmed what we already knew: the plot against Akhenaten at the Temple of Karnak; the unfortunate death of Tuthmosis; the bribing of the Libyans with gold; the suborning of Snefru and the attack on me. To give him credit he took full responsibility and would give no other name. By now he knew he was going to die, determined to salvage whatever dignity he could.

'I can tell you no more.' He shook his head, his face a dreadful mass of blood and bruises. 'As you say, Mahu, I fought and lost.'

I crouched before him. 'Murder, assassination, attempted regicide, blasphemy, high treason,' I declared. 'Fitting tasks for a High Priest of Amun.' I paused. 'Surely you have other names?' I picked the bloody cord from the floor and handed it back to Djarka.

'Rahimere,' Shishnak stuttered.

'He's already dead from fright.'

'Or poison,' Nefertiti said coquettishly.

'And God's Father Hotep?' I asked.

Shishnak nodded. 'Always Hotep,' he sighed. 'From the very beginning it was always Hotep.'

Nefertiti herself brought the cup. She squatted on cushions and, head to one side, watched Shishnak intently as he drank the poisoned wine. Akhenaten lounged in his thronelike chair, one finger to his mouth, the other beating a tattoo on his arm as if measuring the music of his orchestra. Ay composed a poem, 'The Death of Amun'. I walked away. Eventually, Shishnak ceased his death groans. Akhenaten stood over the corpse.

'Nakhtimin!' he shouted.

The new Chief of the Army of the Palace hurried in.

'Burn this.' Akhenaten kicked the corpse.

'I thought . . .'

'You thought wrong, Mahu. I think right.'

The following afternoon I visited Hotep. I found him in his luxurious, well-laid out garden, sitting on a high-backed cushioned chair, positioned to catch both the sun as well as the welcome shade of an overhanging sycamore tree. Dressed in an elegant robe, head and face shaved and oiled, he was staring out across the flowerbed, a goblet of wine on the table before him. A cowed servant had ushered me in, explaining in a frightened whisper how everyone else had fled.

'The mercenaries protecting me are courteous.' Hotep didn't even glance up as I approached. 'I recognised the Captain. We once served together in Kush. He has been very kind, Mahu, but very firm. He was to protect me. I was not to leave.' Hotep gestured at the cushions piled on the other side of the table. 'But I didn't want to leave, Baboon of the South. Well' – his smile widened – 'what do you bring me, life or death?'

'Death.'

'I thought so.'

'But a merciful one.'

'Pharaoh can remove the breath from a man's nostrils and mouth,' Hotep declared, 'but he cannot direct a man's soul.' He lifted a hand. 'Listen, Mahu. There is nothing more soothing than the love call of a dove. I am going to miss all this.'

'You were expecting me?'

'I heard about Shishnak. My servants were allowed down into the marketplace. Poor Shishnak,' he sighed, 'such a fool. What a dreadful mistake he made. I knew we were finished.'

'Mistake?' I asked.

'The Libyans.' Hotep sipped at the wine. 'It was his idea. Oh, don't worry, I went along with it though I considered it a mistake then, and I still do.'

'So why did you continue?'

'Sit down, Mahu, and I'll tell you.'

He waited until I was comfortable and offered me some wine. I refused.

'The Grotesque should have been strangled at birth.' Hotep leaned forward, cradling the cup. He spoke, head to one side, as if talking to himself. 'No, more than that! The Magnificent One should never have married that Sheshnu bitch, Tiye, her head full of visions, her mouth babbling dreams about an invisible, all-seeing god.' Hotep sighed. 'But the Magnificent One always had his heart between his legs. In her youth, Mahu, Tiye was more resplendent than the sun! She was truly beautiful, most skilled in the art of lovemaking.' He grinned at me. 'The Magnificent One himself told me that.' He paused and leaned back in the chair. 'I was the Magnificent One's friend. True scribe, Chief Architect. I built temples, magnificent palaces the length of the Nile but Tiye was always whispering in his ear. The Magnificent One did not understand her idea of a universal god, so she fastened on the Aten, the Sun Disc as its manifestation. She also talked about the Messiah, a Prince who would come and change all things. The Magnificent One laughed. Then Crown Prince Tuthmosis was born: comely, a fitting Prince for Egypt, followed by the Grotesque. The priests, with their soothsayers, horoscopes, predictions and prophecies, wanted him dead.'

'But you didn't believe those?'

'No, I didn't. What concerned me was that Tiye saw the Grotesque as the Chosen One. The Magnificent One wanted him dead. Tiye pleaded for his life. I knew what the wily bitch would do. She kept the Grotesque out of sight, raised in Heliopolis where his cunning little heart was filled with teachings about the Invisible One, the Aten, and how he was the Aten's Holy One. Years later, Tiye tripped into the Divine One's bedchamber with a new scheme. The Grotesque was growing up. Why couldn't he join certain, selected children of the Kap? I put an end to that nonsense. I had him shut up in the pavilion, guarded by men as grotesque as himself.'

'You tried to kill him?'

'Of course I did – poisoned wines, poisoned foods, that fanatic down by the quayside. All my work. Then he joined the army on the Kushite campaign. Tiye was insistent that he join the children of the Kap, that he see military service.'

'You sacrificed Colonel Perra, didn't you?'

'Yes, I did. I bribed the Kushite chieftains with silver. They were to butcher Perra and attack his camp. In one blow I'd rid the world of the Grotesque' – he raised his cup – 'as well as the other children of the Kap.' He shifted the cup to one hand and pointed at me. 'I was already growing concerned about you, Mahu. More importantly, I half believed the ranting of the priests. The Grotesque's life seemed to be charmed.'

'Sobeck?'

'Ah yes, Sobeck. Imri had been suborned. He was a killer. He murdered Weni for mocking a royal prince.' Hotep chuckled. 'I can laugh at the Grotesque, but a fat creature like Weni? Imri was also the one that arranged the poisoned wine and the vipers in the basket. His apparent carelessness allowed that assassin on the quayside to approach. Your Aunt Isithia learned about Sobeck's dalliance and Imri supplied the evidence. I hoped to implicate all the children of the Kap, but I couldn't. Tell me, has Sobeck truly survived? I have spies in the city but they are not very good . . .'

I simply stared back.

'Ah well.' Hotep sipped the wine. 'That's when the priests of Karnak decided to intervene. Shishnak never forgave the Grotesque for singing that hymn to the Aten. He saw it as an act of defiance. Well, the rest you know.

I made a number of mistakes. I didn't plan for the Magnificent One to become so absorbed in his own daughter or having his wine laced with poppy juice. I have always underestimated Queen Tiye and the children of the Kap, particularly you, Mahu.'

'Why do you hate my master?'

'I don't hate him at all,' Hotep replied, 'only what he stands for. Egypt is unified, mistress of a great empire – and do you know why, Mahu? Because everybody can have their own god. They are allowed to walk their own path. People like myself, a mere commoner, can rise to the height of greatness. The gods of Egypt protect me. Tell me, Mahu, what is going to happen when all of Egypt is told there is only one god and no other? That the god of the Egyptians is also the god of the Mitanni, the Hittites, the Libyans, the vile Asiatics, the Kushites? More importantly, what happens when people *don't* accept that?'

'I don't,' I retorted.

'No, Mahu, you don't, but you're just as dangerous. In your eyes Akhenaten is a god and must be served.'

'You know his secret name?'

'It's no more secret,' Hotep laughed, 'than the price of corn in the marketplace. Think, Mahu, today Amun-Ra, tomorrow Osiris, the next day Isis. Judgement meted out to all the gods of Egypt, dismissed as idols! Pieces of clay and stone to be smashed! What will comfort the people then? What hope do they have of an afterlife in an Egypt with one god, bereft of all her statues and idols? No more temples, no Necropolis. Do you think people will accept that?' he added softly. 'Thousands of years of history being wiped out like a stain on the floor? There will be civil war within ten years. What then, about the power of Pharaoh and the might of Egypt? And in the end, Mahu, for what? An invisible god.' He shook his head. 'Yet in the end, we'll arrive back to the beginning. Egypt will have a visible god, the only god, not some mysterious presence or unseen being, but Pharaoh Akhenaten.'

'God's Father, you should have been a prophet.'

'Spare me your sarcasm, Mahu. Certain things are written for all to see. It's just a matter of reading and studying them closely.' He sipped at the wine. 'You've been down to the House of Secrets.'

'You removed certain records.'

'No, Mahu, I *burned* certain records. Let me leave you with a thought. Your Aunt Isithia – well, she was a remarkable woman.' He peered closely at me. 'You arranged her death, the fire which destroyed her house. Oh don't answer, I know you did. She was a singular woman who served her purpose, the handmaid of the God Amun-Ra' – he grinned – 'and a close friend of both myself and the Magnificent One.' He lowered his head, clearly enjoying himself. 'Your mother was also remarkable, Mahu. Have you ever wondered why your father was so distant from you? I'll tell you bluntly. He often deserted her. Aunt Isithia used to bring her to court. She became very close to both myself and the Magnificent One.'

I sat against the cushions, face flushing, the blood pulsing through my head. 'What are you saying?' My mouth was dry, my tongue felt swollen.

'What am I saying, Mahu? I am quoting the old adage,

"it's a wise man who knows his own father".' He smiled at me.

I grasped my dagger, but let my hands fall away.

'You will not be a martyr, God's Father Hotep, struck down in your garden by Akhenaten's assassin – that's how you would like it to read.' I controlled my fury. 'What does it matter where we come from, who is our father or our mother or where we are going?'

'That's what I like to hear, Mahu, the voice of the soothsayer. Tell me.' He sipped from the wine cup and refilled it from a jug shaped in the form of a goose's head. He mingled a little powder from a pouch next to the jug. 'Tell me, Mahu, what will you do if Akhenaten turns against you?'

'Why should he?'

'It could happen.' Hotep stirred the wine with his finger. 'He'll have his head now, Mahu. There will be no one to stop him, not for the present but,' Hotep's eyes creased into a smile, 'I have done what I can for the future.' He picked up the wine cup, toasted me and drank deeply. 'Please go outside for a while, then return. You'll find I am gone. The Great House can publish how I died peacefully in my sleep. Go on, Mahu, get out!'

I rose.

'Mahu! I am sorry – I mean about your mother, yet I have told you the truth. I made two mistakes about you. I should never have left you in the hands of that hideous woman Isithia. I wouldn't have put her in charge of a dog.' He grinned. 'But, there again, you know all about that.'

'And the second mistake?'

'I truly underestimated you, Mahu, and so has Akhen-aten!' He raised his cup in one final toast. 'I'll be waiting for you in the Halls of the Underworld!'

Kemet Meer – Egypt is happy.

Chapter 16

All glory to the power of the Aten.
All glory to he who existed before time and sustains all
    time!
A thousand upon thousand jubilees to his glorious reign.
All power to the Aten, the One, the Indivisible.

Such songs rang through Thebes: all along its avenues,
narrow twisting streets and across the broad, seething
river into the Necropolis. The paean echoed around the
tombs of the dead and up beyond the great brooding peak
where the Goddess Meretseger had her home. The song
of the Aten was everywhere. On shopfronts, on stalls,
carved on the pylons and temples, displayed on their
banners and pennants. Akhenaten had come into his
own. He had broken with convention and, dressed in all
the glorious war regalia of Pharaoh, processed solemnly
through the city. Nefertiti, in the chariot beside him,
received the plaudits of the crowd. There was none of

the usual pomp, the clashing of cymbals, the rattling of sistra, the clouds of incense or the songs of the Divine choirs. No priest went before him. Only Akhenaten in all his magnificent glory, Master of Thebes, Ruler of Egypt, against whom no one dared raise a hand. The news of Hotep's death and the disappearance of Shishnak were warning enough. Akhenaten, together with Ay, ensured that every vacancy, every position of power in both the Great House and the temples were held by their friends and allies.

Akhenaten wished to prove how he feared nothing. He insisted that the imperial bodyguard not accompany him on his royal progress, the roaring crowds being held back by a dangerously thin line of foot soldiers from the Seth and Anubis regiments.

'I put my trust in the Aten,' Akhenaten had boasted.

We had all bowed and nosed the ground before him, though my confidence in the Aten was not so great. I had the side streets packed with mercenaries, and master bowmen from the Syrian company on the tops of houses and palaces, as well as barges of marines along the river between Karnak and Luxor just in case the power of the Aten might fail.

On day thirteen in the fourth month of the Growing Season, year five of his Co-regency, Akhenaten held a sumptuous meal in the great Banqueting Chamber at Malkata. He had been absent for about three weeks, leaving us to scurry about to ensure all was well whilst he processed solemnly upriver to the place of the Aten. On his return he made the decision to turn Egypt on its head, to make a new beginning. First we feasted in those glorious chambers. The silver and ebony inlaid tables groaned with the gold cups, plates and bowls displaying small irises and water lilies. An imposing procession of servants from every part of the empire, male and female, garbed in pure white linen, served red cabbage, sesame seeds, aniseed and cumin in order to create a great thirst to be quenched by the coolest beer, Hittite wines and the best from Pharaoh's vineyards in Egypt and Canaan. After this came roast geese, haunches of calf and gazelle steaks adorned with ham frills, all roasted over wood with bowls of blood gravy and dishes of every type of vegetable. We ate and drank our fill, whilst the Orchestra of the Sun played sweet music and the divine choir chanted hymns to the Aten.

Once the servants withdrew, the gilded doors were locked and secured, the oil lamps freshened, and more wine served. Ay called the revellers to order. We were all present – Nefertiti, Tiye, Horemheb and Rameses, Pentju, Huy, Meryre, Maya and the newcomer, Tutu, who had won the full support of Ay. Tutu had been promoted to the rank of Chamberlain and First Servant of Neferkheprure-Waenre, Akhenaten's new throne-name translated literally as 'The transformation of Ra is perfect, the unique one of Ra'. Nefertiti also had a new name, being called Nefernefruaten meaning 'Beautiful are the beauties of Aten'.

Ay began the proceedings. For the first time we heard Akhenaten's vision of the Godhead, himself as well as his future intentions. I can still recall Ay's powerful voice rolling through the chamber. First he began with a hymn.

'Beautiful, you appear from the horizon of heaven,
Oh, living Aten who causes all life!
You have risen from your eastern horizon
And every land is bathed in your beauty!
You are fair, dazzling high over every land.
Your rays have reached to the limits of the earth.
You are Ra, you have reached the limits
and subdued them for your beloved son.
Although you are far away, your rays caress the earth
and so you are seen.'

On and on he went. One line, I remember, pricked my ears.

'You are in our hearts but no one knows you except
your son Neferkheprure-Waenre . . .'

Most of this hymn was drawn from chants devised by other temples. Ay paused, wetted his throat and continued, his voice no longer so sing-song. He was now acting as the King's mouth, proclaiming the King's words.

'Look, I am informing you regarding the forms of other gods: their temples are known to me, their writings learned by heart. I am aware of the primeval bodies. I have watched them as they ceased to exist, one after the other, except for the god who begot himself by himself, the Glorious Aten.'

I glanced along the table. Most of the guests had drunk too deeply to be taking note, but Horemheb, sat next to me, had a fierce scowl on his face.

'As for Thebes,' Ay continued, 'and the things that have been done here,' his voice rose to a chant, 'they are worse than the things we heard in year four of our reign, worse than the things that we heard in year three of our reign, worse than the things we heard in year two of our reign . . .'

On and on he went. This was the only reference Akhenaten made to the conspiracy and treason he'd confronted.

'However, on this day, Akhenaten,' Ay proclaimed, 'His Majesty obvious in a great chariot of electrum, appeared in glory just like Aten does when he rises in the horizon and fills the land with love and pleasantness. He set off on a good road towards the place of the Aten. He found himself a great monument there. He has ridden a circuit and the land will rejoice and all hearts will exult. He will make an estate of the Aten for his Father, erect a memorial to his name and to the great Royal Wife Nefernefruaten – Nefertiti. It will belong to Aten's name for ever and ever. Now it is the Aten who has advised him concerning this. No official ever advised him. Nor did any person in this land. It was the Aten his Father who advised him so it could be built here. So, in the place of the Aten, he shall make a house to the Aten his Father. He shall also make a sun shade for the great Royal Wife. He shall make himself a residence. There shall be made a tomb for him in the Eastern Mountains. Let his burial be after the millions of jubilees which Aten his Father has bequeathed to him. He shall never leave that place. He shall not go to the North or the South, the East or the West, but in that place he shall make something beautiful for the Aten his Father.

Something beautiful in the North, something beautiful in the South . . .'

By now the Royal Circle was alert but very silent, listening intently to this proclamation. Beneath the courtly courtesies, the pious exclamations, the tributes to the Aten, the reality emerged. Akhenaten was to shake the dust of Thebes from his feet. He would desert the gods of Egypt and build a new city, a great shrine for the Aten.

I closed my eyes and thought of that sandy cove stretching to the mountains. Akhenaten was determined on this. During Ay's declamation, he sat, a faint smile on his face, dressed in a kilt of gold silver cloth and a shirt of the same material: a brilliantly coloured sash with gorgeous tabs circled his waist, over his shoulders lay a jewel-encrusted cape. Diamonds gleamed in his earlobes and on his fingers, legs and ankles. A pectoral displaying a golden Sun Disc surrounded by precious stones lay flat on his chest. A feathered crown on his head made him look taller. He cradled in his lap a jewel-encrusted *ankh* along with the gold-filigreed flail and rod. Akhenaten's face was subtly painted, lips red with carmine, eyelids dusted a light green. Dark kohl rings circled the eyes. He looked majestic, the fine jewels transforming his misshapen body and ugly face into a vision of power and glory. Beside him sat Nefertiti, her red hair tumbling down, a plumed crown on her head, her face exquisitely painted. She was clothed in robes of gold and silver, shimmering with jewels, yet the beauty of her face and the brilliance of her blue eyes cut through all this and made my heart ache. These were not the cruel mockers who had attended Shishnak's trial. They had transformed themselves into immortal beings surrounded by light. Even the air around them was heavy with perfumed glory. I became lost in a reverie as Akhenaten's proclamation offered a new beginning. Our enemies were no more. No hand would be raised against us, no pit dug to trap us. No crook across our path to bring us down.

After his hymn to the Aten, Ay turned to more practical details, listing the treasure of the Temple of Amun which would be used to finance Akhenaten's vision. I half-listened, staring at Nefertiti. I realised that, whatever she did, whatever she said, she was my vision, my Aten. She looked so exquisitely beautiful, those crystal blue eyes staring at me, savouring a quiet joke as if we were both fellow conspirators. Beside her Tiye, dressed in jewel-encrusted silver, enjoyed this moment of triumph. The rest were drunk not only on wine but on visions of further power and glory as they gathered on the threshold of a new era. As for me, Mahu the Baboon of the South? I would have given it all up to be lying in an orchard, Nefertiti beside me serving wine. A sharp dig in my ribs shattered my dream. Horemheb was glaring at me.

'For what we were,' he whispered beneath the discussion going on around us, 'for what we are now. Mahu, listen to me. He's mad! He's insane!'

The comment was so sharp, such a contrast, that I burst out laughing. Ay stared across. Akhenaten's smile faded whilst Nefertiti frowned.

'I am sorry,' I apologised, 'but listing the treasures of Karnak I thought of Shishnak in his wig.'

A murmur of laughter greeted my words. I got to my feet.

'Your Majesty, I must withdraw.'

I left the brilliantly painted Chamber of the Glorious Falcon and almost ran down the corridor, tiled in cobalt-blue, its walls painted a golden yellow with blood-red diamonds at top and bottom. I hastened past guards and servants and out into the moon-bathed courtyard. There I went over to the fountain and sat on its edge and let the laughter come. The more I tried to stop, the worse it became. Horemheb and Rameses followed. They, too, had excused themselves. I watched the water spilling out of the eagle's mouth, making the lotus blossom rise and sink. I tried to compose myself but still I laughed. Horemheb and Rameses tried to speak. They stood, dressed in polished leather kilts, necks and chests adorned with golden necklaces and silver beads, staffs of office in their hands. The very sight of them sent me into further peals of laughter whilst they stood and glowered as if I was some impertinent recruit. The more they did so, the worse it became. Tears coursed down my cheeks, my sides ached, but I could not stop.

'What is so funny?' Rameses demanded.

The laughter bubbled up again. I could not speak. Behind Horemheb and Rameses a shadow moved in the colonnades. Djarka was there, his bow already strung. I raised my hand and shook my head. He retreated deeper into the darkness as Horemheb and Rameses turned.

'Mahu!' Horemheb grasped me by the very front of my robe and pulled me towards him. 'Mahu!'

'I am sorry.' I wiped the tears on the back of my hand. 'I was just sitting there lost in the dreams of glory, listening to the revelations of a god. And what do you say,

Horemheb?' I hissed. 'He's mad! He's insane!' I pushed him away. 'You could lose your head for such a remark.'

Horemheb stepped back.

'Oh, don't worry,' I whispered. 'I have never laughed so much for such a long time. It was such a contrast, so comical.'

Rameses measured his steps as he walked towards me and stopped, his face only a few inches from mine.

'We know it is, Mahu. It's madness, sitting there, eating cabbage and onions, chewing soft meat and gulping sweet wines whilst listening to the ranting and ravings of a god-obsessed fanatic.'

'You could both lose your heads,' I replied.

'We are only telling the truth,' Horemheb protested. He gestured back towards the palace. 'People suspect but they don't really know. Can you imagine, Mahu, what is going to happen when this is proclaimed beyond the Third Cataract or across Sinai? The Pharaoh of Egypt is about to break from the past, lost in a dream of building a new city, a new capital. Are the old gods to be destroyed, the temples closed? Will the Necropolis truly become the City of the Dead? Don't you realise, Mahu, Akhenaten intends to begin again. Can you imagine the cost of it all? If our treasure is diverted to building cities out in the desert, if our energies are devoted to the worship of the one god, who will pay for the troops? The chariots? The horses? Who will send gold, silver and precious stones to our allies?'

'You are beginning to sound like God's Father Hotep.'

'No, we are just talking sense!' Rameses protested, but fear glowed in his eyes. Pride warmed my heart. Rameses the snake, for the first time ever, was fearful. Both of them were here to ask for my help, my advice.

'Well,' Horemheb poked me in the chest. 'Do you believe all this, Mahu? Playing at being priests and temple worshippers is all very well, but what about in a year's time, ten years' time?'

'We are on a river,' I replied. 'We must let the current take us.'

'To our deaths?'

'Rameses, we are all going to die.'

'Not before our time,' Horemheb snapped. 'Mahu, you know, I know – we *all* know this is madness.'

'So the river rushes fast.'

'Look.' Horemheb grasped my wrist. 'I am grateful for what you have done for me and for Rameses. We are also grateful for what you did for Hotep.' Horemheb shook his head. 'I had no quarrel with him, Mahu.'

'Except that he tried to get us all killed out in the Red Lands.'

'Politics,' Rameses grinned. 'It also gave us the opportunity for glory and the rewards that went with it.'

'Akhenaten gave Hotep honourable burial,' I replied, 'because he had no choice. Hotep was the people's hero.'

Horemheb withdrew his hand.

'What is it?' I asked. 'Horemheb, what are you really concerned about? Akhenaten is not threatening the army or preparing to surrender Egypt's power.'

'I am most concerned. I am frightened.' Horemheb wiped his hands together. 'The things I am concerned about will happen in the future. It will take years. Did you listen to Ay carefully, Mahu? I have no difficulty accepting Pharaoh's title of being God's Son or likening himself to the Hawk of Horus or the Ibis of Thoth. As far as I am concerned, he can give himself any title he wants. No.' Horemheb lifted a warning finger. 'Listen to that proclamation carefully, Mahu. There is only going to be one god in Egypt, a country which, for thousands of years, has worshipped what she likes. This god is to be Akhenaten himself.'

'So?' I shrugged. 'His father laid claim to similar powers, that he was God's Regent on earth.'

'No!' Horemheb continued remorselessly. 'Akhenaten not only claims to be the only recipient of this new revelation but that, somehow or other, he pre-existed: he knew the Aten before he was born.'

'What my good friend is saying,' Rameses leaned his hand on Horemheb's shoulder and pushed his face close, 'is that it is only a matter of time before Akhenaten claims he is the Aten, the Sole God.'

'Just titles!' I scoffed. 'Grandiose words which no one really believes.'

'Someone already believes it,' Rameses retorted, black eyes gleaming. 'Akhenaten himself. That's why we call him mad, insane and stupid.'

'It will not come to that. Akhenaten is simply lost in visions of glory.'

'Oh, he believes it,' Rameses laughed, 'he and his red-haired Queen. They see themselves as gods incarnate and that's where the danger lies. If they truly believe it, they'll eventually expect every one of their subjects to believe it too. What happens then, Mahu, to those who object, who protest? Who would like to point out that our army needs strengthening or ships need to be built or that our garrisons in Canaan need to be strengthened? Will we be told to shut up? That the Great God who arranges everything will do something? And what happens, Mahu, when he tells the Kings of the Mitanni and the Hittites, the Princes of Canaan and Kush that he is not their ally any longer? That he is their God instead – and must be obeyed.' Rameses patted Horemheb on the shoulder. 'Now, Mahu, think of that.' And they both turned and walked away.

The revolution occurred; Akhenaten's will was supreme. Thebes went down into the dust to make submission but now he trod on the city's head, made its citizens breathe in and choke on the dust of his own departure. He would forsake Thebes. He would leave it for ever. He would let it wither like the fruit on the branch and no one could oppose him. The Magnificent One, drunk, drugged and failing, was now being fed the milk of mother mice mixed with ale in an attempt to cure his different ailments. Live, freshly shelled mussels were used to ease the pain of his sore gums but, in the end, it was always the sweet juice of the poppy which soothed the pain and sent him into a drugged sleep.

For a short while I fell ill myself – with a fever brought on, Pentju claimed, by exhaustion and excitement. I hoped that Nefertiti would come and tend me. I even sent Djarka with messages excusing my presence from the Royal Circle, but she never replied. Pentju tended me well; Khiya brought him to my bedside. She often visited me, chattering away about the affairs at court. She'd formed a firm friendship with Pentju and, when he finished with me, I would often glimpse them from my window walking in the gardens, heads together, squatting down, studying some herb or plant. Nefertiti didn't visit me because she and Akhenaten were concerned with nothing but the move to the City of the Aten. I was swept up in the same preparations. The erection of stelae and boundary stones on the edges of that great crescent of sand beneath the eastern cliffs marked the beginning. I witnessed Akhenaten, glorious in his chariot, whip in hand, moving round the entire area dedicating the sacred spot revealed to him by the Aten. The news swept through Thebes like a sudden thunderstorm but, of course, it had all been prepared. Ay had seen to that. The wells were already dug, springs uncovered, canals constructed, the fertile edges on the eastern bank of the Nile brought under swift cultivation. The imperial fleet was massed. Barges, collected from all over Egypt, were moored at strategic positions along the Nile. Carts by their thousands and countless trains of mules and donkeys were brought from the imperial stables in many cities and villages.

A veritable armada carried courtiers, musicians as well as the hordes of administrators together with shrubs, plants and seeds to the place of the Aten. The waters of the Nile were almost hidden by the great flotilla. Along the banks moved line after line of carts, donkeys, and mules piled high with wood. Flanking these was the massed might of Egypt's army: footsoldiers, archers, and squadron after squadron of war-chariots. I would have loved to have flown like an eagle to view the majestic power and might of Egypt all moving North to the place of the Aten. A veritable army ringed the land approaches whilst war-barges patrolled the river. Thebes was shocked, its leading citizens given no quarter. Power followed Pharaoh. If Pharaoh left Thebes the dilemma was whether to stay and lose all influence, and any hope of preferment, or abandon the family home and join the great exodus North. Workers in the Necropolis rioted as they realised the impact of the new religion on their labour. Nakhtimin's troops, assisted by my police and Sobeck's gangs, crushed these disturbances.

I met my old friend secretly. Sobeck had decided not to move North but stay where he was and, as he put it, 'look after the City of the Sceptre till the eventual return'. It was the old Sobeck, relaxed and cynical, as intent on building his own empire as Akhenaten was to realise his dream. He admitted that he had met Maya. I explained the circumstances. Sobeck just shrugged, gave that lopsided smile and murmured that, at least, he had another friend high at court. I and the other members of the Kap had no choice but to leave Thebes. The Old City, as it was now termed, was left under the command of Nakhtimin and my subordinates in the East and West.

Time flew. I seemed to spend my life journeying by river to and from Thebes. The entire archives of the House of Secrets were moved to that sandy crescent which now blossomed into a city of pavilions and tents. Chaos was avoided. Akhenaten and Ay had planned so well, so resolute in their plundering of the temple treasuries, that enough provisions and supplies were at hand to feed the growing influx of citizens and workers. Thousands upon thousands of sculptors, architects and craftsmen were hired to work under the direction of Akhenaten's Chief Architect Bek and his two assistants Tethmos and Intu. Bargeloads of sandstone from beyond the First Cataract were on the move North. Ships, their cargo-holds full of sweet-smelling Lebanese cedar, travelled across the Great Green to disgorge their cargoes in the Delta to be placed immediately on the waiting barges. The nearby marble quarries of Hathor were quickly extended, thousands of workers from Thebes hired, the precious stone hacked and sledged into the Holy Place. Alabaster, as well as copper and malachite from Sinai and Kush, together with gold, silver and lapis lazuli from all the mines of Egypt followed after.

All this had been planned from the start. Ay had plotted and worked into the early hours, year after year, as Akhenaten prepared for his great moment. Ay proved himself an administrative genius. I admired him for his subtle cunning, the way he'd kept his plans so close to his heart. The city had been created in the minds of Akhenaten, Ay and Nefertiti and kept secret in detailed plans on roll after roll of papyrus. Akhenaten realised his dream of creating a place for the Aten; he also wreaked hideous vengeance on the great ones of Thebes, its nobles, administrators and priests who, for years, had either ignored or mocked him.

At first Akhenaten's opponents tried to exploit the situation but Sobeck's influence was even greater whilst the prospect of work for the new city emptied the slums of both Thebes and the Necropolis. Tens of thousands of people wrapped their possessions in bundles and trekked

North to begin a new life. They were quartered on the west bank of the Nile and used to shape millions upon millions of hard mud bricks. Surveyors became busy with stakes and ropes laying out the new city in accordance with Akhenaten's dream. The shanty towns around the construction site grew whilst detailed plans ensured a special place for the imperial family and other nobles and scribes. All was protected by Egypt's war-chariots, her massed regiments drawn in from every garrison and outpost throughout the Kingdom of the Two Lands. The Nile had just flooded so transport was easy whilst the deserts on either side, deliberately neglected for years, were full of game for the hunter. At the same time the great storehouses and granaries of nearby cities were ordered to open their doors to send a constant stream of supplies to that great camp now growing midway between Memphis and Thebes. No wonder Ay had been concerned about the previous harvests. They had been good and so now he reaped the fruits of his hard work.

I must confess in my long, sin-sodden life, I have met few real surprises, but to see a city, its palaces, temples, houses, gardens, parks, pools and lakes literally spring up from the desert was truly awesome. It happened so quickly, almost like the sun rising and flooding the land with colour and exciting life. What a city! All the resources of a great empire were directed to its construction. The imperial residences were the first priority; its colonnaded great bridge spanned the King's Highway with the glorious Window of Appearance so Akhenaten and Nefertiti could meet those they wished to favour. The Northern Palace followed next with its inner and outer courtyards, glistening pools, colonnades, altars open to the sun, gardens full of flowers, and row upon row of lush vines. Floors were laid, so highly polished they gleamed like water. The beautiful Green Room was constructed with its long windows all two yards high and seven yards long, overlooking the most sumptuous garden, richly stocked with every kind of herb, flower and tree. The Chamber's other three walls were painted a deep blue to reproduce the beauty of the Nile. The exquisite green borders at top and bottom represented the Nile's fertile banks, alive with all the exotic birds of the riverside. The floor and ceiling were of pure white, so brilliantly constructed and originally painted, the illusion was created that the room was an extension of the garden and that the garden was an extension of the room.

Other chambers in the palace were decorated with different motifs. In the River Room, kingfishers nested in lotus and papyrus thickets, the red spathus of the papyrus so realistic, they seemed to be bending under a breeze. Above these, black and white kingfishers dived towards the water, so vivid you'd expect to hear the splash and see them fly up. Another chamber, the Vine Room, was decorated with girls gathering grapes whilst nearby bird-catchers drew in a clap net full of trapped wild fowl, so lifelike, if you stared long enough you'd think the birds were about to flutter, you'd even strain to catch their cries. The ceiling was decorated with pictures of vine trellises, their grapes of purple faience so luscious you were tempted to stretch up and pluck them. In the centre of this palace, as in other palaces, was the Throne Room with majestic columns on either side resplendent in every colour. At the far end, under a beautiful sculptured canopy of stone, stood the gold and jewel-encrusted thrones of Akhenaten and his Queen.

The temples of the Aten, the Eternal Mansion or the House of Rejoicing dazzled the eye with the whiteness of their limestone founded on pink granite. These were approached through soaring pylons: you would cross spacious courtyards and climb tiers of steps to altars open to the sky, carefully positioned to catch the rays of the sun. Around these sanctuaries stood the storehouses stuffed full of gorgeous tribute brought to the temples from the broad-slabbed quaysides which now ran along the Nile. All such buildings were bounded by walls, each with its own spring, well and gardens. Every palace had its own sunshade pavilions, garden chapels with cool rooms and colonnaded walks decorated with gold asps as well as plants or flowers painted in the form of rosettes and garlands.

The private houses of the nobles to the north and south of the city were all built flat-roofed and mud-bricked, but made all the more resplendent with columns, porticoes, steps and colonnades, all brightly painted and decorated with artwork. The inside walls blazed with light depicting hunting, farming or river scenes though it was almost compulsory that the central hall depicted Akhenaten, his Queen and their children being blessed by the rays of the Aten. Akhenaten's watchword to his builders, architects and craftsmen was 'to live in the truth'. By this he meant art was to reflect life in all its detail and the heart of all life was the glory of Aten. The nobles were only too eager to comply. Their mansions became small palaces with rich drapes covering the windows, exquisite furniture, beds of ebony and ivory, baskets of flowers and, everywhere, the sign of the Sun Disc, the symbol of the Aten's true son, Akhenaten.

The city was composed of three sections: the northern suburbs, the central city with its temples, Great Palace and Mansion of Aten and, beyond that, the southern suburbs with the villas and mansions of the nobles. To the north-east of the city were the houses of the workers whilst others had to find homes on the west bank of the Nile. Streets were clearly named and the entire city was connected by a broad imperial avenue called the King's Highway. In the centre lay the administrative heart of Akhenaten's city, the House of Scribes, the House of Reception and the House of Secrets with its police station and cells where I executed my office. Djarka became my lieutenant. We allowed no one to join us from Thebes but recruited mercenaries, Asiatics and Nubians to patrol the streets. Horemheb and Rameses were responsible for the security of the approaches by land and river; at night, the eastern clifftops gleamed with the campfires of their soldiers.

I have been asked so many times what life was like in the City of Aten. It was peaceful at first, full of petty incident and excitement as the seasons of the year rolled one into another. All of Thebes and Egypt had been shocked by the speed and thoroughness of Akhenaten's revolution; like a wrestler with the breath knocked out of him, they could only stagger and choke but do little. Animals bitten by a certain snake become paralysed, so it was in both Egypt and the Palace of the Aten. Oh, I can describe the different buildings, their beauty as well as the stream of ordinances issued to keep everything fresh and lovely. But in the end? Well, we were like children invited into a beautiful garden to play. The sun shone and shone and shone, plates of sweet dates and iced melon were served and served and served. The music played and played and played but night never came. No breeze blew to cool our sweat and we were not allowed to go home. The sun, indeed, became too bright. Our guests grew sick of the rich food. Our ears were dinned with so much music, we longed for the darkness of the night and the coolness and peace it would bring.

Aten! Aten! Aten! At first everything was centred around this, with only slight changes in the rhythm. Akhenaten, escorted by Nefertiti, would summon meetings of the Royal Circle to lecture us about the new religion, our duties to him and the Aten, our obligations to accept it in all its ways. Huy quietly grumbled how he would love to go and preach about the Aten somewhere, anywhere, as far away as possible. The theme was constant: 'You should be grateful to Akhenaten for revealing to you the light.' We were to thank him for what he had done, rejoice in his presence, be ecstatic over his gifts, as well as realise that the Aten would only hear our prayers if they were directed through himself and his glorious Queen.

Matters were not helped by what I dubbed 'the toadies', the courtiers and officials who now surrounded Akhenaten. They did not include the children of the Kap except for Meryre: he was made High Priest of the Aten when Akhenaten gave up that office, moving from the role of priest to that of He whom the priests should venerate. The ranks of these toadies were swollen as more of the Akhmin gang arrived. Ahmose, fat and slimy, reeking of perfume, who rejoiced in the titles of True Royal Scribe, Fan-bearer on the Right of the King, Steward in the House of Akhenaten, Overseer of the Court of Justice. A viper of a man, Ahmose had a heart of stone and a nose sharp for his own preferment. Tutu from the House of Secrets became Ahmose's good friend – a disappointment to me but he was seduced by the exclusivity of Akhenaten's immediate circle and, of course, he also came from Akhmin. Another was Rahimose, Chief Scribe of Recruits, Ay's nominee from his own town to counter-balance the growing military power of Horemheb. These and others formed what I called 'the Devout' or, in private, 'the Toadies'. The others, including myself, I called 'the Cynics': Horemheb and Rameses, Pentju, Huy and Maya. They grew bored with the constant childish excitement of the parades and ceremonies, the offerings and rewards. Horemheb and Rameses used their military duties to escape into the Red Lands. Huy often went on embassies and would return more woebegone than ever at Akhenaten's attitude to Egypt's foreign policy.

'It's quite simple to understand,' Huy declared on one occasion. 'All people should worship the Aten and all people should accept our Pharaoh as the Aten incarnate. Any problems are not his responsibility. He thinks the Mitanni, the Canaanites, the Libyans and Kushites should love him for what he is and not for the gold and silver they expect to receive from him.'

The others were equally cynical. Pentju, in particular,

would often use the excuse of tending to a patient or searching for some new cure to avoid official functions. Maya found some comfort in his new duties as Overseer of the House of Silver, proving to be a brilliant financier and treasurer – 'Able,' as Rameses remarked sourly, 'to squeeze gold out of a rock.' Maya often had to travel to Thebes; he would use such occasions to meet Sobeck. At least his return brought a welcome relief as he reported the chatter and gossip from that stunned, dying city. He told us about its temples, the subdued life in the markets and the growing resentment of its populace at what they now openly called the Great Heresy.

Ay was the bridge between all groups. Akhenaten's faithful minister, the confidant and ally of everyone who mattered. A watcher and scrutiniser of hearts was Ay, yet even here I sensed a subdued panic. We had all been brought to this place – but what next? Ay expended his energies on strengthening his ties with the men of influence in the city of Aten and elsewhere, particularly Horemheb whose military skill and organisation he came to admire. Mutnodjmet, Ay's second daughter, Nefertiti's comely, fat-faced, calm-eyed sister, arrived in the city with her Danga dwarves. Horemheb fell in love with her only as Horemheb could: stiff-necked, tight-jawed, stuttering and embarrassed. Yet he truly loved her. I used to tease him, tapping him on the chest and saying, 'At last I have discovered that you have a true heart and not one of flint.' Horemheb would splutter with annoyance, he'd even blush. This was one problem Rameses was unable to help him with so I had constantly to advise Horemheb on what presents to buy and how he should act. Ay encouraged all this. Mutnodjmet was not indolent but she had been kept in the shadows by her beautiful elder sister. At first she was very confused by Horemheb. Eventually, with a little coaxing from both her father and myself, she responded sweetly to the great soldier's overtures. Rameses, too, encouraged that match and eventually they married. Maya tartly commented that he didn't know whom Horemheb loved the most, Mutnodjmet or her dwarves.

Shortly after this, news arrived that the Magnificent One had died. Living in the twilight, he had gone quietly into the West. Queen Tiye buried him in glorious splendour in a majestic tomb prepared for him in the Valley of the Kings, protected by the great Colossi of the King. These gleaming red quartzite statues were built to last for ever, glowering over an empire he had created, 'And,' Rameses whispered, 'which his son was about to lose.'

I always wondered if Queen Tiye had helped her husband over the Far Horizon. She certainly struck quick at the cause of her discontent, Princess Sitamun being promptly banished to some distant estate to live out her life in silent obscurity. Akhenaten and his court observed the seventy days of mourning. Certain monuments and inscriptions were erected to his father but these were more as an afterthought, acts of filial piety to his grey-haired, widowed mother. Queen Tiye became a constant visitor to her son's new city, a small sunshade palace being built and placed at her disposal. She was still courteous and affable to me but more concerned that I protect her son. She no longer had to watch me;

Djarka did that for her. Queen Tiye treated me as she would a good knife, ensuring the point and blade still remained sharp and strong. Nefertiti she avoided, being more concerned to talk to Ay. They would often meet in the Hall of Audience near the Records Office, going through documents, talking far into the night over the growing problems from the distant far-flung provinces to the empire.

Afterwards Ay would visit me to break bread and drink some wine. He had been given the title of Chief of Royal Archers and would use such occasions to check the barracks and storerooms. He was amused at how I kept a small armoury in a chamber on the second floor of my own house. I bluntly informed him that I had not forgotten the Jackals or that bloody battle in the Valley of the Shadows. Ay would nod and, without fail, would ask the same question, probing to find out what I and others of the Kap, as he called us, thought of the present situation. I would snap back that I wasn't a spy and ask him what the future held. He muttered about similar cities being founded in Canaan and Nubia, of arranging eternal treaties of peace with other kings and states. Ay was deeply worried; he had good reason to be.

Akhenaten and Nefertiti, together with their children, were now becoming not just the centre of the new cult but the cult itself. In the northern and southern section of the eastern cliffs, on either side of Akhenaten's planned tomb, we founded our own Necropolis. You can go and look at these, they are still there; most are half-finished. I chose one in the southern cliffs, an underground cavern to fool the grave-robbers. Go into mine and have a good look. The paintings are not much and the prayers to the Aten are all wrong – that was my way of kicking against the goad. Go into the rest and study the paintings and inscriptions. Akhenaten had outlawed the Osirian rite. There were to be no ceremonies of Opening the Mouth, preparing for the Journey through the Underworld where your soul was weighed on the scales of Thoth and received the judgement of Osiris. Oh no, Akhenaten changed all that! He made it much simpler. All you had to do was die with Pharaoh's smile directed towards you (which, of course, you couldn't see because you had your head down and your arse up) and everything would be fine. The Necropolis of the Sun Disc proved this. Every single tomb depicted Akhenaten and Nefertiti, together with their family, giving presents, being blessed by the Aten, riding out together under the Aten, eating under the Aten, playing, drinking, sleeping and kissing under the Aten.

As in death, so in life. We were all given psalters with prayers and hymns to the Aten. We were invited to compete, to show our adulation to the Aten and the royal couple. Even wall paintings had to reflect Akhenaten's command about 'living in the truth': they had to be executed according to a certain style. Some people may call it original, thought-provoking and beautiful. To a certain extent that's true but, when you are surrounded by it day and night, ordered to decorate your tombs in the same imagery, it becomes tiresome like hearing the same piece of music, not so well played, being repeated time and time again.

Why did I stay? Well, where else could I go? My interrogators have asked me why I didn't flee. I think for a long time. I reflect. I recall those events and the answer is quite simple.

Nefertiti's smile!

Mahu, Commander of the Police of Akhenaten.

(Inscription from Mahu's tomb at El-Amarna, the City of the Aten.)

Chapter 17

She whose smile gladdens the heart,
Lovely of face and fair of form.

Oh, it was all true. Nefertiti was beauty itself but in the City of the Aten she proved the truth that beauty has its own terror. Physically she changed. Her face became leaner and harder, the cheekbones more pronounced, her head constantly tilted back, the gaze from those seductive eyes more imperious. She lost her laughter, that streak of girlish impishness and love of mystery. She seemed to live in a blaze of light and assumed the aura of an unapproachable goddess, as if she wished to merge with her husband in both appearance and power. She began to wear the Nubian bag wig which left the nape of her neck exposed, two plaits hanging down either side, imitating the hairstyle of the warriors in her retinue. She wore the flowing, gorgeous robes of a queen but she often manifested herself in a bleak narrow kilt like that of a soldier, though longer, falling to her ankles. The Hathor crown with its horns and plumes was put aside for a small feathered blue crown, very similar to the Imperial War Crown of Egypt. In paintings and carvings Nefertiti was now often depicted as smiting an enemy, adopting the stylistic ritual of a triumphant Pharaoh meting out justice to his enemies. In all things she appeared as a female soldier, a war goddess.

At the same time Akhenaten began to dress in floral attire, perfume-drenched wigs and the light flowing robes of a woman. This transfer of robes and roles was like the meeting of two forces. Would it be a true mingling, I wondered. Or would one absorb the other? If Akhenaten saw himself as the Incarnation of the Aten, what role could be, would be, assigned to Nefertiti? Would they see themselves as the male and female expression of the Godhead, or would he resent it?

The imperial harem at the City of the Aten with its concubines and Royal Ornaments expanded to include noblewomen from different parts of the Empire and those kingdoms who expressed their loyalty by despatching their fairest princesses for the pleasure of Egypt's Pharaoh. Nevertheless Nefertiti still ruled Akhenaten's heart, or so it seemed. Perhaps I was the only one to sense an underlying friction, an impatience on his part with Nefertiti who, at the City of the Aten, provided him with two more daughters but not the son he craved for, the future bearer of his life-giving seed. Sometimes Akhenaten spoke to me alone, not about affairs of state or the security of the city, but reminiscences about the past when he was the Veiled One, living, as he put it, 'in complete holiness and purity'.

I wondered if he yearned for those days. Was he resenting the growing power and strength of Nefertiti, who had failed to produce a beloved son? Queen Tiye's influence had certainly declined. Since the death of the Magnificent One she had lost that aura of power, of ruthless will, as if the accession of her second son and the building of the City of the Aten was the realisation of a dream. I suspect she, too, recognised that all was not well. During ceremonies and processions the tension between the royal couple was sometimes apparent, as if my master wanted to be by himself before the Aten, unwilling and unable to share his divine status with anyone.

In his talks with me he would speak of those cherished memories when he, and no one else, walked the Way to the One.

'I never,' he declared defiantly, 'adored another god,' and then as a veiled attack upon his mother, his wife and the entire Akhmin gang, 'nor did I dance, sing, or profane myself before false idols like that of Min at Akhmin.'

Such moods passed. He'd assume that trancelike state, the result of Nefertiti's potions and powders. At other times, when I was summoned to his chamber or into his gardens, he'd sit withdrawn, unshaven, bleary-eyed as if he had been drinking heavily. Once, when I was waiting, kicking my heels in an antechamber, I heard the sound of raised voices from the imperial bedroom, a heated discussion about the liturgy to be used in a forth-coming ceremony at the sun altar. On another occasion I was summoned to the imperial residence. Akhenaten, heavy-eyed, face drawn, sat in the glorious Green Room staring out over the garden.

'Well,' he demanded as I knelt and nosed the ground, 'I have waited long enough. Your spy in Akhmin – what does he report?'

'Your Majesty,' I remained kneeling. 'What spy? What report?'

'You know full well,' Akhenaten shouted threateningly.

I lifted my head. Spots of anger coloured his sallow face, those strange eyes gleamed, dark wells of anger. He seemed on the verge of hitting me.

'You know what?' He stared at me, mouth sagging. 'I am sorry, Baboon,' he stammered. 'I made a mistake,' and summarily dismissed me.

Nefertiti's sun, however, burned as brightly and fiercely as ever though she must have sensed her husband's disappointment at the lack of a male heir. After the birth of her sixth daughter, in year nine of Akhenaten's reign, she held a celebration in the garden below the Green Room. The children of the Kap were invited. It was like the old days: tables were stacked with platters of every food imaginable and delicious wine had been specially imported from Buto in the Delta. Akhenaten laughed and chatted to Ay. Nefertiti sat, serenely accepting compliments when Pentju, full of wine, cracked a joke about the sex of a child being the gift of the gods. Nefertiti heard him.

'What?' she screamed.

The festivities fell silent. Nefertiti sprang from the chair, clutching her walking stick, carved with the signs of the Aten. The birth of her last child had been a painful process, leaving her weak but, strengthened by her fury, she walked along the line of guests and glowered down at Pentju.

'Scorpion man!' she hissed. 'What do you say about gods, when there is only one! And this gift? Are you saying I am not blessed by the One? He has provided me with six beautiful daughters. Have I failed because there is no prince, no forked child?'

Guests on either side hastily withdrew. Pentju, quivering with fright, hurriedly made obeisance.

'Divine One', he pleaded, 'I made a joke . . .'

'A joke! Am I a joke?' And, before anyone could stop her, Nefertiti rained blows down on Pentju's bent back. He scrambled away. In the confusion his robes became tangled while his loincloth slipped, exposing bare buttocks. Nefertiti, screaming with laughter, lashed out at these. The rest of the guests gazed on in horror. Nefertiti swung her stick as if it was a war-club. Pentju, screaming, tried to crawl away but was trapped in his robe. Akhenaten glowered sullenly. Tiye sat, face in hands. Ay looked frightened. Rameses lowered his face to hide his snigger. Tables and platters were sent tumbling. Blood appeared on the grass. I sprang to my feet, pulled Pentju away and crouched down telling him to recover his dignity and flee. I glanced up. Nefertiti stood before me, eyes full of fury, those delicious lips curled in a snarl.

'Your Majesty,' I pleaded. The cane came down but I caught it. Nefertiti, chewing her lips, glared at me. She tried to pull the stick away, I held it fast. Her anger began to fade as if she became aware of where she was and what she had done.

'Baboon?' she shouted. 'Scuttle off! Tell the scorpion man he is banished for ever from my presence. He can look after the family monkey, the Mitanni girl. I am never to see him again!'

I released the stick. Nefertiti swept away and the celebrations ended.

I wished, I hoped, the Beautiful One would send for me. I dreamed we'd meet in some cool garden. She would explain, excuse herself, ask me to act as intermediary with Pentju, but it never happened. Nefertiti made an enemy that day as well as a hideous mistake in alienating Pentju and, may the gods forgive me, for not consulting with me. Instead, I had to listen to the chatter and gossip about the incident, but that was Mahu's role in Akhenaten's paradise.

No threat lurked in the City of the Aten or, at least, I thought it didn't. The troops, both on the land and river approaches, not to mention my swarm of mercenaries, saw to that. Djarka, as my lieutenant, pursued the occasional felon. I was supposed to hunt down what Akhenaten called those 'Criminals of the Heart', who did not worship the Aten in the spirit of truth. Yet what was I supposed to do? Arrest an old priest who cried for the beauty of Osiris and kept his shrine in a cupboard in his house? Flog a woman who begged Isis for a happy childbirth? Fine some poor worker who could not understand how he would fare after death without the protection of the Lord Anubis? Such reports came into my office; I didn't need wood for the brazier. I enjoyed watching these reports burn. My boys in the mercenary corps also understood: they were so suspicious they worshipped every god, just in case. Djarka proved to be an able lieutenant, a true scribe, a just man with a genuine compassion for the poor, some of whom were his own people. He rarely commented on Akhenaten though, when I informed him about Nefertiti and her uncontrollable fury, he looked sad and commented that visions can go wrong, how dreams can turn to dust and that, perhaps, the One had yet to truly manifest himself.

Djarka and I became magistrates rather than police, adjudicating on a wide range of civil matters, domestic disputes and property rights. I grew to enjoy entering other people's lives, savouring the very ordinariness and yet intrigued by their complex relationships, their virtues and vices. Sometimes, to get away, we'd take Karnak out into the Red Lands. We'd choose the bed of a valley or wadi where moisture encouraged the growth of sparse grass and whose deep sides would prevent flight to right or left then, we'd set up two nets halfway down the valley with food and water placed between. The animals would slip through the first net, in which gaps had been deliberately left and, whistling up Karnak, we'd spring the trap. I enjoyed the hunt, a welcome break from the etiquette and protocol of Akhenaten's court.

At the end of the ninth year of Akhenaten's reign, just after what Rameses sarcastically termed 'the beating of the buttocks', Djarka fell in love with a beautiful girl called Nekmet, the only daughter of a very wealthy cook who had opened his own luxurious eating-house in the southern suburbs of the city.

I'll tell the story of how it happened. Nekmet must have been about twenty summers old. Her father Makhre had worked in both Memphis and Thebes, gaining a reputation as a chef who, in the words of Djarka 'could make the plainest bread taste sweet'. Naturally I became a guest in Makhre's house, Djarka sitting alongside me, all hungry for the lustrous-eyed Nekmet rather than the dishes her father's servants would bring. Makhre nursed a great ambition to work in the palace kitchens, so I arranged that. Akhenaten was delighted: Makhre was summoned into the royal presence and rewarded with pots of perfume, a gold necklace and bangle. Djarka spent more and more time with his daughter. I was sad yet happy. If Djarka married, I realised how much I would miss him. The man had become part of me, he'd tried to fill the empty spaces in my soul. I often wondered if I should follow suit, marry some pleasant girl and settle down. True, I had my fair share of lady friends except that, when I lay in the dark and the oil lamps glowed, I'd only see Nefertiti's face, view her body, smell her scent. No, I had been conceived in pain, born in mistrust and lived loveless as a child. My sins are always before me. I have killed, I have lied, I have betrayed – but one sin I shall not, cannot, commit: I will not look at another person and say 'I love you' and know full well it is a lie. So, instead, I went back to my watching and listening, playing the judge, attending the court, mumbling the prayers and singing the hymns and, whenever possible, going out into the Red Lands.

By the spring of year ten of Akhenaten's reign, the other children of the Kap joined me on such occasions and, the more we went out, the less we hunted. Instead we'd gather at some distant oasis, cook food, and drink wine; Horemheb and Rameses, Huy, Pentju, myself and even Maya, even though he complained how the dust stained his robes whilst the heat made his face-paint run.

The only absentee was Meryre. Our High Priest was now caught up in his own holiness, lost in the vision of the Aten, Akhenaten's dog, constantly at his feet, ever ready to serve and please. We didn't want him there because we recognised the true reason we met. We were conspirators without a conspiracy, traitors not yet guilty of treason, grumblers who could do nothing about our grievances.

One auspicious day in that same spring, we were all gathered at the oasis, exhausted after a short hunt. Maya had mysteriously disappeared from the City of Aten two days previously. Speculation was rife on his whereabouts, though Maya was often absent, travelling to Thebes to check the granaries and treasure-houses of the temple. We'd lit a fire. Horemheb had gutted the quails and Rameses was roasting them over the fire. We sat around sipping the wine and chatting about our early days in the Kap. On that particular occasion Djarka was with us, serving as our guard; it was he who raised the alarm. We went to the edge of the oasis and glanced out through the heat haze. A cloud of dust appeared.

'Chariots,' Horemheb declared.

Djarka ran to collect his bow whilst we looked for our weapons. 'No, it's only one,' he called out. We relaxed as the chariot became more visible and I glimpsed Maya standing, his resplendent robes fluttering in the breeze. I made out the leather helmet, baldric and kilt of his driver. The chariot came thundering on, hooves drumming the ground, the horses' plumed heads rising and falling, the dust swirling out towards us. Sobeck, who had overcome his earlier difficulties, skilfully turned the horses round, executing those sensational zig-zag turnings which the professional charioteer loves so much before turning them back and reining them in only a few yards from our party. Maya climbed down, Sobeck followed. He grasped Maya's hand and walked towards us, taking off his helmet. He grinned at the gasps. Horemheb was the first to recognise him. 'I thought you were dead in the Red Lands,' Rameses barked, glancing out of the corner of his eye at me, 'though we had our suspicions.'

Sobeck took the gazelle skin of water I offered. He passed it first to Maya then wetted his own face and chest, before lifting it to his lips, gulping fiercely. He hadn't changed much; his face was a little leaner, there were a few more scars on his chest and arms. Maya stood beside him, a dazzling smile on his face.

'Well?' Sobeck squinted up at the sun. 'Am I friend or foe? Will you keep me in the sun like Akhenaten does his envoys or invite me into the shade for that delicious-smelling quail and a cup of wine?'

'I could take your head!' Rameses taunted. 'There is still a reward on it.'

'No, Rameses.' Sobeck pushed the stopper back into the waterskin. 'You could *try* to take my head, and you'd be dead within a heartbeat of doing so.'

'I was only joking,' Rameses sneered.

'I was not.' Sobeck threw the waterskin at him. 'Well?' He spread his hands. 'Friend or foe?'

'Always a friend.' Horemheb walked forward to clasp Sobeck's hand, the rest followed. When it was my turn, Sobeck pulled me close and kissed me on either cheek.

'You do keep strange company, Mahu,' he whispered. 'I miss you in Thebes.'

His perfumed sweat tickled my nostrils. Then he turned to crack a joke with Djarka and examine his bow. We all settled down, squatting round the fire, sharing out the meat and wine.

'I thought it best,' Maya declared, picking like some young lady at his meat. 'I thought it best if Sobeck – well, if we met him again. I have told him about Meryre.'

'Once a holy man always a holy man,' Sobeck commented.

For a while, we all reminisced about the House of Residence, the different scribes, the night Horemheb lost his dwarf. Sobeck mentioned Weni and offered a silent toast in which we all joined.

'You know he was murdered, don't you?' Sobeck glanced at me. 'You and I, Mahu, we know that Weni was murdered.'

'I thought it was strange,' Huy commented, 'that an old soldier couldn't take his drink and was drowned in a pool.'

'Akhenaten killed him,' Sobeck continued evenly, 'probably with the blessing of his mother.'

'Just as God's Father Hotep tried to kill us all,' I added.

'What?'

I had not told the group about my earlier suspicions or Hotep's final confession, but now I did so: Horemheb and Rameses corroborated certain parts of my story.

'Well, well, well.' Sobeck drained his wine cup and, grabbing the wineskin, refilled it.

'Why have you come here, Sobeck?' Rameses, of course, was the first to look for another reason. 'You haven't come to see our pretty faces and wish us well.'

'And what are you doing?' Horemheb asked.

Sobeck evaded the questions, loosely describing himself as a merchant with a finger in every dish: how he had come out at Maya's insistence and wasn't it good for the children of the Kap to be reunited? For a while he parried our questions and teased us back. When the meal was over he squatted more comfortably, sucking noisily on a slice of the melon.

'Are you sure you can all be trusted?' he asked.

'If one of us was a traitor,' Horemheb replied, 'we'd know by now.'

'There's deep unease in Thebes,' Sobeck continued.

'We know that,' Huy replied, 'in Thebes, Memphis, Abydos, the Delta, not to mention war breaking out amongst our allies in Canaan. Hittites are massing troops along the border. They have realised Egypt is not as ardent as she formerly was in protecting her interests across Sinai.'

'Well, there's definitely unrest in Thebes,' Sobeck declared, 'and something else, too. Mahu, have you ever heard of the Sekhmets?'

'Yes, yes,' I replied, racking my memory. 'They've committed a number of murders in Thebes and elsewhere. Professional assassins, their usual weapon is a knife or poison though they have been known to kill from afar with bow and arrow or arrange some suspicious accident. They always leave their mark.' I lifted my hand. 'A small amulet with the Lion-headed Sekhmet, the Devouress, the Destroyer.'

'Well,' Sobeck commented, picking up another slice of melon, 'I have acquaintances in Thebes – how can I put it, men and women who would prefer not to meet Mahu and his police.' He paused at the laughter. 'They listen to the whispers and the gossip. Now, according to them, someone was looking for the Sekhmets. Apparently,' he smiled at me, 'and I tell the truth, somehow in Thebes a message can be left for this group of assassins.'

'And someone has hired them?' I asked. 'But not for work in Thebes?'

'Mahu, your genius always astounds me. According to the little I know, the Sekhmets, if they have been hired, are to do their bloody work in the City of the Aten.' He sighed. 'Which means two or possibly three things. Either they have marked down one of you, all of you – or someone else in the Royal Circle.'

'Or they could just strike direct at the heart of the court,' I declared. 'Pharaoh himself and his Queen.' I ignored Pentju's muttered remarks.

'But who has hired them?' Rameses demanded. 'Thebes, every city of Egypt, is full of assassins but they have to be hired.'

'The priests of Amun,' Sobeck replied, 'don't take too kindly to having their gods cast down, their treasuries plundered, their temples deserted.'

'But why the Sekhmets?' Rameses insisted.

'They are successful,' I grinned at Sobeck. 'They are the sort of people you should take care of.'

'They're respectable.' Sobeck sipped from his wine-cup. 'People who, apparently, can move easily up and down the Nile, priests or merchants, envoys from some of the other kingdoms; they could be anybody.'

'And you care for us so much,' Rameses taunted, 'that

you have travelled all the way from Thebes just to tell us this?'

'No, Rameses. I arrived at a military outpost last night.'

'Where you have further acquaintances?'

'That's right, Horemheb. A number of army officers are guests at my table. How do you think I was able to ride that chariot?'

'I thought your good friend Maya . . . ?' Rameses' words faltered at Sobeck's cold, hard look.

'I'll tell you why I came here.' Sobeck made himself more comfortable. 'Maya has told me about your little trips out here to the desert. You should be more careful.' He stared around. 'Is this all the great warriors of the Children of the Kap can bring down, a few quail? Ay must be suspicious. An entire day out in the Red Lands to eat roasted meat – or to plot treason?'

'Continue.' I raised my hand to fend off Rameses' retort.

'You come out here to talk like all of Egypt's talking. Some are already ahead of you, plotting what to do next. They call Akhenaten the Great Heretic, insane.' He gestured at Horemheb. 'You know they do! The staff officers, the military command. Hasn't there been unrest amongst the garrison at Memphis?'

Horemheb bit back his reply.

'I know what you talk about,' Sobeck continued. 'Each of you must lie in your beds at night and wonder what will happen next. Have you ever wondered what will *really* happen next? Have you ever speculated about what will happen if Akhenaten dies? He has no male heir, no Crown Prince. Do you think the generals of Egypt, the high priests, are going to allow this nonsense of the Aten to continue for ever and a day? Can't you see the storm coming, Rameses? One day Akhenaten will go beyond his beloved far horizon. Many of Egypt wish he was there already and ask the gods to speed him on his way. Now tell me.' Sobeck flicked the rim of his cup with his fingernail. 'No one dares to raise a hand against the sacred flesh of Pharaoh. Well, at least not publicly, openly. However, Akhenaten may see himself as a god but one day he is going to die! How, we don't know! The question you must ask yourselves is how long will those who supported him, who sat at table with him, survive?'

I watched Rameses' face. He glanced quickly at Horemheb, a sharp furtive glance but it spoke eloquently. Both these ambitious soldiers had already discussed this. I could tell from the faces of the rest that it was also a matter close to their hearts.

'Mahu?' Horemheb prompted.

'There are two problems,' I replied slowly. 'The first . . . well, the first is the immediate future: the protection of Akhenaten against the Sekhmets or anyone else.'

'And the second?' Rameses asked.

'You know full well,' I murmured, getting to my feet. I picked up my cloak and shook out the sand and dirt. 'We must all start thinking about the future.'

'The future may well take care of itself.' Pentju smiled at me and winked.

At the time I thought he was being cynical. Yet, on reflection, Pentju's words contained the first powerful seeds of Akhenaten's downfall and destruction.

When I returned to the City of Aten, Djarka and I became

busy, going through the police archives in the House of Secrets: these were all contained in sealed jars, arranged according to regnal years. None of the scribes were to be told what we were searching for or the reason for it.

At first it was difficult. I found traces of the Sekhmets during the fourth and fifth years of Akhenaten's reign when he was Co-regent and still in the Palace of the Aten at Thebes. These references were usually based on police accounts or the information supplied by spies. The Sekhmets were only known by the amulet they left near their victims: these were often quite powerful men – merchants, army officers and, on one occasion, even a chapel priest in the Temple of Horus. According to the evidence, the victims always had enemies but, because professional assassins were used, it was virtually impossible to link the responsibility for the victim's death to anyone. One police officer investigated the murder of a merchant in the Street of Coppersmiths in eastern Thebes and wrote: 'Many wanted him dead but, at the time of his murder, all could account for where they were and what they were doing.'

The Sekhmets employed a variety of methods in their assassinations. One victim died whilst on a hunting trip along the Nile. He and his servant were found drifting in their boat. Both had been killed by arrows, shot at close range, the Sekhmet's amulet casually tossed into the punt, nestling amongst the feathers of some of the birds. I recalled Djarka rescuing me from the jackals. How easy it had been to approach the boat and loose one shaft after another. Other victims died by poisoning. Another missed his footing and fell from a building he was inspecting.

In one audacious murder a wealthy stall-holder from the Perfume Quarters of Thebes had gone back into his shop to collect something from his stores. When the customer became impatient and went searching, he found the stall-holder lying among bales of cloth, his throat cut from ear to ear, the Sekhmet amulet clutched in his hand. I made Djarka search more carefully and realised that, between the fifth and tenth year of Akhenaten's reign, at least according to my records, the Sekhmets had either deliberately gone quiet or moved elsewhere. I continued my own research and was astonished to discover that the Sekhmets were equally busy ten years previously.

'Fifteen years in all!' I exclaimed as we sat sharing a bowl of wine in my office. 'These assassins have been busy for fifteen years! A gap of ten years occurred and then they began again, just before Akhenaten resumed the Co-regency. Why?'

Djarka shook his head. 'How do we know that they are the same people?' he mused. 'Anyone can take the name Sekhmet and buy a bag of cheap amulets.'

'No, no, no,' I objected. 'These are people who seem to be able to move around the city of Thebes. They are very similar to the jackals. They are a family concern. Could they be merchants? A family which moves up and down the Nile?'

'But someone must be able to contact them?' Djarka pointed out. 'Messages have to be left, the victims' names, the price paid and collected.'

I leaned forward and scratched Karnak lying sleeping at my feet.

'Somebody,' I said.

'Somebody,' Djarka continued, 'must be able to act as the middleman.'

Djarka had posed a problem I could not solve.

I sent out messengers to Memphis, Thebes and Abydos. I asked the same question of the police in each city, those who acted as the 'Ears and Eyes' of Pharaoh. The response came swiftly. The Sekhmets had been responsible for murders in each of their cities but the different authorities were baffled as to who those assassins could be or how they were approached. None could offer even the slightest clue to their identity or present whereabouts. I became fascinated with the problem. So much so that Akhenaten became interested too, and I received a summons to attend the Royal Circle.

This time the meeting was presided over by Akhenaten himself, Nefertiti sitting alongside. The Pharaoh had returned to his usual good humour; his face was shaved and oiled, eyes and voice sharp as he moved through different items of business. At last, he turned to me, leaning his elbows on the arms of his thronelike chair, those long fingers pressed together to hide his mouth.

'Mahu, my friend. I understand you have been very busy. Would you like to inform the Royal Circle why my Chief of Police, Overseer of the House of Secrets, works well past sunset? How the oil lamps have been seen glowing even a few hours before dawn, yet here, at the Great House we have received no warning, no information for such labour?' He clapped his hands together sharply, making Huy jump. Ay sitting on his left held his silence, fingers also to his face to conceal his own expression.

'Your Majesty.' I chose my words carefully, determined

not to lie. 'Your Majesty, I have received information that a guild, a group of assassins who call themselves the Sekhmets, have been despatched into the City of the Aten.'

I ignored the gasps and cries of the other members of the Royal Circle.

'Why were we not informed of this?' Nefertiti's voice cut across the babble. 'Who are these people? Why have they not been arrested? How were they allowed to enter the sacred city?'

'Your Majesty.' I spread my hands. 'I received this information from my own spies in Thebes. It may be nonsense, empty gossip, idle chatter. Anyone can enter the City of the Aten provided they can prove to be of good standing with business here. The Divine One has proclaimed throughout Egypt that any worshipper of the Aten is most welcome. These Sekhmets have never been caught. We do not possess one clue about their identity. For all I know they could be sitting in this chamber, as a servant out in the corridor or one of the soldiers, even members of your own court.'

'And even if they are here,' Huy spoke up in an attempt to assist me, 'we do not know their true business. They may be here to settle a private grudge or grievance.' He paused and closed his eyes as he realised his mistake.

'In other words,' Ay took his hands from his mouth, 'what you are saying, my Lord Huy, is that we have assassins in the City of Aten but they may not really pose a threat to the Divine One or his family. But if you say that,' he continued silkily, 'you do concede the possibility that these murderers are here as part of some heinous plot to strike at the heart of Egypt.'

Akhenaten's hand moved to cover Nefertiti's. For a short while fear flared in his eyes, a fleeting expression which disappeared as he gave vent to his rage. At first he just sat banging his right fist up and down on the arm of his chair. Eventually, he sat back and, with his sandalled foot, kicked away the table before him, sending manuscripts, inkpots, and writing-pads scattering over the gleaming floor. He was not staring at any of us but sat eyes glazed, lips moving as if he was talking to someone we could not see or hear. Nefertiti tried to soothe him but he pulled his hand away. Ay whispered in his ear but Akhenaten made a cutting movement with his hand and sprang to his feet. Immediately we all had to make obeisance, pushing back our cushions, going down to press our foreheads against the cold floor. When I glanced up, both Akhenaten and Nefertiti had left the chamber. We had no choice but to remain kneeling. Akhenaten was absent for at least two hours, yet no one, not even Ay, dared move: meetings of the Royal Circle were not over until Pharaoh decreed it. A worried-looking messenger arrived bursting through the half-open doors behind the throne and Ay hurried out. Horemheb, groaning loudly, sat back on his heels whilst Rameses, in a show of temper, simply pulled his cushions towards him and made himself as comfortable as possible.

At last chamberlains announced the return of the Divine One who, accompanied by Nefertiti and Ay, swept into the chamber. Akhenaten accepted our obeisance and sat down on the throne. He hardly waited for us to take our positions before taking the flail and rod handed to him by Ay and, crossing his arms, issued a decree which would have an effect throughout Egypt: the complete and utter destruction of the cult of Amun. Statues were to be removed and destroyed. All references to the god, be they on a public monument or a private tomb, were to be summarily removed. Anyone who objected or resisted was to be treated as a traitor and dealt with accordingly. The King's writ would run from the Great Green to beyond the Third Cataract and even across Sinai to any temple, chapel or tomb which carried a prayer, an inscription or a carving to Amun the Silent One of Thebes. We sat in shocked silence listening as Akhenaten's voice carried through the chamber. When he had finished Akhenaten pointed the flail at Horemheb and Rameses. 'You are responsible for the implementation of this decree and it is immediate! Mahu, you are to search out the Sekhmets. You are to arrest them. You are to destroy them and anyone connected with them. This is Pharaoh's speech, this is Pharaoh's will and our will shall be done!'

Horemheb and Rameses might curse and complain in private but Akhenaten's decree was written out by scribes and despatched to every village and city throughout the Empire. Horemheb and Rameses were given explicit instructions to move into Thebes and carry out his orders, even if it meant the removal of inscriptions in the Royal Necropolis where the Magnificent One lay buried. Of course, Queen Tiye, Ay and others tried to advise caution and prudence but Akhenaten and Nefertiti were united on this. They believed the Sekhmets had been hired by the priests of Amun so they were determined to cut out that cult, branch and root. Within a year, Akhenaten boasted, Amun would be no more!

Horemheb and Rameses met with little resistance. Their troops, not to mention the mercenaries, were paid directly out of the Royal Treasury. Akhenaten had shown great cunning. He had not struck at the other gods such as Osiris at Abydos or Ptah at Memphis but only Amun of Thebes. The other priests and temples bemoaned such attacks but they were secretly pleased to see the supremacy of the Theban god shattered once and for all, his temples dishonoured, his priesthood scattered. Of course there were riots and disturbances, particularly in Karnak and Luxor, but Horemheb's Syrian archers and Kushite mercenaries brutally repressed them.

My concerns were the Sekhmets. I quietly passed instructions for all entrances to the palace to be closely guarded. Food and wine served to the Divine One was always to be tasted. Day and night I continued my hunt. One thing I did discover. The Sekhmets had left a trail of destruction in the cities along the Nile except for one place, Akhmin, the home of Nefertiti and Ay and the rest of their tribe. Why was this? Did they come from that city? Were they members of the Akhmin gang? But who? Ay and Nefertiti's fortunes, not to mention those of the Queen Mother Tiye, were closely bound up with Akhenaten and his great religious vision. Of course, as I reasoned to Djarka, I may have got it wrong. Other cities could report nothing about the Sekhmets. I found it strange, perhaps a mere coincidence, that Akhmin was one of these. I went through police report after police report. A dim picture of the Sekhmets emerged, though sometimes it was more distinct than others.

'It would seem,' I confided to Djarka, 'that the Sekhmets are respectable and wealthy. They move up and down the River Nile with impunity. There may be two of them, possibly man and wife, that's all I have learned.'

I returned to my searches and in doing so stumbled across something else. I became interested in a family who had moved into the Street of Scribes; they constantly petitioned the Great Writing House for employment at the palace. The group consisted of a man, his wife and their three grown sons. I had the house watched and managed to bribe one of the servants. He eventually told us a different story. The sons in question did not belong to the family but were priest-scribes from the Temple of Amun in Thebes. We raided the house, arrested everyone and went through their documents. Eventually we applied torture, whipping them on their legs and the soles of their feet. One of the younger men broke down and confessed. They had been forced to leave Thebes after the Temple of Amun had been closed and its priestly rank depleted. They had used papyrus and paid forgers to draw up false documents and arrived in the City of Aten eager for employment. Of course I had to submit this report to the Great House. Akhenaten himself, accompanied by Nefertiti and Ay, came down to question the prisoners. In his retinue came Tutu (I'm sure he kept Akhenaten advised of all my doings) and Meryre whose look of smug piety was more offensive than ever.

Akhenaten, fervently supported by Ay, truly believed I had discovered the Sekhmets. Of course, I had found no amulet or any reference to Sekhmet amongst the possessions of these so-called conspirators but Akhenaten refused to listen. The very sight of his enemy, the fact that they had lied, was evidence enough. He brushed aside their protests that they were merely scribe priests of Amun attempting to find fresh work. Ay, too, would not listen to their objections. He regarded the false documents and the small bundle of weapons they had hidden in their house as evidence of their guilt. Akhenaten himself passed sentence. The woman, the wife of the elder priest, was banished to the Red Lands. The four males were taken out into the desert and summarily executed.

Of course I was hailed as the hero of the hour, given fresh Collars of Gold and wine from Akhenaten's own cellar. My brow was blessed with sacred oil. Akhenaten summoned me formally before the Window of Appearances where Nefertiti showered me with scented rose petals. I did my best to reason with Ay.

'They were not the Sekhmets,' I protested. I paced up and down his palatial chapel. 'They have been conspirators, they may have had malice in their hearts. Only the gods know . . .'

'Pardon?' Ay called out.

I beat my breast. 'Only the One who sees all things truly knew what was in their hearts, but I do not think they were the Sekhmets.'

'Why not?'

'They were too clumsy, too easy to discover. Moreover, they had spent most of their lives in Thebes, yet we know from police reports that the Sekhmets have been busy in Memphis and Abydos.'

'They lied,' Ay countered. 'Assassins always lie to pro-tect themselves. Mahu, be content. Pharaoh has smiled on you. You have won Pharaoh's favour. The task he assigned you is now finished.'

I stared at that cunning face, those eyes which betrayed nothing. Was it Ay who'd hired the Sekhmets? Was that why he was so eager to pass the blame onto the scribe priests? Ay with his genius for questioning, for weighing everything carefully in his own dark heart. Why had he been so quick to point the finger of accusation? I bowed, quickly left and returned to my searches. I had almost given up hope, decided to let matters be and dismiss Sobeck's report as idle babble, rootless chatter when, one night, Djarka let slip a remark which made my heart skip a beat. I'd stumbled, quite unexpectedly, on the identity of the Sekhmets.

Mahu, leaning on his staff, listens to the news: the whereabouts of some malefactor has been dis-covered.

(Scene from Mahu's tomb at El-Amarna, the City of the Aten.)

Chapter 18

Horemheb and Rameses hunted Amun and all his followers in the temples and along the avenues and streets of Thebes: not even private tombs were safe. I quietly laughed at the stories of how Akhenaten's agents broke the seals of sepulchres and went in to wipe out the picture of a goose, sacred to Amun, from paintings on the wall. In the City of the Aten Meryre and the rest of the toadies, those sanctimonious hypocrites, rose to the occasion only too eager to prove their subservience and unquestioned loyalty. Houses, shops and warehouses were raided, statuettes of any other god seized and destroyed. Those who had offended the majesty of the Aten were publicly ridiculed, being placed on donkeys, their faces towards the tails and paraded through the streets. It was now a crime in the City of the Aten to praise the wrong god, to honour some other deity. A growing restlessness manifested itself, not helped by shooting stars scrawling the heavens at night and heartchilling rumours about a hideous pestilence which had broken out across Sinai.

I continued my hunt for the Sekhmets. One question still puzzled me. I knew who they were and had a hardening suspicion about who had hired them. I had reached the conclusion that they worked for one person and one person alone, so how had Sobeck's spies come to know that someone was searching for the Sekhmets along the alleyways and the streets of Thebes? Maybe the person responsible for the assassins had deliberately spread the rumour about Sekhmets being hired in order to lay the blame at the door of Amun – which Akhenaten had been only too happy to accept. I dared not trust any of my agents or spies, nor could I inform Djarka, so I went out at night to watch the house myself.

My long vigil proved my suspicions were correct. So, when Makhre and Nekmet invited Djarka and myself to a sumptuous meal of clover and fish served in a special sauce, I eagerly accepted. Their eating-house had been closed for the evening, and Makhre and Nekmet acted as both our hosts and servants. We ate on the flat roof of the house overlooking an elegant courtyard. A small fountain splashed and countless flower baskets sent up their own fragrance to mingle with the sweetness from the pots of frankincense and cassia arranged in the shadow of the parapet along the roof terrace. The meats were delicious, the sauce fresh and tasty to the palate, the bread sweet and soft, laced with carob seeds and a dash of honey whilst the wine was the richest from the black soil of Canaan. It was a beautiful evening with the sky changing colour and, as the sun set, the eastern cliffs dazzled in its dying rays. I was careful of what I ate and drank as I studied this precious pair: Makhre in his white robes, head and face gleaming with perfumed oil, Nekmet soft-skinned and doe-eyed, resplendent in her pleated robes and delicate jewellery. Even then I was arrogant; I did not know the full truth, the hideous secret which would eventually bring so many dreams crashing down. At that moment in time I was only concerned with Djarka and his love for this elegant young woman. Eventually I decided to confront her. As Nekmet served me a dish of lettuce garnished with oil and herbs, Djarka was teasing her about flirting with me. Makhre was laughing. I could take no more. Instead of accepting the bowl I grasped her wrist so tightly she winced.

'You are from Akhmin?'

'No, we're not,' Makhre scoffed but his eyes became watchful.

'But you told Djarka the other day that you were?'

'What?' Makhre turned to his daughter. She shook her head.

'But you did.' Djarka, now alarmed, cradled his cup, not knowing who to stare at. I let go of Nekmet's hand.

'You are from Akhmin,' I repeated. 'You told Djarka, Nekmet, that you were born there. I am sure it was a slip. If you were there, so were your mother and father. So why do you lie now?'

The banquet was over. Makhre and Nekmet's faces betrayed them. For the first time ever they had been confronted with their true identity.

'You are from Akhmin,' I repeated. 'For all I know you may well be related to God's Father Ay, close friend of Pharaoh. So why do you come wandering into the City of the Aten as if you know no one? Why do you have to cultivate my lieutenant Djarka? Gain an entry to the palace when God's Father Ay could have achieved that with a nod of his head?'

'You are mistaken,' Makhre flustered. 'My lord Mahu, you are truly mistaken. I do not know God's Father Ay. I have seen him from afar. I . . .'

'You are a liar! You do not speak with true voice because you do not know the truth.'

'Mahu!' Djarka warned.

'I have watched this house myself. Late at night I have seen God's Father Ay slip in and out. So, why are you here, Makhre and Nekmet? Whom are you hunting? Me? Djarka? Or the Divine One himself?'

Nekmet picked up a slice of pomegranate. She chewed on it carefully, using this to glance sideways at her father.

'You call yourself the Sekhmets,' I continued. 'A family of assassins. You come from Akhmin. You work for one person only, the lord Ay. Years ago, Makhre, it was you and your wife, but she died. Now it's you and your beautiful daughter. You slaughtered certain people in Thebes just before the Divine One left that city. You advertised your slayings so people thought that it was business rivals or enemies settling grudges. However, all your victims in Thebes had one thing in common: they were enemies of Ay. The same is true of your other prey in the cities along the Nile.'

Some of what I said was true, the rest mere conjecture.

'You were brought here by lord Ay,' I continued. 'We are not your victims but, through us, particularly Djarka, you have gained admission to the palace.'

'But we've been there,' Nekmet protested. 'We did no harm!'

'Of course not.' I pushed the wine-cup away. 'A true assassin must first get himself accepted, become part of the normal life, the regular routine. Moreover, there is no hurry. Whoever your victim was, you were not to strike until lord Ay gave you the order.'

'But do you have proof?' Makhre had recovered his wits.

'Don't sit there and fence with me as if we are children with sticks,' I snarled. 'I'll have this house searched; I am sure I will find what I have to.'

'And where are your police?' Nekmet asked.

'You know full well,' I retorted, 'no one else knows. The Divine One thinks the Sekhmets have been apprehended and executed. However, if he discovered the true assassins were patronised, given access to the palace by his own Lieutenant of Police, Djarka would also feel his wrath.'

'Let us go to see the lord Ay,' Makhre offered.

'He'll deny it,' I replied. 'He'll call me mad or insane, but the damage will be done. He'll arrange for you to disappear and Djarka will continue to live under the shadow of suspicion.'

'I really think . . .' Makhre pushed the table back. As he made to get up, he flexed his upper arm, so when he struck, I was waiting. The knife secretly clutched in his hand aimed for my throat even as Nekmet lunged at Djarka with a dagger she, too, had concealed. Djarka was faster than I, pushing the table into Nekmet's stomach, even as Makhre's knife skimmed the side of my neck. I lunged back with my own knife, cutting and slashing into his exposed throat, dragging the knife round and slicing through the soft part under his chin. He fell back against the cushions, a look of surprise on his face; blood pumping out of his mouth and the jagged gash in his neck. He was shaking like a man with a fever, a hideous sound coming from his lips.

I looked to my right. Djarka had his arm around the back of Nekmet's head, pushing her even further onto the dagger thrust into her upper belly; her lips were half-open, eyelids fluttering as if she wanted to speak or kiss him. Djarka's face was a hideous mask, a look of deep pity yet he would not let go of her head or the knife, his eyes only a few inches from hers. Eventually her face went slack, shoulders drooping. Makhre, too, fell quiet, face to one side, his entire chest and groin sopping with blood. I pulled Djarka away, allowing Nekmet's corpse to fall against the cushions. Then I refilled his cup and my own. While I sat and drank, Djarka sobbed into his hands, one of the most heart-wrenching scenes I have ever witnessed. He must have sat for an hour, those two corpses staring at us with their empty, glassy gaze. Birds swooped over the house, the night came, dark and soft as velvet. I kept sipping at the cup. At last Djarka wiped his tears away.

'Why didn't you tell me?' he accused.

In the light of the oil lamps my young friend had aged. His face had lost that olive smoothness, his eyes were red-rimmed; furrows marked either side of his mouth. He had the look of a stricken old man.

'If I had told you, Djarka, you would not have believed me. I know you. You would have challenged Nekmet. They would have either killed you, lied or fled.'

'Why?' Djarka asked. 'Why did she lie?'

'I don't know.'

'I'll kill Ay,' Djarka threatened.

'No, you won't.' I clambered to my feet, my legs tense and hard. 'Come on, Djarka, we have work to do.'

At first I thought he would refuse but Djarka became impatient to discover more evidence, hoping to prove that I was wrong. Yet he knew the truth. Even as he searched he conceded that Makhre and Nekmet had confessed their own guilt.

'They would have killed us,' I declared, 'and taken our corpses out to the Red Lands.'

We searched that house from cellar to the roof. At first we found nothing except indications that Makhre and his daughter had travelled the length and breadth of the kingdom. They possessed considerable wealth. I went down to the cellar, specially constructed to store wine and other goods which had to be kept cool. The cellar was partitioned by a plaster wall. I examined this carefully, removing the makeshift door. I studied the lintels.

'This was only meant to be a partition,' I told Djarka, 'yet it's at least a yard wide on either side.' The dividing wall was of wooden boards covered by a thick plaster; the sides on which the door had been fastened consisted of specially hewn beams. We took these away, and discovered that each side of the partition was, in fact, a narrow secret room. Inside we found our proof: a small coffer with medallions and amulets displaying the lion-headed Sekhmet, Syrian bows, three quivers of arrows, swords, daggers, and writing trays. More importantly, the cache held a carefully contrived and beautifully fashioned medicine chest consisting of jars and pots, all sealed and neatly tagged. We brought these out into the light of the oil lamps.

'I am no physician,' I declared, 'but I suspect these are poisons and potions, enough to kill an entire village.'

We also found documents, all officially sealed, and providing different names and details, as well as pots of paints, wigs, and articles of clothing so Makhre and Nekmet could disguise themselves. Small pouches of gold and silver and a casket of precious stones were also stored there.

'They were always ready for flight,' I declared. 'Prepared to move on once their task was done.'

By now Djarka was coldly composed. We returned to the roof and those corpses lying in pools of blood, the flies already gathering.

'What shall we do?' Djarka asked.

'How many people knew we were to be their guests?'

Djarka, his face still tear-stained, shook his head. I ordered him to help. We took the two corpses, wrapping them in sheepskin cloths and tying them securely with cord, then cleared out the secret rooms and placed the two corpses inside. I found a leather bag and gathered up most of the valuables. We drew buckets of water from the fountain and cleared away all signs of our struggle then waited until dawn to study the results of our handiwork. The rooftop was now like any other. In the kitchen we washed the platters and cups in bowls of water and, going down to the cellar, replaced the heavy beams and rehung the door. I checked the house most carefully. Only when satisfied did we leave.

'Why?' Djarka asked, as we slipped through the streets back into the central part of the city. 'Why did we leave it like that?'

'It's the only way,' I retorted. 'I do not trust Akhenaten's moods nor Nefertiti's furious outbursts. The finger of suspicion would be pointed at you.'

Once home, Djarka stripped himself, throwing all his clothes at me.

'Burn them,' he called over his shoulder.

He went out into one of the courtyards, washed himself and returned to his chamber. I followed him up. He was preparing for a journey, marching sandals on his feet, a set of leather panniers already packed. Across his shoulder hung a bow and quiver of arrows, a dagger thrust into his belt, a staff in one hand.

'Djarka?' I asked.

'I will leave lord Ay for the time being,' he muttered and would say no more. He clasped my hand and disappeared. He was gone forty days and forty nights out in the Red Lands. When he returned, his face was blackened by the sun, there were streaks of grey in his hair, and his body and face were hard. He talked little about where he had been but returned to his duties.

During his absence I was busy. I returned to the assassins' house to ensure everything was well. Of course, questions were asked. I circulated the story about how the owner and his daughter had left in a hurry. Ay had no choice but to co-operate with such a tale, even though he guessed the truth. I confronted him alone in a garden at the palace. At first he acted all diffident, dismissing my accusations with a flutter of his fingers. I told him exactly what had happened and where the corpses of his assassins were hidden.

'I leave it to you, God's Father,' I warned, 'to take their bodies out for honourable burial. I don't think you will.'

'They will eventually smell,' Ay countered coolly though he was visibly anxious about any eavesdropper or servant coming too close. 'Or, there again, their corpses are sealed in . . .'

'Why did you hire them,' I asked, 'and for whom?'

Ay walked away to sniff at some flower. He plucked this and came back twirling it in his fingers, moving his head and neck as if to relieve the tension in his shoulders.

'My lord Ay,' I whispered hoarsely, 'you called me your friend, your ally?'

Ay lifted his head, raising the flower to his nose but using it to mask his lips. 'Look into my eyes, Mahu. What do you see?'

'Fear,' I replied.

'And fear it is. Soon you shall see the reason why.'

'Was that the only way?' I asked.

'It's over, Mahu.' He took the flower away. He gestured with his hand. 'This is all over. It's gone wrong. The wine doesn't taste so sweet or the food so delicious. We were to introduce the worship of the Aten, not go hunting for people who draw geese on the walls of their tombs or keep a statue of Isis in a cupboard. I never dreamed Thebes would be left to rot or our allies across Sinai go down in the dust because we would not help them. Worse still . . .' He shook his head. 'No.' He threw the flower away. 'You will see! The Sekhmets were an easy answer.'

Ay refused to tell me any more and that's the nearest he ever came to a full confession.

The twelfth year of Akhenaten's reign was now upon us and the King became immersed in celebrating his great jubilee, the anniversary of his coronation. Envoys from other kingdoms were invited to the City of Aten. There was feasting and processions, troops marching backwards and forwards, military displays, festivals and gift-giving. This was a last blaze of light before the darkness. Akhenaten performed his public office with all the majesty he could muster. Dressed in the glorious paraphernalia of Pharaoh, he entertained envoys from Kush, Canaan, Libya as well as ambassadors of the Mitanni and the Hittites. He lectured them on the virtues of the Aten, he and Nefertiti portraying themselves as the dazzling incarnation of their god. This was only a mask. During the ceremonies he showed a marked coldness towards his wife. I had been so busy on my own affairs I hadn't reflected on how, in the previous months, Akhenaten had often absented himself whilst Lady Khiya had virtually vanished from the court.

All this was the precursor of the storm. The tempest broke when the jubilee festival was over and Akhenaten and Nefertiti presided over a meeting of the Royal Circle. The only people invited were the Devout and the children of the Kap. It began in the usual perfunctory way. Meryre intoned a prayer to the Aten which went on and on. Horemheb sat beating a tattoo on his knee whilst Rameses pretended to doze. Everyone else was subdued. The great persecution of Amun was now complete, leaving a sour taste in people's mouths. Of course Pentju was not there, being banished from Nefertiti's presence. I'd glimpsed his face three days previously and wondered why he looked so secretive, eyes red-rimmed as if he had been crying. The meeting was also attended by three of Akhenaten's eldest daughters, Meketaten, Meritaten and Ankhespaaten. The twins were comely enough but Ankhespaaten was the one with vigour and life, a beautiful young girl probably no more than ten summers old. She had inherited some of her mother's seductive, alluring beauty, eyes full of expression, her movements exquisitely feminine. Even at that early age she displayed her body, clothed in perfumed robes, to catch and draw the attention of men. All three daughters kneeled on cushions at Nefertiti's feet. The twins were subdued but Ankhespaaten, a glorious fillet of gold binding her hair, stared imperiously around, eyes constantly moving, a faint smile on those lovely lips.

When Meryre ended his boring litany Akhenaten remained seated, hands on the arms of the throne, head down. On this occasion he wore no crown, simply a band of gold with a jewelled uraeus in the centre. He lifted his head. Nefertiti went to touch his hand, a common gesture. Akhenaten thrust this away. Nefertiti ignored the insult, no reaction except for a slight tilt of her head. She stared across at me, a stricken look. I realised how the years had passed; she had aged, her cheeks no longer so smooth, her body slightly plump.

'Your Majesty.' Tutu, from where he sat opposite the King, bowed. 'Your Majesty has words for us.'

Akhenaten's hand went across his face.

'You all must have . . .' he began.

I remember those words so well, for they unleashed the storm.

'You all must have wondered what will happen when I go back to my Father to be reunited with the One across the Far Horizon, Who will sit here and wear the Crown of Egypt? Who will hold the flail and rod? Who will intercede for you' – he lifted his hands as if in prayer – 'with me and my Father?'

Nefertiti, shocked, turned her face. The conventional chatter and gossip of the court was that Akhenaten's eldest daughter would succeed him. Nefertiti made a strange move with her hands as if courtiers were standing too close to her and she wanted them to move away.

'My lord, you have a daughter,' Tutu said, puzzled.

'And now I have a son.' Akhenaten's declaration rang through the chamber.

'My lord!' Tutu gasped.

'I have a son,' Akhenaten repeated. 'Flesh of my flesh, body of my body. The Prince Tutankhaten, the offspring of Princess Khiya the Beloved! Nor is he the first . . .'

I shall never know why Akhenaten chose that time and place to make his declaration. Perhaps all the resentment and disappointment had curdled together to come pouring out.

'He is not the first child,' Akhenaten continued. 'We also had a daughter who died, born prematurely. The Prince, however, is a vigorous child. He is my successor, the blessed seed of the Aten, the breath of God. He is my heir and shall be proclaimed as my heir.'

The Royal Circle was now in consternation. I had to admire Akhenaten's cunning even as I grieved at

Nefertiti's public humiliation. She had made a hideous mistake. Khiya had become a Royal Ornament, a flunky of the court, someone who was seen and patronised. Like the rest, Nefertiti had failed to observe the Mitanni Princess's long absences, her periods of seclusion in the rambling palaces of the Aten. An easy achievement, for who would seek Khiya the Monkey out? She was not liked by Nefertiti and so why should any power-hungry courtier wish to associate with her? Except of course Pentju . . . a man of nimble wits and cunning heart. He must have had a hand in this but, at the time, I sat like the rest in stunned silence. The look on Nefertiti's face was heart-wrenching: her manner wild-eyed and confused. The glory of Egypt, the necklaces, crowns and jewellery which adorned her no longer enhanced her beauty or her status but seemed to emphasise the mockery. Some of the Royal Circle moved to congratulate Akhenaten. Nefertiti suddenly stood up. She moved the children aside and knelt on the cushions before Akhenaten, her back to us.

'My lord,' her voice was strong, 'my lord, I beseech you.' Akhenaten was forced to look at her. 'I am your Queen, your Great Wife. Surely the offspring of a Mitanni monkey will never wear the Double Crown?'

Akhenaten remained silent, face tense, body taut. He had to confront the fury of Nefertiti. She now moved forward; kneeling upright, she placed her hands on his knees, the classic pose of a supplicant.

'I am your Queen, your wife.'

My heart wept at the pleading in her voice.

'I have spoken. What Pharaoh has said,' Akhenaten's voice carried through the chamber, 'will be done!'

Nefertiti remained kneeling, though she withdrew her hands.

'Why, my lord? Why now? Why here? Could you not have told me in the privacy of our chamber?'

'I have spoken,' Akhenaten replied. 'My will is manifest. My will shall be done!'

His twin daughters were now crying, sobbing quietly, moving to kneel beside their mother. Ankhespaaten, however, turned to face us, a beautiful little thing. She sat back on her heels, hands on her thighs and gazed coolly round as if she wanted to remember each of our faces.

'You have betrayed me!' Nefertiti sprang to her feet and moved away, half-facing her husband. She made her appeal to the Royal Circle but what comfort would she find there?

'You have betrayed me,' she repeated.

'The Lady Khiya was the Divine One's loyal rightful wife,' Tutu spoke up. Beside him Meryre was nodding vigorously.

'Silence!' Nefertiti screamed.

If it hadn't been for Ay's outstretched hand she would have advanced threateningly on the sycophantic Chamberlain. She turned back on her husband. 'You have betrayed me! You swore an oath!'

Akhenaten lifted his hand as a sign for silence. Nefertiti refused to concede.

'You swore an oath, a great oath that would last for ever. Only our children, the flesh of the Sun, would inherit the Double Crown!'

'Betrayed?' Akhenaten now changed tack. 'You talk of betrayal, my lady?'

'What do you mean?' Nefertiti hissed.

Akhenaten gestured at Ay, whose head went down.

'Where is the brat?' Nefertiti snarled.

'He is safe.'

'And the Monkey?'

'She is dead.'

I gazed speechlessly at Akhenaten: the murmur of conversation died away.

'The Lady Khiya is dead,' Akhenaten repeated. 'She has travelled to the Far Horizon. She is beyond our care and our tears, but not our memory. She died last night. The physician . . .' I noticed the single title. 'The physician was unable to staunch the bleeding.'

'Then let her body rot!' Nefertiti shouted. 'And I pray her brat follows suit!'

Akhenaten sprang from the chair and, bringing up his hand, he punched Nefertiti full in the face, sending her flying back. Ay tried to catch her but the blow was so powerful Nefertiti was sent sprawling to the floor. The twins were screaming. Ankhespaaten remained kneeling. Courtiers half-rose, not knowing what they were to do. Nefertiti pulled herself to her feet, dabbing at the blood on the corner of her mouth. She whispered at Ay but he seemed like a broken reed, just slumped on his cushions, fearful of where Akhenaten's rage might lead. Nefertiti now lost all control. She was screaming at Akhenaten who shouted back. Both their robes were now dishevelled, one of Akhenaten's slippers had come off. The Royal Circle was so shocked it could only sit and watch Pharaoh and his Great Queen shouting at each other like a peasant and his wife in some back street of Thebes.

Rameses hid his smile. Horemheb just sat gaping at the scene. Meryre covered his ears. I realised that all the resentment which had seethed beneath the surface over the last few years was now surfacing in this violent shouting match. The Captain of the Guard burst into the chamber, alarmed by the noise but I gestured at him to leave. Rameses' shoulders were now shaking with silent laughter as the argument continued; both Pharaoh and his Queen were about to lose all vestige of dignity. Akhenaten gazed wildly around. Perhaps my pleading look cut through the haze of anger for, gathering his robes about him, he walked back to his throne as if impervious to Nefertiti's screams and imprecations. He gestured at me to come forward. I did so, knelt on the cushions and made obeisance. As I raised my head Ankhespaaten caught my eye, a smile on her lips as she moved closer to her father.

'Your Majesty?' I asked.

Akhenaten's face was still suffused with anger; a line of spittle ran down his chin, his protuberant chest was heaving as if he had run a great distance; his white robes were sweat-soaked. He leaned forward, smacking my shoulder with the flail. He didn't speak until Nefertiti fell silent, more out of exhaustion than anything else.

'The Lady Nefertiti has used contumacious words.' Akhenaten's voice rang hollow. 'She has dared to threaten the Crown Prince. She is to be banished to her apartments in the Northern Palace. She will not look on my face again. Mahu, carry out my will!'

I rose and walked towards Nefertiti, hands extended. In that hour she had aged. Her face-paint was patchy and running with the tears and sweat. One earring had come loose and, in her temper, she had torn the silver and golden collar from round her neck and it lay scattered at her feet.

'My lady,' I whispered, 'we must leave.'

Nefertiti made to object.

'Call the guards!' Akhenaten shouted.

Nefertiti gave a long sigh, body quivering. I thought she was choking then her body went slack. She stood, head down, shoulders stooped, hands folded across her stomach. Then she summoned up her dignity and walked towards the door. She made to turn but I caught her by the elbow.

'My lady,' I whispered, 'it's useless.'

Akhenaten must have known what was going to happen. Outside swarmed a horde of Libyan mercenaries, hand-picked men and officers. They immediately formed a ring round us. We walked through the corridors, across courtyards and gardens, following the King's Road up towards the Northern Palace. It's remarkable how the news of someone's fall can spread as quickly as the wind. Frightened servants darted away. Courtiers and officials suddenly found something more interesting and disappeared from sight. Visitors and petitioners, guards, officers, scribes and priests melted away at the tramp of the mercenaries' feet. We swept up the broad avenue into the precincts of the Northern Palace. Akhenaten's decision had been planned. More guards were waiting, whilst in the royal quarters huddled frightened-looking maids and ladies-in-waiting ready to attend on their mistress. Nefertiti's quarters were very similar to the small

Palace of the Aten where Akhenaten had grown up on the outskirts of the Malkata Palace: a central courtyard ringed by buildings and beyond that a walled garden. Soldiers in full battle gear guarded each gate, door and approach. We were treated with every dignity and courtesy. The kitchens were already preparing food. Nefertiti now stopped and gazed sadly round.

'Mahu, this is no surprise,' she murmured. 'It's like going back in time. This is my new home, isn't it?'

We passed through the small audience hall beyond which lay her private chambers. At the entrance to the bedchamber Nefertiti dismissed the gaggle of ladies-in-waiting as well as the burly thickset Captain of the Guard who had followed us up.

'You,' she pointed at him, 'you can withdraw.'

He made to protest. 'You shall withdraw,' her voice rose, 'and only approach my presence at my command. My daughters?'

'Your Majesty', the Captain replied, 'your daughters will be allowed to visit you whenever you wish. But as for withdrawing . . .'

'Do as Her Majesty commands,' I ordered, winking quickly at the man. He bowed and marched away. Nefertiti, plucking at my robe, gestured at me to follow. I did so, closing the door behind me, and leaned against it. She went across and sat on the edge of a small divan. For a while she just sat, face in hands, weeping quietly. I crossed to the table and poured out wine, specially chilled, and brought it across. She snatched it from my hands and drank greedily. I made to go but she called me back, throwing cushions at her feet for me to sit. She lifted her face, pale and drawn, but her eyes were still as beautiful, made even more so from their tears.

'Mahu, did you know?'

'Mistress.' I shook my head. 'By all that is holy, I knew nothing. I didn't notice her.'

Nefertiti handed the wine-cup back to me. She sat running a finger along a plucked eyebrow. 'I didn't notice she was missing, Mahu. I even thought she had been sent back to Thebes. Where was she kept?'

'She had her own small palace,' I replied. 'Madam, didn't you know what was coming?'

'Yes and no,' she replied wearily. 'After the birth of our last daughter, the Beloved no longer approached my bedchamber. He grew cold and distant. He would often ask me about my days in Akhmin. My relationship with my father.'

'And?' I dared to ask.

'I tell you what I told him. My past is my past and so is his. Sometimes he would speak sharply to me. He would remind me that he was the son of the Aten. No, that's wrong! You know the truth, don't you, Mahu? My own father has told me often enough. Akhenaten believes he *is* the Aten himself. He is the God Incarnate, the Possessor of all Wisdom. He came to resent my very presence.'

I sat on those cushions in that beautiful, opulent chamber with its ivory-inlaid caskets, exquisite bed shrouded in white linen and delicate furniture. The walls were painted with the most pleasing scenes, made fragrant with flower baskets and pots of perfume. I realised then why Ay had whistled up the Sekhmets, why Horemheb and Rameses were so worried. The City of the Aten, my master's dream, were teetering on the brink of ruin. Nefertiti, as if speaking to herself, recited a litany of grievances. I kept silent. I did not question her about the potions she had given Khiya, nor did I dream of mentioning Pentju's name, though I suspected what had happened. At last, overcome by the effects of the wine and her own nervous exhaustion, Nefertiti lay down on the divan, pulled a cushion beneath her lovely tear-streaked cheeks, and fell asleep.

For a while I just knelt and studied that exquisite face framed by its glorious red hair. Then, leaning closer, I kissed her gently on the half-open lips still sweet with the taste of wine. I rose to my feet and walked to the door.

'Mahu,' she called out. I didn't turn but paused, my hand on the latch. 'I made a mistake, betrayed by my own pride and arrogance.'

I opened the door and left. I made my way to the mansion of the Lady Khiya, a palatial residence in its own grounds surrounded by a high-bricked wall. The gates were heavily guarded. My presence there was questioned by mercenary officers who treated me more as an enemy than someone they knew. However, I was persistent. At last I was ushered through. Pentju, grey-faced and hollow-eyed, met me in the garden. I told him what had happened. He smiled and nodded in satisfaction. When I struck him in the face, he didn't object or call for the guard, but clambered slowly to his feet, wiping the blood from his nose, laughing quietly to himself. I struck him again, even as I could hear the hymn of lamentation from the house as Khiya's body was being prepared for burial in one of the tombs in the eastern cliffs.

'Will you hit me again?' Pentju nursed the side of his face. 'Or is it a case of doctor heal thyself?'

'Why?' I asked.

'Why not?' Pentju's sly eyes creased in a smile. 'Why not, Mahu? To be treated like a dog in front of the court! My arse exposed like some naughty schoolboy! To receive no apology! To be banished! The same for Khiya. She became pregnant about eighteen months ago but the baby was premature.'

'How?' I asked.

'How do you think babies are conceived?' he spat back. I raised my hand.

'Mahu, Mahu,' he grasped my wrist and gently lowered my arm. 'Khiya was cunning as a monkey. She suspected Nefertiti's gifts of wine and food contained potions which would either stop her conceiving or destroy anything formed in the egg. I told her only to eat and drink what I gave her. The Divine One often came here. Oh, I thrilled at what Khiya told me. How he was growing tired of Nefertiti who saw herself as his equal both before man and god. How bitterly disappointed he was that he had no son.' Pentju shrugged and sat down on a wooden garden seat; he picked up a small pot of flowers and kneaded the black soil with a finger.

'When Khiya became pregnant again, Akhenaten swore me to secrecy. The same for everyone who worked here. The cooks, the maids, they are all Mitanni owing allegiance to Khiya and to no one else. She was instructed not to leave the gardens: the gates were guarded and, of course, no one ever suspected.'

'Except for Ay?'

'Except for Ay.' Pentju sighed. 'Somehow he heard the news but dare not tell his daughter nor raise the matter with Pharaoh himself. Ten days ago the child was born, strong and vigorous. Poor Khiya became weak. She caught a fever and died. Pharaoh had issued strict orders. No one was to come here. No one was to leave without his written permission.'

'Except for me?'

Pentju closed one eye and squinted up at me, nursing his sore jaw. 'She liked you, Mahu, you know that. Khiya really liked you. You were one of the few people who showed her respect. She thought you were funny. How did she describe you?' He closed his eyes. 'Oh, that's it! Not a man who had lost his soul but one who was searching for it. In the last few hours before she died she was sweat-soaked, feverish, hot as a rock burning in the sun. She whispered your name and asked to be remembered to you.'

I felt a chill run through my body. Pentju had lost his cynical look. He rose and grasped both my wrists.

'I allowed you in, Mahu, because of her.' His voice fell to a whisper. 'Because I have a message: "Tell Mahu," Khiya said, "that I speak before I die and I will speak from beyond the grave".'

I recognised the Mitanni turn of phrase for someone taking a great oath.

'What is it?' I asked.

'"Tell Mahu to protect my son. Tell Mahu to be his guiding spirit, to protect him as he once protected the Veiled One. Tell him that perhaps my son is the One who is to come, the Messiah, the Holy One of God".'

Pentju held me so tight, his gaze was so fierce, his voice so strong that I knew he spoke the truth.

'I cannot.'

'No, you must, Mahu! She swore a sacred oath. She called your name. Whether you like it or not, you are bound to that child. Stay here.'

Pentju left and returned a short while later followed by a young woman carrying a baby in swaddling clothes, suckling at her generous breast. The girl looked up at me and smiled. She chattered in a tongue I could not understand. Pentju replied and the woman placed the child gently in my arms.

It was the first time I, Mahu, had ever held a baby. I gazed down, pushing back the linen hood which protected the head. I noticed the skull was strangely elongated at the back but the face was most comely: little eyes stared unblinkingly at me, chubby cheeks, a little mouth opening and closing, eager for the nipple and the life-giving milk. I expected him to cry at being taken away from his suckling but he just stared at me. I felt his warmth seeping through the linen blankets. I pushed my finger into the little hand and smiled at the grip. Pentju said something to the wetnurse who withdrew. For a while I just stared down at this tiny creature who had caused such confusion and chaos to the power of Egypt.

'Tutankhaten,' I whispered, 'the Crown Prince Tutankhaten.'

Those small black eyes gazed at me owlishly. They say that babies don't smile, that their expressions are simply caused by hunger and thirst. However, that little one smiled at me, a fleeting expression, as if he was savouring a joke. I handed him back to Pentju.

'He is well and vigorous?'

'Well and vigorous,' Pentju agreed, 'with no disfigurement or deformity.'

I thought he was going to add something else but he called the wetnurse in. He did not talk again about the oath but escorted me back to the gate. I realised there was an unspoken, unwritten agreement that, whatever happened, Khiya's dying oath would bind me for ever.

For the next few weeks all was chaos and confusion. Ay retreated to his own quarters. Everyone else became busy in that frenetic, mindless way as courtiers do when they wish to ignore something and not face the consequences of what might happen. The Royal Circle didn't meet. Queen Tiye visited both her son and Nefertiti, but it was obvious that the rift between the Royal Couple was bitter and could not be healed. Akhenaten himself seemed wholly taken up with his new son whilst Nefertiti now became a recluse in her apartments in the Northern Palace. No one could approach her. Even when I applied for leave to do so, Chamberlain Tutu instructed me never to ask again. Akhenaten also withdrew. Life in the city became slower, more disorganised. Work on the Royal Tomb and other sepulchres abruptly halted. Everything was in a state of flux and, as happens in the affairs of men, the blundering of blind fate intervened.

The texts in this tomb contain the most extraordinary errors and are often unreadable.

(N. de G. Davies' commentary on the *Hymn to the Aten* as found in Mahu's tomb.)

Chapter 19

The pestilence swept into the City of Aten at the height of the hot season during year thirteen of Akhenaten's reign. A virulent plague, it brought the sweating sickness followed by instant death. Coming so swiftly on the rift between Pharaoh and his Great Queen, it looked as if the gods had finally turned their face against Egypt. The plague was brought to the quayside of the city and swept through the streets on both sides of the Nile. The empty house of Makhre and Nekmet, as Djarka often told me, had been a constant topic of conversation especially when people tried to buy it: they could see no reason why it should be left to lie uninhabited. By the time the plague faded during the spring of the fourteenth year of Akhenaten's reign there were many empty houses in the City of Aten.

The plague, an invisible mist of death and destruction, wreaked havoc among all classes. The symptoms became the constant topic of conversation – a terrible sweating, lumps in the groin and armpits, vomiting and excruciating

549

stomach pains. I know, I became a victim. I only survived thanks to Djarka, who brought in a Sheshnu wise man who fed me a mixture of dried moss mixed with stale milk. Djarka escaped unscathed, but for weeks I was in the Underworld, a frightening reality where the devourers gathered around me, men in strange armour, faces covered with ugly masks, grotesque beasts such as winged griffins, crocodiles with the heads of hyenas. All the dead clustered about me as if to celebrate some infernal party – Aunt Isithia, Ineti, Weni, Nekmet, Snefru, Makhre and all the rest, gloating to see me. I swam in a pit of fire with dark shapes hovering above me and raucous cries echoing through the red, misty air. I survived but thousands didn't.

For most of year fourteen of Akhenaten's reign I remained weak and helpless. I couldn't stand for long; even a short walk exhausted me. Only after the appearance of the Dog Star which marked the New Year did my old strength return. Djarka allowed me to look at myself in a polished mirror.

'You are as lean as a greyhound.'

I had changed. My hair had grown and was tinged with grey. There were marks around my mouth, and my cheeks were slightly sunken. I studied my eyes and pushed the mirror away.

'What's the matter?' Djarka asked.

'I have the face of a monkey,' I replied, 'but worse still, Sobeck's eyes.'

'It's the effects of the plague,' Djarka countered. 'By spring you will be well again.'

Only then did he tell me the extent of the devastation. Great Queen Tiye, Princess Meketaten as well as

Akhenaten's two youngest daughters, not to mention scores of notables, scribes and priests had been swept away. Pentju was safe, so was the young Crown Prince, locked away in strict isolation. Horemheb and Rameses had fled out into the Red Lands. Ay, Maya and Huy had followed suit.

'Karnak's also dead!'

I put my face in my hands.

'He ate . . .'

'Don't tell me,' I whispered. 'Let it go! Meryre?'

'The demons look after their own master, still full of pomp and pus.'

'And Akhenaten?'

'Alive but a hermit.'

I glanced down, my hands were shaking. Djarka crouched before me.

'You often spoke about her, Master – Great Queen Nefertiti! You cried out for her in the night!'

'Well?' I asked.

'She survived, a prisoner of the Northern Palace. But, come, I must show you the city.'

Djarka brought a chariot from the imperial stables. The day was dismal and overcast. A cold breeze sent the dry leaves whirling, and he made me wear a cloak as he drove me into the city. Its streets and avenues were deserted. Houses had been boarded up. The Wadjet Eye had been daubed on walls. The desiccated corpses of rats, crows and bats were still nailed to the doors of houses where families had died. Smoke from countless pyres, built at crossroads and corners to fumigate the air, curled like snakes to sting one's nostrils and throat. Carts, pulled by oxen, heavily laden with putrefying corpses, made their way out up to the rim of the eastern cliffs where fierce fires raged, burning the dead. Black plumes rose against the distant sky before being scattered by the breeze from the Nile. Markets were closed, only a few shops did business. Men and women, dressed like Desert Wanderers, hurried by, cloths hiding their heads, mouths and nostrils. Mercenaries, armed and ready, squatted or lounged, their very presence imposing a deathly stillness.

'A city of the dead,' Djarka murmured. 'At the height of the plague, Master, it seemed as if these were more like the streets of the Underworld. Dead piled outside doorways, scavengers and looters busy. Fires burning as if the earth had turned to flame.'

'Who kept order?' I asked.

'Ay, Horemheb and Rameses. They imposed martial law. The physicians say the plague is over but people are drifting away.'

We approached the great Temple of the Aten. A side gate creaked in the wind. Priests stood about in small groups. A dour spirit now possessed this place. There were no pilgrims, no smell of incense came from the sacrificial fires. The gardens which fringed the avenue leading up to the temple were choked with weeds and badly tended.

'Look at the graffiti,' Djarka urged. He reined in the horses and we got down. The lampoonists had been busy with caricatures of Akhenaten. These self-appointed artists missed no details of the King's physique: the strange, elongated head, bulbous slitted eyes, narrow chin, heavy lips and swollen stomach. In these pictures, however, the King had no grace or beauty; he was depicted as feckless, a drunkard, bleary-eyed and badly in need of the attention of the royal dresser. Other pictures represented the world turned upside down. One showed a harsh-faced cat standing erect, clutching a shepherd's hook, herding a flock of birds. Another depicted a hippopotamus perched in a tree, a servant in the shape of a crow ready to tend to him. A third showed a small boy before a court of justice. The policeman was a cat whilst the judge, garbed in his insignia of office, was a large mouse with protuberant chest and stomach, slitted eyes and a narrow elongated face. Next to this painting an army of mice stormed a fortress, defended by starving cats drawn very cleverly with the features of Akhenaten, Nefertiti and others of the royal court.

We climbed back into the chariot and Djarka drove me home along those same smoke-filled, sombre streets. I must have been noticed for three days later I received a summons from the Royal Palace. As Djarka escorted me along its deserted corridors, the only people we glimpsed were mercenaries and household troops. The Chamberlain who accompanied us whispered how this was the Divine One's wish.

'He has dismissed all his servants,' the fellow confided, 'for he trusts none of us.'

Guards at the entrance to the Throne Room searched me and Djarka. He was told to wait as the door was opened. I was almost pushed into the dark, sour-smelling room lit only by a few oil lamps and the rays of a weak sun pouring through the high oblong windows. I'll never forget what I saw. Most of the chamber was in darkness. The only light seemed to be around the throne where Akhenaten slouched naked except for a loincloth and a pectoral of dazzling fire around his neck. A girlish voice told me to approach. I did so and stood before the throne, too shocked to make the obeisance. Akhenaten's head was shaven; the lower part of his face was covered in stubble, his eyes hollow and sunken peered at me like fluttering oil lamps. Ankhespaaten was sitting in his lap feeding him from a cherry bowl whilst on a cushioned chair to his right his eldest daughter Meritaten lounged, cradling a wine-cup. Both rose as I entered. They were pregnant, their bellies and breasts swollen. Dressed like hesets in diaphanous kilts above loincloths, embroidered shawls about their shoulders, they glittered in a glow of jewellery, necklaces and bangles which rattled at their every movement like the sistra of the dancing girls. Recalling myself, I knelt on the cushions. As I did so, I glimpsed the nails of Akhenaten's fingers and toes; they were unusually long and dirt-filled, and his body sweat was powerful.

At first Akhenaten seemed to be unaware of my arrival. When I glanced up, he stared back in puzzlement. His two daughters sidled up on either side. Meritaten shyly tried to pluck the shawl closer about her. Ankhespaaten was brazen, making no attempt to hide her condition or the beauty of her young body. She stood slightly forward, resting against the throne, her right arm along its top, fingers ready to caress her father's head. In her left hand was a deep-bowled cup of wine which she offered to her father. Akhenaten's hand shook as he took it. He gulped noisily and belched. Meritaten kept her head down, the heavy braids of her perfumed wig half-concealing her face. Ankhespaaten, however, smiled boldly, even flirtatiously. Akhenaten moved on the throne.

'They have all gone, Mahu.'

'Who have, Your Majesty?'

Akhenaten's eyes were vague, his mouth slack, lips wet with wine. He slurped from the wine-bowl again.

'The spirit is gone. My Father has hidden his face. So many dead.' He put the wine-cup down, hands going out to caress the swollen stomachs of his daughters.

'The Beautiful One has gone but my seed still fertilises. I will people the earth with my own seed but they still bother me, Ay and the rest. Reports about this, reports about that.' He blinked. 'I thought you had gone, Mahu. I thought you were dead.'

'I was ill, Your Majesty.'

'How beautiful,' Akhenaten chanted, sitting back on his throne. 'How beautiful are your rays.' He blew his nose on his fingers and stamped his foot.

'What do you advise, Baboon of the South?'

'Advise, Your Majesty? Why, clear the streets. Have them and the gardens purified. Order the merchants back. Open the markets, show your face.'

'And?'

'Bring back your true Queen.'

'Oh, she's back.' Akhenaten swayed drunkenly and tapped the side of his head. 'She is still here.'

'My father will rule.' Ankhespaaten spoke up fiercely, her eyes bright with anger. 'Our line, this seed, his glory will carry us forward to new times.'

For a moment, though her hair was black as night, her kohl-ringed eyes dark pools, the soul of Nefertiti glowed in that girl-woman, impregnated by her own father. She was ruthlessly determined to defend his and her own interests.

'Your son, Your Majesty?'

I ignored Ankhespaaten's hiss of disapproval as she stared like an angry cat, painted nails beating a tattoo on the back of her father's throne. 'He is safe!' Akhenaten shook his head. 'Baboon . . .'

'Bring back your Great Wife.'

'I will think of that, Mahu, but now you have got to go. My seed,' he pointed down to his groin, 'my seed wants out.'

I rose.

'I didn't tell you to go now.'

I slumped back on the cushions.

'I'll summon the Royal Circle,' Akhenaten slurred. 'I'll summon it, but let Ay preside until I decide what to do with his head. No, no, no.' Akhenaten was talking to himself. 'His head is safe. I need him. Meryre will watch him.' He put his face in his hands and sobbed. 'I'll tell them all to come back.' His words were muffled. He raised a tear-stained face. 'I wish I could go back, Baboon of the South. I wish I could return to that grove with the rising sun washing my face.' He shook his head. 'It was not fair. I had no choice. Don't you realise that, Mahu? I had no choice.'

'When, Your Majesty?'

'In the Temple of Amun.'

'Your Majesty?'

'I had no choice. I knew the wine was poisoned. I baited my brother Tuthmosis and he left. I asked him to wait in my chamber, so I could tell him a great secret about our mother. You see, Mahu, I knew the wine was poisoned. I . . . I . . .' He stumbled on his words.

I glanced at Meritaten. She still stood head down but Ankhespaaten knew what her father was saying.

'I'd been back to my chamber, Mahu. I had seen the poisoned wine in the jug, the cup next to it.'

'Your Majesty.' I breathed hard, trying to hide a quiver of fear. My heart was in my throat. I found it difficult to speak. Akhenaten was leaning forward like a penitent confessing his sins to a priest.

'Ay and Nefertiti told me the wine would be poisoned. I was not to drink or eat anything. I felt so faint but they told me how it would happen and they were right.'

The memories flooded back. Ay reflecting on what to do. Shishnak protesting his innocence until the pain made him confess. Hotep grinning at me in that garden, brazenly misleading me just before he died. Now I realised the traps he had hidden away. Hotep hadn't wanted to alert me. He wished to keep me close to Ay and Nefertiti, a willing tool for their ambitions. And who else had Hotep used? Pentju! He had not only been motivated by revenge, he must have been in Hotep's pay from the start. As had Khiya. She had visited the Magnificent One in his House of Love not just to receive the juice of the poppy but to report all she had learned. Hotep had been the one who had brought her there. Hotep had quietly plotted his revenge even before he fell from power.

Hotep and Ay, two cobras circling each other, plotting for the future. Had Hotep also encouraged the Magnificent One to enjoy little Khiya, a subtle revenge on his grotesque son? Had Hotep told Khiya to accept her lonely status, the patronising jibes of Nefertiti and await her chance? Only then, years later, did I see the fruits of Hotep's wily brain. He must have realised that one day, Akhenaten would turn on Nefertiti. Khiya and Pentju were his weapons. Ay, the supreme plotter, could do little to check Hotep except to push ahead his own plans, speeding like a runner to the finish: the murder of Tuthmosis and the advancement of Akhenaten. I could understand Khiya being suborned by Hotep – but Pentju? Then I recalled his infatuation with the Lady Tenbra, a noblewoman, who, in truth, would hardly look at a mere physician. Hotep, of course, would have smoothed Pentju's path. And that poison which had killed Tuthmosis? It was not the work of Shishnak and the priests of Amun but the Akhmin gang. Of course, Ay and Nefertiti would have their spies amongst the priests of Amun. It would be so easy to arrange for a jug of poisoned wine to be left in a chamber and Akhenaten instructed not to eat or drink anything. I glanced at my master's bleary face. Had he been fully aware of the plot against his own brother? Other thoughts came tumbling back. The invitation to the Temple of Amun: had that been Shishnak's work or a sly suggestion by Ay through his placement in the priestly hierarchy at Karnak? An ambitious gamble, so subtle, the priests of Karnak took the blame.

'My Lord Mahu?'

I broke from my reverie. Ankhespaaten was leaning forward.

'What you have heard is sacred and secret. My father trusts his Baboon of the South.'

'And you, my lady?'

'What my father wants is my desire.'

I glanced at Meritaten. She was smiling shyly at me, her beautiful face so vacuous I wondered about her wits.

'Mahu?' Akhenaten was holding a sealed scroll in his

hands, which he must have concealed in the cushions of the throne. He thrust this at me.

'If anything happens to me . . .'

'Your Majesty, nothing will.'

'When I go back to my Father,' Akhenaten's voice was now firm, 'open that scroll. As you can see, it is sealed three times. Promise me, Mahu' – tears filled his eyes – 'for what we have, for the friendship we had, you will keep it safe? Swear now!'

I raised my hand and spoke the oath. He handed it over.

'Go, Mahu, my friend.'

I left and as I did so, Akhenaten and his two daughters, their voices sounding hollow, began to recite a spell from *The Book of the Dead.*

'I abhor the eastern land.
I will not enter the place of destruction.
None shall bring offering of what the gods protect . . .'

By the second month of the season of Peret, in the fifteenth year of Akhenaten's reign, the pestilence had completely disappeared. The City of the Aten returned to some form of normality, but its heart, once strong, now beat faintly. Akhenaten showed himself escorted by his two daughters, who rejoiced in the title of Queen. They had given birth to daughters – each had been given their own name with the suffix 'Tasheit' – but neither child had survived the first month of their life. People whispered that it was a judgement from the gods. Nefertiti still remained a recluse, all access to her denied.

The city was now administered by a small council of Devouts which included Ay and, on occasion, General Horemheb. Ay had passed unscathed through the pestilence. We exchanged pleasantries but I kept my own counsel. Ay was an ally but no longer a friend. I concealed the scroll Akhenaten had given me. For days after my audience with him I reflected on what I had learned. There was no dream or vision of the Aten. Perhaps Queen Tiye had been pure in her thoughts but I was in a nest of writhing cobras. The struggle was about power and glory and, for what it was worth, I was part of it.

At the end of that summer the Royal Circle was solemnly convened. Everyone was present, even Pentju, aloof and quiet, as if he knew his part but did not really care. The rest had continued to prosper, advancing their careers, creating spheres of influence, building up factions and forging alliances. Horemheb was a leading General in the army command, Rameses his Lieutenant. Huy was master of all affairs beyond Egypt's borders. Maya knew every measure of gold and silver, or the lack of it, from the treasuries of Egypt. Meryre, lost in his fool's paradise, still dreamed of being High Priest of a religion which would stretch from the Euphrates to beyond the Third Cataract. Ay was more himself, relaxed and smiling. We all sat as if nothing had happened, yet each quietly plotted for the future. The City of Aten, the reign of the Sun Disc, the idea of the One were all dust. They were impatient to sweep it away and assume the normal business of power: the only obstacle was how?

Ay, however, in a brilliant display of hypocrisy and cant, supported by the children of the Kap, his close allies, deliberately misled Tutu, Meryre and the rest.

He painted a picture which even I found convincing. How Akhenaten had returned to his usual vigour. How the city would prosper. How General Horemheb would reorganise the armies and advance Egypt's standards from one end of the Empire to the other, all under the glowing patronage of the Aten. Tutu, Meryre and the rest drank this in like greedy children.

Afterwards, in the seclusion of his own private garden, Ay convened a second meeting of the children of the Kap, including Pentju. He questioned the physician most closely about the health and well-being of the young Prince. Pentju replied truthfully but made it very clear that the young boy was in his care and would only be handed over to those Akhenaten appointed. Ay pursed his lips, pronounced himself satisfied and moved to the other items of business. We sat in the shade sipping Charou wine and quenching our thirst on slices of lemon and pomegranate, whilst we divided an empire.

Following so swiftly after the meeting of the Royal Circle I felt I could have burst out laughing. No one questioned Ay's decision or the underlying principle that Akhenaten's reign was coming to an end, his revolution no more exciting than a dried-out riverbed. Huy and Maya gave a pithy blunt description of affairs. How Thebes was seething with unrest. The treasuries were empty whilst beyond Egypt's borders the allegiance of our allies was growing weaker by the month. Horemheb delivered more ominous news. How the Egyptian army high command at Memphis were on the brink of mutiny: bereft of supplies, weapons and recruits, commanders were unable to despatch any troops across Sinai either to support

Egypt's allies or defend her precious mines and trade routes.

At last the decision was made. Huy and Maya would return to Thebes. They would form their own House of Scribes and secretly plan for the future. Horemheb, supported by Rameses, would be appointed Commander-in-Chief of all Egypt's forces and take over the garrison at Memphis. Ay urged the need for secrecy but they were all to follow the same path and sing the same hymn. They were to restore confidence, assure the powerful that the old ways would return, that the City of the Aten was merely a stumbling block in the glorious path of Egypt's true destiny. No one, of course, dared raise, even hint, at what Akhenaten might think or say. Ay already had that under control. Each of my colleagues were given their seals of office, their commissions all bearing the royal cartouche of Akhenaten. Once he had finished, each of us took an oath of loyalty, of common friendship and alliance. Hands were clasped and the children of the Kap went their own way.

A few weeks later I broached the matter of Akhenaten's state of mind with Ay. I avoided the temptation of confronting him. I believed we shared a common soul, or at least I thought we did. Ay was as dangerous and as cunning as a mongoose. What memories does any hunter hold of what he's slain? The hunter lives for the moment and plans for the future. Ay had to view me as an ally, not as his conscience. He listened to what I said and brought his fingers to his lips.

'Very perceptive, Mahu. As always you point your finger at the heart of the problem.'

'Don't patronise me, God's Father,' I retorted. 'Huy and

Mahu, not to mention Horemheb and Rameses, even Pentju, must be thinking the same. Tutu and Meryre are easy to fool. They still dream and haven't woken up.'

'We will see,' Ay replied. 'We shall speak to the Divine One and his Co-regent.'

Naturally I reported to Djarka what had happened. Most of it he knew, or at least suspected, but he was intrigued by the reference to a Co-regent. Djarka openly wondered if Ay had managed to worm himself so firmly back into Akhenaten's affections that he was being raised to the rank and title of Pharaoh.

'And yet,' Djarka shook his head, 'I find that impossible. Nobody would accept him.'

'What about Crown Prince Tutankhaten?' I asked.

'But he's only a child.'

On the day of audience Ay collected me from my house, making sure that I was dressed in the full ceremonial robes of a courtier. Surrounded by fan-bearers and flunkies and preceded by heralds and musicians, we swept up into the Palace of the Aten. The gateways and corridors, courtyards and gardens were full of Nakhtimin's men in the full regalia of battle, blue and gold head-dresses, snow-white kilts, spears and shields at the ready. At the door to the Throne Room a host of chamberlains and office-holders milled about. Trumpets blared. Gongs sounded. Gusts of incense perfumed the air. Meryre, dressed in his exquisite robes, escorted us into the imperial presence. The Throne Room had been changed. A raised daïs covered in gold-leaf now held two resplendent thrones. I could only stand and gape. Ankhesenamun and Meritaten were sitting at the edge of the daïs on small cushioned chairs. Akhenaten wore the Double Crown of Egypt, a cloth of gold round his shoulders, the Nekhbet pectoral shimmering brilliantly against his chest, and a brilliant white kilt falling down to his ankles. Beside him was a resplendent figure. I gasped in astonishment. This person too wore the full regalia of Pharaoh, grasping the flail and the rod, but the face was that of Great Queen Nefertiti. Her glorious hair had been shaven, her eyebrows plucked, her face carefully painted like that of her husband. At first glance she seemed not to have aged a day but, as I drew closer, I glimpsed the stoop of her shoulders, the podgy arms and fat hands, the cheeks slightly sagging, the lines round the mouth which even the paint could not disguise. Ay, quietly revelling in my surprise, knelt on the cushions and made obeisance. I did likewise, my forehead touching the ground. We received no command to rise. Akhenaten's voice boomed out.

'Now let it be known to the Kingdom of the Two Lands. Let my words be carried beyond the Third Cataract that I, in my wisdom, under the guidance of my Father, have decreed that my Great Wife and Great Queen Nefernefruaten-Nefertiti is now my co-ruler, assuming the name of Ankheperure-Smenkhkare-Nefernefruaten. Let it be known that her imperial seal carries the will of God; the voice of Smenkhkare will be obeyed.'

On and on he went, proclaiming the greatness of Nefertiti under her new name Smenkhkare. Of course I could only kneel and listen, recalling how Egypt had once boasted of its great Queen Pharaohs, such as Hatchesphut, daughter of the great Tuthmosis III. When Akhenaten finished, we were told to kneel back. I gazed on the face which had always haunted my soul. For a moment, those eyes shifted, a slight smile appeared, before the imperial mask returned. Akhenaten then proceeded to issue a series of decrees, each one being repeated but most of them only confirmed what Ay had already decided.

Once they had finished we were ordered to withdraw. Ay led me out into one of the small walled gardens where tables had been prepared with silver dishes and goblets, fruit and wine being served by servants who quickly withdrew.

'How long have you known this?' I asked.

'For a short while,' Ay grinned.

'Why?' I asked. 'Why has this happened?'

'Why, Mahu? Because you yourself pleaded with Akhenaten. Did you not say his Great Queen should be restored? All right,' he scoffed, 'I see the cynical smile.'

Ay walked over to the sun pavilion and sat on a cushioned seat indicating I sit next to him.

'The honest answer is that Akhenaten has come to his senses. Nefertiti is the life-force of his soul. In fact, I go further – she is his Ka, his Ba, the very essence of his being. He bans Nefertiti and what happens? Three of his children die! The children he had by his two daughters do not survive. A great plague has swept through the City of Aten. There are troubles in Thebes and elsewhere. It's not difficult, Mahu, to make Akhenaten reflect on the reason why the milk has gone sour. Of course,' he plucked at the embroidered sash round his waist and stared quizzically at a painting on the wall of the pavilion, 'he does love her, Mahu. He has missed her sweet breath, her gracious smile.'

'And now all will be well again!' I retorted. 'The lotus

will bloom, the papyrus will grow, the sun will shine, the rains will come and all will be well in paradise.'

'Something like that.' Ay glanced out of the corner of his eye. 'But you don't believe it, do you, Mahu?'

I didn't reply but rose, bowed and left. The last days had begun. Akhenaten and Nefertiti could smile and coo. Pharaoh might send presents with the word 'forever' written in hieroglyphics on a piece of papyrus: a cobra, a bread loaf and a strip of land, but the bread was stale, the land was as hard and the cobra was dangerous. I suspected Akhenaten was now drugged and drunk, soft clay in the hands of Ay who portrayed himself as his saviour. That mongoose of a man was now playing the most dangerous of games, a fervent Atenist who secretly plotted the return of the old ways. Or was it the other way round? I could never really decide what was the truth.

This great change was publicised by processions, Akhenaten and Nefertiti in their gorgeously decorated chariot, harness gleaming, ostrich plumes dancing, clouds of incense billowing about. They were escorted by the nobles in their multi-coloured robes and exotic sandals, guarded by soldiers armed with shields, spears, battle-axes and bows. It was all a dream. He and Nefertiti, dressed alike in war-kilt, jackal tail and the blue War Crown of Egypt, sacrificed white bulls with garlands round their necks. Nothing but show. They stood at the Window of Appearances in beautiful robes bound by red sashes and presented necklaces and gifts to the clash of cymbals. It was all an illusion. Akhenaten was more like a wooden idol from one of the temples he despised, brought out for public display. The real power lay in the hands of Ay and

Nefertiti who now rejoiced in her new throne name of Smenkhkare.

They both worked feverishly to restore the damage done. Writs, proclamations, declarations and public promises streamed from the palace. The double doors of the Great House were thrown open to petitioners and supplicants from every city in Egypt but Smenkhkare's cartouche appeared on the bottom of these documents. 'Smenkhkare' assumed the full regalia of the Empire. It was she who sat in grandeur and glory speaking with true voice and issuing writs whilst Meritaten appeared as her escort. So developed was the illusion that Nefertiti became more and more like a man, her daughter assuming the role of Queen.

Djarka and I were kept busy as if we were being deliberately distracted from the affairs of the Empire by the conditions of the city. We were instructed to search out wrongdoers, apprehend thieves, pursue robbers into the Red Lands. Only twice did I meet Nefertiti in her new role and she was as cold and hard as the flesh of a dead man. The last time was in the Great Writing Office where she dismissed her scribes. Only her Captain of Mercenaries remained, a Canaanite called Manetho, a grizzled, scarred man with a bushy moustache and beard who followed her every movement with all the blind affection and loyalty of a dog. Nefertiti-Smenkhkare had summoned me to deliver a lecture about the need for greater law and order at night in the city streets. She even hinted at my possible removal and sat in the high-backed chair like a judge delivering his verdict on a guilty man. She was still beautiful though her body was corpulent, her face fatter, the cheeks not so smooth, the mouth rather droopy, but her blue eyes still blazed with light and life. She dismissed me as if I was a dog.

The end came not in some dramatic form. Another summons to the palace, this time in the presence of Ay. Nefertiti-Smenkhkare sat on her throne at the far end of the Great Room with Meritaten on a stool on her right and Ankhespaaten on her left. Manetho, armed and helmeted, stood behind the throne. As I swept up towards her, I noticed members of Manetho's corps standing in the alcoves, the oil lamps glittering in the reflection of their drawn swords. The room was as beautiful as ever, perfume-filled with baskets of flowers, well-lit, but there was no hiding the air of menace, of silent threat. We knelt on the cushions on the floor and made obeisance. Meryre standing in the shadows ordered us to sit back and we did so. Ay was relaxed, he knew exactly what was about to happen. Like a master of music, he was directing every movement. From another room in the palace I heard the strains of singing as the royal choir rehearsed. For a moment I thought this was Akhenaten's Orchestra of the Sun but most of these had died during the great pestilence; their music would be heard no more.

'You are pleased to look upon my face, Mahu?'

'The light of your face, O Divine One,' I spoke the ritual, 'refreshes my limbs and gladdens my heart. I bask in the joy of your favour and seek your protection.'

'Then know this, Mahu, son of Seostris. Proclamations are to be issued in my name only for I am Pharaoh, Lord of the Two Lands, Smenkhkare-Ankhkeperure.' Nefertiti stared coldly, waiting for my response.

'The Divine One?' I asked.

'Beloved Pharaoh Akhenaten-Waenre is no more.'

'He has died, Your Majesty?'

'He lives still,' came the reply. 'He has journeyed back to his Father. He and his Father are now one.'

My heart teemed with questions. I opened my mouth to speak but Ay's soft cough and Nefertiti's look of implacable majesty kept me silent. Nefertiti then proceeded, under her new name and titles, to issue edicts of how the news was to be announced in the city as well as be carried to every corner of the Empire. After that I was dismissed. Of course I questioned Ay. I demanded the truth, to see the corpse. 'What preparations have been made for his burial?' I asked. 'In which tomb will he be buried?' Ay shrugged and fended these questions off.

'The tombs in the eastern cliffs,' he declared, 'are full of coffins and sarcophagi, the work of the plague.'

I sat in that small antechamber as the full realisation of what Nefertiti had said dawned on me. Memories came flooding back. The Veiled One in his pavilion or walking with me in the gardens, discussing his vision, chattering about this and that. Now he was gone, his death dismissed as if he was some peasant, some person of low repute. Ay, apart from his casual remark about the tombs on the eastern cliffs, sat in a chair watching me intently.

'I know why I am here.' I wafted away a buzzing fly.

'Why are you here, Mahu?'

'You are using me, as you would a measure, to test gold or silver.'

'What do you mean?' He narrowed his eyes.

'Do you think, God's Father Ay,' I retorted, 'that's how it will end? Akhenaten is dead. Long live Smenkhkare who is not really Smenkhkare but your daughter Nefertiti? Do you really believe people will accept this? That Great Pharaoh has gone but no one knows where?'

'But nobody does.' He pressed his fingers against my lips. 'Mahu, I speak with true voice. Three weeks ago, the Divine One, Akhenaten, simply disappeared.'

'You mean he was murdered?'

Something in Ay's face made me regret the question. A passing look, a rare one of genuine hurt.

'Mahu, he disappeared! He was in his quarters and then the next morning, when the servants entered his bedchamber' – Ay spread his hands – 'it was empty. Immediately we began a search of the palace grounds and the city.'

His words struck a chord in my memory. How Djarka had reported just under a month ago about mercenaries from Manetho's corps searching the city, of chariot squadrons being despatched into the Red Lands. At the time I thought it was some military matter, a reflection of Ay and Nefertiti's desire for security.

'But where? How? Why?' I demanded.

'I don't know, Mahu. Akhenaten had become a recluse; more and more he demanded to be by himself. On occasion he would request a chariot, and horses from the stable to be harnessed, then he'd drive out to his tomb, and on into the Red Lands. He would go garbed like a common courtier or petty official, his face and head concealed in a hood. Sometimes he even wore a veil over his face as he used to when he was a boy.'

I recalled Akhenaten's drunken babbling. How he longed for the old days, the seclusion and purity of his youth.

'The people will demand to see his corpse and, if they don't, Horemheb, Rameses and the rest will.'

'They shall be told what you are being told,' Ay replied. 'Akhenaten did not believe in the Osirian rite. We will say, and it is the truth, that body and soul, Akhenaten has gone back to his Father. He is no longer with us except in spirit.'

'And what happens if he reappears? What happens, God's Father Ay, if our great Pharaoh re-emerges from the Red Lands, purified and more determined than ever?'

Ay shook his head. 'He is past all that.'

'Did he ever hint,' I demanded, 'ever make reference to this?'

'He was morose and withdrawn.' Ay shrugged. 'My daughter, myself, Meryre and Tutu will take the most solemn oaths. We know nothing. We have searched.'

'What do you think truly happened?' I asked.

'Shall I tell you, Mahu?' Ay pushed the stool closer till his face was almost touching mine. 'Akhenaten became tired and disillusioned. He either went out to the Red Lands to die or to be alone. He may have been killed. He may have died or he may be living in some cave like those wandering holy men who speak to no one but the spirits of the desert, the wind and the sky. Whatever, Mahu, the decision has been made: he cannot, shall not return.'

'Shall not?' I queried. 'Do you have a hand in this, God's Father Ay?'

'No, Mahu, but I do have a hand in the saving of Egypt. In putting matters straight, in returning to the old ways. That is my concern, your concern, our concern. No more dreams! No more visions! No new cities or new gods. At the end of this year, perhaps in the spring of next, we shall move back to Thebes where Huy and Maya are preparing for the resurrection of Egypt. Horemheb and Rameses do likewise in Memphis. I ask you one question, Mahu, and one question only. Are you with us? For those who are not with us shall be considered against.'

'How many people will learn about this?' I asked.

'The children of the Kap, no one else.'

'Apart from you and your daughter?'

'You have not answered my question, Mahu. Are you with us or are you against us?' Ay held out his hand, I had no choice but to grasp it.

I made my way home and asked Djarka to accompany me out into the garden pavilion where Ay's spies and informers would find it difficult to listen and pry. I told him what had happened.

'Is he dead?' Djarka asked the same question I had earlier.

'He could be. He could have been murdered or taken out into the Red Lands and left to wander.'

'I will ask my people the Sheshnu to make enquiries. It is possible, my Lord Mahu,' Djarka often used my official title when discussing matters of state, 'that it is all finished. I have also received visitors from the palace.' He smiled thinly. 'We have been instructed to deface any memorial or tomb bearing the inscription of the Lady Khiya. It is to be finished by the end of the month. Anyway, what do you really think?' he urged. 'Is it possible that Akhenaten became tired, exhausted?'

I closed my eyes and recalled that young man living so

frugally many years ago. I was about to reply when one of our officers burst in.

'Master, you have a visitor: a man and a young boy.'

Pentju pushed the fellow aside and came into the room. Beside him walked a young lad of about five summers. He was about medium height, his strange, long, egg-shaped head completely shaved except for the side lock falling down over his left ear. He had dark lustrous eyes in a pointed smooth face, generous but small lips. He looked slender in a white robe which covered him from neck to ankle, stout leather sandals on his feet.

'You know who he is?' Pentju demanded.

I told the officer to close the door and guard it. Then I took the little fellow and lifted him up. He didn't even blink but stared solemnly, scrutinising me carefully. I kissed him on each cheek and put him down. Immediately his little hand went into mine.

'Khiya's son,' Djarka whispered, 'the Prince Tutankh-aten.' I knelt on the floor and made obeisance. Djarka did likewise.

'You must not do that.' The boy's soft hand tapped my head. 'You must not do that,' he repeated childishly, head to one side, gazing at me. 'He told me.' He pointed at Pentju. 'No one must do that for a while.'

I poured Pentju a goblet of wine and asked the boy if he wanted anything to eat or drink. The Prince shook his head.

He sat like a little old man on the stool Djarka brought, gazing at us with all the solemnity of a baby owl. He had the look of Akhenaten, certainly the eyes and lips, but his posture and gentleness reminded me of Khiya.

'Why have you brought him here, Pentju?'

The physician handed over a small carved hippopotamus wrapped in thickened papyrus. 'Every week,' Pentju declared, 'except during the plague, Akhenaten sent his son a present, a small carving, a scarab, an amulet or a ring wrapped in a piece of papyrus.'

I turned the parchment over. On the outside were the words *Enk Hetep*, which meant 'I am content'. On the other side, the words *to kiss*, with the hieroglyphics: an arrow above a head looking downwards at rippled water. 'Akhenaten made me promise,' Pentju explained, 'that I would receive such a gift on the second day of every week. On the outside the words, *I am content*, on the inside the words *to kiss* with the hieroglyphics. If I did not receive such a present for three weeks in succession, I was to conclude that he was no longer with us and that his only son was in danger. I was then to open the sealed document he had given me. It is over three weeks since I received this last present. This morning I broke the seal. The instructions were very simple. I was to bring the Prince to you and hand him over to your care.'

I stared at the little boy and felt a deep sadness, bittersweet because, despite what had happened, Akhenaten had, in the end, trusted me more than anyone else. I told Djarka and Pentju to stay while I returned to the house and retrieved the sealed document Akhenaten had given to me. I broke the three seals and unrolled it. The words scrawled under the crudely drawn hieroglyphs caught at my heart.

'*Haynekah Ahitfe*: hail to you greater than his father. *Mem sen-jay*: do not worry. *Ra mem pet*: the Sun is in the sky. *Heket Nebet Nefert, Mahu*: all good things to Mahu.

Then underneath all this, in a more common hand: Do what you have to, to protect my son. *Senb ti*: goodbye.'

I destroyed the manuscript and returned to the garden pavilion. I now knew the full reasons Ay had taken me to the palace that day: he not only wanted to test me but guessed that I was one of the few whom Akhenaten would trust with his baby son. Ay wanted to keep me close. I closed the door behind me and leaned against it.

'Pentju, you know what has happened?'

'Nothing, except what Djarka has told me.'

'The mercenaries surrounding your house,' I demanded. 'Can they be trusted?'

'They took an oath of loyalty to Pharaoh himself. They have not been released from that oath.'

'But they can be bribed, killed or removed,' I replied bitterly. 'Djarka, Pentju, you must take this little boy immediately out of the City of the Aten. Take him secretly to Thebes and entrust him to the care of Sobeck. Djarka, you know how to find him. Tell Sobeck that as he loves me, if he wishes to repay his debt, he must treat this boy as his own and keep him safe until I or you, Djarka, ask for him again.' I crouched down and embraced the boy; he smelt of perfume and honey. I kissed his cheeks. 'Be brave, little one,' I hissed. 'Do whatever these men tell you.'

A short while later, armed with provisions and small bags of gold, silver and precious jewels, Pentju and Djarka left through the side streets for the quayside.

Ay arrived later that day, accompanied by his mercenary Captains.

'I thought you were with us, Mahu?'

'God's Father Ay, of course I am.'

'Then where is the boy?'

'He is safe.'

Ay peered over my shoulder. 'Where are Pentju and Djarka?'

'They are safe too.'

Ay whistled through his teeth. 'Where is the Prince Tutankhaten?' he repeated.

The Captain of his mercenaries drew his sword.

'He is safe,' I repeated. 'In the gardens outside, God's Father Ay, my mercenaries are also waiting in the shade, bows drawn, arrows notched. Come, friend,' I added mockingly. 'I am with you as I was when I rescued Prince Akhenaten from the Temple of Amun.'

My visitor blinked, then glanced away.

'Moreover,' I whispered, 'if I die, God's Father Ay, so will you. Even if you survive you'll still never discover where the boy is.'

Ay stepped back, waving a finger in my face.

'Mahu, the cunning Baboon of the South.' His hand shot forward in a gesture of friendship.

I clasped it, squeezing just as tight.

'My friend and my ally.' He smiled and, spinning on his heel, left the house.

I was never asked again, at least not during that time, the whereabouts of Tutankhaten, Pentju or Djarka. For a few weeks the city was at peace. I was busy collecting my possessions, stowing them away and burning documents. The dance had only just begun. Other children of the Kap visited the City of the Aten. They, too, asked the whereabouts of the Prince and received the same answer.

They reminded me of vultures. They arrived, busy men on busy matters, but really they were like desert hyenas picking at a corpse. They were openly astonished by the apparent disappearance of Akhenaten but Rameses' cynical words summed up the mood of them all: 'He is gone and the gods be thanked! If he returns, we'll send him straight back.'

On one thing they were all agreed. 'Nefertiti will never be accepted. She can call herself what she likes,' Horemheb snarled over a goblet of wine. 'Smenkhkare–Ankhkeperure! She can proclaim herself to be the Divine Daughter, or even the Son of Horus, but she does not have the Tuthmosid blood in her veins. She is not of the royal line. She and Akhenaten are twin symptoms of the same disease. The army I command will tolerate her for a while and whatever sweet noises she makes to them or the great ones of Thebes but, in the end, she must step down.'

Ay accepted this with equanimity or, at least, appeared to do so. In the first month of the summer season he brought messages to us all, the children of the Kap, that an important meeting of the Royal Circle had been called in the Great Palace of the Aten. He made it clear that all were expected to attend.

I offered my house to Horemheb, Rameses, Maya and Huy, and organised my cooks to prepare a sumptuous meal. I did this at the request of Ay whom I called 'my guest of honour'. The chefs surpassed themselves, but the meal was eaten in silence. We were all apprehensive of what would happen the next day. Horemheb and Rameses had brought their own retinues, encamped down near the quayside, whilst Maya and Huy had been accompanied on their river journey by two bargeloads of mercenaries. Ay arrived late, face unshaven, dressed in simple robes covered by a dark cloak. I heard the clink of armour as his mercenaries camped outside in the garden. The Viper, all agitated, refused the garland of honour but asked me to shutter the windows and close the doors. We gathered round him. For a while Ay just sat on the cushions, face in his hands and, when he took his fingers away, his cheeks were wet with tears.

'The Royal Circle,' he sobbed and rubbed his face as he tried to control his feelings. 'Tomorrow morning you must not attend the meeting of the Royal Circle. You know the protocol. No one is allowed to carry weapons or bring armed followers to the sacred precincts.'

'What?' Rameses rose at a half-crouch.

'My daughter, Great Queen Nefertiti,' Ay wetted his lips, 'has planned your deaths.'

His announcement was met with shocked silence.

'You have proof?' Huy murmured.

Ay dug inside his robe and brought out a small scroll of papyrus. 'You know,' he added wearily, 'how she has ordered that Khiya's name be erased from every monument: even the lady's tomb is to be ransacked and vilified. She plans to make a clean sweep.'

'How do you know this?' Horemheb demanded, clutching Rameses' shoulder and forcing him to sit down.

Ay rubbed his face. 'Because she thinks I am her ally. She claims she has the support of Meryre, Tutu and the rest. Above all, the total unswerving loyalty of Manetho and his mercenaries. The council chambers will be locked and guarded. Certain of the Royal Circle, including you, have been marked down for death: to drink poison or lose your heads.'

I snatched up the scroll. 'It bears the names of those who are going to die,' Ay explained.

I unrolled the papyrus. I am not too sure if the others heard my groan. All I knew was a deep sense of anguish, a numbing coldness followed by an urge to scream and yell. The names were all listed: Horemheb, Rameses, Maya, Huy, Pentju, Prince Tutankhaten, Sobeck, Djarka and a host of others. What caught my throat like a cold hard hand was that my name headed the rest.

'She revealed this to me two days ago,' Ay explained. 'She intends, as she puts it, to make a clean sweep. She will depict you as the real supporters of Akhenaten then move back in glory with her eldest daughter Meritaten to the Malkata Palace at Thebes. The Aten will become one god amongst many. The city here will be allowed to rot whilst the worship of Amun is restored.'

'Why?' I asked. 'Why are you betraying your own daughter?'

'Very simple, Mahu. Because she is betraying Egypt. Oh yes, you can all die but ask Horemheb here – within a month, there will be civil war.'

'I'll kill the bitch!' Rameses snarled, picking up a knife from the table.

Again Horemheb forced him to sit down, ordering him to keep silent.

'What do you propose, God's Father Ay?' Maya demanded.

'What he thinks is no longer important,' Horemheb declared quietly. 'You have soldiers, my lord Ay? So do we. Mahu has his mercenaries. Our troops camp down at the riverside.' He rose to his feet and walked to a window. 'Tonight Manetho and his gang will be disarmed. The

Lady Meritaten must be put under arrest. She is guilty, my lord Ay?'

God's Father Ay nodded, biting back a sob.

'The Lady Meritaten will be invited to take poison,' Horemheb continued.

No one disagreed. A short discussion took place about Meryre and Tutu. It was agreed they'd be given the chance to purge themselves.

'And the Lady Nefertiti?' I asked. I was on the verge of tears. All I could think of was that beautiful face – blue eyes glinting with mischief, red hair falling down, her soft touch and sweet words.

'She must be confronted with her crimes,' Huy declared.

'She must take the poison,' Maya finished the sentence.

I felt so chilled I started to shiver. Ay was staring at me quizzically but Horemheb came over, picked up a shawl and wrapped it round my shoulders.

'Are you in agreement, God's Father?' I asked.

'Are we all in agreement?' Ay replied.

One by one their hands went up; they all sat looking at me.

'I am sacrificing a daughter and a grand-daughter,' Ay whispered hoarsely. 'Those who are not with us are against us. Mahu, what is your answer?'

I was going to refuse but my eye caught that list lying on the table, my name emblazoned on the top, and beneath it Djarka's, Sobeck's and Prince Tutankhaten's. Slowly my hand went up. Horemheb crossed to his belongings and brought back knuckle-bones, clearing the table with one sweep of his hands.

'We will throw,' he declared. 'That's what we used to do when we were children of the Kap.'

We each threw the knuckle-bones. My score was lowest. They all looked at me grimly.

'You are the one,' Horemheb declared, 'to give her the poison!'

I clutched the knuckle-bones in my hand so tightly they bit into the softness of my palm. Rameses served some wine and we moved onto other business, the deployment of troops and what would occur afterwards.

'It shall be proclaimed,' Ay now assumed responsibility, 'that Akhenaten, Nefertiti and Lady Meritaten have gone into the West. The vision of the Aten was built on sand and not meant to last. We shall return to Thebes and bring with us the glory of Amun. We shall send messages to every corner of the Kingdom of the Two Lands that the might and power of Egypt has been restored. We will make the People of the Nine Bows tremble under our feet.'

'And you will be Pharaoh, God's Father Ay?' I asked.

'Prince Tutankhaten will be proclaimed as the legitimate successor to his father,' Ay replied quickly, 'betrothed to the Princess Ankhespaaten, but their names will proclaim the changes which will affect all Egypt. From this day forward they will be known as Tutankhamun and Ankhesenamun. However,' he added dryly, his eyes never leaving mine, 'both children are unversed in statecraft. Until the Prince reaches maturity, all power will be vested in a Council of State. Everyone here will be a vital member . . .'

In that chamber with the oil lamps guttering, the shadows dancing against the walls and the food growing cold whilst the wine-cups were refilled, all the glory of

Akhenaten, all the splendour of Nefertiti crumbled to dust. Each of us took the sacred oath, hand on heart, the other stretched out to swear what we were party to. Eventually they all left. I just sat and drank while the memories poured back. I fell asleep, half-listening to the sounds of chariots and armed men moving in the streets below. Rameses kicked me awake just before dawn. He grinned down at me and pushed a small carob-seed loaf into my hand. He made me eat that and drink the cold beer he had brought. Then I washed my face, put a robe around me and followed him out into the streets.

Horemheb and Rameses had planned well. Regular troops, together with mercenaries, now controlled the roads and avenues, the entrance to every public building, temple and palace. Martial law had been declared. All citizens, on pain of death, were confined to their homes. Only the occasional scavenging dog would nose at a stiffening corpse of one of Manetho's mercenaries or lick the drying pools of blood. The palace, too, was deserted. Horemheb and Rameses' officers guarded the entrances and patrolled the grounds. I passed a courtyard where executions had been carried out. Manetho's head was already impaled on a pole. Other heads lay about whilst corpses were being heaped in corners before being thrown into carts. This included not only Manetho's mercenaries but also courtiers, scribes, officials and, from what Rameses had told me, even a few ladies-in-waiting who had tried to resist. Inside the palace corpses were also being dragged out of rooms. As we crossed a garden Ay's mercenaries were organising prisoners, pushing and shoving them up against the wall. The line of men, naked except for their loincloths, were beaten and abused. A name would be called, one of the men dragged forward and forced to kneel. I looked away but I still heard the hiss of the axe or club, a scream of pain and the thud of the falling head or corpse.

Nefertiti was waiting for me in a small chamber. She was sitting in the centre on a pile of cushions dressed in a simple white gown. In the corner a lady-in-waiting huddled, face in hands, sobbing noisily. Just before I entered the chamber Maya handed me a gold-encrusted cup. He glanced at me sadly.

'I know what you feel, Mahu, but the poison is quick. Meritaten has gone before her.'

I asked for the girl to be removed and knelt down before Nefertiti, clutching the goblet in my hand. Oh, they will tell you how she had aged, how her face was lined, her body fat, how she had shaven her hair to appear more like a man. I can't remember any of that. I sat facing the Beautiful One who had knelt beside me in a fragrant orchard, whose face constantly haunted my dreams, and still does. She was at peace, her blue eyes calm, slightly red-rimmed from crying.

'Mahu.' My name came in a whisper. 'Mahu, I know why you are here. The soothsayer told me, remember? How I would die at the hands of a friend?'

I couldn't move. I grasped the cup and tried to move forward, but all I could do was stare into her eyes and feel the hideous pain in my heart. There was a brazier glowing but I felt as cold as death.

'Mahu,' she smiled slightly, 'at least I am dying in the presence of a friend.'

'Akhenaten,' I replied, 'my lady, where is Akhenaten?'

'Mahu, I do not know.' The smile widened. 'And even

if I did, I would not tell you or,' her glance fell away, 'or the other hyenas.'

Before I could stop her she snatched the cup from my hand, toasted me quickly and drained it. I watched some of the purple drops course down her chin along that lovely neck. She let out a long sigh and threw the cup to one side.

'*Senebti* – farewell, Mahu!'

She sat for a while, head down; when she glanced up her eyes were full of tears. She began to shiver.

'Mahu, please, don't let me die alone.'

I grasped her outstretched hand and pulled her close. Her trembling grew, her body shaking so I clasped her in my arms and pressed her head down onto my shoulder.

'Why?' I whispered. 'Why my name . . . ?'

She pulled her head back. 'I did not draw up any list,' she gasped. 'And even if I had, your name would not have been on it.' She went to pull away, but I pulled her back. I couldn't say anything. I just waited for the trembling to stop.

She gasped once or twice, coughed as if clearing her throat, then she fell slack. I gently disengaged. I was glad her eyes were closed, the white face more youthful in death. I carefully laid her back on the cushions, rose and knocked the cup away. I opened the door of the chamber. Ay and the children of the Kap stood in a semi-circle facing me.

'She has gone,' I declared.

I kicked the door shut behind me. 'It is finished!'

Thou makest great by troops and troops,
Thou, Ruler of the Aten, shall live for ever.

(Inscription from Mahu's tomb at El-Amarna,
the City of the Aten.)

Historical Note

We know a great deal about Mahu from his unoccupied tomb at El-Amarna (the City of the Aten), dug deep into the ground against potential tomb-robbers. The paintings in his tomb are hastily executed but do show Mahu's great achievement, the frustration of a very serious plot against Akhenaten (N. de G. Davies *The Rock Tombs of El-Amarna: Tombs of Pentju, Mahu and Others*, Egypt Exploration Society, London, 1906). Archaeologists have also found both his house and police station in what is now known as El-Amarna, even the fact that he kept an armoury close at hand (see Davies above). The character, opulence and decadence of Amenhotep III, as well as his great love for Queen Tiye, are well documented and accurately described by the historian Joanne Fletcher in her excellent book *Egypt's Sun King: Amenhotep III*, Duncan Baird, London, 2000. The rise of the Akhmin gang is graphically analysed by a number of historians including Bob Briers and Nicholas Reeves, as well as myself in my book *Tutankhamun*, Constable and Robinson, London, 2002. Queen Tiye's control of Egypt, particularly of foreign affairs, is apparent in what is now known as the 'Amarna Letters'.

The suicide of (Amun) Hotep, Pharaoh's Great Friend, the abrupt disappearance of Prince Tuthmosis (Mahu claims it was due to poison not some sudden sickness) and the equally abrupt rise of his younger brother Akhenaten are a matter of historical fact. Akhenaten's decrees founding his new city, rejecting Thebes and hinting that something hideous happened are still extant and can be found in all the standard textbooks on his reign. The same sources accurately describe the founding of the Great Heretic's new city as well as what happened there: the constant emphasis on Akhenaten, Nefertiti and the worship of the Aten. Evelyn Wells' *Nefertiti*, Robert Hale, London, 1965, refers to darker deeds, including the discovery of human remains buried in the walls of a house in the same city!

The collapse of Akhenaten's reign, apart from the outbreak of a virulent plague, is, however, clouded in mystery. The Museum of Berlin holds the famous statue of Nefertiti which reflects her haunting beauty but it also holds a statue of her when she was much older, and when that beauty had begun to fade. Most historians argue that a serious breach occurred between Akhenaten and Nefertiti and the cause, as Mahu says, was possibly the birth of Tutankhaten, Akhenaten's only son by the Mitanni Princess Khiya. Nicholas Reeves in *Egypt's False Prophet: Akenhaten*, Thames and Hudson, London, 2001, cites other sources, and has developed the theory that Nefertiti regained power, acted as her husband's Co-regent and even 're-invented' herself as the mysterious Smenkhkare, only to fall abruptly and inexplicably from power.

This fall did not drag down Ay, Huy, Maya, Horemheb and Mahu: their tombs brilliantly illustrate successful careers which continued long after Nefertiti's disappearance. Mahu may well be right: he survived, and the rest survived, because they were the cause of her fall. These key players in the great game of Empire remained, as Mahu's later confession proves, to play and play again in the vicious, murderous swirl of politics which characterised the end of the glorious Eighteenth Dynasty of Ancient Egypt.

Paul Doherty

Headline hopes you have enjoyed AN EVIL SPIRIT OUT OF THE WEST, and invites you to sample THE MAGICIAN'S DEATH, Paul Doherty's new Hugh Corbett medieval mystery, out now from Headline.

Prologue

THE ROYAL PALACE AT POISSY – THE FEAST OF ST BARNABAS THE APOSTLE – JUNE 1303

Philip IV of France, nicknamed 'Le Bel', knelt on the prie-dieu in the small gorgeous royal chapel overlooking the Fountain of the Courtyard in the Palace of Poissy. Philip loved this little church with its exquisitely tiled floor of black, white and red lozenges, the oaken cushioned prie-dieu, the splendid tapestries depicting the exploits of his great predecessor, the Capetian Louis IX, now St Louis, proclaimed so by the Universal Church. Philip knelt before a statue to his glorious ancestor and stared up at the carved saintly face, studying it carefully. He would have words with the sculptor. He wanted Louis' face to look like his own; that was not blasphemy, for wasn't Philip a direct descendant? Didn't the same sacred Capetian blood flow in his veins? Philip knelt immobile; despite the warmth he had a fur-lined blue cloak embroidered with gold fleurs-de-lys about his shoulders. Philip's light blond hair, parted down the middle, fell below his ears, his moustache and beard of the same colour, precisely clipped, the light blue eyes which so many of his subjects found terrifying in their gaze, moved now and again, distracted by the flame of the countless tapers and candles which surrounded this statue. The memorial to St Louis stood on the left side of the chapel altar in a chantry specially built according to Philip's precise instructions. This was the place to which Philip would retreat to give thanks to God, whom he regarded as an equal, as well as to talk to his sainted ancestor, whom Philip viewed as his envoy at the heavenly court.

Philip joined his hands, fingers raised heavenwards. He had so much to thank St Louis for, and, putting aside his usual icy demeanour, Philip leaned across and kissed the base of the statue. Philip had nourished dreams and these dreams, thanks to the intervention of St Louis, were to become a reality. He had married his sons to the daughters of the three great dukes in his kingdom, provinces such as Burgundy would be brought firmly under the control of the Capetian rule. The only obstacle had been the wine-rich duchy of Gascony in the south-west, controlled and owned by Edward of England. Philip allowed himself a smile – for that too was changing. He had threatened Edward with outright war, exploiting the English King's troubles with his campaign against the Scots. Oh, success tasted so sweet! Last month, by the Treaty of Paris, Edward of

England had been forced to concede that in the matter of Gascony, Philip of France was his overlord. Edward had also solemnly sworn that the Prince of Wales would marry Philip's only daughter, the infant Isabella, she of the light blue eyes and golden hair, a true daughter of her father.

Philip looked up in rapture at the carved face of his ancestor. 'One day,' he whispered, 'my grandson will wear the crown of the Confessor, my daughter will be Queen of England and her second son will be Duke of Gascony.' Philip could have hugged himself. He had finished what this great Saint had begun: he would give France natural boundaries, the great mountain range to the south and the wild seas to the north and west. The Low Countries would become his clients and the power of France would be felt as far east as the Rhine. Philip's smile faded at the cough behind him. He crossed himself slowly, and elegantly rose from the prie-dieu; taking the silk gloves from his belt, he put them on as he stared at Monsieur Amaury de Craon, Keeper of the King's Secrets.

'Your Grace asked to see me?' De Craon did not like the harsh look on his master's face.

'Amaury, Amaury.' Philip's face broke into a smile. Striding across, he grasped de Craon's face between his hands and squeezed tightly. 'We have matters to discuss, Amaury.'

He led this red-haired, most secretive of councillors over to a small bench, halfway down the chapel, in a narrow enclave, where Philip usually met his confessor to whisper his sins and seek absolution. Philip didn't really believe he needed absolution. After all, God was a King and He would understand. Nevertheless, this was an ideal place to meet and plot where no eavesdropper could lurk or spy take note.

'Well, Amaury?' Philip sat down, pulling his robes about him and gesturing for de Craon to sit next to him. 'I read your memorandum.' Philip played with the red tassels on the silken glove. 'You have insisted,' he whispered, 'that I face two problems.'

'The first, Your Grace, is Sir Hugh Corbett.'

'Is he a problem, Amaury, or the result of your hatred for him?'

'Your Grace,' de Craon bowed imperceptibly, 'he is as astute as always. I hate Corbett for what he represents, for what he leads, that Secret Chancery with its legion of spies.'

'True, true.' Philip nodded.

'And the University of Sorbonne?'

De Craon kept his head down though he knew from the long sigh from his master he had hit a mark.

'The lawyers,' Philip hissed. 'Those men from the gutter who believe my will does not have force of law.'

'Your Grace, there are measures we can take.'

Philip leaned closer like a priest listening to a penitent as there, in that House of God, the French King and his Master of Spies spun their bloody tangled web to draw Edward of England deeper into the mire.